THE THUNDER AND THE SHOUTING

*

The epic experience of one Polish family under the Nazi occupation. This is the theme of Christopher Nicole's novel. Anna Janski, herself a German, torn between love for her children and admiration for her Fuehrer; Anton Janski, who lived only for his work, and saw that work destroyed; Josef, who photographed public executions and planned a few of his own; Christina, who came to terms with her destruction. And the strange passionate love of Asja and Frederic whose determination to survive led them down paths so inhuman that survival at last became unimportant.

Christopher Nicole

The Thunder and the Shouting

ARROW BOOKS

ARROW BOOKS LTD
178–202 Great Portland Street, London W1

AN IMPRINT OF THE HUTCHINSON GROUP

London Melbourne Sydney
Auckland Johannesburg Cape Town
and agencies throughout the world

*

First published by
Hutchinson & Co (*Publishers*) Ltd 1969
Arrow edition 1970

*Made and printed in Great Britain
by The Anchor Press Ltd.,
Tiptree, Essex*
ISBN 0 09 003640 9

THE JANSKI FAMILY IN 1939

Descendants of Gustav Johansson, Swedish officer in the army of Charles XII, who settled in Poland in 1720. Gustav made toys as a hobby, his children adopted toy-making as the family business.

The Brothers

Anton Janski, born 1894. During first world war fought for Austria as an officer in the Polish Legion, married a German, Anneliese Harrwitz. Continued military career with Pilsudski until after defeat of Russians in 1920, when he retired to manage the Janski Brothers Toy Shop on Senator Street, Warsaw.

Jan Janski, born 1896. Junior partner in the firm. A bachelor.

The Wife

Anneliese Janski, *née* Harrwitz, born 1899. Married Anton Janski in 1916, but has remained fervent German nationalist.

The Children

Antoni Janski, born 1917. Officer in the Polish Air Force.

Jan Janski, born 1918. Photographer.

Anneliese Janski, born 1919. Débutante.

Frederic Janski, born 1921. Student.

Christina Janski, born 1925. Schoolgirl.

AND

Asja Janski, wife of Antoni, born 1920, a Huzulin, a member of a tribe of Slavic mountaineers inhabiting the Carpathian Mountains on Poland's southern borders, regarded as backward by the sophisticated Janskis.

Antoni Janski the Younger, son of Antoni and Asja, born 1939.

The characters in this book are fiction; the events are fact.

*The train stopped, and the hiss of the brakes was re-
placed by a baying sound, rising and falling on the night
air. Johnson lowered the window. Rotterdam looked the
same. So had The Hook, so had Harwich, so had London. Even the noise, the shouts and the chanting, took
him back all of a generation.*

*He turned at the knock, closed the window again. 'I
am your neighbour, as far as Berlin. Peter Cohn.' The
man wore a grey suit and a white shirt, had close-cropped
black hair. Johnson had already identified him as a
German.*

*He shook hands. 'Frederic Johnson. What is the
demonstration about?'*

*Cohn shrugged. 'Student reform, anti-war, anti-nuclear
weapons, anti-anti. They frighten me, these modern children. But you have the same problem in America.'*

*'Oh, sure. The whole world belongs to kids, nowadays.'
Johnson sat down. He was no longer surprised at the instant recognition of his nationality. In twenty years he
had accumulated an American prosperity and an
American confidence, for all that his hair was greying
and receding, and his still handsome features retained a
certain grimness. His prosperity showed in his three-
hundred-dollar suit and his silk shirt; his confidence in
the cigar ash he had carelessly scattered down one trouser
leg. Cohn looked prosperous too. His suit had come from
Savile Row, he smelt of good tobacco and better brandy.
But he lacked Johnson's confidence.*

*'They frighten me,' he said again. 'Because although
they march up and down and say they are against
violence, they are really seeking just that, and without
any real understanding of what it will be like. I remem-*

7

ber my own youth, Mr. Johnson. We also were searching for violence, without understanding it.'

'And you found it'

'Oh, yes, indeed,' Cohn agreed. 'Is this your first visit to Europe?'

'For over twenty years.'

'And you are going to Warsaw? On business?'

'I used to live there, before the war.'

'You were not a Pole?'

'I was Swedish,' Johnson said. 'But I want to see what has changed. Who has changed.'

The train slipped into motion, the noise of the demonstrating students fell behind. Cohn realised he was not going to be offered a seat, smiled, and withdrew. Johnson lit a cigar, leaned back with his eyes closed. He thought about youth, searching for violence, without understanding what it would mean. And he listened to the sound of the train.

1

Autumn 1939

Trains! Express trains, hurtling through the dawn, over and on either side of the house, trailing behind them an unending whine, smashing through even the deepest sleep barrier. But there were no trains within earshot of Rokonow.

Frederic looked at his watch. It was four-fifteen. Surprisingly, there was no sense of surprise. He got out of bed and stood at the window, looked across the orchard at the empty field, and then the road into Warsaw, also empty, waiting for the morning bus to come rumbling out of the city. If the bus were ever going to come again. The spires of Warsaw were just visible through the dawn haze, rising out of the Polish plain. And over Warsaw there were clouds, at this distance no more than wisps of smoke rising into the air, attempting to engulf the swarm of mosquitoes up there, black specks wheeling and turning, leaving trails of white vapour in the sky. Amidst the black crosses would be red and white quarters. He felt a sense of unreality. Antoni was only a few miles away, killing people. Frederic was here, in safety. There was nothing worth bombing in Rokonow. So there was no reason for personal fear. What *did* he feel? Excitement. Arousal. A sudden awareness of himself as a man. He wondered if everyone felt like that, if war was nothing more than the whole human race seeking a communal orgasm. He wondered if anyone had ever thought that before, or if here was an original Frederic Janski.

The door crashed open. Christina moved like a filly searching for her mother. Her pale yellow hair was scattered, her dressing gown was open. Her face, small, round, bubbled with excitement. 'Wake up, wake up,' she shouted. 'Papa says we must go down to the cellar.'

'Whatever for?'

'That's what Mama says. But Papa insists. And Asja won't open her door. Did you know Asja slept with her door locked? She's a funny woman, don't you think, Frederic?'

Frederic kissed her on the cheek. 'I'll get Asja out of bed.' Christina ran down the corridor. Her feet were bare. Mama would be furious. Only peasants went about without slippers. Mama said that to annoy Asja, and Christina left off her slippers to annoy Mama.

He pulled his dressing gown from the hook behind the door, changed his mind, threw it across the bed. You could not begin a war in a dressing gown and striped silk pyjamas. He dragged on his clothes, wondered if he should wear his best suit, settled for shirt and pants and a beige pullover.

He brushed his hair. He was tall, already past six feet, powerfully built. His hair was a dark yellow, not fine and pale like Christina's. His features were pure Bavarian. But the German bombs would not know that. No matter what Mama said.

He banged on the door. His heart made as much noise as his fist. He knew why Asja slept with her door locked.

'Who is it?' Her voice was low, hardly more than a whisper. Asja always whispered, except when she was angry, and then she shouted.

'Haven't you seen the bombers? The war has begun.'

She opened the door. She wore a cotton nightdress, every bit as shapeless and opaque as Christina's. Asja had never needed frills. She was a Huzulin, and strength flowered from her strong arms and powerful legs. It hung around her face like an aura, delineated her high cheekbones and her square jaw. Compared with the Janskis, Asja's handsomeness was almost masculine. Compared with Asja, the Janskis' delicate looks were insipid.

10

The nightdress drooped, and he could see the swell of her breasts. But she knew this, and clutched her dressing robe close. She was as modest as any peasant girl, being a peasant girl. With Frederic she was more than ever modest, because of that night he had walked into her room without knocking, and she had turned to face him, thinking it was Antoni. That had been six months ago, and yet he remembered every detail as if it were yesterday. And since that night she had locked her door.

'Papa says we must go down to the cellar.'

She bent over the cot, lifted little Antoni, and gave him to Frederic. She had never suspected any of his thoughts, his desires. It had been an unfortunate accident, nothing more, and as it had been an accident Asja did not let it embarrass her. She still trusted Frederic with little Antoni. He was just waking up, looking at his uncle in bewilderment. He opened his mouth to bellow, yawned instead. Frederic cradled him to and fro, always terrified of dropping him. But he made a great pretence of wishing to father little Antoni, because this pleased Asja, allowed him to spend more time in her company.

She brushed her red-gold hair, made a face at herself in the mirror. She wore no make-up. With her pink-brown cheeks and her magnificent hair she had no need. Frederic gave her little Antoni. It was as near as he could come to touching her, and in transferring the baby his hand was for a moment imprisoned against the dressing robe. 'We'd better hurry.'

Her gaze was scornful. She went past him to the stairs. 'German bastards,' she said. 'We will destroy them. Antoni will destroy them.'

Frederic let her go. He stood at the window, listened to the roar of the trains above his head, watched the silent smoke columns rising from Warsaw, and the darting mosquitoes. Antoni was up there, and Frederic was down here.

11

The cellar became filled with the whisper of human breathing. From a place of shelter it became a place of cold stone and rotting wood, of rust and moisture. Slowly, Anneliese Janski unclenched her fingers from her rosary, raised her head to look at her husband. The bombers had gone; the real crisis was about to begin.

Mama was only five feet tall. Her hair was still jet, with never a curl; her tiny rounded face was still a closed casket with a beautiful design. Her enormous dark eyes retained the liquidity which had brought a trail of suitors to her door, twenty-five years before. From those she had selected a Polish exile. She had never really understood why. She had never expected Poland to regain its independence, presumed that when Anton had finished fighting he would settle in Germany. She had never considered children. Certainly not children each of whom would be larger than she. Often, in recent months, she had felt like Daniel. Their faces were replicas of hers. But in their huge blondness they were strangers.

Even Anton. He stood at the barred window, and looked taller and thinner than usual. His expression was despairing. He knew that for the Janskis, even more than for Poland, this was a day not to be forgotten, or alleviated. And yet his thoughts were far away. He worried for her, perhaps he feared for her, but his heart was in Warsaw, and the store.

Mama smiled at Christina. But Christina was too afraid to smile back. And there was no point in smiling at Frederic. Frederic, at eighteen, made two of his father, or either of his brothers; he was the real throwback to the Swedish Johansson who had followed Charles XII over this country two centuries before. And Frederic was angry.

Mama found it ironic that on this most terrible day of her life she should be trapped with her two youngest children, the pair with whom she had always had the least affinity. But to think of the others was too frightening; Antoni, somewhere in a tiny wood-and-metal box in the sky; Josef, somewhere in Warsaw itself, Oh God, under the smoke; and Liese. But Liese was visiting in Lowicz, with the Bieruts. Liese would be all right. Liese had to be all right.

Little Antoni whimpered, and Asja held him close. Strange, Mama thought, how she had hated this girl when Antoni had produced her, with the air of a magician, for inspection. Antoni had holidayed in Zabie two years running, and then had persuaded Papa to take the whole family there. Asja had arrived on her pony, her legs bare. She had sat on the step to put on her stockings and shoes before coming inside. She had worn a red and green skirt and a matching headscarf, a spotlessly white blouse, and a sleeveless tan jerkin. Wisps of red-gold hair peeped out from beneath the scarf, but her face had been isolated, pink-brown amidst the blaze of colour that was her clothing. It was a splendid face, with its strong jaw and high cheekbones, its marvellously small nose and its deep hazel eyes. It had been a face, and a costume, and a mind, out of the past, because the Carpathians had no past, and no future, only the present. But that Lieutenant Antoni Janski, the darling of Warsaw society, should wish to marry a Huzulin!

Little Antoni had changed that. But there had been more. Of course, Asja was pure Slav. It was difficult to regard her as any different from those other Slavs, the maids and cook and Winawer the butler, muttering at the far end of the cellar. But there were exceptions to every rule, even those promulgated by the Fuehrer. Anna Janski knew the brittleness of her family. There was nothing brittle about her daughter-in-law. Asja Janski had brought the solidity of her mountains into the house. And this morning Mama was glad of it.

'I didn't know there were so many planes in the world,' Christina said.

'Some of them were ours,' Frederic said. 'Antoni was up there.'

'I didn't see any Polish markings,' Christina objected.

They were waiting. Mama sucked air into her lungs. 'It's that man Beck's fault. This could never have happened if the marshal were alive.'

'He'd have told Hitler where to get off,' Frederic said.

Here was open defiance. 'He'd have negotiated, you stupid little boy.' Mama loaded her voice with the venom which for twenty years had kept the lions at bay. 'He would never have allowed England to push him into war.'

Frederic opened his mouth, and Christina pinched his arm.

Mama realised she *was* angry. 'The English,' she said contemptuously. 'Warmongers. And because they are not strong enough to fight for themselves they get others to do their fighting for them.'

'They even wanted us to bring in the Russians,' Papa said. 'We had them before, but the English don't understand things like that.'

Mama sighed with relief; Papa had chosen his side.

'Well, let's hope we can throw the Germans out like we did the Russians,' Frederic said lamely.

'The war will be over by suppertime,' Mama declared.

'Oh, yes,' Frederic said. 'With Warsaw destroyed, and all the people killed.'

'And don't you think the Polish air force is bombing Berlin? That's where Antoni is, if you want to know. That's why we haven't seen any Polish planes. That's war, nowadays. Only the innocent suffer. But by suppertime we will have proved our courage, and we will surrender.'

'We?' Frederic shouted. 'You could be shot for saying that. Surrender to Adolf the house painter? I'd rather *see* Warsaw razed first.'

Mama allowed pity into her voice. 'You speak about cities being razed as if they were packs of cards. There are people in those cities, Frederic. Your friends.'

Little Antoni began to wail.

'Now see what you've done, Frederic,' Christina said. 'You've woken up baby.'

'He is hungry.' Asja looked from Papa to Frederic to the servants. Asja's mother had fed Asja on the step in front of their thatched cottage, while she passed the time of day with her neighbours. But Asja was a Janski now, and even with a war on could not be expected to feed little Antoni in public.

'The planes have gone,' Mama decided. 'We will go upstairs. I must telephone Liese and tell her to come home.'

'I am going into town,' Papa declared.

'Don't be a fool, Anton. Do you think there will be customers this morning? We must just make sure that Josef is all right.'

'There may be looting. I should be there.'

'Let Jan look after it.'

'I am going.' Papa would accept her authority in anything except the store.

'I'll come with you,' Frederic said.

'Oh, yes, run along,' Mama said. 'All of you. Leave the women alone.'

'Now, sweetheart,' Papa said, 'no harm can come to you in Rokonow.'

Mama helped Asja lift little Antoni. She knew she had lost them for the moment. Not to the white eagle. To the sheer exhilaration of the male animal at war.

The Mercedes came to a halt with a squealing of brakes.

Frederic, in front beside Papa, bumped his head on the windscreen. Thus far the road had been empty, as if it were Sunday. Beside them the waters of the Vistula raced onwards for the Baltic. The Vistula always raced. It was always in a hurry. But the road and the fields had been empty, the only movement the old Mercedes and the smoke billowing upwards from the city in the distance. But now, coming out of Sielce, there were people streaming towards them, pushing carts and bicycles laden with a selection of their most treasured possessions.

Papa rolled down his window. 'What is happening? Where are you going?'

'We are not staying to be blown to pieces,' a woman said. 'The planes will be back.'

'Did they bomb Sielce?' Frederic asked.

'You go,' said the woman. 'Look at it.'

Papa drove on, slowly now, horn blaring. The smoke hung above them, drifting on the wind, not dangerous in itself. And then suddenly there was a tenement cut in two as if by a knife, leaving living rooms and bedrooms and bathrooms exposed to the morning, smouldering, waiting to be engulfed in flame. The rubble had spread across the road, and what space was left was blocked by a shattered car. Papa pulled into the side of the road, and they got out. There were men in the building, prodding at pieces of collapsed masonry. Above them the first flames licked the woodwork.

'Why don't you put out the fire?' Papa shouted.

'There are people in here,' replied one of the man. 'You can help us.'

'We must get into town,' Frederic explained.

The man shrugged, wiped sweat from his brow. It was hot.

They walked, along Ujawdowskie, with the slope of red and white roses on their right, stretching down to the Lazienskie Palace. There were craters in the park,

16

scattering the roses left and right, and then there was a crater in the road, and beyond, huddled heaps of clothes. Staining the road beside the clothes was brown mess. Frederic regretted breakfast, and he had overeaten, in case he did not get home for lunch. But this was ridiculous. He was a student of history, and here he was, living history. History was made up of blood and death, and sex.

Now the streets were crowded with people, gazing at the burning buildings, and firemen, hopelessly directing their hoses into the flame and smoke. There was very little human noise above the roar of the flames and the clatter of collapsing houses. People stared at each other and exchanged greetings as if nothing had happened. But something had, and they were too shocked to communicate. There were bodies lying on every street now, and no one was going to do anything about them, either. Over Stare Miasto the smoke was thickest.

Janski Brothers was on Senator Street. But Senator Street was a heap of rubble. Uncle Jan was there, one of the sales assistants beside him. She was a pretty dark thing, Uncle Jan's latest. While Papa managed the store, Uncle Jan looked after the customers and the sales staff. Especially the sales staff. He was the family scandal, and the family joke. This morning even he was shaken. He had not shaved and he had forgotten his waistcoat and his fat belly shook up and down as he gazed at the shuddering walls and the twisted girders that yesterday had housed toy tanks and toy airplanes and toy bombs. 'Oh, the bastards,' he said. 'Oh, the bleeding bastards. We'll make them pay. We'll smash Hitler like we smashed Tuchachevsky, eh, Anton?'

Papa gazed at the store. Jan had his arm round the salesgirl, but Papa's only love had been the store itself. And Papa had actually fought against Tuchachevsky. Papa knew what war was like.

17

Frederic held his arm. 'We'd better find Josef, and then go home. We can't do anything here.'

'Why is no one putting out the fire?' Papa asked.

'The engine was here,' Jan explained. 'But they must save the less badly damaged buildings, you see, Anton. All of ours is gone. All the toys, too. We must thank God that nobody was inside.' He was squeezing the girl's backside, massaging the soft flesh. She did not seem to notice. Neither did anyone else on the street.

A woman screamed, and pointed. The noise had been growing for some minutes, but there was so much noise this additional drone had made no difference. But now came the first explosion. The bombers were back.

III

The morning was an endless succession of cups of coffee. Christina kept hopping up and going to the window. Mama stared into her cup. She had not been able to get through to Lowicz, and Liese was her favourite. But more than that, she knew she was caught astride a fence, and the fence could only grow, forcing her to jump, one side or the other.

Asja was glad to escape to the privacy of the bathroom, kneel beside the tub, holding little Antoni, and listen to her son cooing. Little Antoni enjoyed his bath. Like his father. Antoni would spend hours in his tub, and he liked Asja to come in and sit and talk with him. She could not understand why *he* did not telephone. If not to her, then at least to Mama. The planes had gone, the only sign of what had happened was the smoke pall over Warsaw. But probably the wires were down. She must not become afraid, like the Janskis. A Huzulin did not fear something until she saw it in front of her. She

18

smiled at her son. There was more than enough to fear as it was.

Asja had never flown, had never even been near an airplane. The thought of being off the ground frightened her. Antoni had tried to tell her about it, on their honeymoon in Gdynia. He had explained his feeling of immortality, when in the air. 'On the ground, Asja, I'm just a human being. But up there I'm an eagle. A white eagle. And there are eight thousand of us.'

'It is not natural for human beings to fly.'

He had smiled. 'Everything man can do becomes natural, Asja.' And he had taken her to the window to look at the promenade and the pier and in the distance, the teeming docks. 'I came here fifteen years ago, with Papa. This was just empty beach, and the fishermen were drying their nets in the sun. But Poland needed a seaport, and the marshal snapped his fingers, and here we are. Gdynia will be one of the great ports of Europe. Hamburg, Copenhagen, Marseilles, even London, will be no greater. We shall turn Danzig into a fishing village in its turn. But those fishermen thought it was unnatural.'

Antoni had been in love, then, with a face he had watched riding down the hillside above Zabie. 'You have the most beautiful face I have ever seen, Asja. It has the beauty of strength. Only queens should have faces like yours.'

Then he had wanted to put his head between her legs, for queens have to be possessed. He had explained about possession, about having to *know* that he owned her, and she had submitted, but when he had kissed her she had instinctively tightened her legs, clamping his neck as she would have clamped the flanks of her pony when it became restive, and Antoni had fainted. She had bathed his face, and he had smiled at her. 'You are too strong for me, Asja.'

So he had given her books to read. He had done this

19

before he had ever touched her, when he was still coming to Zabie to watch her tend the cow. But she had been afraid to take them home, even though her father could not read. She could read very well, but she had never got beyond the first chapter in any of Antoni's books, even after they had been married. There were some things you did not share even with your husband. Surely.

So the intimate chats had become less frequent. He could not resist touching her, but then he always seemed in a hurry to let her go. Yet they had conceived little Antoni, and they would conceive other children. Surely. But with the withdrawal of Antoni's personal intimacy she had become isolated in a world of witty, brilliant people, like Leise and Josef, who discussed Mickiewicz and Reymont with tremendous knowledge, and Mama and Papa, who went to auctions in search of paintings to hang beside the two Matejko originals hanging in the drawing room, and Frederic, who spoke three languages and knew all about Jadwiga and Casimir and could discuss Sobieski's campaigns as if they were being published in the newspaper, and who was going to be a university professor.

Asja found her conversational level with Christina, who was fourteen and acted much younger. And yet, she thought, as she lifted little Antoni from the bath and wrapped him in his towel and hugged him to her breast, she possessed something that not one of them could challenge, the first of a new generation of Janskis, to inherit the store, and become an important man in Warsaw. Asja had never been to Warsaw until after her marriage.

She opened the door, hesitated at the sight of Winawer, perfectly dressed even on the first morning of a war, waiting at the head of the stairs. Winawer frightened her. Were she not married to Antoni Janski she would be down in the scullery and she would call Winawer 'sir'.

'What is the matter?' Fear made her voice brusque.

20

Winawer shifted from foot to foot. 'It is my sister, Miss Asja. A man has just passed this way who says Praga was badly damaged in this morning's bombardment.'

'I'm sorry to hear that, Winawer.' She hurried into her bedroom, laid little Antoni on her bed, began to powder him. 'I suppose they were trying to knock out the bridges.'

Winawer stood in the doorway. 'I would like permission to go home, Miss Asja. There are no buses running, but I could be there and back by this evening.'

Asja frowned at him. 'I cannot give you permission to go anywhere, Winawer. You will have to ask Mrs. Janski.'

'She has retired, Miss Asja. Her door is locked and she is not to be disturbed.'

'Well, then, I'm afraid . . .'

'You can give me permission, Miss Asja.'

Because she was a mountain peasant he knew she was afraid of him. Because Mama would look him up and down and say, 'Don't be ridiculous, Winawer, we need you here.'

Asja looked Winawer up and down. Mama would also curl her lip in that mind-shrivelling way of hers. But Asja had never learned how to curl her lip. 'Well, of course, Winawer, you must go to your sister.'

'Thank you, Miss Asja. Thank you.'

'I will tell Mrs. Janski. But you must be back by six.'

'Oh, yes, Miss Asja. I will be back by six.' Winawer raised his head. From the sky came the drone of planes.

Frederic lay in a gutter. He clasped his hands over his head and pressed his cheek into the hard, cold, smelly stone. He did not feel the stone. He was floating through the air, suspended in the centre of an eternity of screaming, raging sound, a compound of whining bombs and thudding explosions, of shaking earth, of searing heat and scattering dust, of droning planes, and of fear. The noise and the fear affected his body like an anaesthetic. He had wet his trousers, might even have ejaculated. War is sex. But physical sex only, the sort you want so badly, then are so desperately ashamed of afterwards. War is dirty.

A man lay near to him, his head close to Frederic's. At first Frederic had thought he was Papa, because they had been running beside each other for a while. But this man screamed continuously, a high sound, like a horse with a broken leg. Papa had run the Mercedes into a horse, once, and it made a noise just like that until someone had shot it. Frederic thought that the man's screaming was worse than the whine of the bombs. Somebody should come along and shoot him.

The silence was deafening. He thought the first of his senses to go would be his ears, assailed by the silence after all the noise. Not that it was really silent. There was a tremendous roaring all about him. And a tremendous heat. Even the stone was hot and wet.

He rose to his knees, gazed at the burning buildings on the other side of the street. The house opposite him was a mass of flame, and the roof was beginning to fall in, showering the street with burning fragments. Some even fell into the gutter. There was no one else in the street, except the man in the gutter, who had stopped screaming, and was staring at Frederic, eyes wide and mouth open. There was no fire engine, no policeman to tell them what to do. No one was going to get here, either. Frederic realised that nothing was going to stop Warsaw being burned to the ground. Where the city had stood there would be only an enormous pile of blackened cinders. But that was impossible. Whole cities could not be destroyed nowadays. Only the Mongols had ground whole cities into the dust, and they were six hundred years into history.

But certainly nothing was going to save this street. He bent over his companion. 'Let's get out of here,' he shouted, and wondered who was speaking. The man wondered too. He continued to stare at Frederic, his mouth open. In any event, he would not be able to go very far. He had no legs. The entire gutter suddenly came to an end in dirt and water and blood, and the man's body ended with his buttocks. Frederic wondered if the man had been screaming because he knew he had lost his legs, or if he had stopped screaming when he had lost his legs.

He found a street where, incomprehensibly, there was no fire. There were even several buildings still standing. Naturally, it also contained a lot of people. They stared at the flames looming at either crossing, wiped heat, sweat and fear, from their brows. They stared at each other, too, and said things, and answered questions. Frederic spoke a lot. It occurred to him that he was doing most of the talking. His jaw wagged unceasingly. But he couldn't hear himself, so what he was saying had to be irrelevant. Until someone shouted, 'Where are our planes, then? We have an air force. Where are they, then? Bastards.'

The man was very close, his mouth against Frederic's ear. 'Over Berlin,' Frederic explained. That's what Mama had said. But he knew she was wrong. He could not see Antoni, or any of the young men Antoni had brought home to meet Liese, dropping bombs on a defenceless city. Except that Berlin would not be defenceless. Hitler would have seen to that.

So he hated. Hitler, of course, but all the Germans. Himself, for having so much German blood. He wanted to kill a German.

He was in Chlodna Street, and a man was there, in uniform. A sergeant. He looked Frederic up and down. 'So you want to fight. We all are going to fight. What regiment?'

'I have no regiment yet.'

23

The sergeant looked suitably sympathetic to a young man obviously affected by his first experience of war. 'If you do not tell me the name of your regiment,' he said, 'I cannot tell you where to report.'

'I was eighteen last month,' Frederic explained. 'And my call up has been deferred until after I have been to university. I am going to Cracow in three weeks' time.'

The sergeant scratched his head. 'Then you have no regiment. So you cannot fight. My advice to you is to go home.'

IV

Frederic walked through heat and noise and rubble. He understood now that he was the same as the people he and Papa had encountered that morning. People spoke to him, and he replied, but words did not seem relevant. He moved to a plan. Discover where he was, and then find his way to Josef's studio. Josef might know where Papa was. At a time like this only one's family was important.

But discovering where he was seemed likely to take a long time. The smoke hung immediately above the roof-tops, like a very low thundercloud. And between the smoke and the ground there lay a pall of dust, through which people moved and masonry crashed and voices shouted or screamed. Sometimes he heard an engine, but the fire service had never been intended to deal with catastrophe on this scale. And the flames were spreading. They lurked in the dust, sometimes drifted across the road, and everywhere pervaded the afternoon with their heat.

Only less obnoxious than the flames were the bodies. Not all were dead. Many had collapsed from exhaustion, or had inhaled too much smoke and dust, or were merely

24

too frightened to move. But Frederic did not investigate any of them. He felt resentful towards them. But for the bodies this would be quite exciting.

He stood on grass. The air was clearer, and he could look across the gardens to a church. There were a great many people accumulated here, out of reach of collapsing buildings and spreading flames, many of them children, gazing at the ruins of their city, unable to understand what was really happening. These were the Saxon Gardens. Therefore the studio was only a block away.

He hurried with more purpose. Josef rented a basement, and a basement promised safety.

The street was blocked with great pieces of masonry. Water gushed from a shattered main, running in and out of the crumbled stone like an incoming tide. He wondered why no one had turned off the water; this was a frightful waste. He slipped on a wet stone and sat down, jarred his back. He crawled on his hands and knees, through the water and out the other side, arrived at a street corner, looked to his right. A high explosive bomb had landed at the far end of the street, and the houses had been blasted towards Frederic like a grove of trees of which the first had been felled, diminishing in damage as they approached him. Josef's basement was the fourth from the corner, below a newsagent. He could see the sign on the wall. But the door of the shop had been blown inwards.

Frederic stood at the top of stone steps, gazed at the glass. When he went down the steps it crackled beneath his feet. He did not look inside the shop until he was halfway down, and then he saw that the floor was red, and the red was moving, trickling towards the shattered door from where it slowly seeped on to the top step. But anyone who had lost that much blood was already dead.

The door to the studio was locked. He banged, despair turning into tears which burned his dust caked eyes. He

25

could not face the city again, the death and the destruction. He wanted peace. Just five minutes of peace.

'Is that you, Josef?' It was hardly more than a whisper, but it belonged to Ruth, Josef's assistant.

'Frederic,' he gasped.

The key turned, and he stumbled into semi darkness, bumped into a chair, and sat down.

'Are you all right, Frederic?'

'Yes. Yes, I'm all right. Where is Josef?'

'He went out with his best camera. He said photographs of Warsaw burning will be worth a fortune.'

Frederic rested his head on his hands. 'Have you seen anything of my father?'

'Mr. Janski was here just now. He was terribly worried about you, Frederic. But when I told him I had not seen you, he said he was going back to Rokonow. Did they drop bombs on Rokonow too, Frederic?'

'No.' Frederic wept, softly. Papa had been safe, all this time. He could go home, too.

'Would you like some coffee, Frederic?' Ruth asked. 'I have a Thermos.'

He raised his head. He could see her now, almost, but in any event he knew what Ruth Blass looked like. She was a Jewess, short and plump, with round cheeks surrounding a circular face, and fat arms. Her hair was black, her eyes brown, and laughing. Ruth was always amused. He sometimes wondered if Josef employed her because it was so pleasant to have a jolly girl about the studio. But of course Josef could not afford to employ anyone. His photographs of soccer matches and athletic meetings earned him no more than pocket money. Papa paid the rent and also for the film. Ruth was a luxury. Therefore she had to be more to Josef than a receptionist.

The coffee was lukewarm, but it was sweet and he had not realised how dry his throat was. 'Why are you here?' he asked, 'You don't expect customers?'

'I came down to see if I could be any help. Down here is at least safe. I suppose.'

'What about your folks?'

'I don't know. I'm waiting for Josef, I guess. He'll take me home.'

He put his arm round her waist. Even her thighs were plump. He wondered if he dared rest his head against her thighs, because they were equally afraid. He wondered if she really was Josef's mistress, or if she were as virginal as he.

She rested her hand on his head, pressed very slightly, bringing his cheek into her thigh. He tilted his head, moving it against her clothing, feeling the ridges of elastic underneath. 'Show me inside, Ruthie.'

She smiled. This was a reversion to his boyhood. Always asking for the inner room. Josef's private room. What secrets were locked away in there, known only to Josef and Ruth? 'Josef allows no one in there.'

He caught her hands. 'Look, when the bombers come back they might destroy this place. And I would never have seen.'

Her eyes glowed in the darkness. 'Are they going to come back, Frederic? What more can they do?'

'They mean to destroy all of Warsaw.' He thought of the blood, spreading across the floor, only a few feet above their heads. He was glad it was a solid floor.

'But why?' She sounded like a child. 'Why us? What do the Nazis want with us?'

'Not just the Nazis.' The historian, which always lay just beneath the surface of Frederic's consciousness, came bubbling upwards. 'The Germans. And the Russians. They always wanted Poland.'

Ruth shivered. 'I'd rather have the Russians.'

'The Russians would be far worse. You ask your folks about Tuchachevsky. My dad fought against them, right outside Warsaw. They haven't forgiven us for that.'

27

'But the Nazis, when you think of the things they say, that they won't let the Jews do any work, except for the state, that they'll make us wear special clothes, ugh.'

'That's all propaganda. Those men are running a country. Now can you imagine Marshal Smigly-Ridz having the time to worry about what sort of clothing any of us wear? Come on, show me inside.'

'There's no light.'

The flashlight was hanging beside the door. He switched it on, flicked the beam over her, and she unlocked the door. Frederic stood close behind her. He could smell her perfume, very faint and a little stale. She took the light, shone it up and down the walls. Hands. Hands and hands and hands. Single hands, pairs of hands, hands superimposed upon other hands, hands stretching for ever into the mind's eye, so many hands that Frederic stepped backwards, into the doorway, expecting them all to seize him by the throat.

'Aren't they lovely?' Ruth asked.

'But why?'

'Because they are beautiful. Beauty is *there*, Frederic. It cannot be adorned, or lessened. It cannot be based on emotion. Beauty must transcend every feeling, and be *there*, always.' She was quoting.

'Josef said that?'

'Josef is going to be a great photographer.'

'And he spends his time photographing hands? Whose hands?'

She held her right hand in front of the light.

Frederic scratched his head. 'I thought he had nudes in here.'

'Do you think I would ever pose in the nude, Frederic? Even for Josef?'

'I don't know. I thought ...'

'Well, you were wrong.' He had never seen Ruth angry before.

'Listen!' The drone was back, filling the air, so low it rattled even the remnants of the window-panes down here.

Ruth dropped to her knees on the floor, began to pray, in Hebrew, muttering over and over again. Frederic switched off the torch. Outside, a whine ended in a thud and a crash which shook the cellar and brought plaster from the ceiling. A piece of cardboard drifted across his face. A hand. A photograph of a hand.

He knelt beside her. She lay on the floor, her arms round his neck. He kissed her face, found her eyes were closed and her mouth was open. She was crying.

War is sex, and sex is war. He had always imagined, the first time he took a woman, that he would be naked and so would she, and their bodies would intertwine, from mouth to toe, and there would be nothing but a shared orgasm. But Ruth put one hand under her head to stop it bumping on the floor, and her suspenders ate into his thighs, and the only real softness was her buttocks, and then the backs of his knuckles were ground into the stone, and halfway through another bomb landed very close and he was so afraid he wanted to withdraw.

V

Dusk made no difference to the burning city. The flames lit up every street, the dust continued to hang on the air. The noise, of crumbling buildings, of distraught people, seemed to cling to the dust.

Josef Janski took the steps cautiously. Tall, he stooped slightly, peering at the world through thick lensed spectacles. He carried his camera between his hands, like a sacred offering; having survived eight raids he did not wish to fall in the darkness. He slipped on the very first

step, stooped to discover the cause, found the sticky substance which he knew was blood. He dried his finger on his jacket, went downstairs.

Ruth opened the door. 'You should have gone home hours ago,' he said. 'Where's the light.'

'It went in the bombing.'

She put the torch in his hand, and he played the beam over her. Her hair was untidy and her mouth was bruised. Ruth was such a tidy person. 'Your parents will be worried about you.' He opened the inner door, unpacked the camera.

She held the light, allowing him to see what he was doing. She was restless, nervous. But who would not be restless and nervous this night?

He developed the film with trembling hands. He had shots of burning buildings, and collapsing buildings, and gallant firemen, and frightened people, and shots of smoke patterns, and low flying Heinkel bombers, and strangely beautiful shots of those odd little places in the city where the war had, as yet, failed to reach, of a child sitting by the side of the road with a teddy bear, while a fire engine rushed past and a mother wept. He knew he had a collection of the most brilliant photographs he had ever taken. But it was the very last shot which excited him. He had wanted to take it all day. Heaven knows he had had enough opportunities. But he had not been able to bring himself to do so until the sun was already drooping and the dust had induced an early twilight. He had allowed maximum exposure, and yet he was not sure it was going to come out.

Ruth Blass sat at the table. 'Your brother was here. He took the box camera.'

'I hope he's careful with it. Is there any food? I haven't had a bite all day.'

'Neither have I,' Ruth said.

'Well, you had better go home. The bombers won't be

back for an hour. Very regular people, the Germans. I know. I'm one of them.'

'I know you are.'

'Well, off you go. I'll see you on Monday.'

He could hear her breathing. She was drawing very long breaths. 'I would like to spend the night here, Josef.'

The first of the photographs was coming through. 'Bring the light.'

She stood at his shoulder. 'Are you going home?'

'No. But I live all the way out at Rokonow. And I have work to do.' He held up a study of smoke. It was a magnificent picture, catching the billowing, sinister black vapour against the flawlessly clear sky, showing the chimney pots on the bottom edge of the picture. 'That's a beauty, eh?'

'Yes. Can I stay here, Josef?'

'With me? Your parents will be furious. They know I often sleep in town.' He frowned at a photograph of the bombers. The camera had moved. Actually, it made a dramatic picture, the slightly blurred planes, the slightly blurred buildings, the whole suggesting the very moment of an explosion. But it wasn't beautiful. Only clarity was beautiful. Clean lines, clean movements, clean designs.

'They will be even angrier if I go home,' Ruth said. 'Frederic was here. I told you. He stayed for an hour.'

Josef sorted through the remaining prints, found the little boy and the teddy bear. This was sentimental, good for a magazine. He would get more for this little boy than for all the beautiful ones put together. But now he was coming to the last of the pictures.

'Are you listening to me?' Ruth asked.

She was distraught. Everyone was distraught today. But he didn't want her whispering in his ear when he developed the last print. 'Frederic was here. For an hour.'

'He made me bring him in here. The bombs were dropping. We were both afraid. I was, anyway.'

'You showed him my studies?'

'I'm sorry, Josef. I just didn't know how to stop him.'

Josef took the torch away from her, sent the beam over the walls, counting. He found the three that had fallen on the floor, replaced them. 'He laughed?'

'I think he admired them.'

'Well, don't worry about it. Frederic is very persuasive.'

'Yes, but afterwards . . .'

Josef held the last photograph by its edges, allowed it to dry. The man lay on his back. What had happened to the rest of him was not relevant, because it was a head and shoulders study. The man was about to die. There was still life in his open mouth, but a moment after the shutter had closed the mouth had sagged, the eyes had frozen into just that look. The man's tie was loose, his hair was grey, but with dust rather than age. He might have been handsome, once, but now he looked tired and old and afraid. Josef wondered if everyone died at the same age, so that when a child was about to die he grew old at ten, fifteen years a second. Suddenly he wondered why he had never photographed death before.

'How horrible,' Ruth whispered. 'You must have been only inches away from him.'

'I was kneeling above him. But it's a picture of war. Horrible, but real. Reality can never be ugly. What were you saying about Frederic?'

Ruth sat at the table, her chin on her hands. 'Nothing.'

The Mercedes remained where Papa had left it that morning in the Sielce suburb. It had been thrown on its side, its windows shattered, the flames of the burning building across the street flickering from its paintwork. But there was no crater close by. 'Must have been some blast,' Frederic said.

'No blast,' said the man. 'We did that. Bloody German car. People who own German cars should all be shot.'

Frederic thrust his hands into his pockets, began the long walk home. The camera slapped him on the back as he walked, into the darkness, away from the flames and the heat and now, worst of all, the smell, of burning wood, and scorching flesh, faintly sweet, like overcooked pork.

Men who raped girls should also be shot. He wondered what constituted rape? There would be bruises on Ruth's body, but these would be because they had lain on the floor. Of course, she had wanted it too, at the end, because she was afraid and excited and tormented and sexually aroused, as he. But she had not wanted it before, and she had not wanted it afterwards. She was a Jewess, a member of the most moral race on earth. Antoni, in one of his big-brother moods, had joked about the Jews. 'Jewesses don't even strip for their husbands,' he had said. 'They screw in the dark. Fancy not being able to see Asja when I lie on her.'

Since joining the air force Antoni had become remarkably vulgar. Frederic hated him when he had spoken of Asja like that. But of course it was Asja *he* wanted to screw. When he held Ruth's buttocks, one in each hand, he had closed his eyes and imagined it was Asja he was holding. But when he had thought about Asja he could only remember the swell of her pregnant belly, a perfect semicircle of smooth flesh from breast to hair. He had wanted to stroke it, so gently.

The planes droned overhead. They were so confident they had not troubled to black out. Their lights winked in time to the roar of their engines, and from far behind Frederic the dull thuds began again. But he paid them no attention, walked down the centre of the empty, deserted road. Out here in the darkness they could not see him. In less than twelve hours he had changed from someone who would jump at a popping ballon to someone who could walk away from the destruction of a million people, intent on going home, for the last time.

Was he distressed at what he had done to Ruth? What had happened could be explained. Fear and desire and darkness and solitude had combined to turn him into a caricature of himself. So he was distressed. But he was more afraid. She would tell Josef, at the very least. And suppose she was pregnant? He might have to marry her. Mama would never speak to him again. She had become reconciled to Asja, but she still despised her for a Slav. Frederic and Josef, she had often said, had better come home with either a German or a Swede. She might go for a Finn. But she didn't even want them to marry a Pole, much less a Polish Jew. Mama should be taken out and shot. Undoubtedly she would be a traitor if she had the chance.

The planes went again, the darkness was intense, the glow settled on the horizon behind him. He had walked for hours and he was very thirsty. The only thing to pass his lips since breakfast had been a cup of coffee. But he was not hungry. Now it was after midnight, the 2nd of September 1939. In a few hours the war would be two days old. He wondered what this second day would bring. Nothing worse than the first. Nothing *could* be worse.

The house was in darkness. Papa was taking no risks. At night the Germans might drop a bomb wherever they saw a light. That would be ironical, were a German bomb to land on Mama. He wondered if he did hate her. He hated Germans, certainly, more for what they had made of him than for what they had done to his country. But it was necessary to come to a decision about Mama. Today everything had been confusion. Tomorrow the country would become organised, to fight a war against the Germans, against those who supported the Germans.

The side door was locked. He kicked dust from his

shoes, banged. A window opened above his head. 'Who's there?'

She, of all people, awake. 'Frederic.'

'Oh, thank God. Wait a moment.'

She had pulled on her négligé, but not fastened it. She carried a candle, and it illuminated her face, from underneath, and her hair, loose and everywhere. 'We thought you were dead.' She took him in her arms. She was so soft, and yet so hard, and she had never held him in her arms before.

She released him and stepped away. 'I will wake Mama. And Liese. She got home this afternoon. Did you know the Germans have crossed the border? Liese says they could hear gun-fire. Oh, you'll find candles on the kitchen table. They've cut off the electricity.'

He held her wrist.

She lifted the candle above her head, frowned. 'You look terrible. And you smell. You need a bath.'

'I can't stay.'

'And a meal,' Asja said.

'There's a war on. I must fight. Everyone must fight.'

'You haven't any papers.'

'I volunteered. I must report at dawn. So I came to say goodbye.'

'You just sit down and I'll fix you something to eat. I'll call Mama and Papa.'

He would not let her go. 'Have you heard from Antoni?'

'The telephone wires are down. Anyway, he is too busy bombing Berlin. So Mama says.'

'You're not afraid?'

Her wet eyes gleamed in the candlelight. 'Of course I'm afraid, Frederic. But what is the point in worrying? Soon enough we'll know.'

It occurred to Frederic that she did not love Antoni, that she had not loved Antoni for a long time. But she had loved him when they had returned from their honeymoon. He wondered when she had stopped.

'Frederic?' She was frowning again. She was the only woman he had ever seen who looked more beautiful frowning than smiling.

'I wanted to say goodbye. To you.'

'What happened today, Frederic?'

'Nothing.' He sighed. 'I came to see you because you are Polish and we are bastards.'

'But you are going to fight. For Poland.'

'Yes. Mama wouldn't understand. Asja, may I kiss you?'

She turned her cheek, and he caught her face between his hands and kissed her on the mouth, while it was open. He dared not let himself touch her body. He held her mouth for a long moment, and then he released her and ran down the stairs. He looked back when he reached the road. The candle still flickered in the doorway.

VI

'Frederic was here?' Mama cried. 'And you just let him go again, without waking us?'

'He was afraid you would try to stop him,' Asja explained.

'Just as you let Winawer go. Now he's been away a whole twenty-four hours.'

'I bet he's dead.' Christina slurped her coffee. 'I'll bet he was blown up by a bomb. Listen! Here they come again.'

'I must do something,' Papa said. 'I cannot just sit here while they destroy us. I must find Jan again, and we must organise something.'

'And get killed,' Mama said bitterly. 'Because that is

what is going to happen. The child is right. Winawer would have come back if he could. So he is dead. Antoni would have telephoned us or got a message to us if he were still all right so Antoni is dead. Josef is still in town, somewhere. So he is probably dead. And now Frederic is going to die and I am never going to see him again. All my sons. Dead. In a single day.' Tears ran down her cheeks, shining as they trickled as far as her chin. 'Only you had the sense to come home, Liese. Only you.'

Liese, with the thick wavy yellow hair and the arrogant mouth, gazed at her mother with pity. With her delicate features and billowing figure, she had never lacked for escorts, had made it perfectly clear since her return that she regarded the war as nothing more than a nuisance, certain to cause a postponement of the Raschinsky's ball.

Asja's gaze was equally cold. 'Antoni is crying.' At the door she paused. 'Because no bombs have fallen on Rokonow you think this is not our war? Poland is being invaded, Mama. I do not believe that nonsense on the radio that we attacked a German frontier post. Hitler wants to wipe us off the map, like he did to Czecho-slovakia, like he did to Austria. I agree with Papa. We should be doing something, volunteering, as Frederic did, instead of just sitting here enjoying breakfast as if nothing was happening.' She banged the door.

Mama stopped crying. 'Really, that girl forgets her-self.'

Liese went upstairs. 'Asja,' she called. 'I'm sorry.'

'What for?'

'For Mama. For all of us.'

'I thought Mama liked us to have our own opinions.' Asja went into the bedroom, lifted little Antoni from his cot. 'Sopping. Just sopping.'

Liese remained in the doorway. She and Asja had never been friends. 'She's afraid.' She shrugged. 'Every-one is afraid.'

'I know that.' Asja undressed little Antoni, quickly, expertly. Asja might not be able to do much with a polonaise, but she handled her first baby as if she had had dozens. It was born in her. Liese wondered how many other things had been born in Asja.

'Do *you* think Antoni is dead?'

'He is not dead until I know he is dead.' Asja cradled baby in her arms, went to the bathroom.

'What do you think is going to happen, Asja?'

Asja turned on the tap. A few drops of rusty water came out. 'They have burst the main. Liese, could you have one of the girls fill a bucket from the well?'

'Yes. What will happen to *us*, Asja?'

'If we win we will dance in the streets and be very arrogant. If we lose we will crawl in the streets and be very humble.'

Liese went downstairs, avoided the breakfast room, gave the maids the order for the water. She went into the drawing room, stood at the bay window, and watched the bombers over Warsaw. The city was hidden by smoke. That anyone could be alive in there was impossible. But Rokonow was still untouched. A bomb had fallen in the road about a mile from the house yesterday afternoon. The explosion had rattled all the windows and cracked some of them. But that was the extent of the damage. So far.

Liese clasped her hands round her throat. That Asja also should be afraid was disturbing. But perhaps Asja had reason to be frightened. Not Liese. Two years ago Mama and she had visited Munich, to see Mama's brother. He was a big man in the government, and he had had a party for them. There had been officers, magnificent young men in black uniforms, with perfect manners and the confidence of belonging to the best army in the world. They had been anxious to dance with the lovely Polish girl with the curling yellow hair and the frosty grey eyes and the arrogant twist to her lips. To be simultaneously desired by so many men had made that evening the most splendid of her life. But soon those young men, or others indistinguishable from them, would come marching down this road as conquerors. She knew this, as everyone else in the family knew it, as Asja knew it. Of all the women in Europe, Polish women knew conquest best.

But the young men who had danced with her in Munich had not been red Russian revolutionaries, she reminded herself. They had been German officers. And they had been charming.

Soon after dawn Frederic hitched a ride on a column of trucks making for Lowicz. They did not stop for the lone man standing by the roadside, but they were travelling slowly, and he waved and shouted and at last a sergeant gave him a hand up into the back of the last truck, where he collapsed to the floor, exhausted by his night's trekking.

'You're a sad looking sod,' the sergeant remarked. 'What regiment?'

'No regiment.' Frederic tapped his camera. 'Press.'

The sergeant gave him a drink of water and one of the soldiers offered him a biscuit. There were twenty men in the truck, obviously reservists being rushed to the front, for their grey uniforms were at once freshly pressed and ill fitting. 'You don't look like any newspaperman I've ever seen,' the sergeant said. 'What's your name?'

'Janski. I'm acting for my brother. He's a freelance photographer.'

'Janski?' asked one of the soldiers. 'You're not related to the toy people?'

'I'm a son.'

The soldier dug the man next to him in the ribs. 'We're travelling with a toff.'

The man did not open his eyes. 'Bloody bourgeois scum.'

'I bought a toy at Janski's once,' said a third man. 'A mechanical rabbit. It never worked.'

'You should have taken it back.'

'I did. And a fat man said I must have dropped it.'

'I'm sorry,' Frederic said. 'If it's any consolation the Germans have burned the store down.'

'Bloody Nazi scum,' said the man with his eyes shut. Frederic was intrigued. He'd never actually met a communist.

The people of Lowicz were packing up. The farmers and their wives were coming in from the neighbouring districts. The men drove the cattle in front of them, the women carried their shoes in their hands, as Asja had done the first time Frederic had ever seen her. He wondered if Liese's friends the Bieruts had locked up their house and gone to Warsaw. As if Warsaw would be any safer than here.

'What's the rush, then?' the sergeant shouted. 'The border's a hundred miles away.'

'The Germans aren't,' someone shouted back. 'Haven't you heard? Nothing can stop them. Nothing.'

The planes flew overhead all the time, but still making east, for Warsaw.

Beyond Lowicz they encountered the first real refugees. The road was packed with a solid mass of humanity, punctuated with ancient motor-cars and horse-drawn carts and bicycles, every vehicle piled high with clothes and pots and pans and mattresses, and on top of one car, precariously balanced and held in place by a single chafing rope, a grand piano. The stream flowed along the road like lava, slowly and yet relentlessly, shouting at the soldiers to get out of their way.

The truck stopped, an officer appeared. 'Unload,' he said. 'No unnecessary violence, but we have a war to fight. Get these people off the road.'

'Come on, lads.' The sergeant released the tailgate.

'Look there.' The communist had opened his eyes. The planes still droned overhead, purposefully. But now one of them detached himself from the echelon, swung low. He reminded Frederic of a shark. And he was followed by five others.

'Stukas,' said the sergeant. 'Hit the ditch.'

'Not Stukas,' corrected the communist. 'Messerschmitts.'

He led the rush for the side of the road.

A long wail rose from the refugees as the fighters came lower. They scattered, slowly at first, peeling off like the first feathers drifting from a split pillow in a high wind, and then making a human cloud, cleaving down the middle, as the planes formed line above the road, their wings spitting red.

Frederic jumped from the truck, fell to his hands and knees. The first plane seemed to be coming straight for him, the bullets carving the earth like the bow wave of a fast moving motor boat. Frederic stayed on his hands and knees, fear paralysing every muscle. In front of him the sergeant, refusing to make for the ditch until the last of his men had reached safety, raised his rifle, squeezed the trigger, and then came backwards as if kicked in the chest. His backside struck Frederic on the face, and they fell over together. Blood exploded across the back of the truck, and Frederic found himself on his face underneath the chassis. The sergeant sat against a wheel. Frederic could see his ribs, heaving through the tattered blood-mess of his freshly pressed jacket.

The camera had been smashed in the fall. Frederic took it off, gripped the sergeant's rifle, rolled out from under the truck. At the edge of the parapet he looked along the road. Four of the trucks were already in flames, and so was one of the cars. Horses thrashed their legs in the air

41

as they died, and the ropes holding the piano had burst, allowing it to crash into the earth. And there were scattered mounds, lying amidst the bicycles and their carts and their precious bundles, making large bundles of themselves on the road.

Frederic rolled into the ditch, landed on his back, stared at the most brilliantly blue sky he could remember, watched the six planes turning for their second run. They were single seater fighters. Six men were destroying an infantry column and several thousand civilians. He thought there was something unreal in those figures.

A man got up and began to run. He put his foot on Frederic's groin and Frederic cried out in pain and rolled on his face. But he retained the rifle. He was going to kill somebody. Anybody. In the midst of so much death a man had to kill if he was going to remain a man. He got up, too, and ran for the safety of the fields. He tripped, landed on his hands and knees. It was a woman, lying on her back, both hands pressed to her belly. There were no ribs down there, only oozing red and brown. Her eyes were open, but he did not think she saw him. He did not want to look at her again. She had strongly Slavic features, reminded him of Asja. He turned away, saw the child, perhaps two years old. She was unhurt, although dazed at being thrown through the air. She was getting to her feet, staring at Frederic. She smiled. She said, 'Dadda, Mamma, gone dey.'

Frederic stepped round her and ran for the trees.

VII

'Be seated, gentlemen.' The general himself sat at a large desk, littered with papers and reports. Behind him on the stone wall were two more maps, one of Poland, the other a street plan of Warsaw. Both were covered with flags, apparently scattered at random. In front of the desk were rows of chairs, in which the civilians now took their places, ill at ease in the presence of so many soldiers, thinking back to their own service days. Above their heads the reinforced concrete roof of the bunker shuddered as a bomb landed, and the movement reached the waiting men. The officers standing along the walls, the armed guards on the door, never moved.

The general smiled. 'You may smoke, if you wish.' He paused, surveying their faces. 'On Friday morning, gentlemen, our country was the object of a vicious and unprovoked attack. The shape of this attack you all know. It is a merciless onslaught upon our defenceless cities, upon our wives and children. But what we experienced on Friday and yesterday, what we are experiencing today, is nothing more than an overture. The Nazi aim is conquest.'

He sighed. 'Alone and unaided, we would stand no chance, a nation of thirty millions, an essentially peaceful nation, opposed to one of seventy millions, girded for war. But we are not alone, gentlemen. I can tell you that the British government has this morning declared war on Germany.'

'What about France?' asked a voice.

'France will follow the British lead. Now, gentlemen, there is no possibility of French or British help being available for the next few weeks. Thus for those weeks our task, here in Poland, is to bring Hitler's armies to a halt, to pin him down, on his eastern front, while Great Britain and France hurl their armies at the so called West Wall and crush it out of existence.'

The general drank some water. 'Due to the surprising nature of the attack, our armies, we have to be frank about this, are falling back. Our air force was mostly destroyed on the ground. The first round belongs to the enemy. But we must win the second. Our armies have been defeated, but they have not been destroyed. As soon as they are regrouped we shall counter-attack and bring this impetuous Hun to a halt. However, it is possible that enemy columns may penetrate as far as the Vistula.'

They gazed at him, faces devoid of emotion. Again he sighed. 'That is why I have called you together, gentlemen, as the leading citizens of our great city. I am not going to discuss matters like rationing and allotment of air-raid shelters and the evacuation of women and children. Your mayor has already taken these matters in hand and the necessary instructions will be issued today. I want to talk to you about the defence of Warsaw. For Warsaw must be held. For Poland, for our wives and children, for our honour, and, above all, for the defeat of Germany. We, my soldiers and your civilians, are going to fight for this city, street by street.'

He stood up, turned to the map of Warsaw. 'Now, gentlemen, let us first of all consider the essential points, the places which must not be allowed to fall into the hands of the enemy, the positions where we will establish our fortifications.'

Anton Janski discovered he was not listening. He had heard all this nineteen years before, when Tuchachevsky' Russians had been advancing from the east like a plague of ants. *They* had also reached the Vistula. And there they had been stopped. The marshal had struck up from the south, leaving his flanks exposed to Budienny and Yegorov, staking all on a desperate counter-attack. But that had been nineteen years ago.

Somehow it seemed less important, now. Young Antoni, then, had never left the ground. He had been killed, perhaps even as he taxied that machine which had been the centre of his life. How to tell Asja? How to tell Anna? Anna would say, why? There was no need. No German is going to trouble the family of Anneliese Harrwitz. Just

44

identify yourself to them. Just be a traitor.

The man seated beside him stood up, and then the next. They were applauding. Anton did the same, standing and clapping. The general saluted, went to the door. His place was taken by a captain. 'The raid has ceased for the moment, gentlemen. It is safe for you to return to the streets.' His smile was contemptuous. He saw no future in defending Warsaw with a rabble of overage reservists.

Jan clapped his brother on the shoulder. 'So there we are, Anton. We, the businessmen of Warsaw, will lead the defence. And we will be the first the Jerries will put up against the wall.'

It was hard to tell when Jan was serious and when he was joking, perhaps because he was never entirely either.

'And let me tell you something else.' Jan dropped his voice. 'So we will defend Warsaw while the British roll that West Wall flat. Do you know how many divisions Britain has under arms? Six.'

'He was thinking about the French.'

'I was in Paris two years ago, Anton. Never forget that. I know the French. But for the architecture, and the girls, I could have been in Moscow. Don't tell me about the French.'

'So you are not going to fight?'

Jan shrugged. 'Of course I am going to fight, Anton. We have no business any more. What else can we do but fight?' He winked. 'I am going to see how many of the girls I can recruit. A woman's army, by God. I'll die in harness.'

Overnight, the column had become experts. Not at fighting the enemy, but at avoiding him. They felt safer now the trucks were burned. They marched briskly, one man in each platoon at all times watching the sky. At the first alarm they scattered into the ditches, lying low until the fighters had passed on, seeking some less alert regiment, or, better yet, some accumulation of refugees, straggling, helplessly encumbered.

Frederic marched with the rear platoon. He still carried his rifle, had found for himself a bandolier and a cap, and on the advice of his new comrades, a uniform jacket, taken from a dead man. It fitted badly, pulling across the shoulders, but he was no worse off than the other reservists, and now, they reminded him, he was protected by the laws of war; all their trousers were so covered in mud and dust there was no telling which were uniform issue and which were not.

More important than his clothes, he had also secured a water bottle and a haversack containing rations, and a spare pair of boots. He was well off, really, with water to drink and food to eat and companions to talk with. He was better off than anyone he passed coming the other way, streaming to the east, hurrying, terrified, carrying their pitiful bundles. Frederic did not look at them. In each of them he saw the little girl standing above her dying mother outside Lowicz. He wondered where she had found her next meal.

No one questioned his presence in the ranks. No one questioned anything, least of all where they were going or when they would encounter an enemy on the ground in front of them as opposed to those in the air above them. The regiment had left its colonel on the road outside Lowicz. But the adjutant had all the necessary maps, and he had commandeered a bicycle from a group of refugees and sent a messenger across country in search of brigade headquarters.

Meanwhile, they marched, and rested, and sheltered in the ditches, and asked the refugees why they were running away. The answer was always the Germans, yet the villages were usually empty, at least of Germans. But those who had stayed behind were having a very successful time. Frederic imagined Rokonow in the hands of the looters, the Janski villa, with all its carefully gathered treasures, being picked apart by scavengers. But the Janski villa was something else he preferred not to think about.

An empty sky, a bright sun, a warm breeze, and now, all of a sudden, an empty road as well, devoid of refugees. Of walking or running or cycling refugees. Of course they were still here, on the road and in the ditches and in the field. The planes had passed this way. Dead refugees, even dead children and a long-legged girl with her skirt blowing in the wind, no longer interested the column. But it was Sunday, and when the padre called them together then they could not help but think of the bodies lying all around them. Frederic thought of the girl's legs, of the flies on them.

The prayers were interrupted by the planes, and they returned to the ditches. The planes passed on, and in their place arrived a lancer, capless, his horse a lather of sweat. He halted at the head of the column, panted his orders, and the orders came down the line. 'Now then, boys,' said Frederic's sergeant, a new sergeant, this, promoted from the ranks only yesterday. 'We are in contact at last. The enemy is coming up this road, and we are going to hold that ridge over there.'

They lay on the ground, amidst the trees. These were great poplars, and the foliage gave them protection. It occurred to Frederic that they were lucky to be fighting this war in September, instead of next month, when the leaves would be clouding downwards. He was not afraid. Lying on the dusty earth against a tree, he was only aware of how pleasant it was on this glorious summer's day. Here he was invisible, surrounded by his comrades, tough, professional soldiers. All they had to do was watch the Germans come along the road in front of them. There was a regiment of cavalry in the village down the slope, also waiting. Some day, when the war was over, he was going to feel sorry for the Germans. These Germans.

It was like a morning on a farm, down at Zabie, perhaps, where he had first seen Asja. There had been a tractor in the distance, grinding away as it moved up and down the field. There were not that many tractors in all Poland, and this had been the only one in Zabie. The children had walked behind it, singing and shouting. He wondered if there were children walking behind this tractor. These tractors.

They came up a shallow slope and across the field on a wide front. The earth was dry and the wind was from the west. Clouds of dust drifted towards the Polish line. But even through the dust Frederic counted more tractors here than he had seen in his entire life. They looked peaceful enough. The trapdoors on the roofs were open, and each trap contained a man, looking out, enjoying the sunshine.

'Hold your fire,' said the sergeant. 'Not a sound, now. Not a movement.'

On came the panzers. Into a trap. Several thousand tons of rolling steel about to be enveloped and pounded into submission by a few hundred tons of flesh and blood and lead. And now he was afraid.

A trumpet sounded, above even the clatter of the tracks. The panzers did not stop, but you could sense, even at this distance, a movement amongst the heads in the traps. The cavalry trotted out of the village. The sun gleamed from their lance-heads. They looked very businesslike on their magnificent horses, with their long lances and their drab grey uniforms and their rifles hanging at their sides. There was even a cornet bearing the standard with the white eagle flapping in the breeze. All they needed to be sure of victory was Prince Poniatowski at their head. In his thesis, on the part Poland had played in the Napoleonic War, Frederic had called these men the most feared cavalry in the world.

They advanced at the trot, broke into a canter. Suddenly this was a mock battle, between toy tanks and toy soldiers. You expected a gigantic little boy in short trousers to step down from heaven and move each horseman forward, towards the tanks. Only the dust was real, rising from the horses' hooves and drifting towards the concealed infantry. The opposing lines met in the dust, and were lost to view. There was a roar, of exhausts and armour and cannon-fire and rifle-fire and of men, and of horses. The panzers had plunged headlong into the trap. The infantrymen waited. Should any German emerge from the dust-cloud they would close the trap, finally. They waited, for what might have been an hour but was only a few seconds. Then the dust rolled on, and the tractors returned to view, clanking towards the hill. The cavalry had disappeared.

VIII

Uncle Jan rode out to Rokonow on a bicycle. He looked absurd, as his fat belly seemed to hang above the handlebars, but he explained that he couldn't get petrol for the car, and with all the craters this was the best way to travel.

Christina waited at the gate to welcome him. 'Isn't it terrible?' She was talking about the garden, which was ankle deep in weeds, and she was thinking about the house, which was starting to accumulate dust since the girls had left.

'Terrible.' He put his arm round her waist to squeeze her against him. Uncle Jan had done this since she could remember. So did Papa, of course, but where Papa squeezed with the palm of his hand, Uncle Jan squeezed with his fingers. To be squeezed by Uncle Jan gave Christina the same feeling as lowering herself into a very hot bath tub. 'Where's your mama, then?'

'In bed. Mama has stayed in bed since it began. Uncle Jan, is Warsaw really burned down?'

'Just about. You're lucky you live in Rokonow.'

She followed him up the stairs. 'Oh, the Germans have bombed Rokonow, too. Don't you see the craters in the road? And they've knocked the glass out of nearly all the windows. And you know what?' She giggled. 'The whisky decanter shattered.'

'Now there is a catastrophe. Where are Liese and Asja?'

'Asja is feeding baby, and Liese is in the kitchen.'

'And what are you doing?'

Christina's laugh was a high, happy sound. 'I'm doing nothing, Uncle Jan. Term starts next week, but Mama says she won't let me go.'

'Nobody's going to school right now, Christina. You tell Liese to come to Asja's room.'

Christina ran into the kitchen. Liese wore her hair up, and an apron over her slacks. 'Uncle Jan's here. He wants to talk to you. Upstairs.'

'Did he bring a message from Papa?'

Christina giggled. 'I forgot to ask.'

Asja had turned her chair to face the wall, while little Antoni sucked. Uncle Jan had never been allowed in Asja's bedroom before, would not have been allowed in now if he'd taken the trouble to knock. He sat on the bed, pretending not to look at Asja. But he could see her in the mirror. Between them they formed a pattern, Christina thought. Every time little Antoni took his mouth away, Uncle Jan's nostrils widened.

'How is Papa?' Liese asked.

'Working. We are all working.'

'He should come out to see Mama. Even Josef came out yesterday afternoon. He walked all the way.'

'Your father is a very busy man,' Uncle Jan said

50

severely. 'We are putting Warsaw into a state of defence. We are going to defend the city to the last bullet. So I have come to invite you to take part. Papa said no, but I thought you girls might like to do your bit. This is a war of the people. Men, and women, fighting shoulder to shoulder. And children, too.'

He was on his feet now, so excited that he had forgotten to look at Asja, and little Antoni had stopped sucking altogether.

'What would we have to do?' Liese asked.

'Well, for women it's mostly filling sandbags.'

'Mama is very upset by everything that has happened,' Liese said. 'I could not possibly leave her.'

'I would like to help, Mr. Janski,' Asja said. 'But I am still feeding Antoni.'

'I understand.' Uncle Jan stood above her, a very good observation point. 'Is there any news of young Antoni?'

She shook her head. 'I know the air force is destroyed, Mr. Janski. I heard it on the radio. But not the crews. Antoni will be fighting with the army.'

'With Frederic, eh?'

She smiled. 'With Frederic.'

'Well, I thought I'd come out and put you in the picture, so to speak. Give my love to Anna. Don't come down, Liese. Christina will show me out.'

She held his hand. 'I'd come with you, Uncle Jan. I can't go to school, and I'm no use around here. Liese won't let me do anything except sweep, and I hate sweeping. Asja won't let me touch baby. Can't I come?'

Uncle Jan stood under the Matejkos. 'Those should be stored somewhere safe. In a bank vault.' He put his arm round her waist, right round, so that his fingers touched the softness of her bodice. 'I know you would like to come with me, Kitgirl. But you have to stay here. I'll come out and see you again.' A last squeeze, and he was clambering on to his bicycle and kicking the pedals. Christine closed

51

the front door, slipped the bolt. Liese came out of the pantry.

'You want to stay away from him, Christina.' For a moment she sounded exactly like Mama. 'He's a lecher.'

'I like Uncle Jan. At least he's cheerful. And he's only trying to make sure we win the war.'

Liese's mouth was arrogant. 'Not even God can do that.'

It had rained overnight, and now the ditch contained six inches of unpleasantly cold water. But Frederic welcomed this. The water was not deep enough to drown him, but a man lying on his face in a ditch full of water at least looks dead, and Frederic had now lain in this ditch for twenty-four hours. Besides, the water, however muddy, was cleaner than his body. He felt if he lay in here a few more weeks he might even be clean enough to get out.

His body might be clean. His mind was never going to be clean again. Memory began with the tree, against which he had pressed his back as he had heard the tanks clattering towards him. They had splashed through the dust. And they had splashed through the men, too. The man next to Frederic had been called Smorodin, and he had come from somewhere to the east, Brest Litovsk or somewhere like that. Not that it mattered. Smorodin had been unable to find a tree. Frederic remembered a frog squashed by a car outside Rokonow. The frog had exploded at both ends, its guts forced through its mouth by the pressure on its body. Then it had been an empty flat slab. Smorodin had been considerably larger than the frog, but, then, the tank had been considerably larger than the motor-car. Some of what Smorodin had spewed up had hit Frederic's tree, and that had been sufficient. So he had run away. Nobody had minded. Other people had been running away, through the tanks, throwing away their rifles, seeking shelter. They had even seen German soldiers following the tanks, smart-looking fellows for all the dust that caked their uniforms. One or two of the Germans had fired at the running Poles, like exuberant boys hurling stones after birds. But they had not been seriously trying to kill anybody. They had left that to the panzers, and they assumed, correctly, that anyone who happened to be alive after the panzers had rolled through a battalion was not going to do any more fighting for a very long time.

Frederic supposed he was a coward. Any soldier who runs away is a coward. And to be one of several hundred cowards was no consolation. No general could expect men to fight moving masses of steel, off which their bullets bounced like pebbles, but Frederic had been too afraid even to squeeze his trigger. Then he had thrown the rifle away, reasoning that the laughing German soldiers might take aim at a man running with a rifle in his hands. Now he had thrown away the bandolier as well.

Something fell into the water beside his head. Frederic watched the splash, listened to the slither of boots. Fingers touched his haversack, began fumbling at the strap. He turned over, throwing his arms upwards to envelop the scavenger. The man was capless, but his uniform was a tattered grey, and he was unarmed. 'I thought you were dead,' he explained.

Frederic sat up.

'Good idea, though.' The newcomer was as tall as Frederic, but not so broad, and he was dark. His nose was long and slightly drooped. 'I am Rosenthal.'

'Janski.'

Rosenthal was gazing at Frederic's haversack. 'An unusual name. There is a toy store of that name on Senator Street. Some say it is the biggest toy store in Poland.'

'It was.'

'Do you manufacture your own toys, Mr. Janski?'

'We had a workshop behind the store.'

53

'Ah, yes. I too am a manufacturer, in my own way. I make ornaments, jewellery. Not real stones, you understand. Purely for decoration.'

'Were you in my regiment?'

'I was an aristocrat amongst soldiers, Mr. Janski. I was a cavalryman. Yesterday morning I struck my lance into a tank, and, do you know, it would not go in? So I threw the useless thing away. The tank, in turn, threw my horse away. A very noble fellow. I am speaking of the tank. My horse was obviously of no more value in this mechanical age.' Rosenthal sat in the ditch. The water rose over his boots. 'Amongst my other accomplishments, Mr. Janski, I also eat. This may surprise you, as there is no visible evidence of such a talent, but it is there, I assure you.'

Frederic took off his haversack. 'You'll find it soggy.'

Rosenthal undid the strap with trembling fingers. 'It is good biscuit consommé, Mr. Janski. We will share.'

'You eat it.'

'Your first war?' Rosenthal lowered his face into the haversack. When he had recovered his breath he sighed. 'Mine, too, as a matter of fact.'

'What are we going to do?'

'A very important question. I think we may agree that the Polish army no longer exists. Such portions of it as have not yet surrendered will do so when they in turn meet General Guderian. Therefore it no longer requires us to be gallant defenders of the state. My first idea was to try to reach either the Lithuanian or the Rumanian borders. Then we should be interned, presumably.'

'Let's go.'

'Unfortunately, we are a fair distance from either of those attractive countries, and we are surrounded by Germans, and we have no food, as I am about to finish this delicious soup. Therefore, I think our only alternative is to ask for assistance from those fellows over there.'

Frederic peeped over the parapet. The men were armed, and wore olive-green uniforms, and were laughing as they poked amongst the dead. 'Germans!'

'They are the victors, we the vanquished. One must learn to face facts, Mr. Janski. Now, if I remember the drill correctly, we clasp our hands on the backs of our necks, and we walk towards them, saying, what do we say, Mr. Janski?'

'*Kamerad,*' Frederic said.

IX

Even the planes sounded different. This morning there were no roars and no zooms, no whines and no bangs. This morning the planes flew in orderly squadrons, wing-tip to wing-tip, hundreds, perhaps thousands of them, obliterating the sky, forming a thundercloud which lay over all of Poland.

And yet their noise was subdued by the tramp of marching feet, a river of sound which flowed along every main road into Warsaw. These men had just fought a war, but their uniforms were spotless, their rifle barrels and their bayonets gleamed. They lifted each leg high in the air and thumped it down again, in perfect unison. They were the victors.

They were alone in their glory, at least in Rokonow. Few people were on the street, and those hastily went inside again, to watch from the windows of their houses, as the Janskis were doing. They stood at the drawing-room window, watching, and in turn being watched by the Germans who commanded the street corners. Alone of all the houses in Rokonow, the Janski's villa flew a swastika flag, from an upstairs window. No one had known Mama possessed such a flag. But this morning she had unpacked it from the trunk in which she kept her best linen and had draped it from her bedroom window. Now she was silent, sympathising with her husband and his people, but her whole body swelled and her eyes gleamed with passion. The Reich was expanding, as the Fuehrer had promised, to include Volksdeutsche wherever they might be, and now that irresistible force had reclaimed Anneliese Harrwitz, and her years of exile might never have been.

Papa stood beside her. There was no apprehension or even resentment in Papa's face; he merely looked very tired. For Papa, Poland had fallen on that Friday morning a month ago when the store had collapsed into a heap of rubble. Poland would rise again when the store was rebuilt. What happened in between was irrelevant to Papa. But not to Josef. Cameras had been forbidden this morning, and Josef without a camera seemed naked. His hands made a box in front of him, his fingers twiddled with each other. Here was an historic occasion, and he was not recording it for posterity to hate.

The girls made a separate group at the other big window. Liese glowed, like her mother. Of course, the marching men were common soldiers, and Liese had no intention of ever looking at them twice. But if private soldiers could be so splendid, and so perfectly disciplined, and so dedicated, think about the officers. The young airmen Antoni had brought home to meet his beautiful sister had just been boys.

Christina was excited, hopping up and down, running her hands through her already untidy hair, bubbling with excitment. Christina had wept a full twenty-four hours after Frederic had gone off, because Frederic had been her favourite brother. But that had been a whole month ago. And so much had happened in that month

Asja left the window, went upstairs to her bedroom. Mama had wanted to bring little Antoni down to watch the parade, but she had refused. Little Antoni had a nap in the middle of every morning, and if German bombs had not been able to disturb him German soldiers certainly were not going to. So Asja sat on her bed, gazed at the cot, and listened to the tramp of feet. If she knew so well what the others were feeling then it was strange that she could not isolate her own thoughts. Fear, certainly. The red, white and black flag draped from the window along the corridor did not protect her. Nor did it protect her family, down in Zabie. Her only hope was the speedy return of Antoni. The war was over. Whatever had happened to Antoni when his airfield had been overrun, if he was alive he would now be coming home. And Frederic, too. It was strange. She could not imagine Antoni as being anything else than alive, confident, arrogant. She had no fears for Antoni. But Frederic was so vulnerable. She dreamed of him almost every night, standing in the doorway, kissing her. She could remember the taste of his lips. Poor Frederic. He had not run towards the defence of his country. He had run away from what lay in his home, and she could not be angry with him. But she prayed that Antoni would be the first back.

The door opened. 'Bastards,' Josef said.

'It could have been worse. They could have been the Russians. I always knew the Russians would come back. They could have been given as far as the Vistula, instead of the Bug.'

'And you would have liked that less?'

'The Russians shoot people like the Janskis.'

The Germans won't shoot us,' Josef said. 'They are too civilised. They will suck our blood.'

There was no sound above the shuffling of two hundred thousand feet. It filled the air, drove the birds far away, raised a cloud of dust which hung above the column like a flag, signalling its presence throughout the land, warning the fortunate, keep away, avoid this place, this road, this is a legion of the dead, marching to death. Only comparable with the sound was the smell. Here were a hundred thousand men who had removed no article of their clothing, for any purpose whatsoever, for three weeks. At first, each smell had been identifiable, at least in Frederic's immediate neighbourhood. He could say with certainty, old Willi is at it again, weak bowels, you know; even if nothing goes in, something comes out. But now there was no identification. The column carried its own miasma, an almost visible effluvium which hung above their heads like a mist, perhaps stretching farther afield than the shuffling of shoeless feet warning farmer and villager for miles around.

Two weeks ago to belong to such an army had been to dip your head so deeply into shame that recovery had seemed impossible. You shambled, and between you and Rosenthal, shambling beside you, there arose a sense of comradeship stronger even than your mutual smell. You were bound together by the understanding that you were no longer human beings, no longer, apparently, even useful animals. Just walking shitbags, to use the German expression. But over two weeks' degradation had slipped into the background. Your spirits rose above such mundane matters as your belly grew lighter. Whether or not you stank had no relevance besides the question of whether or not you ate. Men who had defended their positions to the last bullet became unimportant when placed alongside a hero like Frederic Janski, who had never fired his rifle in anger, but who had had the alertness to seize that rabbit last Monday. Twelve men had shared the tearing apart of that not quite dead rabbit, and eight more had had a long gnaw on the gutted skin and fur. Frederic Janski had provided food, of a sort, for twenty men. When the medals were coming round, nineteen men at least would remember Frederic Janski.

Food was the only subject worth thinking about, or speaking about. You could not wonder what you were doing here; that was to collapse in a welter of self-recrimination and self-pity. You dared not look at your feet, or consider your feet. You had to perform a tremendous act of will to think coherently at all, except about food, and your thoughts about food were liable to lead into strange and unholy paths.

To be very hungry was rather like being drunk. Frederic had only been drunk once, but he remembered it very well. In the midst of the lightheadedness, the uncertainty of his surroundings and the disregard for them, he had found it best to fix his mind upon one irrelevant point. He could not remember what it had been then. But on this march it was Asja. Because he felt that, being a mountain peasant who had relieved herself in a shed at the bottom of the garden and bathed in the kitchen tub once a month, Asja would know all about odours and lice and blisters, and would not be nauseated by them in the way Liese, for instance, would be nauseated. Or even Mama. Definitely Mama. But he felt that if, by some miracle, he could find himself walking across the croquet lawn towards the house, and the door opened and Asja stood there as she had done that Friday night so long ago, she would utter not a word of distress or protest, but would take him inside, and herself wash him clean, with those strong hands which had learned about life on the udders of her father's cow.

The column halted. How long it had been halted was difficult to decide. Frederic was near the rear and the men at the head of the column might have stopped an hour ago. Yesterday, perhaps. But now the process of ceasing to move had reached the end of the column, and the much more difficult process began of not moving and yet not falling down. But you did not fall down here. Some had,

59

but that had been two weeks ago, at the end of the first week's marching and starving. Adolf, as they called their number one guard, had put his gun muzzle to their heads and squeezed the trigger. Adolf was a very merciful fellow. Other guards might have shot from a distance and left their victims to bleed on the road. Adolf went up to each man and put the gun muzzle against his head.

Adolf rode up and down the column on a motor-bike, sometimes with Hermann on the sidecar, sometimes alone. Presumably there were other guards, farther along the column; it was not credible for two men to have charge of so many. But then it was incredible that the five hundred men who composed Frederic's rearguard should be afraid of two men, even two men armed with tommy guns. At the cost of no more than a dozen lives, it should be possible to overpower both Adolf and Hermann. But which dozen lives? To be a hero you must walk like a hero and dress like a hero. Above all, you must smell like a hero.

A ripple spread down the ranks. Perhaps it too had started yesterday. 'Peace!' 'We have surrendered!' 'The Russians have come in, and taken half the country.'

History, Frederic thought, is an unchallengeable force. Poland was not meant to be independent. It had had its chance, once, when its boundaries had touched the Black Sea and even the Volga. And nations, like men, do not receive more than one chance.

'We'll be going home, Mr. Janski,' Rosenthal said. 'Think of it. We'll turn round and march back again. It's all over.'

Frederic watched the open car bouncing down the road. It contained two men in black uniforms. It stopped opposite his group. There were other motor-cars, farther up the column. Dozens of them. And the men in black uniforms were getting out.

'Officers,' Rosenthal said. 'Now they have to account

for us the bastards are worried about us. Tell them, Mr. Janski. You speak the best German. Stand forth and tell them.'

Frederic hesitated. These officers, if they were officers —certainly they wore tremendously smart black uniforms with little skull badges on their caps—did not look particularly concerned at the condition of their prisoners.

'Geneva Convention,' Rosenthal said. 'They had no right to treat us like animals. Tell them, Mr. Janski. Don't be afraid of them. Look, I'll come with you.'

Frederic sucked air into his lungs. Five hundred men were watching him. Since the rabbit they had counted him a magician, a born leader of men. He stepped out of the ranks, heels together, shoulders back. 'Permission to speak, sir!' He was surprised at the sound of his voice.

The SS men looked at him in mild surprise.

'A trouble-maker, sir,' Adolf said. 'A young firebrand.'

'A Jew?'

'No, sir,' Frederic said.

'But this man is a Jew.' The SS man pointed at Rosenthal, rigid at Frederic's shoulder.

'Yes, sir,' Rosenthal said. 'I am also a trooper in the Fourth Cavalry Regiment.'

'We have come here to separate the Jews from the Aryans.' The SS man raised his voice. 'Jews leave the ranks and assemble here.'

Twenty men lined up behind Rosenthal. Other groups were being detached at varying intervals all along the columns. And the column was moving again, beginning the vast shuffle which commenced in the distance and stretched all the way back to the rear. Frederic became afraid. 'I am not a Jew,' he said urgently. 'My mother was a German Aryan.'

'Twenty Jews and one anti-social,' said the first SS man, who had been counting.

'I merely wish to ask about food,' Frederic protested.

'We have none. Those men are dying of hunger.'

The second SS man smiled. 'Then you have accomplished your purpose. You are not going to die of hunger.'

Johnson drank coffee, watched the morning sunlight slanting through the trees as the train slowed. Soon the houses would begin. He found himself waiting for his first glimpse of Berlin with remarkable anticipation.

'Good morning, Mr. Johnson.' Peter Cohn hovered in the doorway. 'Did you sleep well?'

'When the border guards let me.'

Cohn came inside. 'I wish to say goodbye, as I shall be getting off in Berlin. There is something very satisfying about returning home, after even a short absence. And the country around Berlin is so pretty. Did you know Germany at all, before the war?'

'I lived in Germany for over a year,' Johnson said. 'But it was during the war.' He glanced through the window. 'As you say, the trees are very pretty.

Cohn hesitated, then held out his hand. 'Goodbye, Mr. Johnson. I hope you enjoy your holiday.'

Johnson squeezed the limp fingers. He had used up all his hatred nearly thirty years ago. He closed the door, sat down, gazed through the window at the trees.

2

Christmas 1939

The train jarred to a stop. Frederic had been dozing, his head on Rosenthal's shoulder, his knees buckling. Now he jerked into wakefulness. Stoppages were usually worse than movement because there was a general relaxation, which spread from shoulder to shoulder, groin to groin, all pressed close one against the other. Vast areas became damp, vast aromas rose towards the low roof.

But this time the doors were squealing as they opened. 'Out! Out!' The man was one of several, all of whom wore black uniforms. Black would be imprinted on his mind for ever, Frederic thought. When he got out of here, he was going to get himself a gun, and he was going to shoot everyone he could find wearing black. He thought about nothing else, except when Rosenthal talked to him, about sunshine and blue sky, about children and the art of making cheap jewellery. But Rosenthal had talked less during the past twenty-four hours. Sammy had a problem; the man standing against his back was dead. This depressed Sammy, because no one knew how long this journey was going to last, and it was very close in the cattle truck. So Frederic had had more time than usual to think, and he could not understand how he had once actually held a rifle in his hands and not killed somebody. He thought that he had been mad, all his life, and only just regained his sanity.

But the doors were open, and they were getting out, thirty-three of them. Only three men took the opportunity to fall down in the truck. Frederic was amazed. He had expected many more to be dead.

They marched. The road was rough, but the woods on

either side were beautiful. It was autumn, the leaves fell thick and fast, the sun came through the trees in great slants of muted light, the birds had already left and the wood was silent, except for the tramp of marching men. You learned something new every day. That bare, bloody, shapeless feet could make a sound like boots.

'My first visit to Germany.' Rosenthal was himself again now he had lost the company of the dead man. 'I shall complain to my travel agent about the journey. But perhaps the accommodation will be satisfactory.'

'Looks pretty good to me.' You could not despair in Rosenthal's company. But it did look good. A paved street, on either side neatly tended gardens, and delightful villas, set on the slope of a gentle hill, surrounded by the forest. In one of the gardens a children's birthday party was in progress. None of the girls and boys looked at the column.

'I don't think these are our quarters,' Rosenthal said. The good road ended, and they went up the hill and down the farther side, and faced a gatehouse, very like a reconstruction of a western frontier fort, except that instead of wood these walls were barbed wire. There was a plaque over the gate: 'WE WORK FOR VICTORY.'

'And I have an idea we are going to do just that,' Rosenthal said.

'Inside, inside, you whoresons,' shouted a large man. 'Inside, bastards. Down you go. Salute the encampment. Saxon salute, you sons of bitches.'

'What's that?' Frederic asked Rosenthal.

'Who spoke?' roared the Block Leader. 'What drivelling dropping of a fat-arsed Jewish ape?'

'I'm a Pole, not a Jew,' Frederic explained, and hit the ground. His head went round and round, and seemed also to be falling from side to side. He hadn't observed that the Block Leader carried a stick.

66

'Up, up, Pole, or I'll give you something to lie down for.'

Frederic joined the others in their deep knee-bend, hands clasped on the back of his neck. He gazed across an expanse of beaten earth to a group of barracks. In front of the buildings were gathered hundreds of men, all wearing what appeared to be striped pyjamas. Their heads were shaved and they suggested convalescents recovering from some debilitating illness, and they were gazing at the new arrivals with a mixture of unconcern and anticipation.

The pain spread from his calf muscles into his thigh muscles and up his back, and down his neck into his arms and shoulders, and he knew that his understanding in the train had been correct. This was sanity, this was reality, and all else was the oblivion of madness. And even if Mama pulled the right strings and got him out of here he would never be mad again.

Never before had he questioned his eventual release. He listened to the SS men moving behind him, insulting those they felt like insulting, kicking or beating those they felt like beating. His own head still swung, and the tears still rolled down his cheeks. He could only pray that they did not start on him again.

He stared at the barracks, and the administrative block to the right. Focus. Concentrate. Don't fall down.

There was a man over there. He wore black. Frederic thought the world must be divided into just two races, those who wore black, and the others. Those who wore black controlled. And this man controlled even those who wore black. This he knew, although he could not see the man clearly; his eyes were too full of tears. But he could see the way the man stood, the way he walked, the gleam of his uniform, from high peaked cap to black boots. It came to Frederic, crouching in the dust, with the afternoon sunlight beginning to fade behind the wood that surrounded the camp, that over there was a man who would make the bully on the gate seem like a childish play-mate. And the man was gazing at Frederic.

Mama had the family up at dawn. Liese and Christina polished and swept, Josef scrubbed the kitchen floor, Asja got little Antoni out of bed an hour before his usual time. By breakfast the house was almost as clean as it had been in August, and there were flowers in every vase.

'All this fuss,' Josef sneered. 'For a German.'

'Be quiet,' Mama snapped. 'You'll say, yes, sir, and no, sir, and nothing else. And that goes for you too, Jan. And will you please shave.'

'I have given up shaving for the duration,' Jan said.

'The war is over. Asja, I wish little Antoni dressed in his best gown.'

'But, Mama, that gown has to be laundered.'

'Please do as I say, Asja. You, of all people, must make a good impression.'

Asja supposed she was right. Already there had been rumours, whispered stories. But she was the widow of a Polish pilot, who had been Volksdeutsche, and she was the mother of another little Volksdeutsche. No one could take that away from her. Nevertheless, she dressed little Antoni in his christening gown, and then, because he was fretful at being disturbed, she walked him up and down the bedroom, and looked out of the window, and thought about her mother and father and her brother in the mountains behind Zakopane. She did not suppose the Germans had got there yet. Perhaps the Germans never would get there, and the Huzulins would live out this war as they had lived out many wars in the past, minding their cattle and letting the world forget they existed. In the mountains was security.

Little Antoni wailed, hungrily. Asja's mother had fed Asja until her second birthday. Asja's breasts, so large, so

68

perfectly shaped, were running dry in less than six months. But Asja's mother had had a husband at her side. Uncle Jan had brought the news two days ago. Antoni had died in the very first hour of the war, struck by a bomb while running to his aircraft. There had been almost no grief, not even from Papa. And Asja? Asja had thought, he was dead, then, before Frederic woke me up that morning. He had been long dead when Frederic kissed me goodbye. But Frederic was a taste, not a memory. And the staff car was drawing up at the gate.

Josef opened the front door. There were three officers, but only the colonel mattered. He was the smartest soldier Asja had ever seen. He had grey threads on his temples, but the rest of his hair was black, seeming to stand straight because it was cut very short. His face was tired, but kind. He clicked his heels, and saluted. 'Frau Janski?' Mama curtseyed.

'Your house has been recommended to me. You flew a German flag. Why?'

'I am a German, sir.' Mama was proud. 'I was born in Munich.'

'Your father?'

'Dr. Harrwitz, sir. He died on the western front in 1915.'

'Make a note of that, Wittzen. Introduce me, madam.'

'My husband, Anton Janski. His brother, Jan. My husband and his brother are of Swedish descent.'

The colonel nodded. 'You are the Janski brothers who operated a toyshop on Senator Street. And this young man?'

'My son Josef.'

'You have three sons, Frau Janski.'

'Two are dead, sir.' Mama spoke without emotion.

'You don't know Frederic is dead, Mama,' Liese objected.

'Your daughters?'

'Yes, sir. Anneliese and Christina.'

'Their occupations?'

'Christina is still at school. Anneliese has not yet decided what she wishes to do.'

'They will help you about the house. And you, young man, why did you not serve?'

'I have poor eyesight, sir.'

'Josef is a photographer,' Mama said.

'The best in Warsaw,' Liese said.

'In Poland,' Christina said.

'Your daughters lack discipline, Frau Janski,' the colonel said. 'I will see some of your work, young man. And this is your servant?'

Asja opened her mouth in surprise.

'My daughter-in-law,' Mama said. 'The widow of my eldest son. She holds my grandson.'

'She is a Slav.'

The blood in Asja's legs seemed to turn to water.

'A Huzulin,' Mama explained. 'But she is a Janski now.'

'Rokonow has been reserved as an area for Aryans. A Huzulin, you say.' The colonel looked Asja up and down, and the water climbed into her heart. 'She belongs to the Russian part of Poland. She must be handed over to the Russians.'

'No,' Asja cried. 'No, please.'

'Mama!' Christina burst into tears.

'She is feeding my grandson,' Mama said. 'Please, sir, we will vouch for her.'

'Enter this woman as the Janski servant,' the colonel said. 'Rules were meant to be broken, eh, madam?' He smiled. But the smile was directed at the beautiful Bavarian, not at anyone else in the room. 'Now, madam, how many bedrooms?'

'Seven. And the servants' quarters, of course.'

'We will require six bedrooms. You and Herr Janski may retain yours. Your family will use the servants' wing. We shall require the dining room and this room, and another room downstairs for an office.' He stood beneath the paintings. 'Originals?'

'Oh, yes, sir.'

'Matejko is unsuitable for private collection. Your loyalty to the Reich would best be expressed by donating these to the Berlin Museum.'

'My Matejkos?' Papa cried.

The colonel smiled. 'Your name will appear as donor, Herr Janski. Now, madam, show me the bedrooms.'

II

The conductor looked Ruth up and down. 'Can't you read?'

'I am Josef Janski,' Josef explained. 'I take photographs for the Germans. Miss Blass is my assistant.'

'Well, you get her a pass,' said the conductor. 'I have my orders. See, they're printed right over there. *Juden Verboten*.'

Here was one German phrase everyone had learned overnight.

Ruth jumped down. The passengers were staring at her yellow armband. 'I'll go home,' she said. 'This will only get you into trouble, Josef.'

'Nonsense. We'll walk. Once we get to Rokonow we'll be all right.'

She supposed she was being a traitor to her own people. But they had all been in a tremendous hurry to get on to the Judenrat or into the Jew militia. When the ship is sinking it is every rat for himself, and only those who fail to reach the surface call the rest traitors. She walked

71

quickly, her coat held close. The morning was already chilly with the promise of winter.

'The trouble with the Germans is not that they are bad people—of course I make exceptions for Hitler and the Gestapo—but that they are too organised, too methodical, and individuals become submerged in masses of red tape. One has to delve.' Josef laughed. 'I know. I'm half German myself, remember?'

He was always reminding her of this, to prove the good intentions of his race. But now everyone was staring, because here in the autumn sunshine the yellow shame band gleamed, and people could not believe their eyes that a Jewess should be openly walking down Ujawdowskie, and with an Aryan.

But soon they were beyond Sielce, and could see Rokonow. She had often dreamed of being taken home by Josef to meet his mother. Now she wished he would let her go, to run all the way back to the security of the ghetto.

'We'll leave the road here,' Josef said. 'And go across that field and through the orchard.'

'I'll ruin my stockings. It's my last pair, Josef.'

'I'll get you some more. But, you see, now we are the colonel's residence, there's always a guard on the front door.'

He held her hand, led her down the parapet and into the field. They walked through long grass, hand in hand, like lovers. They had never been lovers. Josef loved inanimate objects, things which could be identified as beautiful. He knew, instinctively, that the cut and thrust of passion would have its ugly moments. Josef was not really like either of his brothers. And if he was like his father it was a miracle that old Janski had fathered five children. Silly thoughts, obscene thoughts, for a sunlit morning when so much was at stake.

He released her hand, put his finger to his lips, and

scurried across the orchard. She followed, suddenly a small child again, trespassing and stealing apples. Asja was filling a bucket of water from the pump. Ruth had never met Asja, as she had never met any of the Janski women, but she recognised her at once.

'Josef!' Asja looked delighted. But she frowned at the yellow armband.

'This is Ruth Blass. I've told you of her.'

Asja took Ruth's hands in hers. She had very brown hands, with long fingers. Ruth realised that Asja's hands were more beautiful than hers. She felt like curtseying. 'The house is full of Germans, I'm afraid.' The contempt in Asja's voice might almost have made her a Jewess. Ruth knew she was going to like Asja.

'That's why we came round the back. Is Mama about?'

'In the kitchen.' Asja smiled at Ruth, but the confidence was gone, and with Asja's, Ruth's oozed away in shoulder sweat. Asja went up the steps. Strange, Ruth thought; it had occurred to neither Asja nor Josef that the man should carry the bucket.

Asja opened the back door. 'Josef is here.'

'Josef?' Anna Janski stood in the doorway. 'But you must not sneak into the house like this.'

'I have brought Ruth Blass to see you.'

Anneliese Janski had the coldest eyes Ruth had ever seen. They stared at the shame band.

'Ruth received an order yesterday.' Josef spoke hurriedly. 'She can no longer be my receptionist, but must stay in the ghetto and work at the clothing shop.'

'Orders must be obeyed,' Mama said.

'But Ruth isn't just *any* Jew. She's my friend.'

Ruth supposed she would get used to being referred to as if she was not quite human, given time.

'And she's my receptionist. I couldn't carry on the work without her. Bruckner himself got me the appoint-

73

ment. Mama, I thought that if you were to speak to Bruckner ...'

'*Colonel* Bruckner. And what you are suggesting is quite out of the question. You'll be wishing her to stay here next.'

'Her father has been sent to a labour camp, and times are very hard in the ghetto.'

'Times are hard everywhere.'

'I will go back to Warsaw, Josef.' Ruth's cheeks felt as if they would catch fire.

'You can't turn her out, Mama,' Josef cried.

'The Jew is right. Every second she is standing here she is endangering us all. Particularly Asja. Tell her to go, Asja.'

Asja's eyes were sad. Jew and Slav. Subhuman and subhuman. But Asja had reached the surface. 'It would be better for you to go,' she said softly. 'The Germans would never stand for a Jew in the house.'

Josef gazed at her with his mouth open. 'What is the matter with you people?'

'I'm sorry,' Asja said. 'I have little Antoni to think about.'

But she was thinking of herself as well. She would not look at Ruth Blass again. She did not wish to be handed over to the Russians, and she did not wish to be sent to a labour camp. She wanted to be forgotten. She would do anything to be forgotten. Ruth Blass turned and went down the steps.

'Name? Name, you pus-filled son of a Jewish cretin!'

'Walenski.' The man did not speak good German, but he had got the message.

'Occupation in civilian life? When captured? What regiment?'

The questions came like machine-gun fire. Frederic understood that he would soon be on the receiving end.

74

He was not sure what to say. He was not sure of anything at this moment. Sometimes he thought they had been kept crouching in the Saxon salute all night, because they arrived late. Of course this could not be so, or they would not be walking now. His legs seemed unreal as it was. So they had slept last night in the barracks. But he did not want to think about the barracks. He was going to have to sleep there tonight as well.

'Name?'

'Samuel Rosenthal. Fourth cavalry. Taken prisoner before Lowicz, 4th September.'

The clerk sneered. 'An intelligent Jew.'

'My father was not a cretin, you see. Only a half-wit.'

Without Rosenthal, life would be unbearable, would not have been bearable over the past few months. Of all the thousand and one prisoners in this camp, only Rosenthal really existed.

'We know how to cure humorists here,' said the clerk. 'Next!'

Frederic's knees rattled. What am I doing here? he wondered. Why am I not at home in Rokonow? Obviously I am being punished for raping Ruth Blass. We are all being punished. He wondered what crime Rosenthal had committed.

'Frederic Janski.'

'Occupation?'

'Student.'

He was aware of eyes. There were dozens of eyes. There had been the doctor, and there were the guards, and there were the other prisoners. Now there was an extra pair. Frederic could just see the black uniform to his right. He could see the tremendous sheen of the black boots, of the black holster. And he could feel the tension in the room.

'Regiment?'

'Fourth cavalry.' His uniform jacket was in such a

mess no one would ever be able to tell the difference, and he and Sammy had agreed to stick together, if possible.

'Crime?'

'Anti-social behaviour.' He had learned to make that reply without hesitation.

'Next!'

Frederic stared at the commandant. The man was young, his face pale. He was not handsome, but his features possessed an attractive peacefulness. He looked the sort of man who would say, 'Come on, chaps,' and march towards the approaching tanks, at peace with himself and with the world, dying in the execution of his duty. But he was commandant, and his duty was here, and he was gazing at Frederic Janski. Nobody else. And how slowly the line moved, from desk to door, shuffling, with the questions ringing out behind them, and the eyes, gazing.

He escaped to the baths, where Rosenthal was already waiting, naked, for his turn underneath the showers. How hairy Rosenthal was. Or, from Sammy's point of view, how hairless Frederic was. It was not relevant. After the bath they were delivered to the barber, and hair ceased to be important. The barber was not gentle, and his clippers were blunt. And Frederic made the terrible mistake of thinking about Asja, of imagining Asja in here, naked, being shorn of her lovely hair, no matter where it might be. 'Filthy-minded bastard,' said the guard, standing beside the barber, and kicked Frederic in the groin. After that, for several hours, it did not matter if he thought of Asja or not. Perhaps, he thought, it will never matter again.

Rosenthal helped Frederic to the clothing shed, assisted him into his new uniform. They were given the same striped pyjamas, but their insignias were different. Frederic wore a black triangle, apex downwards, on his left breast. He was an anti-social. Rosenthal was also considered anti-social, apparently, but as a Jew he wore, under the black triangle, a yellow triangle, and this time the apex pointed upwards, to make a perfect Star of David. Beneath the insignia was printed a number. Rosenthal's was three thousand one hundred and eight. Frederic's was three thousand one hundred and nine.

Then they were delivered to roll-call.

III

'Come in, Frau Janski.' Colonel Bruckner stood at his desk, very erect. His adjutant held the door. 'And you, Herr Janski. Please sit down.'

How strange, Anton Janski thought. To be invited into my own drawing room, and then told to sit down. How strange not to hate this man.

'Heinrich, Mr. Janski will have a cigar.'

'Thank you.' Papa discovered his fingers were trembling. His fingers were always trembling, nowadays.

'I have good news for you. Your antecendents have been investigated, and it has been decided that you are pure-blooded Aryan, at least back to 1800, which is as far as anyone need worry.' The colonel beamed. 'Does that not please you, Herr Janski?'

Papa regarded the cigar between his fingers. But you could not hate a man who is but carrying on a mode of existence to which he has been educated.

'He is overwhelmed,' Anna said. 'Does this mean that we can leave Rokonow? Perhaps go back to Germany?'

'On the contrary, Frau Janski. This means that you will be allowed to *stay* in Rokonow. Your husband's place is here, amongst people who know and trust him. But we will come to that in a moment. As I promised you, I have also looked into the matter of your youngest son. You will be pleased to learn that he is alive and well.'

'Frederic? Oh, thank God!'

'He was apparently serving with the Fourth Cavalry Regiment in the Posen campaign, and thus was taken prisoner during the first week of September. As you may know, due to the rapid advance of the German army it was some time before we could round up all the hundreds of thousands of prisoners. During those weeks it would appear that your son fell under the influence of some subversive characters, Jews and communists.'

'He has been sent to prison?'

'No, no, Frau Janski; he is a prisoner of war. But he has been classified as anti-social, and has been given a short sentence in a labour camp.'

'You mean a concentration camp?' Papa asked.

Colonel Bruckner smiled. 'I mean a labour camp, Herr Janski, which is what I said. I personally think the experience may do the young man a great deal of good, and he is performing a useful service to the community, building, well, whatever it is he is building. He will also be taught a trade, and will receive appropriate political education, to prepare him for a useful life when he returns here.'

'And when will that be?'

'It could be next week, providing he shows a proper understanding of his crimes, and a proper attitude of contrition. I suggest you write to your son, reminding him that he has this very pleasant home to which he can return, upon completion of his sentence, and imploring him to behave himself, that his release may be expedited.'

'Oh, I shall,' Mama said. 'We both shall. Today. Won't we, Anton? Oh, the girls will be so happy to hear that Frederic is all right. They have been so terribly worried.'

'I can well imagine. I think we should all have a glass of brandy, Heinrich, to celebrate our host and hostess's good fortune. Take one for yourself.' He stood up, his glass in his hand. 'I give a toast. Long life and prosperity to the Fuehrer.'

'Long life and prosperity to the Fuehrer!' said Mama and Captain Wittzen.

'Quite!' Papa sipped, and sat down again.

'Now we must discuss your future, Herr Janski,' Colonel Bruckner said.

'My future?'

'But of course. Our task is to convert Poland into a prosperous and contented colony of the Reich. It will be the task of leaders of the civil community like yourself to mobilise public opinion into an understanding and acceptance of their new responsibilities.'

'I am no leader,' Papa said. 'I do not even belong to the Chamber of Commerce. Jan is your man.'

'You belong to the Chamber of Commerce as of this morning. I will speak frankly, Herr Janski. Your brother has been classified as unreliable, if only on account of his drinking habits. You would do him a favour were you to point this out to him.'

'I will do so. But I do not even have a business now.'

'That is something else to be discussed. If we are to make Poland once again into a land of happy, smiling children it will certainly be necessary to give them toys. Of course, with things in their present state, it will not be possible to rebuild Janski Brothers. But, on the other hand, there are a great many fine buildings left in Warsaw, or, for that matter, here in Rokonow, which are derelict. There is a particularly splendid villa just down the road.'

'It belongs to Dr. Landski.'

'A Jew. He is being resettled in the Warsaw ghetto, and the house will soon be available. I could recommend that it be handed over to Janski Brothers.'

'You hear that, Anton? You will be able to go back into business.'

79

Anton Janski finished his brandy. There was sediment in the bottom of the glass.

'Sing, you shitbags, sing!' Bauer had a loud voice. His shout reverberated through the wood.

So they sang. They shouldered their tools, left behind them the unfinished road surface—it would still be there tomorrow—and burst into song, marching and singing as though not a muscle ached, not a head bled from the sudden crack of Bauer's whip, not a belly rumbled, as if they had been picnicking in the wood for the afternoon, instead of labouring on the road since dawn. Sang as if there was nothing in front of them but supper and bed. As if there was no roll-call.

That roll-call should loom so large, so soon, was a measure of human adaptability, Frederic thought. Had anyone told him that life could be more degrading than the march west from Poznan he would have laughed. Except that he did not laugh any more. Had anyone told him that life could be more degrading than a week in a cattle truck, packed so tightly that even the dead could not fall, he would have smiled. Except that he did not smile any more. In fact, the ultimate degradation, worse than the frantic struggle for the inedible black bread every night, the eternal intimacy of sleeping four to a plank and eight hundred to a barracks, where every movement of wind in the belly was an instant communication, was to perform the most personal of human functions balanced precariously on a pole, which you shared with a dozen others, over an open cess-pool, bowels tight because this was an operation which could be suspended at any moment by the appearance of Bauer, or one of his cronies, round the corner of the barracks. Then you left or you were ducked in the pool. Presumably to drown in your own excrete would be yet more degrading. Blaschmann the Czech had drowned in there yesterday. Blaschmann had ever been a slow mover.

This, then, was the ultimate in degradation. What rubbish. The ultimate in degradation came when degradation no longer mattered. There were worse things in life than degradation. Labour was bad. Labour was pain without cessation, unless you intended to cease labour permanently. Bauer had impressed this upon them the first day, and had shown them what he meant. To cease labour was mutiny, and mutiny was punishable by death. Walenski had died on the first morning. Bauer had told him to move a heavy rock and Walenski had dropped the rock on his own foot. He had cried out in pain, and knelt. Bauer had hit him three times on the head with his stick, kicked him twice in the kidneys, and then placed his boot on Walenski's neck and pressed. Seventy men had watched Walenski die. Here truly was the ultimate degradation. But you could not be a hero in striped pyjamas behind which there was an empty belly. Or perhaps you could not be a hero once you reached the railhead. Perhaps all the heroes died before then.

Labour was bad, but roll-call was worst of all. Roll-call was a timeless ritual. This was a small camp, and there were only three thousand inmates. Thus this was a short roll-call, according to Mittwitz, who had been in Buchenwald. No one knew for sure why Mittwitz had been transferred. He wore the mauve triangle of a Jehovah's Witness, and it was understood that even the Gestapo did not know what should be done with Jehovah's Witnesses. Obviously, they could not be left free to convert other Germans to their devastating doctrine. But equally obviously it was impossible to put the fear or death into men and women who welcomed the prospect. Mittwitz had been in several camps, had endured beatings and retained only one of his teeth. But he was alive, and he considered this camp the best he had been in. Yet counting three thousand inmates, when the counting was done by men like Bauer, who found twenty a large sum to reach, was sufficiently awesome. And this supposed every man was present. Roll-call lasted from the return of the labour parties to camp until the correct total was reached, and during this period you stood to attention, unless you were dead, in which case you lay to attention, in your proper place. Roll-call could last until midnight. And no one ate, no one moved, until roll-call was completed.

So you sang. And your voices reverberated over the trees and down into the valley, where the handsome blonde women with the pretty blonde children would be preparing dinner for their hard-working husbands, and talking with each other over their charming green fences, and agreeing with each other how fortunate it was that Hans and Siegfried had this job, looking after these happy political prisoners, who sang on their way to work, and sang on their way back to camp, and never gave anybody any trouble.

If only they would sing in tune. Mittwitz had a very high voice. Rosenthal sounded like a rusty saw. Frederic was too deep. And Groetz did not sing at all. He opened his mouth, but never made a sound. Groetz did not have to sing. He was Senior Block Inmate. Mittwitz had not been able to believe his eyes that a man wearing a pink triangle should be Senior Block Inmate. 'In other camps convicted homosexuals are segregated, not allowed to mix with the other prisoners.' But here they could be Senior Block Inmates. Groetz swung his arm against Frederic's, again and again. 'It takes two to survive in a labour camp, Frederic. There can be no individuals here, only pairs. And you must survive, Frederic. You are too beautiful to die. Did no one ever tell you how beautiful you are, Frederic?'

'Powdered milk,' Asja said. 'Please, Mama, as much as you can manage.'

From the bedroom came little Antoni's wail. Little Antoni did a great deal of crying nowadays. Mama would never have supposed that a peasant girl like Asja, so strong and heavy breasted, would run out of milk before the boy was six months old.

'We'll go to Grybowski's,' she told Christina, who was going to carry the shopping bag; Liese was off to Warsaw with Captain Wittzen, as usual, and Asja, of course, was out of the question. Most of the Slavs and all of the Jews from Rokonow had been resettled, and people always looked very hard at Asja. So she seldom went out. At this time of the year she was the lucky one—the snow was six inches deep on the street.

Christina was already waiting at the gate. She had been talking with a young woman, but her friend scuttled off when Frau Janski came down the path. The sentry clicked his heels and presented arms. Mama enjoyed entering and leaving the house better than living in it, nowadays. It was humiliating really, to be at the beck and call of a lot of men. She didn't mind the colonel, but the adjutant, that Heinrich, was a low-class Württemberger. She couldn't understand what Liese saw in him. But to have a German soldier present arms every time she went in or came out was just marvellous. It showed the people of Rokonow who really mattered nowadays. Mama knew her neighbours had never really liked her. The Janskis had been Polish for eight generations, but when Anton Janski had come home with a German bride everyone had remembered he was, after all, more of a Swede.

'Who was your friend?'

Christina giggled. 'Lila. You remember Lila.'

Snow crunched under their boots. A German soldier came towards them, very erect, arms swinging rhythmically. Christina stepped into the gutter. Mama remained on the pavement, glared at him. He opened his mouth to bark an order, recognised her, saluted and stepped into the road. 'Come on, Christina.'

'Mama!' Christina squeezed her arm. 'Do you remember the Ploetner boy? He was in the form above me. He left school last term. Well, he and another boy, do you know what they did? They stuck a penknife into the tyres of Governor Franck's car.'

'The little horrors. I hope they were caught.'

'Oh, yes. Lila was telling me. The Gestapo caught them.'

'And gave them a good thrashing, I hope.'

'They're going to be shot tomorrow afternoon. In public.'

'Shot? But you said he was a schoolboy.'

'Sixteen. And the other boy is younger. Isn't it exciting?'

Christina had not uttered a coherent word until she was three. Dr. Moens had hinted that she might be just a little slow. 'Did you know this Ploetner boy well?'

'Not well. I didn't like him, really. He was always pulling my hair.'

'Of course he did a terrible thing. They could have caused a dreadful accident.' There was probably more to it than Christina had said. She would ask Colonel Bruckner. He would tell her exactly what the boys had done, what was going to happen to them.

Grybowski was a Slav. He had been allowed to continue in his store because no one could be found to take it over. Those who had residences in Rokonow were not exactly small shopkeepers. He rubbed his hands together when Mrs. Janski came in. 'You must excuse me, Mrs. Arpel,' he said to the woman he was serving, and hurried over. 'Good morning to you, Mrs. Janski. You are looking well, Christina. Christmas holidays, eh?'

'Oh, yes, Mr. Grybowski. Isn't it exciting about the Ploetner boy?'

A blind seemed to descend across Grybowski's eyes. 'I know nothing of the Ploetners,' he said. 'Terrible people.' He lowered his voice. 'There is Jewish blood in the family. What can I do for you, Mrs. Janski?'

'We need all the powdered milk you have, for baby Antoni.'

'I saw some in your window only a week ago,' Christina said.

Grybowski's smile suggested the Gestapo had slipped up. 'But I sold those only yesterday. My very last stock.'

'The baby has to have milk, Mr. Grybowski,' Mama said. 'Can you suggest another shop?'

'In Warsaw, perhaps, Frau Janski.'

She stared at him. A deliberate switch of title. He would not sell something as precious as powdered milk to a German. She could have him gaoled. But she could never prove it. She turned away, so angry she forgot the rest of her order.

Christina squeezed her arm. 'He does have it, you know? Hidden away. He sells it on the black market. Lila was telling me he sells all sorts of things on the black market. All you have to do is offer him the right price. You call it a commission, Lila says.'

'Bribe that?' Mama snapped.

'There is none in Warsaw, Mama. I know. Asja asked Josef to see if he could get some, and the Slavs like Josef, Mama. But he couldn't get any. Antoni didn't have much breakfast, Mama, and Asja was squeezing away.'

Mama gazed at the poster on the wall, pretended to be reading the curfew regulations, as if she didn't already know them by heart. She was waiting for Mrs. Arpel to leave. And Grybowski knew it.

'Janski to the gate! Janski to the gate!' The loudspeaker reached every corner of the camp, reverberated in every mind and every heart. Frederic scrambled to his feet.

'No hurry,' Mittwitz said. 'They'll only keep you waiting for an hour.'

'But what can they want with Frederic?' Rosenthal asked.

Mittwitz shrugged. 'Who can say? It may be a punishment.' He smiled. 'Or it may be an order for your release, Frederic. Oh, yes, people do get released.'

'I told you my parents wouldn't let me rot in here. I'll see that you are released too, Sammy.'

'One at a time, Mr. Janski. When you are on the outside, looking in, then will I consider looking out.'

'Janski to the gate!' He ran across the compound. It was starting to snow, as it did most evenings. But he could stand the cold this evening.

The door opened, Bauer came out. Frederic's knees touched. This was terrible luck. Bauer would certainly take offence at seeing one of his labour gang here.

Bauer looked him up and down, and Frederic tensed his muscles, waited for the pain. Bauer always struck first and talked afterwards. 'They are waiting for you inside,' Bauer said, and marched away.

Frederic went inside. He wondered if cowardice was like deafness or Josef's myopia: once it had afflicted you, you were stuck with it for ever.

'Janski?' asked the clerk. 'Inside with you.'

Frederic gazed at the door, his optimism, increased by Bauer's strange behaviour, draining away in dripping fear. To go through that door was surely irrevocable.

'Get on with it,' said the clerk. 'The commandant is waiting.'

Frederic knocked. The sound of his knuckles raced round his brain. Knocking his way into eternity.

'Come.' The commandant sat at his desk. His holster

hung over the back of the other chair, his cap from the hook behind his head. Apart from these he sat, as he stood, very erect; his jacket was buttoned, his tie neat. He was surprisingly young; Frederic had never seen him this close before. His face was sensitive, with relaxed, intelligent features, a high forehead, a strong jaw. Only the eyes so grey, so cold, remained terrifying. 'Janski!' he said. 'Taken prisoner in the Posen campaign, 4th September 1939. Yours was a short war, Janski.'

'Yes, sir.'

'I have a letter for you, from your mother.' Commandant Reitener opened his desk drawer. The envelope was already slit; he dangled it between thumb and forefinger. 'Frau Janski has received a full report concerning your misdemeanours, and she implores you to right your ways, to stay away from the Jews and homosexuals, in order that your time here may be shortened.'

'Yes, sir.' Frederic gazed at the letter.

'And you have a great deal to go home for, Janski. Your family has been recognised as pure Aryan. I'm sure that pleases you.'

'Yes, sir.'

'So that you see, but for your anti-social activities, there would be no need to keep you in here at all.' Commandant Reitener took a cigarette from the box on the table, tapped it, struck a match. It was Turkish tobacco; Antoni and his air force friends had sometimes smoked it. 'I am going to help you, Janski.'

'Sir?'

'You are very young. Your education was doubtless neglected. Oh, I am sure your mother did her best. She sounds an eminently sensible person. But no doubt, living in Poland, you were subjected to a great many unhealthy influences. Now, it so happens that I require a houseboy. My present servant is leaving. You will find the duties less exacting than the labour detail.'

87

Frederic gazed at him. To leave Sammy Rosenthal, to exist without the constant support of Sammy Rosenthal, did not seem conceivable.

'Well?'

'Yes, sir.'

'You will report tomorrow morning, Janski. That will be all.'

'Yes, sir.' Frederic remained at attention.

Commandant Reitener frowned. 'I said that was all, Janski.'

'The letter, sir.'

'The letter? I will keep the letter, Janski. You may read it tomorrow.'

v

'Are you ready, Janski?' asked Captain Hoeppner.

Josef nodded. He could not trust himself to speak. He buried his head behind the camera, yet peered round the sides, at the silent people, and the two men—hardly the right word—against the wall. It was snowing, lightly, adding a fresh layer to the white sheet on the ground. Warsaw was receiving its first Christmas present from its conquerors. But not until the photographer was ready.

Captain Hoeppner raised his hand, dropped it. The volley reverberated, rising into the buildings on either side of the square.

The watching crowd made no sound. They turned their sobs inwards, felt them in their bellies. The two young men lay on the snow. Josef bent his head again, took Captain Hoeppner walking forward, pistol in hand. Captain Hoeppner fired twice, dull sounds. Then he holstered the pistol, and returned to the firing squad, and the camera.

Josef swallowed. 'I would like a close-up.'

Captain Hoeppner raised his eyebrows, then shrugged.

Josef walked across the snow. He was between the firing squad and the wall now, felt something of the awful exposure of being condemned to death, something of the awful hatred swelling upwards from the watchers on either side of the square.

The wall was pocked with bullet holes. Josef stooped, released the bandages. The first young man was not identifiable. Captain Hoeppner had rested the muzzle of his automatic pistol slightly upwards at the base of the skull, and the face had disintegrated. But the Ploetner boy's face was untouched by bullets.

It was a face Josef knew well. Ladi Ploetner had been a talkative, excitable boy, obsessed with where he was going. He had gone nowhere, except to the house on Szucha Avenue which the Gestapo had taken for its own. An old man looked up at Josef. And he had aged before death.

Josef snapped the shutter, straightened, walked back to the firing party.

'Satisfied?' asked Captain Hoeppner.

'Thank you, sir. May I go off now?'

Hoeppner nodded, signalled for the death van. Josef hurried down the side street, camera hanging on his arm. He ran down the steps, unlocked the basement door, stepped into the darkness, and shivered. The wood fire had gone out, and it was colder in here than on the street. He stamped his feet, brushed snow from his cap, lit the oil lamp. He opened the inner door, checked. The man carried a pistol very like the one used by Captain Hoeppner.

'How did you get in here?'

'I picked the lock.' With his dark hair and his pinched features the intruder made Josef think of the rats which occasionally invaded the cellar.

He hung the lamp from the hook in the ceiling. 'Killing me will serve no useful purpose.' His voice was steady. He was glad of that.

'None at all. Now develop your pictures. I have been looking at these others. You are a good photographer, Josef. I am not surprised the Germans employ you.'

Josef unloaded the camera, moved to the basin in the corner. The man watched him for some time. 'You may call me Kopa,' he said at last. 'I did not subscribe to the articles of surrender.'

'Neither did I.'

'That pleases me. But it is not merely a matter of words. Ladi Ploetner worked for me. Although slashing tyres was his own idea. It is difficult to create discipline in an organisation such as ours. Communication is even more difficult.'

'Why am I being told this?'

'You are a valuable person, Josef Janski. Oh, I know that you are half German, that you have them living in your house, that your mother flew the swastika flag from her window. But I know too that your brothers died fighting for Poland. It is time for you to decide to which eagle *you* will fly.'

Josef held up the first print, of the two boys standing against the wall. The bandages had not yet been fixed, and they gazed at the camera with a mixture of fear and defiance.

'An excellent photograph,' Kopa said. 'Well?'

'I could say what I wished now and denounce you later.'

'I do not really expect to survive this war. It is a matter of whether one chooses to die like a man or a crawling thing. And, of course, my associates know where I am this morning. They will hold your family equally guilty.'

'What do you wish me to do?'

'Nothing dramatic, Josef. But situated as you are, you make a perfect communications centre, able to come and go as you please, able, perhaps, to supply us with certain pieces of information. What happened to your receptionist?'

'She is in the ghetto.'

'You must find another. Someone you can trust. One of your sisters.'

'I would prefer not to involve my family.'

'They are involved, Josef. If the Gestapo decides to question you they will certainly question your sisters as well. You understand this word, question?'

Josef took out the second photograph, the one taken as the bullets struck. 'Yes.'

'Good. The important thing is that there be someone here at all times. You must approach your employers, and say that you have an opportunity to expand, to gain the reputation you seek. Be a Nazi, Josef. And I will send customers, faithful collaborationists, to your studio.'

The front door closed, softly. Josef took the last photograph from the basin. It was of Ladi Ploetner's companion, the faceless head. Josef hung it with the others to dry, then he sat at the desk, opened the drawer, took out the rest of the collection he had started on September 1st.

Aladdin had needed a lamp, Ali Baba a magic word. Frederic Janski did not even need a key. There were books, of course. A weird selection. *Mein Kampf*, in a bound edition. Nietzsche and Chamberlain and Rosenberg. But some Goethe, and most remarkably, a complete Shakespeare. Also *Leaves of Grass*.

And then food. He felt faint, standing in the centre of the kitchen. He took a grape from a large bunch on top of the apples and pears in the bowl on the table. Even the cold grey eyes were not going to miss a single grape.

And then cleanliness. The bath needed washing, so he got beneath the shower. He had forgotten about a towel, and he dared not take one from the cupboard. He cleaned the bath, dripping water. There was snow on the ground outside, but the heating was on high. He was dry in an hour, and clean enough to stretch out on the bed before making it.

And, lastly, solitude. As he chose. He could stand at the window and watch the schoolchildren playing, and the pretty blonde women passing the time of day, and the other servants, mostly Jehovah's Witnesses, coming and going about their duties. But to stand at the window was also to look at the wood, and to know that beyond the trees Mittwitz and Sammy Rosenthal were building their road, ankle deep in snow, fingers dwindling with frostbite. Why? he wondered. Why they there and me here? Sammy had never hesitated for an instant. 'Of course you must go, Mr. Janski. As if you had a choice. But it will be the saving of you.'

'House servants always survive,' Mittwitz had said. 'They have only to please their master. One master at a time. Or one mistress.'

'Besides,' Rosenthal had said, 'it will get you away from *him*.' And he had glanced at Groetz, whose very fingers seemed curled into talons at losing his prey.

But he was young and strong. Stronger by far than either Sammy or Mittwitz. He thought he would have had an even chance of surviving the winter in the snow.

There was so little to be done, there was an immediate temptation to do nothing. To sit in the easy chair in the living room with Whitman, and let his brain drift out of the window and back to Rokonow. But he was never going to think of Rokonow again.

He made the bed and washed the dishes and swept the floor and beat the rugs and dusted the furniture, and the books, and found the ivory chess set and cleaned each piece with loving care. The snow had stopped, so he swept the steps, and looked up, and saw a pretty blonde woman at the fence. She was a small woman, concealed by a cheap fur coat and fur hood. Her prettiness lay in the fact that she was a woman. 'You're new,' she said. 'German?'

'Polish.' Should he have said that? Should he have spoken at all? Conversation between inmates and the wives of the guards could hardly be encouraged.

'You speak German well,' she said, as if the one word was all she required. 'If you need any assistance you must not hesitate to ask for it.'

'Thank you, Fräulein.'

She smiled. She was truly pretty when she smiled. 'Frau, you silly boy.'

Frederic ran up the steps. The day was spoiled. The work was finished by lunchtime, and he ate a piece of bread and cheese. Then there was the book, opened on the table. But he was too afraid to understand the words. He sat there, staring at them, until a shadow fell across the page.

He leapt to his feet, brain sagging. Tomorrow the snow. Commandant Reitener took off his cap and his gloves and his belt, hung his holster over the chair. He said, ' "I sound my barbaric yawp over the roofs of the world".'

Frederic licked his lips.

Reitener smiled. 'Or perhaps, "I am larger, better than I thought; I did not know I held so much goodness." Whitman expresses much of the American character. Do not be afraid, boy. Had I not supposed you to be intelligent I would not have removed you from the cesspool. Do you also cook?'

'No, sir.'

'You must learn. There is a cook book on that shelf. Tonight I will eat at the cafeteria. But tomorrow night I wish a meal.'

'Yes, sir.'

'And it must be a good one. There is a bottle over there. Pour two glasses.'

Frederic obeyed. Reitener took one and raised it. 'I drink to your success. Now you do the same.'

It was a Frascati, thin and sweet.

'I always holiday in Italy,' Reitener said. 'I like all things Alban. I like the plain and I like the mountains and I like the heat. And I like the Alban wines. Well, Frederic, cook me a successful dinner and a glass of wine shall be yours every night. Ruin my digestion and I shall whip you. Is that fair?'

'Yes, sir.'

'I think you are going to make a good cook. I think I am going to enjoy having you about the house.' He frowned, took Frederic's chin in his hand. 'Yes,' he said. 'There is something about you, Frederic. Something quite beautiful.'

VI

Christina opened the door, gazed at Captain Wittzen. Early as it was, he wore uniform, and he stood to attention, heels together, hands in front, holding the parcel. Christina pulled her dressing gown close, backed into the servants' living room. 'It's the captain.'

Mama turned in her chair. Papa stood up. Liese stepped behind Asja, who was holding little Antoni. Uncle Jan put out his cigarette. In their brightly coloured dressing gowns Christina thought they looked like a flock of terrified peacocks. And peahens.

'I am here to wish you a very merry Christmas,' Captain Wittzen said.

'Thank you,' Mama said.

'And the same to you,' Papa said.

Christina realised that Captain Wittzen was more afraid

of them than they of him. His face was crimson, and he held the parcel in front of him like a shield. 'With Colonel Bruckner's compliments.' He gazed at Liese, whose neck was just as crimson. Christina knew the captain was taking Liese to the ball.

Mama stood up. 'How lovely. You must tell the colonel that we are delighted. And we hope that you both will take a glass of wine with us this evening.'

Captain Wittzen bowed. 'It will be our pleasure, madam.'

The door closed. Mama placed the parcel on the table. 'I wonder what it is.'

'Chocolates,' Liese said.

'I've never seen a box of chocolates that big,' Asja said.

'I have, in Warsaw. It had a ship on the box.'

'There's your ship.' Mama lifted the lid. 'It must have cost a fortune. Oh, he is sweet, isn't he, Anton?'

'Pity it isn't coffee.'

'Oh, you! You'd carp if it was pure gold.'

'Pure gold wouldn't be much good either.'

'Can I try one, Mama?' Christina asked.

'I think we should all try one, sweetheart. We'll put Josef's share aside.'

'And one for little Antoni,' Liese said.

'It'll ruin his teeth!' Asja flushed. 'When he gets them. He can lick mine.'

'Well,' Mama said, 'this certainly makes our presents look a bit meagre.'

'Speak for yourself.' Uncle Jan had been wearing an air of importance all morning.

'Don't tell us you have a surprise too, Jan,' Papa said.

'For these ladies.' Uncle Jan pulled his hand out of his dressing-gown pocket, laid four pairs of silk stockings on the table. 'I'm sorry I don't have a fancy box, but you don't get these in shops nowadays.'

95

'Jan!' Mama cried. 'You shouldn't. Isn't it dangerous?'

'What isn't?'

'And is one for me?'

'There is a pair each. Even for you, Christina.'

She held the silk against her cheek, ran into the little room she shared with Liese. She pulled up her nightdress, stretched the stocking along her leg, leapt at the knock.

'Can I come in?' Uncle Jan closed the door behind him.

'Oh, Uncle Jan. It feels so delicious.' She threw her arms round his neck. Suddenly she wanted to feel his fingers, and she had never actually *wanted* to feel them before.

'A lovely lady needs lovely things. But how are you going to wear them?'

She released him, hugged the stockings to her breast.

He smiled. 'I'm not going to take them away from you, Christina. I've brought you something else.' He took the suspender belt from his pocket. It was black lace. 'Let's see if it fits. Take off your dressing gown.'

She had never seen anything so beautiful. But it was a terribly tight fit. 'It's too small.'

'It's this thick cotton nightdress.' His voice was reassuring. 'Lift it up.'

'Oh, Uncle Jan, I couldn't.'

'I'm old enough to be your father, you silly girl.'

She shut her eyes tightly, felt his fingers stroking her thighs as he fastened the belt. At least she had hair. Perhaps he hadn't expected that. But suppose Liese opened the door? But then it occurred to her that perhaps Uncle Jan had bought Liese her first suspender belt, too.

You never thought about punishment. It was an event which took place twice, sometimes three times a week, but it never concerned *you*. You watched, of course. You had

96

to. The punishment square was surrounded by a wire fence. The camp proper was on three sides, and every inmate had to be present, behind the wire, watching his comrades. This was good for discipline. But once an inmate was marked down for punishment he no longer existed. He knew it, and you knew it. He spoke to no one once his name went on the list. He spent his last hours on earth in private communion. And you respected this. Besides, what could you say to a man about to die in an utterly repulsive manner?

Frederic often wondered how such a cataclysmic event affected the men who were close friends. How did you shut a friend out of your life, shut his screams out of your life, at a few hours' notice? But it was a problem for others. Not for Frederic Janski, and not for Sammy Rosenthal. Surely.

In the event, he never found out how friends spend their last hours as human beings. He returned to the block late, as usual nowadays, and an air of more than usual desperation hung over the barracks. No one spoke at all. That something terrible had happened was obvious. But he had no part of it. Nor did he wish any. So he did not find out until next morning, when the stools were arranged behind the barbed wire, and standing against the fence he discovered that Sammy was not beside him. Nor was Mittwitz. Nor was Groetz. They were out there, beyond the wire, their pants down about their ankles as if they were truant schoolboys, their bare backsides unnaturally white in the winter sunlight, shivering as they were strapped to the stools, their eyes open but their faces shut, men already dead, seeking to exclude the coming half-hour from their minds. He looked away from them to the men in black, to *the* man in black, standing at the open end of the punishment square. His face was immobile, peaceful. Had Reitener, then, so attuned his mind to the completion of his duties that his pleasures *could* only be transient, and physical?

You could hear the first blows, clearly, because there was no other sound. You could hear the second blows, too, because no one screamed until the third. Even dying men have their codes of honour. From then on the sounds of the blows became submerged in screams and moans, in the shuffling of the three thousand pairs of feet.

Rosenthal only looked up once. He threw his head back to scream, and Frederic closed his eyes. He stayed with his eyes shut, felt the cold. Sammy was not feeling the cold now. Sammy was never going to feel the cold again. But Frederic felt the cold, and it seeped through his skin into his heart, and it stayed, after the screaming had stopped, and the death van had backed up to the stools, and the hoses had sprayed the stools and the snow around, and the inmates had returned about their duties, and Frederic stood above the radiator in the commandant's kitchen.

There was no more need for thought. There was a bottle of champagne, a very thick, heavy bottle, one of several laid in for the commandant's party. At last the warmth was reaching him; the cold dissolved in tears. Not that tears affected his resolution. Just as Sammy had known he had to die all of Christmas Eve, so Frederic knew he must also die. But not until he had killed.

He listened to the boots striking the steps. He tiptoed into the living room, took his stand behind the door. Reitener stepped inside. Frederic moved forward, swung the bottle. Blackness flashed in front of him, then a variety of coloured lights, and then the polished wooden floor, just before he hit it. The bottle had shattered, and champagne bubbled on the floor. And the blackness towered above him, for ever and ever. You could not defeat the blackness.

Reitener took off his cap, then his belt, threw them

on a chair. He poured a glass of brandy. 'Of course. He was your friend.'

Frederic sat up. The holster stared back at him, only feet away. But it was black.

'He may even have died for you, Frederic. He had a fight with Groetz on labour assignment. And Mittwitz joined in. Groetz said something disparaging about you, I imagine. About your new life.'

Frederic was on his knees. The holster was within reach. It would need to be unbuckled, but there was nothing Reitener could do. Reitener might be an expert at unarmed combat, but Reitener was on the other side of the room.

Reitener finished his brandy, poured another glass. 'So now you wish to join him, wherever he may be. You are a fool, Frederic. Do you think I enjoy sending men to their deaths? Do you think I enjoy anything about this miserable existence? I'm a Sturmbannfuehrer in the SS, not a gaoler.'

Frederic stood up, the pistol between his hands. He had both forefingers round the trigger.

Reitener smiled. But he had to be afraid. No man could look death in the face and not be afraid.

'Gestapo rat,' Frederic said.

'I work for the Schutzstaffel. There is a difference, as the names imply. The Gestapo are mere policemen; the SS are guardians of the state. I have been playing the policeman for six months, because I had typhoid earlier this year, and was considered unfit for active service. But I am fit now. I am leaving this camp next month, Frederic. Providing you do not send me on my way earlier.'

'You are a murderer.'

'An executioner, Frederic, in my present role. It was not of my choosing.' Reitener sighed. 'One obeys orders because one is a soldier. Oh, one attempts to justify them. One says, these Jews and communists and religious fanatics and anti-socials would hold back the forces of progress, would negate the efforts of the Fuehrer to create something lasting, here in Europe. Think about that, Frederic. Great Britain and Germany, the only two nations in Europe worth considering, committed joint suicide in 1914. The British, being removed from the maelstrom of European politics, have no sense of urgency, and so continue their decline without even noticing it. But we of Germany have to rub shoulders with the Asiatic hordes, just over there. Without a powerful Germany there could be no Europe. Without a dominant Germany Europe can never advance. And these men, for their own prejudices, in their search for a petty profit, would keep Germany weak.'

'You are wrong,' Frederic shouted. 'You are spouting Nazi claptrap.'

'Of course I am wrong, Frederic. This is what makes my job so difficult. I am right about the Rosenthals and the Groetzs and the Mittwitzs of this world. They are the weeds who would stifle the growth of the human race. But I am wrong to consider every man here as belonging to that category. Because then I come face to face with a Frederic Janski, and I ask myself what is a man like this doing here, and I try to help him, and I fail.'

'Liar!' Frederic screamed, and pulled the trigger, again and again and again. Nine times.

Feet crashed on the steps, fists banged on the door. 'Sturmbannfuehrer Reitener! Sturmbannfuehrer Reitener! Are you all right?'

The pistol slipped from Frederic's fingers, thudded to the floor. Commandant Reitener stooped, picked up the pistol, opened the door.

'Sturmbannfuehrer Reitener!' they gasped. 'We heard shots!'

Reitener showed them the pistol in his hand, the mass

of bullet holes in the floor beneath his chair. 'It is Christmas. Frederic, these gentlemen will have some brandy.'

VII

They flowed, on a river of sound, swept along by the melody, whipping round and round in an ecstasy of synchronised movement. Light, laughter, other dancers, passed in a haze. Even Wittzen of the two left feet, standing against the wall, frowning, disappeared into the kaleidoscope. And Liese did not even know his name. She gazed at his face, distinguished, proud, flawlessly featured. His eyes were deep blue, almost the same colour as his dress uniform. Only his close-cropped hair spoiled the symmetry. He needed hair as long as hers, perhaps, sweeping down his shoulders.

The music stopped. The dream was over, and she must return to her Heinrich.

'A drink, perhaps?'

'I'd love one.'

He imprisoned her arm, led her to the stairs. 'Liese,' he mused. 'Would that be short for Anneliese, by any chance?'

'Oh, yes. It's my mother's name. So Papa calls her Anna, and me Liese. It saves confusion.'

He smiled. He smiled often, but always gravely. 'It is a German name.'

'Mama is German.'

'Then I think it shall be champagne.' They had reached the huge table with the white cloth and the myriad bottles, and the other officers were making way for the beautiful Janski girl. 'And we shall drink a toast, to all the Annelieses, wherever they may be, and especially to this one.'

'Then I can't drink. Unless I toast you. But I didn't catch your name.'

The gravity disappeared, and he looked very young. 'Paul von Bardoman.'

She studied his sleeve. 'And you are an over-lieutenant.'

'It sounds better in German. Oberleutnant. No syllables now.'

'Oberleutnant. Would you prefer to speak German?'

'The general said we may speak Polish tonight.'

'I'd rather speak German. Couldn't we find somewhere quiet, and speak German?'

'I should like that very much.' He followed her, carrying the glasses. 'Do you smoke?'

'Oh, no. But please go ahead.' Liese sat in one of the chairs lining the hall. 'You dance beautifully, Oberleutnant.'

'Then call me Paul.' He sat beside her, the gravity back. 'You are escorted by Captain Wittzen.'

'He's Colonel Bruckner's adjutant.'

'He is looking for you now. He's just gone into the bar.'

'There's the billiard room. He'd never think of looking for me in there.'

Balls clicked, and the two junior officers looked startled. 'Excuse us, von Bardoman,' they muttered, and left.

Liese picked up the white ball, rolled it across the cloth. The red was just within reach. She leaned over to secure it.

Von Bardoman stood on the opposite side of the table. 'Do you play?'

'I wouldn't know how to begin.' She rolled the red ball after the white. He stopped them both, returned them. He put a back spin on the red ball, so she had to lean forward again.

'I am leaving Warsaw tomorrow morning,' he said.

She straightened.

'I am stationed on the West Wall.' He shrugged. 'The British and the French will not stop this war, so someone must defend the Reich. I was glad to be returning to active service this afternoon.'

'I'm sorry.'

He came round the table, took the balls from her hands. 'This is presumptuous of me, I know. I have only just met you, and there is an ocean of feeling and event between us. But I would like to write you a letter now and then. I am an only son, and my mother is very old. There are certain things one writes to very old mothers, and there are other things one wishes to write and cannot.'

'You think there is going to be fighting?'

'As soon as the weather permits it.'

'I should love you to write to me, Paul. And I would like you to know that there is nothing between us to remove.'

He raised her hands to his lips.

'Paul!' Her fingers were tight on his.

He parted her arms, kissed her mouth, just a touch, and straightened again. 'I will have leave again next year. And I will come to Warsaw. I promise this.' He smiled. 'I will inform Captain Wittzen of my intention.'

'Say something.' Commandant Reitener smoked a Turkish cigarette. Even in bed he looked totally correct. He could step straight from bed into a parade and be the smartest man there. It occurred to Frederic that, even as an inmate, Sturmbannfuehrer Reitener would stand out as the smartest man present. Or was that a façade, and would Reitener also shrivel up and become a coward when exposed to Bauer.

'I hate you.' Frederic poured coffee, added the drop of milk and the four lumps of sugar.

'I meant something intelligent. But tell me why.'

'For last night. For not executing me yesterday.'

'I do not intend to execute you at all.'

'Then I hate you more. For keeping me alive.'

Reitener smiled. 'You mean you hate yourself for loving me. You fell in love with me the moment you entered
the compound last October. I saw you staring at me. I
have had men flogged for less than that, Frederic. But I
recognised the love in you. You loved my authority, my
uniform, my personality. You proved your love last night
when you could not make yourself kill me. And you know
that everything I said yesterday was true.'

'None of it was true.'

Sturmbannfuehrer Reitener swung his legs from the
bed, sipped his coffee. 'Then let us argue. Tell me where
I was wrong.'

Frederic gazed at him.

'Oh, no tricks. Now really, Frederic, why should I
waste my time baiting you? I can, whever I choose, do
anything I wish to you. Have you ever tried to envisage
such power, Frederic? I have it over three thousand men.
Over more than that, because I possess no less power over
my guards, and their wives, and their children. Whoever
steps down from the train at that station belongs to me,
Frederic.'

Frederic knelt beside the cupboard, took out the black
boots, applied polish. 'And you love it.'

Reitener shrugged. 'Love, hate, like you, Frederic, I
cannot be certain where the difference lies. I know that
empires are based on fear, that I must implement that
fear, that I must be cruel. I know that when I see a man
strapped to the stools being flogged I am thrilled. Is it
revulsion or pleasure? Or purely sexual excitement?
Do I hate myself every time I have an erection? Do I hate
myself for loving you? It is a criminal passion, Frederic,
which proved against me would send me behind those
very fences, complete with pink triangle. I cannot answer
any of those things, and neither can you. For men like us,

duty is the only consideration. Every so often Genius comes into the world, and rises above the rest of us, and tells us where our duty lies. And we obey. We know that we must obey. To understand more is beyond us.'

'Your trust in the Fuehrer is the most frightening thing about you.'

'I can remember Germany as it was six years ago, Frederic. There is not a man in the Reich, except possibly the Jews, who would revert to such chaos.'

'Surely he has led you to disaster now, sir.' Frederic scuffed vigorously, lost in unreality, that he should be kneeling on a bedroom floor arguing with the commandant. 'To invade Poland, to conquer Poland, to divide Poland with Russia, was to compound disaster upon disaster. Only Poland stood between Europe and Russia. When Pilsudski defeated Tuchachevsky he saved all Europe from Bolshevism. Now your Fuehrer has torn down that bulwark.'

'I had forgotten you intend to be a historian, Frederic. And I agree with your estimation of Pilsudski's achievement. But not with your estimation of Poland. Poland is not a nation; it is an accumulation of nationalities. I doubt that half your inhabitants are true Poles. There is no bulwark in a patchwork. And so I do not agree that the Fuehrer has made a mistake. What happened to Poland merely means that we Germans are now ready to settle with the Bolsheviks. *We* will take on the burden of safeguarding Europe, and not by withstanding Bolshevism. By destroying it.'

'You are allied with it.'

'We have an understanding with it. Because of Britain's foolish attempts to maintain her famous balance of power. But once Britain comes to her senses and makes peace, then we shall see, Frederic. We, the armies of the Reich, are going to keep an appointment with Armageddon. It will be the greatest conflict in the history of the world, Frederic. And we shall win it, and decide the future of mankind.' He rested his hand upon the dark yellow head. 'Would you like to take your part in that conflict, Frederic?'

Frederic polished.

'I have been thinking about it. I spend a great deal of my time thinking about you. As a Pole you are a joke. You are a Swede, and a German. This is obvious to anyone who looks at you twice. As either of those, you are welcome in the Wehrmacht. We need young men like you. I personally would prefer it were you to become a German citizen. So would your mother. I could arrange it for you.' He dropped to his knees beside the boots. 'You would change your name to Johansson, perhaps. You would leave this stinking hole and these shameful stripes and wear the finest uniform on earth.'

'And I would disgrace it. I am a coward. I tried to fight for Poland, and at the first shots I ran away.'

'Over a million men ran away in Poland. But the fault was poor leadership, poor equipment. Bravery is a matter of education and confidence. You would go far, Frederic. Ours is a revolutionary society. There is every opportunity for a man to rise from the ranks to the highest position. And you would be a *man* again. And think of the alternative. I am leaving next month. My replacement is a married man with three children. To him you will be just another inmate. And with that peculiar streak of yours you will wind up on the stools yet. I want you to think very carefully about what I am offering.'

'I would be a German.'

'You are a German, Frederic. I know what is at the bottom of your reluctance. You see Germany as a cruel, perhaps vicious, society. That is a harsh judgement. We are a society at war, and to all intents and purposes we have been at war, non-stop, since 1914. Thus we are corrupted. Because that is the most terrible of war's effects,

106

Frederic. What is remarkable about death? We are all going to die. What is remarkable about suffering? We suffer more when ill than we could possibly do under the Gestapo. Even bad toothache is more painful than any torture I have seen inflicted. The hideousness of it is the fact that these horrors are not brought upon us by germs, or natural processes, but by other men. That other human beings can *want* to do these things to their fellows. But I will tell you something else, Frederic. War corrupts everything it touches. It has corrupted you, and you are a tyro at war. You will become more corrupt with every day. It is corrupting your family now. You think, perhaps, that you must remain their own Frederic, that they may recognise you when you finally return to them. But *you* will not recognise *them*, Frederic. They are living in conditions of war, there in Poland, and they are corrupting, in their minds, their desires, their fears, their hopes, most of all, in their understanding of what is right and what is wrong. Your father, your mother, your brothers, your sisters, your mistress, if you have one, are on their way down, Frederic. You can imagine them, drowning in a sea of vice and selfishness, and you are there with them. You can only save them by reaching the shore, you can only reach the shore by being on the winning side when the war ends. There lies the only hope of humanity. And to save humanity you must be prepared to commit any crime, inflict any injury.'

Mama corrupt? Papa, who would not hurt a fly? Christina, who would not know how to hurt a fly? Josef, who wanted only to record? And Asja? Asja's world was so innocent she could not even understand his desire, because he was her brother-in-law.

'I hate you,' he said. 'I shall always hate you, Sturmbannfuehrer Reitener. Oh, I admire your clothes and your ways and your aura. But I hate you. For daring to suppose that I or my family could enter your world. For murdering Sammy Rosenthal in the name of mankind. For living. I could never be one of your army.' He paused for breath, aghast at what he had said. Already he could feel the edge of the stool cutting into his groin.

Sturmbannfuehrer Reitener stood up. 'And I love you, Frederic. So think about what I have been saying. You have a month.'

VIII

The paper was the first official communication Asja had ever received. 'What is it?'

Josef's spectacles gleamed when he was excited. 'It says that Mrs. Asja Janski can come and go between Warsaw and Rokonow as and when she pleases.'

She folded the pass. 'You must be very thick with the Germans.'

'I take all their official photographs. But I'm attracting a lot of local trade as well. I'm quite well known now in Warsaw. That's why I need an assistant.'

'I know nothing about photography, Josef.'

'You'll learn. And the important thing is that you'd be there. I have to go out on assignments, you see, and the studio is left unattended. I'm losing a lot of business.'

'Then why not ask Liese to help you?'

'That's impossible.'

'So she goes out with German officers. You work for them.'

'It's not as simple as you think.'

Asja frowned. There had been a distinct change in Josef's personality over the past few weeks. He *was* sly now, instead of looking sly, and he seldom came out to Rokonow. 'Are you doing something foolish, Josef?'

'Is it foolish to want your country to be free?'

'It is foolish to go around slashing tyres when if you're caught you'll be shot.'

'Slashing tyres! The Home Army is just starting.'

'Then I would stop shouting about it.'

He sat beside her on the bed, held her hands. 'I'm important to the Army, you see, because I'm in with the Germans. I hear things, and I can find out things. Now you see why I can't employ Liese.'

'But you can employ me.'

'As my receptionist. You'd take orders for photographs, hand out prints to people who would call for them. That's all. So some of the things you'd handle would be in code. But you'd never know. You'd be absolutely safe.'

'Then why have you told me?'

'Because I must be able to trust you. God, how I want to trust somebody! Do you know how lonely it is, sitting down there, like a spider, waiting?'

She stood up, and he released her hands. 'Like a fly, you mean. And when they take us down to Szucha Avenue?'

He took her in his arms. 'Asja! Antoni died fighting the Germans. Frederic is in a concentration camp because he fought the Germans. You don't expect me to sit back and enjoy living under them?' He squeezed, pressing her against him. He wants me too, she realised, and wondered why she had not understood before. Antoni had had first pick. Now he was dead Josef was next in line.

'I could never leave little Antoni.'

'You're not feeding him any more. Mama would look after him. She'd love that. And you'd see him almost every night.'

'Almost, Josef?'

'Well, there would be times, of course.' He let her go, stuck his hands in his pockets. 'The Germans aren't going to leave Poland, you know, Asja. They're going to have to be thrown out.'

'By whom?'

'By us. The French and the British are ready now to launch their offensive. They're just waiting for the weather to improve. Then the Germans will be defeated and all Poland is going to rise up in revolt. And then, Asja, we are going to remember those who collaborated.'

And what will happen to Mama and Liese?'

'We'll be able to save them, Asja. You and me. Because we'll have worked for the partisans. There's little Antoni, too. You want him to be proud of both his parents.'

The door opened. 'Josef!' Mama cried. 'Christina told me you were here. And you didn't come to see me?'

'Josef wants me to work for him, Mama.'

'In Warsaw?'

'I'd go in every day. He's brought me a pass from the Governor-General's office.'

'I think that's a splendid idea, Asja. I've been so worried about you, never getting out of the house, never seeing anybody. I think it would do you good.'

'You'd have to look after little Antoni.'

'It would be my pleasure, Asja. Now you come downstairs and tell me what's happening in Warsaw, Josef.'

But he hung behind, half closed the door, held her shoulders. 'I've dreamed about you and me, Asja, together, working for Poland.'

She gripped his wrists, moved his hands. She was stronger than he.

There were two bodies on the floor outside the kitchen. When Frederic pushed the swing door it came back at him, struck the tray, and knocked over a glass. He put the tray on the kitchen table, returned to the door, got his head through the aperture. The woman was on top. Her skirt was pulled up to her thighs, and he could see her suspenders. But she had fat legs. She straddled the man, working her body and putting her tongue into his mouth.

She pushed the door against Frederic with her shoulder.

Frederic picked up the tray, went through the bedroom. There was a couple on the bed, and they were taking themselves more seriously. They did not notice the waiter. He went into the living room. The gramophone still blared, but no one was dancing any more. The room was littered with couples in various stages of copulation. Only Reitener sat by himself, legs crossed, smoking his Turkish cigarettes, looking at his guests with a mixture of amusement and contempt. He beckoned Frederic, took two glasses of champagne, drank one, sipped from the other. 'The master race, celebrating. I think I will kick them out now, Frederic. Don't open any more bottles.'

Frederic nodded, returned through the bedroom. There was no movement from the bed now, only breathing, slow and deep. A woman vomited into the kitchen sink. She was the blonde from next door. Her dress was unfastened and she held it against herself as she looked up. 'Get me a glass of water.'

Frederic poured, held it for her.

'And don't look at me like that, you miserable bastard. If your tight-fisted employer served better-quality champagne this wouldn't have happened.'

'Would you like anything else, madam?'

She sat at the kitchen table. 'You bet your balls I want something else. Frederic! That's what he calls you. I've heard him.'

Frederic listened to voices, and doors banging. 'The guests are going.'

'Max is on duty. Reitener gave him duty tonight. So you come here. Or do I have to fetch you?' She released her dress, stood up. She wore no brassière. But her breasts were small, nothing like Asja's. He thought, with her plump face and shoulders and her small breasts, her figure must be like Ruth's.

'I bet you're a virgin.' She put her arms round his neck.

He could feel her nipples through his shirt. He gazed above her head, at Reitener.

She released him, scooped up her dress, but did not seem embarrassed. 'You're a damned nuisance, Joachim. So I get tired of screwing Germans. I'll go.'

Reitener's eyes burned. The heat was more frightening than the more normal cold. 'Do you have any idea what the penalty is for a German woman who has sexual intercourse with a Polish prisoner?'

'Tell me, Joachim.'

Reitener smiled. 'The prisoner of war is hanged.'

'It is what he deserves. And the woman?'

'Is flogged, Gerda. Publicly. Twenty lashes.'

'A sentence you would just adore to carry out, Joachim. What a pity you interrupted us.'

'I gained the impression you were just getting dressed.'

Gerda's smile died. 'You would not dare, Reitener. You would not dare.'

'The evidence is not conclusive, I agree. And I would hate to ruin a brother officer by forcing his wife to undergo such a public humiliation, which, incidentally, is often but the prelude to other charges. How would you like to be on the inside of that fence, looking out?'

Gerda sat down. The dress sagged away from the small breasts, the small breasts sagged away from the plump chest. 'You are joking, Joachim. You would have to hang Frederic.'

Reitener's eyes were like nothing Frederic had ever seen. They made him think of *Inferno*. 'And for that, Gerda, I would personally see to your place in Ravensbrück.'

The pretty blonde woman fell from the chair to her knees. 'Please, Joachim, I beg you. I will do anything.'

'Then I shall be lenient. I shall try you myself, *in camera*, and find you guilty, but with extenuating circumstances, and my sentence will be that you shall receive ten lashes, here in my kitchen.'

She gazed at him.

'So take off your clothes, Gerda.'

'In front of him?'

'He is an instrument of the court. Frederic, there is some Wagner to the left of the dance records. Put them on the gramophone, and turn the volume high.'

Frederic obeyed. He was back in the cellar with Ruth. Reitener had deliberately taken him there. Reitener, of all people.

The music crashed through the night. But no one would complain about a little music in the commandant's house. When he returned to the kitchen Gerda was spreadeagled on the table, each wrist and each ankle tied to a table leg, clamping her body to the bare wood. Her head hung over the edge. Her eyes glowed at him. But he did not think she saw *him*. 'This is a game, Joachim. Say it is a game. You will not hurt me.'

'We will share this, Frederic.' Reitener handed Frederic one of the belts. 'Five strokes each. And we are going to hurt you, Gerda. By God, we are going to hurt you.'

Her screams rose with the Valkyries. Whiteness turned to red, and a streak of blood ran down her thighs. The plump body quivered and sagged, and quivered and tensed, and billowed with sound. Reitener slit the bonds with a kitchen knife. 'Now get out.'

She did not wait to dress. She forgot the snow on the steps. The front door banged. Reitener poured two glasses of brandy. 'We will drink to Gerda's chilblains. It is already two, Frederic. You will spend the night here.'

Frederic sipped the liquor, felt it burn his throat. The fire still smouldered in Reitener's eyes. 'You enjoyed whipping her.'

Reitener smiled. 'So did you, Frederic. So did you.'

Gdanska looked the same. But Gdanska had always looked the same. Johnson took his bag to the compartment door, waited for the train to stop. There was more track than the last time, but not really more stock. Certainly there were less people, and these were civilians, in summer frocks and open-necked shirts. And like all people in summer, regardless of their nationality, they were good-humoured.

His throat was dry. When the door opened who would be standing there? Ziegler and Kolisch? Josef and Liese? or Asja? He wondered what he would do if it could be Asja.

It was a young man, neatly dressed and anxious to please. 'Mr. Johnson? Welcome to Warsaw. I have a car waiting. And perhaps on the way to the hotel I can show you something of the city.'

Johnson gave him his bag. 'I should like that very much,' he said. After lunch he would go out to Rokonow. In Rokonow he could begin his search.

3

Summer 1941

Gdanska looked the same, except that the last time Frederic had been here there had been no soldiers. This morning there were no civilians, other than the porters and the ticket collectors. Even the men in plain clothes waiting by the doorways were so obviously Gestapo they could as well have worn uniform. 'It is because of the explosion up the line,' Ziegler said. 'This country is alive with partisans.'

They left their rifles in the care of the duty section. 'I am going to find myself a Polish bit.' Kolisch came from Hamburg. 'The most beautiful women in Europe, Poles.'

'I'm going to take a walk through the old city,' Ziegler said. 'What do they call it?'

'Stare Miasto,' Frederic said.

'You know Warsaw, Johansson?' Kolisch asked.

'I've been here. I have friends here. I think I'll look them up.'

'Her, you mean,' Kolisch grinned.

'Well, remember we're not in Germany now,' Ziegler said. 'You wander down a dark alley and you'll get a knife in the back.' Ziegler was the oldest soldier in the section, Frederic the newest.

Frederic adjusted his cap, passed the Gestapo men on the gate. They looked like ordinary detectives. Only the name Gestapo was sinister, shrouding all connected with it in a mist of terror and suspicion. To other people. To the partisans. Not to him. He had come into close contact with the Gestapo, knew what they were capable of. But that was part of Frederic Janski's past. The Gestapo had no part in Frederic Johansson's future.

A man passed him, sloshing in the gutter. It had rained overnight, and there was water in the gutters, but the Poles preferred to get their feet wet than share the pavement with a German soldier. Did he have to feel sad about this? About Warsaw? About Poland? What did he have to feel sorry about? He had plunged into the middle of hell and he had got back out again. Why? When Rosenthal had been flogged to death? But you did not think about Rosenthal, any more than you thought about Smorodin, who had been crushed like a frog. There was a war on, and they had died. But Frederic was still alive.

The Saxon Gardens were ablaze with spring flowers. The sky was blue, the sun was shining, and the grass glistened. He wondered if the roses would be out on Ujawdowskie yet. But Warsaw was a sad place. The gutted houses reminded him of fleshless skulls, with their glassless windows and empty doorways. This had been a beautiful city.

He wondered if he should drop in on Josef first, decided against it. He wanted to get home, to see them all. To see Asja. To know what he was, how he was.

He caught a bus. A woman hastily got up to allow him a seat. He smiled at her, and she averted her eyes. No one in all of Warsaw, in all of Rokonow, would recognise Frederic Johansson. Frederic Janski had left, a boy. Frederic Johansson was not yet twenty, but there could be no doubt that he was a man.

In how many ways? He gazed through the misty window at the wrecked houses, the sad-looking, shabby people. But there were many people in Germany who looked just as drab; those who weren't in uniform.

He supposed to Reitener he had been nothing more than a passing fancy, a pretty little thing, a moth caught in a flame, from which Reitener had rescued him. He had not seen Reitener for over a year, and in that time a great deal had happened. The frightened boy had become a soldier. He had not seen action yet but the time was close. Would he be afraid? But that was something every soldier considered, even Ziegler, who had been through the French campaign. He had said, with them all:

'I swear by God this sacred oath that I will render unconditional obedience to Adolf Hitler, the Fuehrer of the German Reich and people, Supreme Commander of the Armed Forces, and will be ready as a brave soldier to risk my life at any time for this oath.'

He counted scenes from his life, as he would look at photographs in an album. A scattering from his childhood—how long ago that seemed—a naked, pregnant Asja turning to face the open door, the man in the gutter with no legs, the little girl waiting by her dead mother, Smorodin, Rosenthal, Gerda stretched across the kitchen table, Reitener smiling. Strangely, Ruth Blass had no place in his album, or Reitener out of uniform. These had happened in darkness. But they had all happened before that afternoon, *the* scene of his life, the purification of his soul, the transformation of a boy into a man, of a coward into a heroic defender of the Reich. The flags, draped from every corner of the vast square, the measured tread, the waiting guards, the gleaming helmets and bayonets, the high officials, the Fuehrer himself, a surprisingly small, nondescript figure, but with a gleam in his eyes, visible even at a distance, which dwarfed every passion of which Reitener had been capable, and, above all, the aura of belonging to such an army, to such a race, to be dedicated to such a blood-tingling purpose, the creation of an edifice which would stand a thousand years, and be the high point of all human history. To have experienced such an afternoon, and *belonged*, on such an afternoon, was to leave dark barracks and cold floors and screaming inmates deep in the subconscious. They came back to you in your nightmares. To Ziegler as well? And Kolisch? Or did Ziegler and Kolisch not even know about them? And

Johansson? Johansson thought about them as he thought about tuberculosis and heart disease and cancer, about car accidents and train crashes. He wondered why, how, these things happened, and he knew, as Reitener had known, that he was not one of the appointed few who could ameliorate the inevitable course of history.

And the knowledge made him strong.

There was a flag flying over the house, red, white and black; *the* flag. Frederic opened the gate, and the sentry presented his rifle. 'Halt! This is Colonel Hoeppner's residence, soldier.'

'I have come to see Frau Janski.'

'Then use the back door, soldier.'

Fingers, drumming softly on the brain, summoning you back into the world, perhaps summoning you to Szucha Avenue. Asja dreamed of Szucha Avenue every night. She did not know what lay behind the door, but she had walked past it and looked at the barbed-wire barricades, and at the swastika flag floating lazily from the roof.

She sat up, took the revolver from beneath her pillow. She slept in her underwear when in town, and so she rested the barrel of the revolver on her brassière, pushed the muzzle inside, to touch, so very cold, her left breast. Her left hand pulled the blanket round her shoulders, concealing the gun. Should the man out there say, 'Frau Janski, we would like you to accompany us,' she would squeeze the trigger, and that would be that. Perhaps today would be the day. She knew they had to come, eventually. She had known this from the first day she had spent here, had waited for them, almost anxiously. Antoni was dead; what had happened to Frederic was worse than death. Little Antoni was her only reason for remaining in the prison that was Poland, and she knew now that his sentence was going to be very short.

She unlocked the door. In the gloomy cellar she would

identify them before they could see her. 'Asja!' Kopa stepped inside.

Asja sighed. She dropped the blanket, laid the revolver on the table, struck a match. 'Well?'

'Didn't you hear it?'

Asja turned up the wick, hung the lamp from the ceiling. She could feel his gaze, moving like a suction cup over her skin. 'There was thunder in the night.'

'That was the explosion. The line is wrecked for half a mile. And there was a train. Carrying troops, Asja. We must have slaughtered fifty of the bastards.'

'Josef?'

'He'll be along later.' He picked up the revolver, broke it, spun the chambers. 'You're always ready, eh?'

She buttoned her blouse.

'And if Josef had been killed?'

'I'd weep. He's my brother.'

Kopa threw both arms round her waist, from behind. 'Asja! Do you know what it is like, lying out there in the wet, waiting for the charge to go off? Waiting to kill, or to be killed?'

'I know what it is like waiting here.' She moved his hands, sat on the bed, rolled on her stockings. She was well supplied with stockings; both Kopa and Josef brought them to her.

'You were married, Asja. You have borne a child. But that was two years ago. Don't you ever catch fire between your legs?'

Asja straightened her seams. 'Would you like some coffee?'

Kopa sat on the bed in turn, hands dangling between his knees. 'You're not a woman. You're some kind of stone.'

She poured the coffee. 'I'm a fool, you mean. We are all fools. When I came here to help Josef we were going to free Poland. We were going to rise up when the French and the British defeated Hitler. Eighteen months ago, Kopa.'

'The British are still fighting.'

'About as effectively as we are. The Home Army! Robbers and murderers.'

'You'd rather collaborate?'

'I'd like to know how long you mean to keep this up.'

'We fought the Russians for a hunded and forty years.'

'And some of us were hanged every year.'

'Asja!' He caught her thighs, sat her on his knee. 'That train we blew up was just one of many. There are hundreds of trains, all full of soldiers, all passing through Warsaw, heading east. Tell me why, Asja.'

'Hitler would never be that stupid. He has an understanding with the Bolsheviks.'

Kopa drank, noisily, wiped his mouth with the back of his hand. 'How's your baby?'

'He has a cough. He always has a cough.'

'I might be able to get you some medicine.'

'I'd be very grateful.'

'I'll bring it tonight. Will you be here tonight, Asja?'

'If you'll bring the medicine.'

II

Anton Janski listened to them coming up the stairs as he had watched them walking down the street. I wonder if he'll notice how grey I've become, he thought. How thin. How thin we all are.

'Papa!' Anton had expected him to give the Nazi salute, but he came into the room with both arms outstretched.

'I recognised you on the street. Let me look at you.'

He could have been any of the soldiers you saw on the street every day. Forage cap, olive-green uniform, black

122

boots, close-cropped yellow hair. But how fit he looked. The old Frederic had never looked so fit.

'You're looking well.'

'And so are you, Papa.'

'Do you think so?' Anton stroked his hair. 'I'm looking my age.'

'We're all doing that, Anton,' Mama said. But her silver threads were becoming. 'Isn't it splendid to see him?'

'Isn't he smart, Papa?' Christina cried.

'Why didn't Liese come, Anna?'

Frederic grinned. 'She wouldn't be seen walking along the street with a common soldier.'

'She's baby-sitting little Antoni,' Mama explained. 'That child worries me so. He had a cold all last winter, you know, Frederic, and even now he coughs.'

'Asja must be worried.'

'Oh, yes,' Mama said. 'When she has the time to worry. She and Josef work very hard, you know, taking photographs for the authorities.'

'I must drop in and see them this afternoon. So this is the new firm, eh, Papa?'

'Janski Brothers, once again. Jan and I are starting at the beginning, like our ancestors. There'll be a job for you when the war is over.'

'I think it's a marvellous effort.' Frederic fingered the battleship Papa had been carving, glanced at the tanks and soldiers and airplanes. Janski Brothers had always made warlike toys.

'All hand-carved,' Papa said. 'Just as Grandfather used to make them. You won't get toys like this anywhere in Germany.'

'The detail on this thing is just marvellous. *Tirpitz*, is it?'

'Well, it began as the *Bismarck*,' Papa said slyly. 'I've repainted the name.'

'Didn't this house belong to Dr. Landski?'

123

'That's right,' Mama said. 'But he was a Jew, you see. Jews aren't allowed in Rokonow.'

'Oh, yes, of course,' Frederic said.

Anton Janski wondered what Frederic thought about the Jews. What had Frederic done about the Jews during his eighteen months in Germany. But Josef worked for the Germans, and Jan seemed to get on with them, and Liese went out with them, and even Asja seemed to accept them. So why shouldn't Frederic fight with them? If only he hadn't changed his name, renounced his Polish citizenship.

'Where's Uncle Jan this morning?' Frederic asked.

'In town. He has a permit from the Germans to gather wood for our toys. There are no other materials. And in the winter people can always burn their children's playthings, eh?'

'What a good idea.' But Frederic was restless. Duty had demanded he come to see his family. But now he was anxious to get away again, from these tired, underfed, humble people.

'You'll be staying for lunch?' Papa asked.

'Of course he's staying for lunch,' Mama said. 'But we must eat early. He has other people to see this afternoon in Warsaw.'

'Well, then, off you go. Frederic will help me lock up.' He ushered the two women on to the stairs, began closing the shutters. 'There are a lot of soldiers passing through Warsaw this last week.'

'We're going to fight the Russians. That's why I joined up, Papa. To fight the Russians. You don't blame me for that?' He threw his arm round his father's shoulders. 'You fought the Russians, Papa. Remember Tuchachevsky?'

'Those were the days.'

'But you don't like me in this uniform, eh? I can see it in your eyes.'

124

'Who am I to like or dislike any more, Frederic? I am a tired old man.'

'You're younger than the Fuehrer, and no one could accuse him of being old and tired. I've seen him, you know. Quite close. When we took the oath of allegiance. I've never felt so . . . Well, so *part* of something.'

Anton remembered how, when he had told the boys about the campaign against Tuchachevsky, Frederic had said, 'Why wasn't I named after the marshal, instead of that four-eyed fish? If you'd christened me Josef, Papa, I'd have been a second Pilsudski.'

Frederic remembered this street so well, the houses leaning towards him after the blast. He remembered the newsagent's shop, the blood seeping across the floor and on to the step. He remembered the hands. And Ruth. He wondered what had happened to Ruth. But he hadn't wanted to ask them. He hadn't wanted to ask them anything. Lunch had been the most difficult meal he could remember.

Tarpaulins had been nailed across holes in roofs and planks over windows. There were people in the newsagent's shop. They stopped talking to stare at the German soldier. He nodded at them, went down the steps. He felt uncomfortable. In Germany to be a soldier, even one who had not yet seen active service, was to be a hero. Everyone had a smile for a member of the Wehrmacht. But the Poles had never learned, would never learn, to like their conquerors.

He knocked, listened to the key turn. 'Yes?'

To hear the single word after two such years was to drift back over all that time, to a dark doorway and a flickering candle and a tousled head of red-gold hair, and a strong face, because she was frowning, and although it was one o'clock in the afternoon she might just have got out of bed; she wore a blanket over her shoulders, concealing her chest and her right hand.

She was looking not at his face but at his uniform. 'What is it you wish?'

'Asja?' He had wondered how it would sound when he said it again, to her, after nearly two years. It sounded flat.

'Frederic?' It was an utterly incredulous whisper.

He threw the door open, took her in his arms. Her body was stiff, her right hand, caught between then, seemed to be clenched. She moved her mouth, and he kissed her cheek. She freed herself, closed the door and turned the key, hung it on a hook. She took off the blanket, wrapped it around her right hand, then slipped it off and threw it on the bed. 'You gave me a start. Why didn't you let us know you were coming?'

'I didn't know myself until two days ago.' He walked into the centre of the room. 'Same as always. Are the photographs the same, too?'

'There are some of my hands as well, now.'

'That brother of mine is a nut.' Frederic licked his lips. 'Do you see much of Ruth nowadays?'

'We don't see anything of the ghetto people. Would you like some coffee?'

'I'd love some.' He sat at the table. If only bombers would appear overhead now. Whose bombers? The British, perhaps. Russian. Any bombers, to bring them together. But Asja wasn't afraid of bombs.

'It isn't really coffee,' she said. 'I'm afraid there's no sugar, either.'

'It's hot.'

She sat opposite him. 'When are you going to Rokonow?'

'I've been.'

'Mamma must have been overjoyed.'

'She was. Asja, what has been happening?'

'What do you wish me to tell you?'

126

'The truth. About Mama and Papa. They're miserable. And Christina is different, too. And Antoni . . .'

'Antoni has a weak chest. We are all sick, Frederic. To be conquered is to contract an illness in the mind. To be conquered by the Germans is to make the illness fatal.'

'You work for them.'

'I work for Josef.'

'Do you sleep with him?'

'Is that all you men think about? Why don't you go back to your German friends? You have German friends, haven't you?'

'Asja!' He snatched her hands across the table. 'Listen to me. Just listen. For five minutes.'

The door opened. 'Frederic!' Josef slapped him on the shoulder. 'You look splendid.' He carried a canvas bag.

Frederic squeezed his hand. 'And you look thinner.'

Josef laughed. 'Ah, well, you Germans keep us at it, eh? Asja?' But he did not look at her. 'I like your uniform. Let me take a snap of you.'

'With Asja.'

'No,' Asja said.

'It'll make a good picture.' Josef herded them through the door, made them stand on the steps. Frederic put his arm round her waist. 'You rest your head on his shoulder, Asja,' Josef said. 'Mama'll be delighted with this. Now, I know you only came down here to see Asja, Frederic.'

'You do?' Frederic looked down at Asja. Her face was cold.

'Of course. Why don't you take her for a walk? Go and look at the old city. She has a pass.'

'No,' Asja said. 'I must go home.'

'You go for a walk with Frederic,' Josef said. Strange how his voice could alter, Frederic thought. Strange how Asja could alter, too.

'I'll get my coat,' she said.

III

To leave the ghetto on a Saturday afternoon was not really so very dangerous. Ruth reminded herself of this every week. The Germans were methodical people, and Saturday afternoon was a holiday. It was largely a matter of luck whether you encountered a soldier walking with his Polish girl friend or whether you met a group of soldiers who had no girl friend and resented it. You had a choice. You could march along the street, your yellow star gleaming on your breast, and, if stopped, insist you had a pass, or you could conceal the star and pretend you were an Aryan, although the success of this depended on your appearance. In either event, if you were stopped you had to be a very convincing talker. And you had to keep a cool head. Jacob Finer had been a convincing talker, and had left the ghetto whenever he felt like it for over a year. But he suffered from indigestion, and the pain in his chest made him bad-tempered, and the afternoon had come when he had lost his temper with two German soldiers. Jacob was one of those who had preferred not to wear the star when he left the ghetto, so they had cut a star into his forehead with their bayonets. Jacob had never left the ghetto again. They were less violent with women. The day Abbi Landski had been caught out of the ghetto they had taken off her knickers and made her crawl all the way back while they had walked behind her with a pointed stick. Driving the ass home, they had said. But Abbi was a very pretty girl.

Ruth was not a pretty girl, certainly not since she had lost thirty pounds. Her face, which had once been round and vivacious, had sunk inwards and become a small hatchet, with concave cheeks and a narrow chin. Her plump hips had also dwindled; no German would get much excitement out of walking behind her while she crawled along the street. So what would they do to Ruth Blass when they caught her? She lived with this problem, dreamed about it at night. Yet she left the ghetto every Saturday afternoon. She walked through the scarred streets with her coat closed, hurrying without haste, looking purposeful, doubtless sent on her way by the Govenor General himself. Pass? Oh, yes, she had a pass. But this afternoon she had forgotten it. As if she would be able to say anything. But in nearly two years she had never been stopped.

She slowed, waited for a moment when the street was deserted, which was immediately, because this street had been blown flat, and stepped into a ruined building, picking her way over the rubble until she reached the cellar wall, and there she sat. Once she reached here she was safe until she had to move again. She could sit for ever. She wondered why she didn't, at least in summer, gazing up at the sky, and the clouds, coming from Russia, perhaps, drifting on to Germany. Clouds had a freedom of which human beings could only dream.

She heard him whistling. He was an Aryan, and could whistle as he walked. A Pole, ratting. That would be the excuse for the bag across his shoulder. The Poles weren't starving, but their diet was monotonous. So Josef went ratting. He took his camera, too. Studies of rats. Scientific. But all the Germans knew that Josef was a dedicated photographer, and respected him for it.

She uttered a single bar, waited. This was another private nightmare, that one day it would not be Josef's face peering at her over the rubble, but a strange head surmounted by a forage cap. It had to happen, by the law of averages. But not today.

Stones dribbled from the rubble heap. He sat down, pushed his cap back on his head. He laid the bag between them, took off his spectacles, polished them. Ruth waited. The bag was hers now. Still she waited. You main-tained the code. Whatever tore at your stomach you did not tear at the bag.

'Guess who's in Warsaw,' Josef said. 'Frederic. I told you he changed his name to Johansson?'

'Yes.' With trembling fingers she unfastened the bag. How long ago Frederic seemed. She had been obsessed by the fear she might be pregnant. How long ago.

'He was at the studio,' Josef said. 'I barged into him with the bag.'

'What did you do?' Chocolate. Oh, how marvellous, to begin with chocolate, a square at a time. You had to eat just a square at a time or it gave you diarrhoea, and that was a terrible waste. And Abbi adored chocolate.

'I sent him for a walk with Asja. But I can't stay long.'

'I'll take this stuff with me.' She pushed it inside her blouse.

'You don't share my food, Ruthie?'

He always asked her this. He risked imprisonment to bring her food but he was jealous of what she did with it. 'Of course I don't, Josef.'

He emptied the bag, placed the bread and the cheese and the two potatoes on her lap. 'Next week, then.'

She squeezed his hand. I love you, Josef. I would give all of this food back to have you take me in your arms. But these were thoughts, not words. Maybe, afterwards, because there was going to be an afterwards, there had to be an afterwards, he would say that he loved her too. No man risked his freedom for a woman, every week, from guilt alone.

She listened to his feet tramping over the stones, waited until the noise faded. She got up, her coat held close over the food inside her blouse. She crossed the stones and reached the street, turned to face the ghetto. She hurried, because it was getting late. She ran round the corner, bumped into the men before she saw them. They wore forage caps.

130

They walked through Stare Miasto, crossed the square, went under the arch, stood on the battlements and looked down at the old gate to the city, standing proudly in the middle of the bomb damage, and the Vistula, at the bottom of the hill on their right, hurrying, always hurrying. Across the river Praga huddled in sombre desolation. Frederic wondered if there was anything more desolate than a bombed-out slum.

'Do you have a cigarette?' Asja asked.

He lit it for her. 'When did you start?'

She shrugged, dragged smoke into her lungs. 'A year ago. They are a food substitute.'

'There is rationing in Germany too, you know. Asja, you only came because Josef told you to.'

She leaned against the wall. She was exactly as he remembered her. If she had lost a little weight the slight gauntness of her face only made her more lovely than ever. 'He employs me.'

'You should be home, with Antoni.'

She dropped the cigarette stub to the ground, trod on it. 'Are you a Nazi, Frederic?'

'I suppose so. But I wouldn't inform on my own brother.'

'You asked about Ruth. The Jews in the ghetto are starving. So Ruth comes out on Saturday afternoons and meets Josef. and he gives her food. He was afraid you wouldn't understand. It was in the bag.' She looked past him, at the river. 'There are times when no matter how proud you are you will beg, or risk imprisonment, just to eat.'

'I was in a concentration camp, Asja.'

'A labour camp.'

'There are three categories. Mine was the second. Not as harsh as the third, not as easy as the first. I had a friend who was a Jew. He was flogged to death.'

'But you survived.'

131

'And that was wrong?' He was holding her hands, and her fingers were tight.

'Of course not. But wearing that uniform!'

'A labour camp is like nothing you can imagine, Asja. Try to think of chickens living in their own filth, having their necks wrung at the whim of their owner, and at the same time having to work until they dropped. I kept alive by thinking of you, Asja. Without you I'd have died.' Were there tears in her eyes? Were her fingers squeezing harder? 'And then there was a man. Not the Jew. The Jew was the best friend I ever had. But the other man loved me. Can you understand that?'

'I can understand men, shut up together, needing love.'

'He was the commandant.'

His hands were empty; hers were round her throat.

'Do you hate me for that, Asja?'

'I don't understand what men need, Frederic. From each other or from women. I don't want to any more. I want to understand how you could forgive.'

He could take her hands again, away from her throat. 'He was brilliant. We talked, and argued, and he convinced me. You may not like the Germans, Asja, but they are *here*. We belong to them, now and for ever. Nothing is going to change that. So I could die in that camp, or I could get out. I could only get out by wearing this uniform. And what is so terrible about it? We are going to fight the Russians. Oh, it is a deadly secret, but everyone knows. We are going to smash Russia this summer.'

'And the Jews? And us Slavs? And the men you left behind in the concentration camp?'

'I don't know. I wish I did. But these things go in cycles. Seven hundred years ago, only twenty generations, Asja, the Tartars were watering their horses just down there.'

'And now they're back. Is that good?'

'It means we are at a fundamental point in history. A time when certain races get exterminated because they cannot maintain themselves.'

'That's what I can't understand, Frederic. I belong to one of those races, according to the Nazis.'

'No, you don't. You're a Janski. Asja, I came back only to tell you how much I love you. I want to marry you, Asja.'

'I could never sleep three to a bed.'

'Antoni has been dead for two years.' He took her in his arms. For how long had he wanted to do this, to feel her knee against his, her thigh against his, her breasts moving against his. But she wore a coat and he a thick jacket, and he could not feel her nipples as he had felt Gerda's. Nor could he feel the suspenders as he had felt Ruth's.

Her mouth was an inch away. 'We are going to smash the Russians,' he said. 'This summer. And then Britain will give up as well. The war is going to be over by Christmas, Asja, and I will be coming home for good. And when I come home I am going to marry you. I am going to show you what a man needs from a woman, and what a woman needs from a man. It's something which no one except the two of them can understand, Asja. It's sharing everything worth having in life, with nothing held back. And it begins with our bodies.'

Her mouth was only half an inch away, and it was open. But he would not move his head. He wanted her to kiss him. She kissed his upper lip and then his lower lip, and she licked his tongue, and she took it into her mouth to caress it.

'You love me, Asja. Say you love me.'

'I love you, Frederic. Sometimes I think I have always loved you.' Her hands were between them, on his chest. 'Now go win your war.'

Josef sat at the table in the inner room, his head in his hands. Asja took off her scarf, unbuttoned her jacket. 'He asked me to marry him.'

Josef's head came up.

'He held me in his arms.' Asja's voice was toneless. 'I kissed him.' She buttoned her jacket again. 'I must go to church.'

'Why did you kiss him, Asja?'

'I can't belong to all of you, Josef. I don't know if I can belong to any of you.'

'But why Frederic? Tell me why?'

Her shoulders rose and fell. 'There are times a woman does not know why she does what she does. Antoni frightened me. So does Liese. And your mother most of all.'

'You are not afraid of anything, Asja.'

'You mean I have less fear than you of being hurt in my body. Even of dying. There are worse kinds of fear.'

'And I frighten you too?'

'You want me to hurt you, Josef, and I am not going to do that. You have never frightened me. But Frederic is the only Janski I have ever *liked*. Can you understand that?'

'Antoni was killed by a German bomb.'

'I'm sorry, Josef. Nations, peoples, races, I don't understand all that. I don't want to. When I woke up this morning I wanted to die. Now I want to survive. Nothing more.'

He got up, held her shoulders, thrust her against the wall. 'Kopa was here. They got Ruth this afternoon. After she left me she was going back to the ghetto, and she ran into some soldiers.'

Asja's tongue came out, questing, exploring her lips.

And suddenly Josef understood what Asja wanted, what Asja had never had, not even from her husband. Asja wanted a man stronger than herself.

'What did they do to her?'

'Kopa didn't know. They took her to the barracks. German soldiers, Asja. Friends of Frederic.'

'Garrison soldiers are scum. Frederic is in the line.' She took hold of his wrists, as she had done before, to move his hands. But he would not let her. She thought Frederic was the man to conquer her, because he was physically the biggest of the Janskis. Or perhaps she knew that no man would ever be her master, so she had settled for the opposite, the man who would lie down at her feet for the rest of her life. Asja, so strong, so regal, wanted nothing more than to be thrown on the floor and taken. By any man who was strong enough and ruthless enough to do it. And now, as she gazed at him, she knew he understood what she wanted, and she was waiting.

'I must go, Josef. I wish to confess, and I do not want to break the curfew.' His hands fell to his sides, and she adjusted her scarf. 'Kopa was going to try to get some cough medicine for the baby. If he brings it tonight will you keep it for me? Tell him I will pay him on Monday.'

'What with?'

'With money.' She opened the door, hesitated. 'I'm sorry about Ruth, Josef.'

Frederic dozed while the floorboards rasped to and fro across his backside, and the movement sent his backbone jarring upwards through his brain. He wondered if he would ever take a first-class journey again, sitting comfortably in an upholstered seat, or if first-class travel was now a historical event, like travelling by stage-coach.

Sitting on the floor of the cattle truck, his Mauser rifle between his knees, propped against the man next to him, surrounded by smells and grunts and snores, took him

135

back two years; the man next to him could be Sammy Rosenthal. But it was Hans Ziegler. And beyond him was Cowboy Kolisch. And there was nobody dead on this train. There was nobody even unhappy, despite the discomfort. They were a spearhead, bright and sharp, about to be hurled into the wilderness. Some of them would die in the wilderness. For the first time it occured to Frederic that soon he might be chasing Sammy Rosenthal upwards, or downwards. Sammy would understand.

Had Asja understood? She had kissed him. This did not mean she understood, but perhaps it meant something much more important. It could mean that it did not matter to her whether she understood or not. He had held her in his arms, not as a sister but as a woman, she had held him back, and when he returned from this campaign he would hold her in his arms again, as his wife.

When he thought that he wanted to jump out of the train and run all the way back to Rokonow. But he could wait. For Asja he could wait a hundred years. He wondered what right he had to be this happy when Sammy was dead and Mittwitz was dead and Antoni was dead. He wondered why he thought of them now when he had not thought of them for over a year. Returning to Warsaw, to Rokonow, had been a mistake, except for Asja. Papa had looked old, Mama had looked tired, Josef had looked sly, Liese had looked contemptuous, little Antoni had looked ill, and Christina had looked incredibly contented, as if she alone of all the family had discovered the secret of life. The look had not suited Christina, had made her a stranger. But Asja had looked the same. He could not imagine that face ageing, as he could not imagine anything, however cataclysmic, however painful, changing Asja. Asja personified all the immensity of the pagan gods. Daschbog and Strobog and Wolos, beside whom the Christian trinity had no substance. He even thought there might be something of Pierounn, the Slav

136

god of war and lightning, buried inside Asja.

'Did you find your girl?' Ziegler whispered.

'Yes.'

'And was she glad to see you?'

'I think so. She'll be there when we come home again.'

'I congratulate you.' Ziegler scratched the bristle on his chin. Even in the darkness Ziegler looked like a veteran soldier, hard and tough. Ziegler had followed his rifle from the Ardennes to Dunkirk. Ziegler had killed, with his bayonet as well as his rifle. And Ziegler was the most gentle, the most cultured, the most peaceable of men.

'Did you enjoy your walk through the Old City?'

'Not really. Destruction is the real evil of war, you know, Frederic. Human life sprouts again and again. A great painting, a beautiful building, never returns.'

'You talk like my brother.'

'Right now I would settle for a world full of paintings, and no humans at all. I went to the barracks this afternoon, before I returned to the station. I didn't stay long. Some men brought in a Jewish girl they had caught outside the ghetto. They were playing with her, Frederic. You have seen a cat playing with a mouse? Think of a dozen cats with just one small, frightened mouse.'

Frederic did not want to think about it. It could so easily have been Ruth.

'Do you hate the Jews, Frederic?'

'I don't hate anybody right now.' Which was a lie. He hated Bauer. And sometimes he hated Reitener. And often he hated himself.

'The story of Jewry is like a canker running through the history of mankind. And therefore it is right that no Jew should be allowed to hold a position of authority. And it is right that we should take away their businesses. Why should Jews have more money than Aryans? And yet one wonders. Do you play chess, Frederic?'

'I know the moves.'

137

'I was a good player once. And an insignificant little Jew in the shop on the corner could beat me. Would I be right in saying that the Jews are the most intelligent race on earth, Frederic? Because chess requires a great deal of intelligence, and so many of the best players are Jews. What is more, they are mostly Jews born between Berlin and Moscow. You could say, if you wanted a better than even chance of discovering a great chess player, look for him in a Polish ghetto.'

'The Jews, the Semites, have more intelligence because intelligence grows from generation to generation, and the Semites happen to have had a written alphabet before anybody else, so they were the first away.'

'But how did they *get* the alphabet, Frederic, if intelligence is just a matter of reading and writing and they were as dumb as everybody else before? You know what bothers me most about this whole business? I said look for good chess players between Berlin and Moscow. We're going to start killing a whole lot of them, maybe tomorrow. It would be so much simpler if we could just play them a game of chess, eh?'

'The train's stopping,' Frederic said.

The door opened, and Vice-Sergeant-Major Walbrodt shouted, 'Out! Out!' There was not much difference between a sergeant-major in the Wehrmacht and a Block Leader in the SS, when you came down to it. He wondered if there was really much difference between being in the army and being in a concentration camp. In the army they trained you to keep alive as long as possible; in the concentration camp they trained you to die as quickly as possible; but the end result was the same. For what? He wished Ziegler wouldn't talk so much.

But after they had pitched camp he followed the rest of the squad up a slight rise, to look down at the river, and then at a plain. Behind them the Polish plain drifted, marked by the railway track, and at no great distance a

138

village, showing grey in the twilight. In front of them was another plain. It was Polish too, strictly speaking. But there was no railway line there. There was nothing. It just stetched for ever into the dusk.

'Not even a frontier guard,' Kolisch said. 'Those poor bastards just don't know.'

'It's a long way to Moscow,' Ziegler said.

And it's full of Russians, Frederic thought. Playing chess.

V

The noise awoke Christina. She got out of bed and stood at the window, gazed up at the night sky. The planes showed no lights, but she felt she could see them, thousands of them, judging by the noise, forming a solid wall between her and the heavens.

Liese hadn't come home yet. The other narrow bed was empty, the sheets unruffled. Liese stayed out most Saturday nights, went to mass half asleep.

She opened the door, very softly, as if a squeak could register above the drone of the planes, stood in the blackness of the corridor. But he always insisted she be careful. He was terrified Mama would find out and make him leave.

She stepped inside the next room, listened to his breathing, an occasional snore. She did not need a light. She knew every inch of this room as well as she knew every inch of his body. She took off her nightdress, left it on the floor, lowered herself on to the bed. She didn't want to wake him yet. She had often dreamed of having him all to herself, asleep. Theirs was a one-sided relationship. He wanted everything she could do to him, and he liked to caress her and explore her, but he would never come inside. And she wanted him to come inside more than anything else in the world. He was so large, when he was ready, and so velvety, and she was sure that to have him come inside would be the most delicious experience, and as she knew from some of her other midnight visits he was sometimes ready while he slept, just before he woke. She thought perhaps, while he was still asleep but just ready, she could get him inside. Once inside he would not want to leave again.

Slowly, very slowly, she lay down, inserting first one leg and then the other beneath the sheet. She rested her head on his shoulder, and it slipped forward so that her forehead touched his chin. She loved the bristles on his chin, because they, like his tool, like his great fat belly, were all hers. He sighed, and his arm went round her shoulders, but he was still sleeping.

She lay still for some seconds, listening to the drone of the planes, and then she got her right arm out from under her body, and slipped both hands down, over his belly, found the silky hair, and the tool. It wasn't ready, but it wasn't entirely asleep either. She liked this part best, the movement beneath her fingers, the response, which was so immediate, even when he slept.

She lifted her leg, carrying the sheet with her, and put it across his thighs. She pressed down with her right knee, teeth clamping her tongue, sweating with excitement, yet her body chill compared with the heat rising beneath her. She lay on his chest, felt his great fat belly swelling into her slender pit as he breathed, felt the tool stroking the inside of her thighs, and felt her arms gripped by his always strong fingers.

'You're a little tart, Kitgirl.'

'Please, Jan. Please!'

He sat up. 'It's begun!'

'They woke me up. What's begun?'

'The war with Russia.' He moved her thighs, got out of bed. She watched his silhouette against the window and

140

the night sky, like a monstrous, alerted satyr. She supposed he was. But he was her satyr. He had taken possession of her, every inch of her, with finger and tongue, slowly and methodically, over nearly two years. She had never considered the rights and wrongs of the matter. She only knew that she belonged to him, that she could never enjoy another man, no matter how long she lived.

'Please, Jan.'

He came back to the bed, took her in his arms. 'Who's seducing whom, Kitgirl?'

But she knew his tricks. He expected her to end it now, as she usually did, with her two anxious fingers. She let him go, lay down. 'If you don't I'll never touch you again.'

He lowered his belly on to hers, and the breath left her body. 'I've had girls pregnant before. It's a terrible business, sweetheart. You'd never be the same again. Maybe I wouldn't like you any more. I like my women to be very young, and very thin, and very hard, all legs and arms and little pointed tits. like yours, Christina. I like kittens, not cats.'

But she was the stronger, in the mind. Poor little feeble-brained Christina, because she knew this was what they said of her. But Uncle Jan, who was an old rake, so he said, and a big man in the Home Army, so he said, could not withstand her. His body was moving, adjusting, and the heat was coming into her. She was so delighted she wanted to laugh. But she didn't, for fear it might annoy him, as he was working so hard, and gasping for breath. She lay still, and gazed at the ceiling, and through it at the sky, and listened to the planes, flying east, and she thought how silly men were, to fly east, and bomb, and kill, and be killed, when they could be in bed.

Ziegler said, 'I have never heard anything like that.'

The barrage had stopped now, although their ears still

141

buzzed, and the planes still droned overhead. They couldn't see what the guns and the planes had accomplished, sitting in their truck, the flaps down at the rear, racing along the road. So they discussed the story which had come down the column of how, when the first truck had crossed the bridge, one of the Russian frontier guards had called out, in German, 'Hey, Fritzie, you're going the wrong way.' Frederic had not seen the guard; by the time Frederic's truck had crossed he had been lying dead beside the road. 'He wasn't an ordinary soldier, you know,' Kolisch said. 'He was a member of the NKVD. Those boys are supposed to be tough.'

'In Belgium and Holland we had to drop paras on the other side of the bridges,' Ziegler said. 'And even then it was a dicy business as to whether we'd get them intact. You always felt, when you crossed the bridge, that it might go up under you at any moment. I believe one of them did.'

By lunch they had crossed the old border into Russia itself. The column stopped to refuel, and the men were allowed out, to leak and stretch their legs. Now they could see the bomb damage, great craters in the fields, in the distance what looked like a small fort blasted into rubble, but the Luftwaffe, still droning endlessly overhead, had carefully avoided damaging the main roads. These were needed for the Wehrmacht.

'Old Joe has three, maybe four million men under arms,' Kolisch said. 'I wonder where they all are.'

They found out that afternoon. The truck rumbled to a halt, and Sergeant-Major Walbrodt lifted the flap. 'Out! Out!' he bellowed. But only the last two trucks had stopped. The rest had left the road to rumble across country, pluming yellow dust into the overheated air, intending to bypass the village ahead and rejoin the road beyond. So the section fell in, looking at each other and wondering why they were being abandoned in the middle of a Russian nowhere, until Lieutenant Koehnlein came down the line. The lieutenant was very young, and, like Frederic, had not yet seen service. Also like Frederic, Frederic thought, he was nervous. He had already drawn his pistol, and gesticulated with it in an alarming manner.

'There are Russians in that village,' he said. 'I have sent for a bomber. When it is finished we will go in. The road must be opened by dusk.'

They lay in a ditch, very hot and dry, and, except for the noise of the bombs, even peaceful. Their heads were down and they shook with the earth after every explosion.

'This is a job for the panzers,' Kolisch complained. 'They could just roll those houses flat.'

'The panzers are chasing the real opposition,' Ziegler said. 'I'll bet they're a hundred miles away by now. Scared Frederic?'

Frederic took off his helmet to scratch his head. He had to occupy his fingers, because they trembled constantly. But his head did itch.

'I made a mess the first time,' Ziegler said.

Frederic listened to short barks, smothered in bursts of automatic fire.

'They're using single-shot rifles, the poor bastards,' Ziegler said. 'Probably left over from 1914. And you've ten bullets under your hand, Frederic. Just remember that an infantryman is only as good as his weapon, and theirs belong on the scrap-heap.'

Walbrodt came along the ditch, not bothering to duck. 'Up! Up!' he snapped. 'To the left.'

Ziegler went first, Frederic was second. He ran, bent double, along the ditch, his rifle thrust forward, his bayonet threatening to jab Ziegler in the backside. He thought about Asja, had an overwhelming urge to jump into the air and collapse on the ground, roll over and lie there, staring up at the sky. No one would know for sure whether or not he had been hit, and by the time the medics

143

came along he'd be on his feet again, at the end of the line instead of second from the front.

Walbrodt passed him, panting, scrambled up the parapet, rifle and bayonet in one hand, waving the other, impelling his men into line, so that they emerged together, rifles crackling, again and again. I'm shooting, Frederic thought. He didn't know what at. The village was only a pile of stones. Not even Warsaw had looked like this. But there were sparks amongst the stones, and somebody close to him uttered a terrible sound, as if he were passing wind and belching at the same time, and hit the ground like a sack of potatoes. That's funny, Frederic thought. Smorodin had never said a word.

He tripped over a loose stone, staggered, regained his balance, halted, because Ziegler had stopped in front of him, back pressed against the remnants of a wall. Frederic followed his example, looked over his shoulder, discovered they were alone. But the others couldn't all be dead.

Ziegler was feeding a fresh clip into his magazine. Now he took one of the grenades from his belt, held it to his lips, then lowered his hand again and gently rolled the grenade round the wall. Frederic closed his eyes, opened them again after the bang, and looked at the man standing behind him. He wore a green uniform and a peaked cap, and he carried a revolver, which he threw on the ground before raising his hands. But Frederic was already running forward, screaming. The bayonet took the Russian squarely in the middle of the chest, and sank right up to the gun muzzle. A tremendous gush of blood spurted over Frederic's hands. He let go of the rifle, sank to his knees. 'Oh God,' he said. 'Oh God.' He made the sign of the cross, and he had not done that for so very long.

Ziegler seized Frederic's rifle, put his foot on the Russian's belly, pulled the bayonet free. With it spurted more blood, but only a little now.

'He had surrendered,' Frederic said.

Ziegler clapped him on the shoulder. 'Always kill the first man to surrender, Frederic. It convinces the rest.'

VI

Reitener lit a cigarette, read the newspaper again. 'Complete surprise was achieved. In twenty-four hours the Wehrmacht has bitten deep into the Ukraine and Byelorussia, and the advance continues at breathtaking speed.'

He got up, went to the window. From his office he could look up the Avenue Kléber towards the Arc de Triomphe. He liked to stand here for half an hour every morning, deciding what he would do with his evening. He had always loved Paris, saw no reason to love it less as a conqueror. Much of the gaiety was gone, but the gaiety would return when the war ended. And the news suggested that the end of the war was closer than ever he had suspected.

He sat at his desk, lit a fresh cigarette. This was a beautiful office, high up, bringing all the charm of Paris in summer through its huge window. All the odours, too. But he would not be without a single one of them. He watched four men come in. Three wore uniforms. The fourth wore a muddy rain coat and dirty boots, and his thin face had the white mask of exhaustion. He was surprisingly young, sandy-haired, neither very tall nor very broad, a man picked for his nondescript qualities.

'Thank you, Kohtz,' Reitener said. 'You may go. Not you, of course,' he said to the young man. 'Sit down.'

The door closed behind the three policemen; the young man continued to gaze at Reitener.

'You are young for a major,' Reitener remarked in English. 'I was young for a major, too. The next step is more difficult. But the essential thing is that we are both soldiers, whatever our present disguises. I will not waste my time or your intelligence in threatening you, Major Layton. You see, we even know your name. We knew you were coming before you ever left England. And we knew where to arrest you. Why not sit?'

The young man's knees gave way, and he fell into the chair.

'And have a cigarette. Turkish, very strong. Good for the nerves.' Reitener leaned forward, flicked a gold lighter. 'Your betrayal was the work of our English organisation. They are very efficient. Unfortunately, we do not know who were to be your local contacts.'

'You know I cannot divulge that, sir,' Layton said.

Reitener looked at him through the cigarette smoke. Last night he had watched the girls dancing in the *Folies*, through the same smoke. He had dined well. This morning he felt more than usually at peace with himself, and with the world. The news from Russia was better than anyone could have hoped. He thought he could spend a relaxed morning sitting here, talking with Major Layton about England. England was a country he had always wanted to visit. Maybe after the war. He sighed. 'If you do not tell me I will have to act on my own initiative, which means, as I know where you landed, that I will round up all the prominent citizens in that neighbourhood. I may even have to shoot one or two of them.'

'You cannot murder innocent civilians,' Layton said.

Reitener left the desk, stood at the window. 'In a war like this there is no such animal any more.' He was behind the young man. I like you, he thought. Strange, how you can like a man at first sight. I liked Frederic Janski at first sight. Frederic would be in Russia now. Frederic would do well, until he stopped a bullet. But that was the ultimate fate of every soldier. 'Think well, Major,' he said to the back of the young man's neck. 'Before I take those hostages I will either break your resistance or I will kill you.'

Layton leaned forward, stubbed out the half-smoked cigarette. When he leaned back his fingers were tight on the arm of his chair. He was a very brave young man, Reitener thought. But he was very afraid at this moment. And Reitener? Reitener is afraid of you, young man. Reitener is afraid of what you are going to do to him. Because it was starting, the pulse in the belly, the surge of the heart. He was going to send this young man downstairs, and then he was going to go there himself, and when he saw the young man, stripped naked and strapped to the table, he was going to allow himself to practise every conceivable act of barbarity. And then he was going to hate himself. Worse, he was going to hate Heydrich for tapping this vein of emotion within him. He thought: But for Heydrich, and, behind Heydrich, the Fuehrer, I would have lived out my life as an ordinary policeman in the Federal German Republic, investigating murders, chasing burglars. I would have wanted other things, of course. I would have dreamed strange dreams. But they would have stayed dreams.

But even while he waited he had passed the point of no return. His entire body had become a pulse at the thought of what he was going to do.

He opened the door. 'Take him downstairs, Kohtz.' The normalcy of his voice at these moments always amazed him.

Kohtz grinned. Kohtz had no trouble with his personality, or his desires. But for Heydrich, Reitener thought, I would be locking Kohtz up.

Kohtz tapped the Englishman on the shoulder. Layton raised his head, looked at Reitener. Now the fear had even reached his eyes. But he was brave enough, and sufficiently well trained to resist for a long time. It was going to be a beautiful, horrible, unforgettable morning.

His boots receded down the corridor. Rietener took a drink of water, gazed at himself in the mirror. He looked at a sophisticated, confident, contented man. But the canker in his mind, in his belly, was growing with every day. He pressed the bell on his desk. Hanna was an extremely attractive young woman, with long yellow hair which she wore in a tight bun on the nape of her neck, when in uniform. Reitener had never seen her out of uniform. She had hoped much from the handsome young colonel when she had first worked for him, but she knew better now, even if she did not know why.

'Hanna,' Reitener said. 'There is a war on, and I am rotting in Paris. I wish you to type an application for transfer.'

'My transfer, sir?'

'Mine, you silly girl. To the eastern front.'

'But Herr Standartenfuehrer, what will become of me?'

'You will stay in Paris, Hanna. Your next superior may be someone you can understand.' He followed the boots down the corridor.

The column was strung out along the road for as far as the eye could see, each truck having disgorged a handful of grey-green figures, standing or lying by the roadside, helmets off, rifles stacked, smoking. On either side of the road the plain was unbroken, save for a little village in a hollow some distance to the right. In the fantastic speed of this war the Blitzkrieg had passed this village by. Not a stone was out of place, not a flower. And beyond the village, in the very far distance, there was the fringe of deep green which marked the forest. Always the forest hung on the horizon, immense, unending, beckoning them onwards. But now the trees were hazed in the columns of yellow dust.

'What's up over there?' Ziegler wanted to know. 'Storm coming?'

'That's the Russians,' Walbrodt said. 'Running like hell. Or maybe it's our panzers, running behind them.'

'Then why are we stopped?' Frederic asked.

'You can't trust anything Russian, Johansson. Seems the road we've been following runs right into Red Square, according to the map. But it's *going* to do that when the bastards finish it. It's just a dirt track, right now. And it's crumbling away since the panzers have been over it.' Walbrodt was more human now. He had had too many recruits in his section, and he had probably been more nervous than they. Now they were blooded. They had killed, sent prisoners marching to the rear. As the communiqué would have it, 'isolated pockets of resistance have been liquidated by our infantry'. And one of the enemy had been killed by Frederic Johansson. A man who had already surrendered. He wished it could have been different. But he couldn't remember when he had not wanted things to be different.

'The American west must have been like this.' Kolisch scratched his head. All their heads were itching. Some blamed the dust. Frederic suspected lice. 'Imagine,' Kolisch said. 'Standing on the edge of the great plain and looking west, at the forest, and the Rockies.'

'Why aren't you living there?' Frederic asked.

'We were all set to go, back in '31. Then the old man come down with TB, and we didn't get our visas. So we stayed, and a couple of years later I found myself in a brown shirt. It seemed the best thing.'

Frederic wondered how many men in the regiment, all of whom had paraded before the Fuehrer had taken the oath of allegiance as good Nazis, had worn their brown shirts because there was nothing better to do.

'They gave me a gun,' Kolisch said. 'I'd always wanted a gun. Of course, it was a pistol, not a six-shooter. But I managed to exchange it for this.' He took the Colt from his haversack. 'Isn't she a beauty? That's real pearl, you

149

know. And I'm good. I'll show you.' He thrust the revolver into his belt. 'You put your hand in your trouser pocket, Frederic, and when I say "Now", pull it out and point your finger at me.'

Frederic put his hand in his pocket.

'Now!'

Frederic jerked his hand from his pocket, looked down the muzzle of the revolver.

'Pretty fast, eh? If you were Billy the Kid, I'd be Pat Garrett.' He faced the plain and the forest. 'And then we'd watch the redskins coming out of those trees, and we'd throw the truck on its side, and get behind it with our carbines. Could happen, you know. These Russkies aren't much different to the Sioux. Just a lot of wild savages.'

'And here they come,' said Corporal Wohnt, who had been asleep just behind them.

'Where?' Even Ziegler sat up, fingers scrabbling for his rifle.

They came up the slope from the village. In front walked a man with a white beard. Behind him were half a dozen men, and then a group of women. They were like no women Frederic had ever seen, even in the mountains behind Zabie, with voluminous, ankle-length skirts, in the drabbest browns and greys, and great scarves, like cowls, round their heads.

'Pinch me, Frederic,' Kolisch said.

The men walking behind the major carried jugs. The women bore trays of fruit. Now they halted, fifty yards from the column.

'Hey! Hey!' Walbrodt ran down the line. 'Anybody speak Russian?'

'I do,' Frederic said.

'Well, ask him how much for that fruit. Good German marks. Leave your weapon.'

Frederic leaned his rifle against the truck, walked away

150

from the column. He had an awful feeling of exposure. Suppose there was a tommy gun under each of those huge skirts billowing in the wind.

'Good morning,' he said. 'My sergeant-major wishes to know if we may buy some of that fruit.'

'It is not for sale,' said the mayor. 'My people wish to present it to you. We welcome the men of Germany as our brothers.'

Frederic didn't feel able to say anything more. He saluted and marched back to the column. 'They want to give it to us.'

The soldiers exchanged glances. 'Could be poisoned,' Wohnt suggested.

'Poisoned, hell,' Ziegler said. 'They're just happy to get the commissars off their backs. All the Russkies are.'

Kolisch slapped Frederic on the shoulder. 'The natives are friendly, Frederic, boy. This is going to be a good war.'

VII

The servants' living room had never looked so good, with flowers in every vase and the thin patches in the old carpet disguised by a skilful arrangement of chairs. And the party was a success; even Colonel Hoeppner had come down, and in the year he had lived here he had never treated her as other than his housekeeper. 'This is very good whisky, Frau Janski.'

'A friend gave it to me.' She smiled at Jan, who was looking after the bar. 'It's pre-war.'

'That it is.' The colonel accepted a fresh glass. 'You must forgive me for not mentioning this before, madam, but you have two most charming daughters.'

'Why, thank you, Colonel. And how is the general?'

'You mean General Bruckner? He is in Athens. Ah,

Janski! I've been meaning to have a chat with you. Do you think you could carve me a statuette of the Winged Victory? In oak, I think, perhaps a foot high. I've been telling the Governor General what a talented craftsman we have down in Rokonow, and he would like a sample of your work.'

'It will be my pleasure, Colonel,' Papa said.

Mama joined Josef, who was listening to Oberleutnant Brandt. 'Two million, Janski! Two million! Good evening, Frau Janski. I was telling Josef that over two million Russians have surrendered in the first three weeks of the campaign. Think of it, madam, half of old Joe's army gone in three weeks. If we wished we could be in Vladivostock by Christmas. But what is the use of conquering a lot of useless territory? Now tell me, why isn't that utterly magnificent Slav daughter-in-law of yours here tonight?'

'She and Josef have some sort of an arrangement.'

'Indeed?' Brandt's eyes gleamed.

'One of us always sleeps in the studio,' Josef explained. 'Tonight is Asja's turn.'

'You mean you stay there separately? You'll forgive me, Frau Janski, but you Poles are very peculiar people.'

'I have some valuable prints down there,' Joseph explained. 'And as you must know, Brandt, we Janskis are no longer considered Poles. Not even Asja.'

Mama squeezed Christina's arm. 'Circulate,' she hissed. 'Talk to people. Smile at the colonel. He thinks you are charming.'

'I hate him,' Christina said. 'I hate them all. I hate them being in our house.'

'You'll go over there and be nice to the colonel or I'll have the skin off your back.' Mama for once got all the old venom back into her voice. Christina was easily the prettiest girl in the room, prettier even than Liese. But her face was closed, tight, a mask of secrecy; Mama often

152

wondered just what went on inside that twisted little brain.

But if Christina was the prettiest girl there could be no question as to the handsomest couple. They stood in the corner, holding hands, smiling at everyone, but more particularly at each other. Liese wore a pale blue, so as not to clash with Paul's dress uniform; the colour set off the pale yellow of her hair. All the arrogance was back in Liese's eyes, and Mama loved to see it there. She understood too well the stresses that were acting not only on Papa and Jan but on Josef and Asja as well. But at least Frederic and Liese had found their way, and they had always been her favourites.

'Well, Paul,' she smiled. 'I've been told that by the time you reach the front the war will be over.'

'Oh, I hope so, Mama,' Liese said. 'I do hope so.'

Bardoman smiled. 'I think the bear may well be beaten, Frau Janski. Whether he will be wise enough to lie down is another matter.'

'You men.' Liese squeezed his arm. 'He just *wants* to fight, you know, Mama.' But she looked so happy. Over the two days of his furlough she had spent every waking moment in his company, as over the past eighteen months there had been a letter for her every week, posted in the most unlikely places, from Trondheim to Dubrovnik. Paul was a major now. And he loved Liese. Of course, he had not said anything to Mama yet. She understood. There was a war on, and Liese, if indisputably Aryan, was still Polish. But the war was ending, and Paul's love showed in the gleam in his eyes, the way he held her hand.

And because he loved Liese, Mama loved him. She pressed his free hand. 'You fight, Paul, and beat the Bolsheviks. But keep safe.'

Bardoman gave that gentle smile of his. 'I've been shot at by Norwegians, French, British, Yugoslavs and Greeks,

Frau Janski. They all missed. They tell me the Russkies are the worst shots of all.'

How far would you say we have come in the past three weeks?' Ziegler asked.

'About six hundred kilometres,' Frederic buttoned his jacket. It wasn't cold; in fact it was rather stuffy in the stalled truck. But the rain made a dampness which cut the marrow.

'Six hundred kilometres in three weeks. You're a historian, Frederic. Has any army in the entire history of war travelled that far in so short a time?'

'None I've heard of.'

'And yet we are still not in Moscow, much less at the Urals. Now tell me something else, Frederic. Have you ever known rain like this?'

Frederic raised the flap. The dirt road was disintegrating before his eyes. The embankments were dribbling away in liquid mud, and you could feel the truck settling, like a sinking ship, beneath your backside. The truck behind was already down to its axles, so much so the man behind the wheel was fast asleep, his head resting on his hands. But even he was barely visible. The rain made a teeming curtain which obliterated everything, made even thought difficult.

'It rains like this in West Africa,' Kolisch said.

'Thank God the Fuehrer has no interest in West Africa, Ziegler said. 'That was the Kaiser's idea, eh, Frederic?'

The flap lifted again. Walbrodt suggested a bird, the beak being the peak of his helmet protruding under the canvas cowl. 'Out! Out!'

'Out, out, up, up,' Kolisch said. 'If you'd learn a two-syllable word of command you'd make captain.'

They could say things like this to Walbrodt now. For three weeks they had fought at his command, followed him into action time and again, and always they had won.

154

If there was a superior soldier in the German army to Vice-Sergeant-Major Walbrodt it could only be Lieutenant Koehnlein. And if there were better foot soldiers in the German army neither Lieutenant Koehnlein nor Vice-Sergeant-Major Walbrodt knew where they were to be found.

'I'll give you a two-syllable word, Wild Bill Hickok,' Walbrodt said. 'Out, bastard. We have a war to fight.'

Frederic was first down. His boots entered the earth with a gigantic squish.

'Get them up,' Walbrodt shouted. 'Get them up, you Swedish lout, or you'll be there the night.'

Ziegler took one arm, Kolisch the other, and pulled him free. Rain splashed off his helmet, poured down his back, tickled his chest. At least the lice would be equally uncomfortable.

'Form up there,' Walbrodt shouted, his mouth full of water. The men were leaving the trucks before them and behind them, as well. 'Let's have a bit of discipline. Sling your rifles. Let's go. By the left, left, left, right, left.'

They marched, and slipped, and marched, passed the truck convoy to come upon the most amazing sight Frederic had ever seen. Strung out along the road, for as far as the eye could see, was the panzer division. The great tanks wallowed in the mud, tracks totally obscured in oozing black liquid, while the crews sat on the hatches and huddled beneath ponchos and greatcoats. One lucky driver even had an umbrella.

'For Christ's sake,' Ziegler said.

'Back to first principles,' Frederic said. 'You should be happy we didn't belong to Napoleon's mob. They marched the whole way.'

'And back again,' Kolisch said.

'Some of them,' Wohnt put in. 'Just try to figure what would happen if the rain stopped and a Russkie bomber came over.'

155

'If the Russkies still have a bomber,' Ziegler said.

They marched for several hours, and it was nearly dusk when they were halted. The rain had abated, very slightly, into what would have been a cloudburst anywhere else. The regiment was soaked from helmets to underpants. Where the rain hadn't reached was pumping sweat.

Lieutenant Koehnlein's uniform was splattered with mud. Lieutenant Koehnlein was a modern type of officer, who believed his men fought best when they knew what they were at. 'The Russkies are holding a town just up the road,' he said. 'They're in force, because of the factory. As you know, normally our panzers would drive round a position like this and isolate it, and our bombers would reduce it, and for us it would simply be another mopping-up operation. But our planes can't fly and our tanks can't move in this mess. So we are going to carry this place by assault. The Russkies won't expect an assault in weather like this. Now we will have something to eat, and an hour to rest, and then we are going to move off south-west. The objective of this section is the church of St. Sebastian in the lower suburb. Our schedule is to be there by midnight. Good luck to you all.'

'Fall out!' Walbrodt said. 'Fall out, you lucky bastards.'

'You may not believe this, Frederic,' Ziegler said. 'But we are about to fight our first battle.'

VIII

Asja took the prints from the basin, clipped them to the line. Once she had messed up as many as she had developed, although so long as they had been publicity shots for the Germans Josef had not minded. She used the magnifying glass to peer at the assembled soldiers, the cheering people in the background. It had been a spectacular

156

turn-out. The Governor General would be proud of this photograph of his subjects, listening to the Fuehrer's broadcast, cheering him on to ever greater victories.

Kopa came in. He had a key now, entered the studio whenever he felt like it. 'What do you think?'

'They're very good. Josef couldn't take a bad photograph if he wanted to.'

'I meant the news.'

'That the war is over? Not even Hitler would claim Smolensk has fallen, if it hasn't.'

'Oh, Smolensk has fallen. But think of Russia, Asja. From Smolensk to Vladivostock is about the same distance as from Warsaw to New York.'

'There comes a time when people don't want to fight any more.' Asja lit a cigarette. Nowadays they brought her cigarettes instead of stockings, and she let her legs go bare in the summer.

Kopa placed the bottle on the table. 'Cough medicine.'

'Oh, you sweetheart. You promised me a month ago.'

'These things take time.'

'How much do I owe you?'

'Not a zloty.' He leaned across the table. 'Asja, Frederic isn't going to come back, you know. This talk about the war being over just because Smolensk has fallen is all balls. The Russkies aren't going to give up. The commissars won't let them.'

'Only ten per cent of the Russians are commies.'

'Ten per cent of a hundred and fifty millions is a lot of people. He isn't coming back, Asja. And if he does we're going to kill him. He's a German soldier. They're all going to die. It's them or us.'

Asja dropped the bottle of medicine into her pocket. 'Well, call me them.'

'You hate the Germans as much as anyone.'

'Maybe more. But they've won, and the best thing you can do with that pistol you carry around is either drop it in the river or blow out your brains. They've won, Kopa. It's a historical fact. Some day a professor is going to write; "With the defeat of Soviet Russia the Nazi domination of Europe was complete." Maybe Frederic will write it. He will write it if I have anything to do with it. There are certain things in life which aren't very pleasant, but you have to come to terms with them. Like growing old. I can look in the mirror and count the grey hairs popping out of my head. I'm twenty-two years old, and I'm old. I grew old sitting in this goddamned cellar pretending to be fighting the Fritzes while my baby contracted pleurisy. Well, I'm going home to be a mother, and I'm staying in Rokonow until Frederic comes back for me.'

Kopa took the pistol from his hip pocket. 'Nobody can quit the Home Army. You're in something like this for life, Asja.'

Nowadays Asja could curl her lip quite as devastatingly as Mama. 'So?'

'You don't think I'd do it?'

'I know you won't do it, Kopa. That's why the Germans have won and you've lost. You still think about people. They only think about things.'

'Stop!' He was on his feet, his fingers white on the gun butt. 'No one will hear the shot down here.'

Asja opened the door.

'Asja!' Kopa wailed. 'Don't go, Asja. Stay with me. Stay and fight.'

Asja looked over her shoulder. 'I'm surrendering, little man. Now.'

They lay on their bellies in a ditch. Frederic wondered how much of his military career was going to be spent in a ditch. This reminded him of his first, outside Lowicz. He wallowed, as in a tub, holding his rifle clear, listening to the machine gun fire away to the left. The rain only dripped, now, and the town was shrouded in a dawn mist, clinging to the ruined buildings and the gaping windows and the piles of rubble. And the cathedral was still a hundred feet distant. All night they had crawled towards it. All night they had flushed Russians from doorways and bedrooms and kitchens, from coal-holes and from right in the middle of the street. All night they had killed Russians, and they had watched their comrades killed, all night. This wasn't according to form. These Russians were fighting, and dying, where they stood. He hadn't seen a solitary one surrender. He didn't think it would do them any good, now, anyway. For the first time since crossing the border the battalion was angry.

Now they waited, in the pre-dawn greyness. Despite the weather they had managed to bring up some mortars. 'There they go,' Ziegler said. 'Keep your head down, boy.'

But Frederic peered over the edge of the parapet. It had been a beautiful cathedral, all onion domes and stained glass windows, and, amazingly, there was still glass in a couple of the windows. Frederic supposed he was unique, the last man on earth to see glass in the windows of the cathedral of St. Sebastian in . . . he didn't know the name of the town. Because, as he looked, the last of the onion domes toppled, and with it the last of the windows shattered. And then a shell landed on the roof and that fell in as well, and the entire cathedral became covered in a fine white dust, rising from the stone. He remembered the dust rising above Warsaw two years ago.

'Get your head down, you silly Swedish bastard.' Walbrodt crawled along the waterlogged ditch, making a bow wave like a motor-boat. 'We'll be there soon enough. Even those Bolshies can't stand up to much more blasting.'

'Some battle,' Kolisch said. 'Lying in a goddamned

ditch catching pneumonia. You know something, Frederic? Them plains Indians never fought in the rain.' He lay on his back, his helmet over his face. His body was totally sunk in the water, except for the toes of his boots. 'Maybe, if it rains long enough, all our weapons will rust up solid, ours and the Russkies, and we'll have to call it a day. Man, Smolensk is far enough. I don't want to see Moscow. All I want to do is get back to Hamburg and catch a ship for the USA.'

'Shut up,' Ziegler said. 'We're on our way.'

The last of the explosions died away, the morning became a vast echo, punctuated by the occasional rifle-shot and the rumble of collapsing masonry.

'Now you listen to me, you bastards,' Walbrodt said. 'We're six hours behind schedule. Thanks to you sons of bitches the entire Wehrmacht is being held up. We are going in now, and if any one of you shitbags stops shooting before I say so I'll have his balls for nutcrackers. Let's go!'

They leapt to their feet, scattering water to the left and right, and ran forward, bent double, rifles blazing. At the usual empty chucks of stone, Frederic thought. There could not possibly be anyone left alive in there.

A bullet hit the ground at his feet, throwing up a spurt of dust and shattered stone, and for a moment he was blinded and dropped to his knees. His hammer clicked on an empty chamber and he threw himself on his belly, hugging the earth while he reloaded, hearing Walbrodt shouting away to his right, 'Run, bastards. Inside, you sons of bitches.'

His fingers scrabbled over the magazine, slapped it shut. The strap of his helmet had broken and he clamped it between his teeth, biting into the leather, shooting as he did so. The red flashes in the doorway ceased, and Frederic got up and ran inside. It was surprisingly light, because there was no roof; the Russian defender lay on

160

his back, his knees bent so that his legs were doubled underneath, his breasts ripped open by the impact of Frederic's bullets. *His* breasts? Frederic gazed at the woman, and she gazed back at him. Her helmet had come off, and her hair, thick and brown, trailed on the ground. Her blouse was shot to pieces, as was the flesh and blood behind it. Her fingers still gripped the butt of her empty carbine.

'For Jesus' sake,' Kolisch said. 'I told you, Frederic. Bloody savages.'

'There's nothing but women.' Wohnt dropped to his knees and wiped his brow. 'We've been held up for six hours by a lot of skirts.'

But these women wore pants. They lay, scattered about the cathedral, in grotesque postures, at once masculine, because of their uniforms and their weapons, and entirely feminine, because in death their femininity had stolen over their features as it had released their hair. 'Oh Jesus,' Frederic said. 'Oh Mary. Forgive me.'

Ziegler stood above him. 'Two hundred kilometres to go, Frederic. Just two hundred kilometres to Moscow.'

It began to rain, a gentle August shower, coming from the east, sweeping across the Vistula to shroud Rokonow. The pale sunlight mingled with the rain mist to turn the afternoon into a damp gold. 'Stop here, will you,' Johnson said.

The guide tapped the driver on the shoulder; the car pulled into the kerb. Johnson rolled down the window, gazed at the towering block of flats. There was another a little further down the street, and then a third. He found Warsaw surprisingly familiar, because the authorities had rebuilt the city as it had been in 1939. But Rokonow was unrecognisable. 'This used to be a residential suburb before the war,' he said.

'It is a dormitory for Warsaw now,' said the guide. 'Did you know Rokonow before the war?'

'I visited here. That corner site used to have a white house on it. A very large house. It belonged to a toy manufacturer named Janski.'

The guide shrugged. 'Who knows? This Janski might occupy one of those flats. If he is still alive. If he is still in Poland.'

'He would be very old if he were still alive,' Johnson said. 'But I would like to go inside. Will you wait for me?'

'All afternoon if you wish,' said the guide.

Johnson got out of the car, turned up the collar of his raincoat. Water scattered across his face.

4

Winter 1941

Like the women, the men looked ugly, because of the death stamped on their features, because of the rain and mud. They were dirty, unkempt figures, lumps of clay. Yet now they meant nothing. The women had meant a great deal, the first women. But they had been three months ago, and since then Frederic had lost count of dead bodies. Nowadays he thought only about the rain. So did everyone else. Ziegler sat on the remains of a step, tilted his helmet back on his head, scratched the stubble on his chin. 'You'd think this goddamned country would turn into one vast bog.'

'Don't you think it's already done that?' Frederic sat beside him, lit a cigarette. His boot rested against a helmet. Inside the helmet was a head. But the Russian had been there for some time. They had entered this particular town with little opposition; the howitzers had done most of the work for them. Against that, of course, it meant that hardly a house was habitable. 'Where do you think we are now, Hans?'

'God alone knows. I think we've missed Moscow. Or maybe Moscow isn't really there. Maybe it's all a myth. France was never like this. That was a good summer.'

'Commies!' Kolisch turned on his knees and opened fire. Frederic and Ziegler followed his example instinctively, although they had seen nothing, heard nothing. They blazed away through the shattered doorway, flooding the rubbled, soaking, mudcaked street with bullets.

'For Christ's sake call it off, you bastards.' Walbrodt clumped through the mud behind them. 'What the hell are you shooting at?'

'Someone moved out there,' Kolisch explained. 'And don't tell me they've surrendered.'

'They haven't,' Walbrodt said. 'They're all dead. And you want to give up shooting at dead men. How's your ammo?'

They checked their pouches. 'We'll collect some when the truck gets here,' Ziegler said.

'What truck, you bleeding twit? There isn't any truck. There isn't a vehicle moving between here and Warsaw.'

'This man is trying to tell us the Wehrmacht has run out of ammo,' Kolisch said.

'It's *there*,' Walbrodt said. 'Scattered about all over Russia, stuck in the mud. They're using mule trains, and one's supposed to be coming in. But it won't be here before tomorrow so you bastards had better hope there isn't a counter-attack.'

'What's the Russian word for counter-attack, Frederic?' Ziegler asked.

'They don't have one. The only word for movement the Russkies have is retreat.'

'You come with me.' Walbrodt led them out of the house, down the street. They walked in line. There was no other safe way to walk down a street. Frederic imagined himself after the war, taking his children, Asja's children, for a walk along Ujawdowski, in line, number two looking after number one, and so on to the last one. Number five or six, he thought.

At what had once been a crossroads two women crawled out of a cellar and stared at them. The women's clothes were soaking and mudstained, their faces were pale with exhaustion and hunger, their eyes blank with terror. They had sat out the bombardment beneath the street. They had nothing to offer the conquerors. The days of the trays of fruit were centuries in the past. That sunlit morning had been the real myth.

Walbrodt led them into the village square, pointed to

166

the burned-out bus, lying on its side. The driver was a shattered mess, sprawled in the mud beside the bonnet.

Kolisch stooped to peer at the sign, scorched but otherwise forgotten by the flames. 'Mockba,' he read.

'That's Russian for Moscow,' Ziegler said.

Kolisch stared down the street as if expecting to see the towers of the Kremlin at the far end. 'Where?'

'If it wasn't raining so damned hard, and you had eyes which could look maybe fifty kilometres, you'd see it.'

'Fifty kilometres,' Frederic said. Fifty kilometres to an end to the war and a chance to get back to Warsaw. 'What are we waiting for?'

'For God to stop pissing on us,' Walbrodt said. 'There's no hope of getting the panzers moving again until we get a frost to harden the ground. So you can go down on your knees and pray for winter. But because Moscow is there, the Russkies are going to fight for it.'

Almost as if he had given a signal, there was a whine and a vast explosion, from not more than a hundred yards away.

Frederic hit the cobbles, losing his rifle and rolling against Ziegler. Kolisch was rubbing his ears.

'Land mine, by God,' Walbrodt said.

'That dropped,' Ziegler said. 'Must have been a mortar.' He hit Frederic on the shoulder, forcing him flat. The cobbles shook up and down against Frederic's belly.

'Don't make me laugh,' Kolisch said. 'You ever heard a mortar with a charge like that?'

They crawled across the square, past the burned-out bus and the dead driver.

'It has to be a mortar.'

'And mortars mean infantry.' Walbrodt lined them up behind the wall of what had once been a post office. 'Kolisch, you rout out the rest of the section and get them up here. Tell the lieutenant I sent you. And then get back to company headquarters and tell Captain Winz we're holding the square against a counter-attack supported by mortar-fire. On the double, soldier.'

Frederic fed a fresh clip into his magazine. He had two clips left. And out there was only the rain, and now another explosion which had them ducking their heads and huddling against each other.

'Mortars,' Walbrodt said. 'You think the Russkies have something new, Ziegler?'

'Like you said, Sergeant-Major, they've found that missing word.'

Asja and Christina took the bus into town. They held hands because Christina was so terribly afraid. Asja was just as afraid, but she had to pretend she wasn't. So when she shivered it was because of the cold. Suddenly it was very cold. The leaves came clouding down as if the trees were diseased, and every leaf had to reach the street as quickly as possible.

They left the bus in Sigismund Square and walked, still holding hands, not speaking. In the summer Warsaw, despite the unrepaired damage, was bearable. Open-necked shirts and summer frocks took longer to look threadbare, and even where nothing remained but a pile of rubble the wild flowers sprouting amidst the crumbling stones had added a certain beauty. Once the cold came there were no flowers, and the topcoats were so terribly shabby, and the boots were down at the heels, and the woollen stockings were darned and patched. People seemed to hobble, in the autumn, suddenly aware of the emptiness in their bellies, the desperation in their minds.

She no longer had a key, so she knocked, and prayed that Josef would be in. He opened the door, blinked at them. 'Asja! You've come back!'

She pushed past him. The studio was less tidy than when she had lived here, and it smelt. Josef was not one of those men who naturally smell attractive. And it was cold. 'Could you light a fire?'

Christina stood by the door, her sixteen years draining away, one by one. 'What's up?' Josef asked.

'Christina and I would like to borrow the studio for the morning.' Asja kept her voice even. 'We'll use the inner room. I'd like you to wait out here and make sure nobody interrupts us.'

Josef looked from Christina, so frightened, to Asja, so determined. 'Holy Mother!'

'There is nowhere else, Josef,' Asja said. 'You are the only one I can trust.'

'It is murder,' Josef said. 'A deadly sin.'

'Father Paul will understand.'

'Oh Mary, forgive me,' Christina said. 'Asja, let me have it.'

'Go inside and undress,' Asja said. 'And you light that fire, Josef.'

'It was a German, Asja. You must find out which one. Kopa and I will look after the bastard.'

'Yes,' Asja said.

He caught her arm. 'You know.'

'Now really, Josef. How could I possibly know?' But even as she spoke she realised she had made a mistake. Josef's grip slackened, and he sat down. His face closed. She ran her fingers into his curly yellow hair. 'I came to you because I can trust you. This is a secret, for you, and for me, and for Christina. You must swear that to me, Josef.'

He raised his head. 'I suppose he brings you things too.'

'The family is all any of you has left, Josef. One explosion, and you'd fly apart like a shrapnel bomb. Girls have been aborted before, and lived. And been happy.' She went inside. Christina sat on the table, wearing only her vest, shivering.

'Asja,' she begged. 'Please! Let's go home, Asja. I can manage.'

Asja hung the lamp from the ceiling, took the steel knitting needle from her bag. 'This is no time to be born, sweetheart. Only to die.'

II

'Ruth!' Abbi whispered. 'Ruth, wake up. There are military men downstairs. Shouting.'

Ruth turned over, clamped her eyes shut. She hated waking up, knowing that she had the whole day in front of her, that she was trapped, moving, sitting, standing, eating, inside that same pink and brown prison which she hated, but from which there could be no escape. Asleep or dozing, she could be on a cloud. Ruth thought of very little else but clouds, nowadays. She preferred watching the clouds to eating, not a very difficult choice. Sometimes she thought she knew each cloud, separately and intimately. She calculated where they might have come from, allowed her imagination to carry her all over the world; she had been good at geography, in school. The huge stormclouds came from India, and the gentle, mincing clouds came from Japan, and the sinister grey ones came from Malaya, and the bubbling, bouncing, rushing clouds surely came from Australia. Australia had always fascinated her. It was so remote, so enormous, so complete. Imagine being able to step on a train in Athens and get off again in Edinburgh, and still be in the same country. She supposed America was as big, but America had an explosive quality which frightened her. She thought, afterwards, she would go to Australia.

'Wake *up*!' Abbi cried in desperation, and Ruth sat up, to stare at the militiamen, stalking into the room, taking their positions along the wall. They had no business in here. She'd complain to Rabbi Waldstein. They might have signed up to help the Germans keep order in the ghetto, but they hadn't the right to invade the girls' rooms.

'Get up. Get up. All of you. Get dressed.'

The girls gazed at them. It seemed absurd, after what had happened to Ruth in the barracks, after Abbi's trip home with the stick between her legs, yet they did not want to dress in front of the militia. These young men weren't Germans, faceless creatures from another world who wore black uniforms and carried whips; these were their on kind, who only three years ago had walked them home from service and flirted with them on the street corners.

'Hurry up! Hurry up! Or you'll go in your night-dresses.'

The girls dragged on their clothes, searched for coats and hats. They assembled in the street, all females, all somewhere between sixteen and thirty-six. They formed a straggling line, each with a small suitcase or a bundle under her arm. It was the first time Ruth had left the ghetto for six months, since that day which she felt was burned into her brain. Some of the others had laughed at her distress when she had come home. 'Nothing has happened to you,' they jeered. 'Nothing which couldn't happen to any woman. You're not marked, and your hair will soon grow again.'

Her hair was growing. But having her head shaved hadn't been so terrible. The soldiers had even been kind, then, had laughed and joked as they held her down, had explained that this was the legal punishment for a non-Aryan having intercourse with a German. She even thought they had been a little ashamed of themselves for what they had done earlier. And the jeering women had not known. They still thought it was a simple matter of lying on your back, and that was always preferable to being branded. They didn't know. If the Germans had cut a star on her forehead, as they had done with Jacob Finer, or even on some other part of her body, that would have been that. She could have looked at it and said to herself, That's what they did to you. Instead they had cut their star into her brain, and only she knew it was there, and nobody who hadn't been there could know, or understand.

They marched, a long straggling line of young women. It was early in the morning, and bitterly cold. The wind off the river made nonsense of their threadbare coats and tattered stockings, seemed to scorch their undernourished bodies. But at least there weren't many people on the streets. Those who were out hurried by, pretending not to notice. Only a few of the young men stopped to stare. One or two even whistled, and the escorting militiamen grinned. Ruth was glad to be out of the ghetto. Until she saw the photographer, waiting by the entrance to the railway station, waiting to photograph the happy young Jewesses, off to labour for the Reich.

Dawn came through a mist of cold rain, colder than they had known all summer. It fell silently, lay in vast puddles on the mud-strewn ground, covered the entire country in wet mist. Frederic's eyes ached. And yet he had to keep looking out *there*. Beyond the mist lay Moscow. And between himself and Moscow there were Russians. And suddenly the Russians were important. They hadn't been for the last three months. They had been males and females, at whom you shot, or into whose bodies you drove your bayonets, and sometimes they had fired back and then melted away into the yellow dust or the sweeping rain. That those phantom figures actually obeyed generals, and that those generals had maps and plans which might include counter-attacking, did not seem credible.

172

But if they did counter-attack, and Private Johansson did not see them before they saw him, he was for the penal battalion. So he wrapped his fingers round his rifle, and peered into the gloom, and wished the sun would come out. It couldn't possibly rain for ever, not even in Russia.

'Coffee!' Ziegler squatted beside him, played the steaming mug of boiling brown water between his hands.

Frederic sipped, burned his lips and tongue.

'What do you think about on sentry go?' Ziegler asked.

Frederic drank coffee. 'Asja.'

'The Slav bit in Warsaw? You think she's still waiting.'

'I told her I'd be back by Christmas.'

'Then you'd better get a move on. Ever screw her?'

'I've known her a long time. I can remember things about her. Don't you ever want to remember something about a woman, Hans?'

'Not if I can help it.'

'He was married, you know,' Kolisch said. 'What'd she die of, Hans?'

'She didn't. She had a peculiar interest in living. Still has.'

'I'd have beat her brains in.'

'I joined the army instead. I beat other people's brains in. They call that sublimating, eh, Frederic?'

He loved them both. He could not envisage life without Kolisch on one side and Ziegler on the other, just as he could not envisage life without a rifle in his hands and an enemy in front of him and rain trickling down his neck.

'So what do you think about, Hans?' Kolisch asked. 'If the three b's are out?'

'I think about Russia. How far would you say it is from Leningrad to the Crimea, Frederic?'

'God knows.'

'I hope the Fuehrer does too,' Kolisch said.

'I figure it's about fifteen hundred kilometres,' Ziegler said. 'And it's about another thousand kilometres from

173

Moscow back to Warsaw. That's a lot of territory.'

'A million and a half kilometres,' Frederic said.

'Just what I was thinking,' Kolisch said.

'So how many men have we got under arms in Russia?'

'Three millions?'

'Maybe we had three millions last June. But let's say three million men in one and a half million kilometres. I think about being only the second man in each square kilometre.'

'But we don't have to have somebody in every square inch of the country,' Kolisch said. 'We have a line. And we have better tanks and better rifles and better planes, as well as better generals.'

'We don't have better mortars. Not since those *katyushas*. And what in the name of God is the use of tanks which can't move?'

'Hey!' Frederic cried. 'Look! Look there!' The silence was deafening. The last of the rain had stopped. In its place soft white flakes settled on the ground, drifted towards the three soldiers, kissed their cheeks before melting.

'Eureka,' Kolisch said. 'I think you could brew up some more coffee, Hans. And we'll toast the winter.'

III

Obersturmfuehrer Schmidt saluted. 'The prisoners are assembled, sir.' He shivered, trembled from his shoulders to his heels. There was snow on his boots.

'You'd better come by the fire, Schmidt.' Reitener wrapped his scarf round his neck, strapped his belt round his waist, adjusted the weight of the pistol against his thigh. 'Did you see the general?' His tone was casual.

Schmidt unbuttoned his breast pocket, held out a piece of paper. 'He gave me this.'

Reitener scanned the note, raised his head. 'Do you have any idea what would happen to you were you to be arrested with this in your possession?'

'But I am carrying out an investigation into a plot against the Fuehrer, Herr Standartenfuehrer. On your instructions. That letter will be valuable evidence.'

Reitener knelt, held the edge of the letter into the flames, watched it turn brown.

'Herr Standartenfuehrer?'

'We took an oath to Adolf Hitler, Schmidt. But Adolf Hitler as Supreme Commander of the Armies of the Reich. At least, that is my interpretation. These generals may be frightened old men, but they are also the finest professional soldiers in the world. If they find the military situation disquieting then I also find it disquieting.'

'And I also, Herr Standartenfuehrer.'

'I am glad you agree with me, Schmidt.' Reitener took the poker, prodded the ashes of the letter. 'Our duty is to the Reich, and the greatness of Germany. We must never forget that, Schmidt. So we will listen to what the generals have to say. If we are lucky events will prove them wrong, and then we will not find it difficult to secure more evidence. If we are unlucky then we shall have to consider our position.' He stood up. 'Have some brandy.' He set the bottle on the table, pulled on his gloves.

Schmidt gulped, noisily. 'It is a dangerous business, Herr Standartenfuehrer.'

Reitener polished his dark glasses, put on his cap. 'So is war, Herr Obersturmfuehrer. Shall we go?'

Schmidt clicked his heels, opened the door. There was snow on the porch, driven by the wind. And beyond the porch there was nothing but snow, carpeting the ground, clinging to roofs and to vehicles, smothering the ruined houses. The black uniformed guards stamped their feet and slapped their hands together, massaged the barrels of their tommy guns. The Russians, already stripped of their coats and boots, shuffled their freezing feet in the snow. Some were already collapsed. Reitener sighed. There was no pleasure in this business, no thrill. It was impossible to regard any of those grey creatures as men, and therefore there was no conflict in conscience, no personal decision. It was a job of work. He nodded to Schmidt.

The lieutenant raised his loudspeaker. 'All Jews and all commissars will step forward,' he shouted in Russian.

There was a short hesitation, and then a man left the ranks. He was an extraordinarily big man, who lumbered rather than walked. Behind him came a dozen others.

'There are five hundred men there,' Reitener remarked.

Schmidt nodded. 'Come now,' he shouted. 'Five minutes at the dump for the man who turns me up a Jew.'

This time the hesitation took longer. Then there was a scuffle, and a man was thrown out of the ranks. He landed on his hands and knees in the snow, scrambled to his feet, tried to regain the anonymity of the ranks, and was thrown back again. The scuffles spread, disturbing a fine white mist which rose around the prisoners and into the still air. The guards stopped rubbing their tommy guns and pointed them instead.

The snow dust settled. Another thirty men had been excluded from the ranks. They stood in a huddle, glancing at each other, at once resentful and afraid. 'Fall them in.' Reitener went down the steps, got into his car. It bumped over the road, slithered through the snow, and came to a field. The orderly left the engine running. The firing party came to attention, faces rigid with cold, but also with apprehension.

Reitener got out of the car, sank ankle deep in the soft snow. It struck through the leather of his boots, seemed to grip his toes in a vice. The prisoners were barefooted.

Captain Hilse saluted. 'All present and correct, Herr Standartenfuehrer.'

176

'Are you sure?'

Hilse looked embarrassed. 'They have had this assignment before. They are afraid there will be an incident. It disturbs them for days.'

'Do you think I enjoy it, Hilse? We happen to be soldiers. You had better remind them of that.' He watched the prisoners marching up the snow-covered road. They had been stripped of their shirts, and their chests gleamed white-blue in the pale sunlight. They carried spades, sloped against their shoulders like rifles.

'Halt!' shouted the lieutenant. 'Now dig.'

The prisoners exchanged glances. Forty spades. They could at least die with weapons in their hands. Reitener observed them with interest. Prisoners always exchanged that glance, and then commenced digging. Yet amongst these men were half a dozen commissars, trained leaders. He supposed it was because in every man's heart they could not believe this was going to happen until it was too late. Not even while they were digging could they believe it was more than a ditch.

Even the half-naked bodies were sweating. And now the ditch was six feet deep. They were lucky: the ground was still soft. When the frost set in digging a ditch would be next to impossible, with spades.

'Get in,' shouted the lieutenant. 'Get in.'

Captain Hilse gave an order in a low voice, and the firing party advanced to the edge of the ditch. Reitener thought these young men were far more dangerous, to everyone present, than the Russians could ever be. Their faces were unnaturally white, their eyes unnaturally bright. Like himself, they were soldiers and this was not soldiering. He fully expected one day to have a mutiny to quell, unbuckled the flap of his holster.

The big Russian scrambled out of the ditch and ran towards him, shouting incomprehensibly. He threw himself on the snow at Reitener's feet, scrabbling for the black boots. How strange, Reitener thought. Were I in his position I would try to *kill* the commandant; this man was begging for mercy.

The guards, the firing squad, Captain Hilse and the lieutenant, and the other prisoners, heads just visible in the ditch, stared. The big man had his eyes shut, and was kissing Reitener's boots. He expected either to be reprieved, in some miraculous fashion, or to be shot by the commandant himself, at close range, perhaps a more merciful death. Reitener drew his pistol, but did not fire it. He brought the butt down on the big man's head, not hard enough to knock him out, just hard enough to break the skin and send him tumbling in the snow, blood streaming from the cut. Reitener snapped his fingers, and two of the SS guards came across. They took an ankle each and dragged the big man through the snow. He wailed and cursed and wept, and the guards rolled him down the slope into the ditch. Reitener nodded at Hilse. He had acted correctly, and the firing party would now also act correctly. The tommy guns began to chatter.

'Up! Up!' Walbrodt bellowed. 'Fall in. We've a war to fight. And get those Kopfschützer on.'

Consciousness was a painful business. Frederic had never been so cold in his life, not even in the labour camp. He struggled to his feet, stamped his boots while he pulled the woollen inner helmet over his head. Kolisch tapped the window. The glass, blown out weeks ago by the blast of a mortar shell, had mysteriously reappeared, twice as thick, opaque and gleaming as it diffused the sunlight.

'Where's our winter gear, then, Vice-Sergeant-Major?' Ziegler asked.

'You have gloves and you have kopfschützer,' Walbrodt said. 'What are you, soldiers, or young ladies? This freeze-up is a month early, that's what. Your gear is on its way. But if you don't mind I'm for Moscow.'

'This morning?' Corporal Wohnt asked.

'This morning, Corporal. This morning the panzers go into action again, so come on, you lazy bastards.'

They formed ranks on the street, ankle deep in the snow. The battalion casualties remained amazingly light, which was as well, because they had received no replacements. They didn't need them; this was an élite regiment, with every man twice the soldier he had been when they crossed the border. Lieutenant Koehnlein always glowed with pride when he inspected them.

'Cold enough for you?' he demanded, and got the chuckles he wanted. 'You'll be happy to know we're getting out of this goddamned village this morning. But it's all hands to fatigue duty, first. That'll put a sweat on you. March them off, Sergeant-Major.'

Walbrodt saluted, called the ranks to attention. The snow deadened the sound of their boots. Marching, with hot acorn coffee inside their bellies, it seemed less cold. Besides, the sun was trying to shine. The snow and the sun made the shattered town almost beautiful.

The panzers remained where they had been for the last month. But this morning the crews were busy, oiling and cleaning, and even lighting fires beneath their tanks.

'That's another thing about the Indians, Frederic,' Kolisch said. 'They didn't fight in the snow, either. When you think there must be snow maybe four months of the year, and rain another four months, it cuts into your fighting time.'

'I'd just like to *start* fighting again,' Ziegler said. 'That's what we're here for, in case you forgot, Berthold. If we don't fight we don't win. Frederic doesn't get home to his Slav.'

'Column, halt!'

They stopped marching, stood at ease. If the Russians showed up they'd fight to the last man. The rest of the time they had their rights, as heroes of the Reich.

They were past the panzers now, and had reached the artillery and the supply trucks. These were still axle deep in the snow, despite the digging and the efforts of the tough little ponies harnessed to each vehicle.

'Now then,' said Vice-Sergeant-Major Walbrodt. 'Let's show them where the German army keeps its guts. Stack your rifles, Wohnt, I want ten men to each gun. Get them out.'

Wohnt signalled Ziegler, and Kolisch and Frederic followed. The ponies looked at the men, and the men looked at the ponies. Neither side cared much for the obvious distaste of the other.

'Sling those lines,' Wohnt bellowed. 'Come on, now. Give me a whip and I'll have every goddamned cannon on the road in ten minutes.'

'You'd look good with a whip, Corporal,' Ziegler agreed, and slung the rope over his shoulder and round his waist, like the anchor man on a tug-of-war team. 'You should have been in the SS.'

'You'll see the SS, by God, if we don't get moving. They're just down the road, rounding up civilians to help us. You're not going to be licked by a pack of *moujiks*? Heave.'

The ponies panted and pulled. The men dug their boots into the snow and yet found no purchase; the ground was frozen solid for the depth of a foot. They slipped, and staggered, gasped and sweated, listened to similar sounds rolling up the road. Wohnt took off his gloves and himself seized hold of the rope.

'What the hell is going on?' Walbrodt shouted. 'Corporal, where are your gloves?'

'Right here, Sergeant-Major.' Wohnt reached for his belt, carried the rope with him. He gazed at his hands in horror.

'You bloody fool! Johansson, double down to that fire and raise some warm water. Ziegler, wrap his hands

180

in your jacket. You men, don't just stand there. Massage those fingers. Pretend he's your favourite whore. Get to him.'

Frederic fetched the water, and Wohnt was prised free. But he wouldn't use his hands again for a long time. Two medics arrived to take him down the line.

The platoon gazed at each other, worked their own fingers uncertainly. 'Ziegler, you're in command,' Walbrodt said. 'Now get that cannon clear.'

'Come on, chaps,' Ziegler shouted. 'One for the old man.' There was a tremendous heave, and the ponies stumbled forward. The men followed, gasping and cheering, sliding through the snow into the party in front of them.

'How's that for power.' Kolisch scrambled to his feet and brushed snow from his pants. The rest of the section dropped their ropes and gathered round, while Ziegler's platoon stood proudly beside their mules. Walbrodt sent down the line for coffee.

'Well done,' said Lieutenant Koehnlein. 'Where's the carriage?'

A great silence fell over the group; slowly they moved to the edge of the road. The rope had been secured to the howitzer itself, and the huge chunk of metal had come free. But the carriage remained embedded in the frozen earth.

IV

The ball clicked, settled, the wheel slowed. The large room became silent for a moment, even the blackjack players on the far side seeming to sort their cards more softly at this moment of reckoning. Then the wheel stopped, the room seemed to sigh, and the next round began.

181

'Two brandies.' Josef rested his elbow on the counter and looked at the blue velvet curtains, the dim ceiling lights, the soft carpeted floors. 'This must be the most elegant room in all Warsaw.'

'It is a prison.' Kopa lit a cigarette. 'That is why the Germans are not allowed to gamble here, you know. It is a scheme to turn the Poles into a race of gamblers and moral misfits.'

'Here's to the Goddess of Fortune.'

'So let's get out of here. There isn't a man in this room who's not a hundred per cent collaborator at heart, even if he keeps his nose clean.' Kopa finished his drink.

'Two more,' Josef said. 'Let's collaborate a little.'

'It's not a joking matter,' Kopa said. 'The number of collaborators is quite sickening. Take your sister Liese. You should speak to her. Going out with Germans every night.'

'Her turn will come. I will attend to her personally.'

'And now Asja. I don't like the way she stays at home all the time in a house full of Germans.'

'Asja would never let a German lay a finger on her. Do you think that is a good photograph?'

Kopa held it under the light. 'Jewesses?'

'All women, this time.'

'The pretty ones to the brothels, the ugly ones for the labour. Why did you keep this one?'

'Because Ruth is there. See the third row, on the end? I didn't know until I developed it. She looks all right in the picture. But she never came out again. I take food every Saturday afternoon, but she's never there. She always was a sensitive girl. Now she's to be a whore.'

'The swine should all be castrated and have their balls strung end to end from here to Berlin,' Kopa said. 'Along the telephone wires. But it beats me why you took all those risks for a Jewish bit. My principle is, let the Jews get on with it. We've problems of our own.'

'Yes.' Josef thought of Ruth's hands. He still photographed hands. But they had no meaning any more. He did it because he hoped that one day beauty would again have a meaning to him. It had to, one day. 'Have you ever killed a man, Kopa?'

'I'm Kopa, remember?'

'Forget about the train.'

Kopa frowned. 'Shut up, you damned fool.'

'It's all very well,' Josef said thoughtfully, 'to sit in a ditch and wait for a bang. Have you ever walked up to a man and stuck a knife in his ribs?'

'Of course not. Neither have you.'

'That's what we will have to do with the collaborators. I think we should start now. Tonight.'

Kopa finished his drink, patted sweat from his forehead. 'Let's go home.'

'For instance, that man over there, playing blackjack, is the biggest collaborator in Warsaw.'

Kopa blinked across the dimly lit room. 'Your uncle? Now I know you're joking.'

'He and Hoeppner are in each other's pockets. It's easy for him, you see, living in the same house.'

'I would never have thought it.'

'Have another brandy,' Josef said. 'Only I know this. And now you, Kopa. Well, what with Mama and Liese, the Janskis have a pretty black reputation already, so I'd prefer to keep it in the family, so to speak. Will you help me?'

Kopa stuck his forefinger inside his collar to loosen it. He grabbed the third brandy and drank it at a gulp.

'It'll be a rehearsal,' Josef said. 'Because there is going to have to be a lot of killing one day, and we won't be able to do it sitting in a ditch.' He waved his hand. 'You're looking prosperous, Uncle Jan.'

'Josef!' Jan Janski slapped him on the shoulder. I didn't know you gambled.'

'It seemed a good idea to do something the Germans actually approve of. By the way, meet Ladislas Kopa. He helps me in the business.'

Jan Janski shook hands. 'You must let me buy you a drink. I won, you know, and when the cards are kind to me, Mr. Kopa, they are really kind.' He produced a thick wad of notes. 'Three brandies. But you're not playing?'

'Kopa became nervous.'

Kopa drank his fourth brandy, mopped his neck. 'I am a very nervous person.'

Jan Janski offered cigars. 'So you lose a little money. What is money for but to be spent? That is why I have never married. Wives, children, take away all the money you would otherwise have for pleasure. But you will ask, Mr. Kopa, am I never lonely in bed?'

'Not a man of your accomplishments,' Josef said.

Jan Janski laughed. 'I am not ashamed of it. So I tell you what we will do. We will have another brandy, and then we will pay a visit to a certain house where I assure you we will be welcome.'

'That's a splendid idea,' Josef said. 'But we have had enough to drink, thank you very much.'

'Then I'll just get my coat. It's beastly cold out, isn't it? I'll meet you in the lobby.'

'I'll have another brandy,' Kopa said.

'You've had enough,' Josef said. 'Let's go.'

The mortars boomed ceaselessly, and the explosions shook the town like a never-ending earthquake. The Russians had been banging away ever since the German assault had been brought to a halt. No doubt the bastards supposed *they* had stopped the advance, and not their detestable weather. But the mortars were dangerous. The battalion had suffered more casualties since allowing itself to be pinned down in this town than in its entire journey across Russia.

Frederic sat on the floor of what had once been a school-house, he supposed, because one wall was still a blackboard. He chewed chocolate, and listened to the pounding, and to the snores of Ziegler from beside him. There was ice on the floor, ice clinging to the upturned, shattered desks, icicles dripping from the holes in the roof. How Ziegler could sleep, how he could snore, while he was slowly freezing to death, was quite unimaginable. Frederic hadn't slept properly for a week, not since poor old Wohnt had been carried off with rope-burned hands. Somehow that had been more sinister, more threatening, than even the mortars. Or perhaps he was just depressed, because he was cold, and hungry, and sitting here in the darkness he was suddenly uncertain of the future.

'Frederic!' Kolisch knelt beside him. 'Look out here a moment.'

Frederic slapped his hands together, picked up his rifle, crawled on his hands and knees to the doorway. The mortars still banged away, their explosions bringing brilliant yellow flashes across the night sky. But as he reached the door they were silent.

'What the hell?' Walbrodt woke up with a start.

'I don't like it, Sergeant-Major,' Kolisch said. 'There's something out there.'

'The yeti,' Walbrodt said disagreeably. 'So the Russkies have run out of ammo. It had to happen.'

'There are men out there,' Kolisch said.

'Scavengers, maybe,' Frederic said. It didn't make sense. The Russians had never actually attacked a German position before.

'Sound the alarm!' Kolisch's voice was brittle. He dropped to his knee, fired into the darkness. Instantly the

185

fire was returned, bullets crackling into the frozen wood of the schoolhouse.

'Fix bayonets,' Walbrodt snapped, 'and get down. Down, you bastard.' But one of the recruits had already got to his feet, half asleep, and was spinning round before crashing back to the floor.

Now Frederic saw them, and yet he didn't. They wore white, and so were only there when they moved. Snow moving against snow. He fired, emptied his magazine at a particularly large lump of snow, didn't know whether he had hit anything or not. He reloaded, snapped his bayonet home, saw a wall of snow rise from the other side of the street and come towards him.

'Up! Up!' Walbrodt yelled.

The section rose as one man, bayonets gleaming. The white-clad Russians surged at the door. Frederic thrust his bayonet deep into a chest, was surprised when the blood welled; there was something inhuman about these figures. But he was long past the stage of staring at one dying man. Even as the thoughts raced through his brain he was withdrawing the blade, and swinging the butt of his rifle against the jaw of the man behind. A bayonet passed under his arm and ripped his tunic, and then his rifle butt crashed into the bone, driving the man backwards. Beside him Kolisch and Ziegler cursed and screamed as they too thrust and swung. And then the doorway was clear. The white-clad figures melted away as if they had never been, except for the half-dozen who were no longer.

'Down! Down!' Walbrodt shouted, as the mortars began again. 'Bier, get down the line and have the medics up here. Corporal Ziegler, find Lieutenant Koehnlein. I want orders. Tell him we're still holding the school-house. On the double.'

A mortar shell landed very close, and a building down the street burst into flames, making the night light for a

186

moment. Kolisch and Frederic lay next to each other in the doorway, their rifles resting on the man Frederic had bayoneted. 'Look at this.' Kolisch used his bayonet to cut into the Russian's jacket. 'Fur-lined, by God. And his pants. Pity you tore him up, Frederic. He's just about my size.'

The flames were already dying down, and the darkness was closing. Frederic wished it was dawn. He was a veteran, and he was afraid. Because he was a veteran of the advance, of an irresistible force. Because no white-clad figures had ever come at him out of the darkness before. Because these men had equipment he lacked. Because an infantryman was only as good as his gear.

Ziegler knelt beside them. 'Orders from H.Q. We're pulling back. Quietly, now.'

'Eh?' Kolisch turned his head. 'You're joking.'

Ziegler's face was grim. 'The Russians have penetrated. They're behind us. So let's get the hell out of here.'

v

'In here, Mr. Janski!' Gavlikowski opened the door. Anton Janski hesitated, nostrils dilated as he tried to breathe without appearing to do so. The morgue was painted white, and seemed colder than it was. The ceiling was low, the air close.

Josef held his arm, urged him through the door. Josef's nostrils were also dilated; his eyes gleamed behind his spectacles.

'We're a little crowded.' The police inspector led them between the tables. 'It is a time of year when people feel they can no longer continue.'

'My brother would never have committed suicide.'

'I entirely agree, Mr. Janski. If I had been asked yester-

187

day to select the happiest man in all Warsaw, at least from amongst the Poles, then I would have chosen Jan without a moment's hesitation.' He lifted the sheet. 'Would you?'

Anton Janski lived in a world of make-believe, and even to scrap a toy soldier because of a flaw in its manufacture left him depressed. Jan Janski looked ugly, although they had cleaned the mucous from around his nostrils and closed his eyes. Anton glanced at his son. Josef had moved round the other side of the table, gazed at the drowned man as a child might look at a lollipop. 'It is my brother.'

'You understand it has to be done by a relative, no matter how sure we are of his identity.' Gavlikowski led them back to his office, poured three glasses of brandy. 'We will be holding an autopsy, of course.' He peered into his glass as if the liquid held the secrets he was after. 'It will be done this afternoon. Tomorrow you may have the body and make the arrangements for the burial.'

'Why do you need an autopsy?' Josef asked.

'Because your uncle did not die a natural death, Josef. Can you tell me where he went last night?'

'He was at the casino,' Josef said. 'We left together, as a matter of fact. But we separated at the door. I sleep at the studio nowadays.'

'What time was this?'

Josef shrugged. 'A little after eleven. We had been drinking. Uncle Jan had won.'

'And did he tell you where he was going?'

'I thought he was going out to Rokonow.'

'But he didn't. And were you not worried, Mr. Janski, when he was not there this morning?'

Anton's turn to shrug. 'Jan was nearly forty-five years old, Inspector. Often, after the casino, he does not come back. Especially when he has won.'

Gavlikowski opened the file on his desk. 'A considerable amount of money was found in his wallet. And certainly he had been drinking, heavily. You could almost say his drinking cost him his life. Just after midnight last night a man was heard crying out for help in the river, and my police went to his aid. They sent one of the dogs after him, and the dog got up to him, and then turned away and swam back to the bank. These dogs are teetotal. They simply will not take hold of a man smelling of liquor.'

'You mean Jan was alive then?'

'If it was he. We didn't recover the body until dawn. But the times fit. So he certainly didn't attempt suicide. Indeed he fought for his life before he went into the water; there are bruises on his arms and back, consistent with blows. Had your brother any enemies, Mr. Janski?'

'He was very popular.'

'Only with the ladies, surely. A jealous man can nurse revenge for a long time, waiting the right opportunity. Unfortunately, there are also other possibilities. The resistance.'

'Now really, Inspector, can you seriously imagine the Home Army trusting a man like Jan?'

'You speak as if you approve of their activities. Mr. Janski. You understand if there is a link between your brother and the resistance it will become a matter for the Gestapo.'

'Of course it was not done by the Home Army, Inspector,' Josef said. 'They'd have taken his money, made it seem he was attacked by footpads. Actually, he seemed upset when I saw him, although he'd won. My friend Kopa remarked on it.'

Gavlikowski frowned. 'Who was that?'

Josef's glasses glinted. 'Ladislas Kopa. He helps at the studio. He knew Uncle Jan quite well. "You mark my words, Josef," he said, "Jan has a jealous husband after him."'

189

'I suppose you're right.' Gavlikowski smiled at Anton Janski. 'And the Gestapo have enough to do without being involved in domestic tragedies, eh, Mr. Janski? I think we will be able to clear up the affair without troubling you again.'

Anton buttoned his coat, picked his way through the snow on the pavement. He seldom came into Warsaw nowadays, but as he was here, he walked down Senator Street, stood in front of the pile of rubble that had been Janski and Son. It looked like a vast tomb under its mantle of snow. The graveyard of the Janskis, he thought.

Josef took his arm. 'Come down to the studio and I'll make you a cup of coffee.'

'Isn't it strange, the way Gavlikowski suddenly lost interest in what had happened to Jan?'

'When he was sure we knew nothing about what had happened he wanted to forget it as quickly as possible.'

'When he was sure.' Anton repeated thoughtfully. He allowed himself to be led down the street.

The town burned, seething into the freezing air, popping and sending showers of sparks into the snow. The heat would melt the snow on the shattered buildings, and tomorrow the town would be a great black scar on the white plain. Until it snowed again, and then it would disappear altogether.

And they would forget it existed. The battalion moved with a vast hiss. Frederic imagined a gigantic snake, winding its way through the darkness. He had no knowledge of his feet. They were lost, down there, ankle deep in the soft white powder. They were moving because his thighs were moving. He could feel his thighs. He was conscious of dictating to them, first one and then the other. But feeling ended with his knees. It was the same with his hands, clamped together on the strap of his rifle, the same with his helmet, resting like a stone on his brain. It was the same with his eyes, staring at Kolisch's back, so close he could smell Kolischs' sweat, inhale Kolisch's fear seeping back through the freezing air.

Yesterday, even if upset by the cold, by the way their impetus had faded into nothing, this had been an army of heroes. Today it was suddenly afraid, of the darkness, where before they had welcomed it. Out there, in the darkness, where white-clad figures, snug and warm in their special winter clothing. To be beaten by the Russians perhaps to have to surrender, was an impossible thought. For they were the aggressors. No amount of propaganda could reverse that truth. The Fuehrer had elected to smash Bolshevism. Frederic still felt this was a good thing for the whole world. But they had struck the first blow and they had all but annihilated a totally unsuspecting foe. To fall into the hands of that foe was unthinkable. And how quickly his mind took him back to that march west from Lowicz, the thousands of hopeless, shambling men, the smell, the shuffling. The last two were already with them.

'Take ten!' Walbrodt came down the line, speaking quietly. 'Corporal Ziegler, you'll post a guard. Rest, but no sleeping. And no noise, no smoking. The Russkies are all around us.' He continued on his way.

'Come on, Frederic,' Ziegler said. Frederic sighed, left the column and the road, slid down an embankment. There were trees here, looming in the darkness, concealing their pursuers and leaving the column exposed. He could see them now, black dots on the snow, an endless smudge. But not endless at all. There were only fifty men left in Captain Winz's company. In one night they had suffered more casualties than in the whole campaign.

'Keep awake,' Ziegler said. 'If the Russkies locate us we've had it.'

'Don't you think they're watching us now?'

Ziegler chuckled. 'Like Berthold's redskins you mean,

191

waiting for the dawn? When the Russkies find us they're going to move in. They'll never have an opportunity like this again.'

Frederic massaged his rifle. 'I hope you're right.'

'Look, boy, I've been wearing this uniform for four years, and this is the first time I've ever marched backwards. We overextended, that's all. We thought they were licked, and they weren't. So we'll pull back and dig in and wait for the weather to improve. They can't expect infantry to take a city like Moscow. We need the panzers, and the planes.'

To listen to Ziegler was to feel the blood pumping through your arteries. It occurred to Frederic that he had been lucky in his companions. Rosenthal, Mittwitz, and now Ziegler and Kolisch. Not every man could be as lucky as he. He wondered why. Because he was young and good-looking? Did that mean that every man was a homosexual at heart? Mentally, yes. Man kept trying to find a masculine mentality in a feminine body. That was man's trouble. And there again Frederic Johansson was the lucky one, because his quest had been successful. Asja was so strong, so single-minded, she could easily be a man. And her body was the most feminine in the world. But he could not let himself think of Asja. He had promised her he would be home for Christmas.

And how strange that this man beside him, Ziegler, who liked him, might even love him, would instinctively hate the other man, Rosenthal, who had also loved him. He thought to find the answer to why men loved, and why men hated, would be the greatest of all discoveries. He wondered if the time would ever come when a surgeon would operate, and remove hatred, and substitute love.

'Fall in! Fall in!' Walbrodt was back, and they were marching again, back, back, for the first time in the history of the Wehrmacht. Back.

Just before dawn they came to another town. They had

been here before. The burned-out bus still clung to the corner of the square. But the rest of the battalion was already here, digging, setting up machine gun nests, embedding mortars. 'Fall out!' Walbrodt could shout again, now. 'Fall out, you bastards. Let's get to work. We're staying right here.'

Even the sweat smelt better.

VI

It snowed incessantly, pushed from the east by a fresh breeze drifting against the headstones, lining the freshly dug graves with cotton wool, settling on coats and scarves and shoes. The wind made nonsense of stockings, slid between neck and collar, funnelled upwards beneath Christina's woollen skirt to chill her thighs. But her thighs had been cold before she had ever left the house. Her thighs were never going to be warm again.

She stood apart from the rest of them, hands tight on her rosary, gazed at them bitterly. They were cold, and this was a duty. They wanted it done so they could get back to the house. Papa looked anxious. Papa always looked anxious, nowadays. Mama looked exhausted; Mama always looked exhausted. Liese looked contemptuous. Josef looked grim; but then, Josef always looked grim. Captain Brandt looked at Asja. And Captain Brandt always looked at Asja, nowadays.

Only Asja looked sad. Only Asja knew how much what was happening meant to Christina. Only Asja looked beautiful. Which was remarkable. All the women wore black coats and black hats, and Mama looked as neat as ever. But Liese, although her coat was new, with a fox-fur collar, and her shoes were new, and her gloves were new, and her handbag was new, and her hat was new, wasn't beautiful any longer. The twist of Liese's lips had become permanent. All life was contemptible, particularly life as lived by the Poles, particularly life as lived by the Polish Janskis. But Asja, with her threadbare coat and her shabby shoes and her old-fashioned hat, and the faint blaze of red-gold hair penetrating her veil, and the line of her jaw and the compression of her lips, looked magnificent. And dangerous. Christina could still feel the pain in her groin. And Asja was breathing deeply to keep from tears. Her bosom expanded and settled, expanded and settled. To have breasts like Asja's was to make all other women inferior. Captain Brandt watched Asja breathing.

Father Paul came round the grave, put his hand on Papa's shoulder. Father Paul buried at least one person every day. He did very little else. Nobody got married, nobody gave birth nowadays. And less and less people went to church. The Germans kept their eyes on the churches; they knew no man could worship Christ and the Fuehrer. They knew the priests were natural agitators. Three of Father Paul's colleagues had already left Rokonow. Nobody knew for sure where people who left Rokonow were taken. They marched off with small bundles or suitcases to the railway stations, like the Jews, and they disappeared.

The family left the cemetery. They walked right across the graves, because there were no headstones any more, and the newer part of the cemetery was just a solid mass of freshly turned earth. Winter was a bad time for finding burial space.

The hearse had already left, the horse clipping silently through the snow. The street was empty, save for Captain Brandt's motor-car. Father Paul was still talking with Mama and Papa. Liese was getting into the car. Captain Brandt was whispering to Asja, and, as Christina watched, his arm went round her waist. Her right arm immediately clamped to her side, so that his fingers

194

had to squeeze her elbow instead of going any farther, but her expression never changed.

Josef watched them too, his eyes sly behind his glasses. Josef and Asja weren't friends any more. But Asja was refusing, quite definitely. Captain Brandt looked annoyed, but he shrugged, and offered the spare seats to Mama and Papa. They got in, and the car drove off, sliding in the snow. Josef walked beside Father Paul, talking in low tones. Asja looked over her shoulder. 'Come along, Kitgirl.'

She meant well, but she shouldn't have said that. Christina waded through the snow, stood next to her. Asja put her arm around her waist, tightly. 'You've been very good,' she said. 'Now let's go home and I'll make you a cup of coffee.'

They walked. 'What does Captain Brandt want with you, Asja? Does he want to screw you?'

Asja smiled. Since they had become so intimate she had also become used to Christina's language. 'I suppose so. I sometimes think that's all a man ever wants from a woman. That is all Jan ever wanted from you, you know.'

'No,' Christina said. 'He loved me.'

'Of course he loved you, Christina. But in the way a man loves a woman.'

'He didn't want to do it. I made him.'

Asja sighed. 'Well, it's over and done with now. I wonder if Jan isn't better off than any of us. I'll bet he's at least warm.' She glanced at Christina, as if just realising what she had said.

Christina stared at the road, and the swastika flag flying above the house. 'The Germans killed him.'

'He was drunk, and he fell into the Vistula, and he drowned.'

'He was thrown into the Vistula. He told me he was a colonel in the Home Army. And he knew the Germans were after him. I hate them.'

'We all hate them.'

'Liese doesn't. She is going to marry one. The bitch. Oh how I hate them, Asja. And Liese.'

'I have something to tell you all.' Captain Winz shouted into his loudhailer, surveyed the hundred and fifty men gathered in front of him, stamping their feet and shuffling in the snow, collars turned up, hands deep in pockets. You could not make men stand to attention when inactivity would send them straight to hospital with frostbite, but it was difficult to tell exactly where the soldiers ended and the always curious crowd of townspeople began.

The captain cleared his throat. 'Last week we were forced to retreat for the first time in the history of this regiment. I may add for the first time in the history of the Wehrmacht. This retreat, as you know, was in no way brought about by superior enemy action but by the early frost which limited the mobility of our panzers, and, even more important, of our supply columns. It became necessary, therefore, to adjust our line, eliminate unnecessary salients, and prepare for the coming offensive, which will take us beyond Moscow, and bring the Soviet Government to its knees. It also gives men like yourselves, who have been in the front line since the 22nd June, an opportunity to enjoy a well-earned rest, here behind the line. However, the first thing I have to say to you is this: There will now be no more retreat. The line holds this position until we recommence our advance. This company will hold this town, if need be, to the last man and the last bullet.'

The company shuffled their feet; snow drifted into the morning air.

'These orders are direct from the Supreme Commander of the Wehrmacht. I know how pleased you will be to learn that General von Brauchitsch has been forced to retire, for reasons of health, and so, in the present decisive stage of the war, the Fuehrer has himself taken over the Supreme Command. With such a leader, such a strategist, the greatest of all time, in charge of our destinies, as he has already been in charge of our destinies for the eight most glorious years in German history, there can be no question of any Russian recovery. And as if this were not sufficient, I have some more momentous news to give you. The people of Germany and Italy, and their Rumanian and Hungarian and Finnish allies, have now been joined in the struggle to establish the new order by the greatest nation of Asia. The Rising Sun of Japan has taken its place beside the swastika. I need hardly tell you that the Japanese army is inferior only to our own, and the Japanese navy is the greatest in the world. With such tremendous forces at our disposal, complete victory can now be only a matter of weeks.'

The company shuffled, clapped hands together, rubbed cheeks and noses.

'Now to a more personal, a domestic, matter. The Fuehrer's first directive as Supreme Commander, in view of the inclement weather we are experiencing, has been to remedy our shortage of winter clothing. You will be overjoyed to learn that four complete sets of winter clothing, superior by far to anything that the Russians possess, arrived this morning for distribution to each company.' The captain began to speak more quickly, before the mathematicians could divide four by a hundred and fifty. 'I have decided, therefore, that the fairest way to distribute this first supply will be to have all ranks draw lots for each item. This draw will take place immediately, under the supervision of Sergeant-Major Walbrodt.'

Frederic collected his borsch and sausage from the kitchens and joined Kolisch, who sat beside the smouldering fire in a shattered cottage. Three ragged Russian children stared at them from the window. But you got used to being followed by hungry children; most of the time you scarcely saw them. 'No luck?'

'Not a bleeding sock. Smoke?'

They shared a cigar. Kolisch had a remarkable knack for securing things like cigars and almost empty flasks of brandy. Frederic thought he would have done very well in the wild west.

'So here we sit and here we die, eh, Frederic?'

'That kind of talk could get you a penal spell.' Frederic watched Corporal Ziegler stamping through the snow towards them. 'Any luck?'

'You're speaking to Hans Ziegler.' Ziegler tossed a pair of woollen drawers on to Frederic's lap. 'Try those.'

'You won them.'

'So what do I have to protect? But you don't want to offer your Slav goddess a frostbitten tool, do you?'

'If she's still waiting,' Kolisch said.

'Asja will wait for ever,' Frederic said. 'Well, thanks, Hans. I'll pay you back some day.'

Ziegler sat between them. 'So the cowboy's feeling low.'

'He figures we're going to lose the war,' Frederic said. 'Or something.'

'How do you think we could possibly lose this war, Berthold?' Ziegler placed his feet as close to the fire as he dared. 'You've seen the map.'

'That map doesn't mean a thing,' Kolisch said. 'I was talking to Walbrodt. The captain forgot to drop one little piece of information to you yobs. Sure the Japs are on our side now. But they didn't declare war on the Soviet Union. You want to know who they're fighting? England and the USA.'

'Whatever for?' Frederic asked.

'To become top dog in Asia. The Yanks wouldn't stand for that.'

'But the Americans don't really have an army,' Frederic said. 'Just a few marines.'

Ziegler chuckled. 'Maybe you'll wind up fighting red-skins yet, Berthold.'

'That's a big country,' Kolisch said soberly. 'Bigger than Germany. Damned near as big as this one, and there's a lot less wasted space. What in the name of God is that? I thought we were behind the line?'

The firing came from the next block. They scrambled to their feet, reaching for their rifles, as Sergeant-Major Walbrodt led the rest of the section along the street. 'Partisans!' Walbrodt shouted. 'In broad daylight. Let's go!'

VII

Liese spent the morning in bed. Only in bed was it possible to be warm; the fuel ration was insufficient to burn more than an hour a day, and Mama was saving it to keep a fire going all Christmas Day. Mama was determined to celebrate Christmas.

So was Liese. She had received half a dozen invitations, from Captain Brandt upwards. She thought she would accept Major Hilse. He had just returned from the Russian front, where he had obviously been a friend of Paul's, so they would have something to talk about.

Meanwhile, she re-read the letter, pretended she had just opened it. He still wrote her every week, but sometimes they came out of order, and referred to other letters which had not come at all. This one had been delivered by Major Hilse personally. Having read it, she could understand why. They were in love; they were unofficially engaged; they were going to be married, when the war was over. There was enough material for any man to fill a dozen pages and still have things to say. Instead of which Paul had written page after page of pessimistic drivel, which would never have got past the censor had he tried to mail it, and might well have got him into trouble. She hated his introspective moods.

She sighed, and turned the page. 'God knows, there can be no man in the Wehrmacht who has a greater admiration for the Fuehrer than I, my darling No one could possibly deny his political genius. But one cannot help wondering if here in Russia he has not been let down by his advisers. And we must not delude ourselves that what is happening here is a *result* of the war. These directives were printed long before last June. There was time to cancel them. I have it on good authority that our troops were welcomed as liberators by the people of the western Ukraine, and even in western Byelorussia. Yet once the line advanced these people were treated as wild animals, men, women and children, their food confiscated and no provision made for their welfare. This was not immediately apparent during the summer. For every kilo of grain the farmer handed over to our commissariat he kept one for his family; I have no doubt they are all experienced at this kind of cheating with the commissars. But now that winter has come, these people, and there are millions and millions of them, are quite literally starving. So we have a vicious circle. The Russians attempt to steal food or hold up supply trains, they fail and some of them are caught, and they are interrogated, in many cases with considerable brutality, by the Gestapo, and then they are executed.

'I wish it would end, but I am terribly afraid, my darling, that it cannot now do so before next summer. Our High Command has made the same mistake as Napoleon and Charles XII in underestimating the power of the Russian winter, and perhaps also in underestimating the fanaticism with which the Russian, communist or not, will defend his holy cities of Moscow and Leningrad. This has to be seen to be believed. They throw women as well as men into the line, and here at Leningrad, only a mile or two beyond our lines, they are literally dropping down dead on the streets from starvation. But still they fight. And in the air, you will not beleive this, but as the Russian fighters are so slow they have no hope of bringing even our bombers to combat, they commit suicide, flying their machines straight into ours.

'And so, my dearest Liese, I am not going to get home for this Christmas, and must ask you to accept one of the hundreds of invitations which I know will have been showered upon you, and go out and enjoy yourself, for my sake. The front is bogged down in snow and ice, and will probably remain in this miserable state until the spring, but we are using our time well, to regroup and prepare ourselves for the offensive next summer, which will finally end this unhappy affair. I will see you then, my darling.'

And if that was a typical letter from a German soldier to his loved one, she thought, it was going to be a pretty gloomy Christmas for everyone.

Frederic had not realised there were so many Russians left in the town. But this morning there were men here, as well as women and children. About a thousand, he calculated, and curled his fingers round the butt of his rifle. The company was strung out, one man every five yards, right round the square. Kolisch was nearest to him, but even Kolisch was very far away. They stood, facing the people, their backs turned to the slanting snow which drifted ceaselessly through the shattered buildings, piled itself against the foot of the gallows, dusted like powder across the platform. They shivered, and so did the crowd. It was a silent crowd. But there were so many of them. I would not stand here, Frederic thought, if I were a Russian.

But he was standing here, as a German. And he had shared guard duty last night, with Kolisch, outside the house appropriated by Obersturmfuehrer Schmidt, and they had listened to the woman screaming. Kolisch had been philosophical about it. 'It does not matter what they do to her,' he had said. 'Or the man. As they are going to be hanged, anyway.'

'Then they should have been hanged, right away,' Frederic had said. 'We stand for civilisation. *They* are the savages.'

'They are that,' Kolisch had said. 'What about those chaps they caught and stripped and left to freeze to death? Whatever happens to a partisan, he, or she, deserves it.'

Then the screams had got louder, achieving a note of desperation which had made Frederic physically sick. 'What can they be doing?' he had shouted.

Kolisch had looked through the window. 'They have set her body hair on fire. But it doesn't matter, Frederic. She's going to hang anyway.'

He had joined the Wehrmacht to kill Russians. It was necessary to remember this. For a hundred and forty years Russia had lain across Poland like a fallen tree, and from every branch had sprouted a knout or a deportation order to Siberia. The Russians had dished it out for too long. Now they had to accept some back.

But he had not joined the Wehrmacht to set girls' pubic hairs on fire. That girl had carried a pistol, and certainly had used it to kill one of his comrades. And as Kolisch had said, the partisans could be just as terrible to any stragglers they caught. But standing there, listening to her screams, or standing here, waiting for her to be ceremonially strangled, did that not mean the wheel had turned full circle? Because he had been afraid to die as Rosenthal had died he had fled, through the only door opened to him. He had betrayed his friends and his family and his nation, but he had convinced himself that life was always better than death, and that his life could still be spent usefully, fighting the Russians. Standing here, he might as well be wearing a black uniform. Because he knew how adaptable the human body and the human mind could be to its environment. So in a month's time *he* would be looking through the window to see what they were doing to some other girl, and in two months' time the screaming would be only a nuisance, and by next spring he'd be fully qualified to take his place beside Reitener.

And there was nothing he could do to stop the process. Except die.

A ripple spread through the crowd. Now, if ever, there would be trouble. He wished there would be. He thought the passivity of these people was worse than the screams. So they were unarmed and the square was controlled by machine gun nests; there were still many more people than soldiers. But the column, marching west from Lowicz, had been controlled by just two men on a motor-bike.

The army officers came first, Captain Winz and his three lieutenants, faces pale. They were soldiers, too. No man could have better superiors than Koehnlein and Winz. But they had been forced to watch the girl being tortured. Then came the men in black, headed by Ober-sturmfuehrer Schmidt. And in the middle of the men in black were the girl and the boy; they certainly were not out of their teens. The girl could not walk, and her companion half carried her, his arm round her waist, while her feet dragged a trail in the snow. Although the wind had got up and it was very nearly a blizzard, their heads and feet were bare, and both wore placards, saying 'Partisan', hung round their necks. The girl had black hair, long and thick. It floated forward, obscuring her face.

Obersturmfuehrer Schmidt climbed the steps, and two of the black uniformed guards accompanied him. The mayor came from the other side of the square, accompanied by a priest. The crowd watched silently. The mayor went up to the two prisoners, spoke to them in a low voice. The priest raised his right hand. Then they were thrust up the steps by the guards. The boy let the girl go, and she sank to her knees. They had been turned to face the wind, and her hair drifted behind her. Her face was swollen with tears and pain and bruises, and it was difficult to decide what she might have been like, met with on a peaceful street. But she had beautiful hair.

Then it was gone, swept away by black gloved hands to allow the noose to be adjusted, and then, very quickly, she was standing, sucked upwards by the tightening rope, her face swelling even more. A sigh rose from the crowd, and it was the young man's turn. He seemed about to speak, and then he joined his companion, feet dangling, body still moving. Frederic wondered how long it took to strangle, dangling from a rope. The people waited for perhaps a minute. Then they melted away, going back to the empty, freezing cellars which were all they had left. In ten minutes the square was empty, save for the German soldiers and the dangling bodies.

VIII

Asja awoke, listened to Antoni coughing. The little boy's entire body heaved with each convulsion. She threw back the blanket, got out of bed; her body seemed to swell into a huge goosepimple. And it was only December.

Antoni shivered, even beneath the two blankets and the coat she had put over him. He shivered all the time nowadays. She scooped him from the bed, held him in her arms, walked him up and down the room, pressed him against her breast. And still he shivered, and the shivering communicated itself to her.

It was not yet midnight. And it was growing colder

204

every second. She opened the bedroom door, stood in the corridor. She wondered who else was asleep, and who awake, and cold. Christina? Liese would be sleeping; Liese kept herself warm with her dreams. Mama and Papa? They had each other. Or did they? She wasn't sure any more. She wasn't sure of anything, except that it was December, and the war was not going to end this year, and her son was dying.

The parlour was colder than the bedroom, and Antoni broke into a fit of coughing which woke him up, so that his little fingers scrabbled at her shoulders, and he whispered 'Mama?' His teeth chattered.

She gazed at the baize door which led to the house proper. Even the door was warmer than the air in the corridor. But to go through that door was to shed the nebulous protection afforded her as a relative of the Janskis.

'Mama?'

'Hush, sweetheart.' Already the warmth was creeping over her. And it was dark, and silent. She tiptoed up the hall, into the drawing room. A gaunt moonlight came in the french windows, cut slithers across the floor, brushed the wall where the two Matejkos had hung and where now an enormous photograph of the Fuehrer gazed disapprovingly at her. The fire still burned. It was dying, but it would smoulder for at least another hour, and then would retain its heat longer than that.

She sat on the hearthrug, Antoni on her knees. He sighed, coughed, and said 'Mama!' Then he went to sleep. Her own eyes drooped, as the heat seemed to surround her on a blanket. She wondered if she dared. She could lie here on the rug, beside Antoni. But would she awake in time?

She listened to a car engine, muted on the snow covered street. For a moment it meant nothing to her, then she realised it had stopped at the gate. She could hear the

205

slap of the sentry's hand on his rifle butt as he presented arms.

She rose to her knees. But the baize door was on the other side of the hall, and already the front door was open. She hugged Antoni to her breast, crawled behind the settee, crouched, bending over her child as if her strong back could remain forever between him and eternity.

The door opened, the room flooded with light. 'Brandy?' She did not recognise the voice; she avoided them as much as possible, scarcely knew their names.

'Brandy will be fine.' The second man sat down; the back of the couch bulged against her shoulder. 'Damned cold for December.'

Another man sat on the settee. 'You should thank God you're not on the Russian front.'

Antoni coughed, and Asja stood up. She looked at herself in the mirror on the opposite side of the room, a mass of red-gold curls hanging every which way across the shoulders of the blue dressing gown, a tight lipped, anxious face beneath.

The officers also stood up. One of them was Brandt. 'By God!' he said.

Asja licked her lips. 'My baby is ill. He needs warmth.'

'What a magnificent woman,' said the second man, as if she had not spoken. 'Come round here, Slav.'

The fear was locking her thighs together. Slowly she walked round the settee to stand in front of the fire. Antoni had gone back to sleep.

'You baby is sick, you say, Slav?' Brandt asked. 'Then we shall cure him. If you choose.' He took a coin from his pocket, spun it. 'Say.'

'Tails,' said his companion.

'You lose. Now be a good fellow and go to bed. You will have your turn tomorrow.'

The man stood beside Asja. 'You will bring your son

in here every night at this hour, Slav. If you do not we will have you arrested for attempting to steal from German officers. It will be Szucha Avenue for you.'

Asja's head jerked. It could be interpreted as a nod. The man left the room.

Brandt sat down. 'Put the boy on the rug, where he can sleep, and come over here. Pour yourself a glass of brandy.'

'I do not drink.' Asja stooped, laid Antoni very carefully on the rug. A single tear rolled out of her right eye and raced down her cheek.

'Numbers two hundred and forty to two hundred and fifty-five.' Ziegler traced the route on the map. The houses weren't really numbered like that, but Ziegler had been an accountant before his wife left him, and he had renumbered the lots on his map. 'This way we know where we are.'

'I think we may as well go home,' Kolisch said.

Frederic agreed with him. This had been one of the main access roads in to town, and as such had been well defended. Not a house had a roof on it, not a window contained glass. That anyone could be alive in these empty shells was ridiculous.

'You'd be surprised,' Ziegler said. 'We start with two hundred and forty. Cover me.' He clambered over a dislodged stone gatepost, lying across the driveway, embedded in the snow.

Frederic unslung his rifle, knelt in the snow behind the pillar. Kolisch moved twenty feet to his right, sloshing through the remnants of the garden, seeking the shelter of some bushes. The other four members of the patrol, youngsters hardly older than Frederic himself and raw recruits into the bargain, followed the example of the veterans, finding shelter and pointing their rifles at the shattered buildings while Ziegler went up the steps. They had learnt to be careful from bitter experience. They could occupy a town for a week and still not be sure which house was a nest of partisans.

The front door hung from a single hinge. Ziegler raised his boot, scattered snow, kicked it in. 'Anybody home?' he bellowed. 'Frederic!'

Frederic left the pillar. He hated walking across empty spaces, his olive-green uniform a vivid target against the snow. Ziegler waited in the hall. It was dark because, surprisingly, the first floor was still there. The staircase at the end of the hall climbed to a landing, and then another, and then into the air, the last three steps seeming an ascent to heaven.

'Not a sound,' Ziegler said. 'Give it a go, though.'

'Anybody here?' Frederic shouted in Russian. He pointed to the closed cellar door.

Ziegler nodded, signalled Kolisch. The platoon came in fast, scuffing the snow, stamping their feet to kick their boots clean. Frederic moved along the hall to the door, put his boot against it, kicked. Kolisch joined him, lamp in hand, and they stepped inside together. Stairs led down to a corridor, more doors.

'Csank! Varin!' Ziegler snapped. 'Stay here, cover us. Start from the right, Frederic.'

Frederic took the light, went downstairs. It was colder than on the street. To live in this darkness and this damp, for days, weeks, perhaps months, afraid to show your nose upstairs, must be worse than dying, he thought. The first door was ajar. He threw it back on its hinges. 'Wine cellar,' he said over his shoulder. 'This place must have belonged to a commissar.'

'Let's have a look.' Moll stepped past him.

'We're counting heads, not bottles,' Ziegler said from the stairs.

'Just checking the vintage, Corporal.' Moll reached into the rack, picked up the cleanest of the bottles.

There was a flash of light, and Frederic discovered himself on his belly, in utter darkness except for the flame in his mind. His head went round and round, and he could feel blood trickling down his neck.

He rolled on his back, put his hands above his head, touched stone. Cautiously he explored himself. He had had a remarkable escape. The thing to do now was get out. But which way? Distant crashes and shouts seemed to come from all around him. His nostrils were choked with dust. And now his senses began to throb. He was buried alive in a Russian cellar, twelve feet under a shattered house on a shattered street.

But Ziegler would never stop looking until he found Frederic's body.

He turned on his stomach, rose to his hands and knees. His back brushed the masonry above him, and he dropped again, wiped blood and sweat from his face; he could not tell what was holding the huge mass of stone from crushing him. He wormed his way forward, hands thrust in front of him, touched human flesh. Warm flesh, as warm as flesh could be in this tomb.

It was impossible for Moll to be alive; the wine rack had exploded in his face. The rest of the patrol had been on the stairs. 'Who are you?' he whispered in Russian.

'Thank God,' a woman said. 'I thought you were a Fritz.'

'Are you hurt?'

'No. I had just set the trap, and couldn't get out. So I hid in the press.' Her fingers moved from his hand to his sleeve, touched his buttons. 'Oh God,' she said. 'Oh God. You spoke Russian.'

Frederic gripped her hands. 'Are you a partisan?'

The hands pulled. The flesh was firm. He tried to imagine what she might look like, but could only see the black haired girl, hanging.

'Fritz,' she whispered. 'It is an act of God that we survived the blast. You cannot turn me over to the Gestapo. I beg you, Fritz. Kill me now.'

Frederic held both her wrists in one hand, moved his left up her sleeve and over her shoulders to her face. Big chin, small nose. Hair short, but silky. Smooth throat. Full breasts, obscure beneath the heavy coat. 'What is your name?'

She had not moved during his inspection. 'Galina.'

'Are you a partisan, Galina?'

'Yes. We are all around you.'

'I know that.' Frederic listened to the scraping.

'Frederic!' Ziegler shouted. 'Are you all right?'

'Yes. But you'll have to dig me out.'

'Five minutes,' Ziegler promised. The confined space was filled with the noise of spades.

'Please,' Galina said. 'Do you know what they did to Tereskaya?'

She had blown Moll into little bits. And he would be betraying Ziegler and Kolisch, as he had betrayed his own family. But the black-haired girl swung before his eyes, and he could see through her clothes to the scorch marks on her belly. 'If you don't move no one will know you are in here.'

Her hands touched his. 'God bless you, Fritz.'

'Frederic. Remember my name, Galina.' There was a light now, faint, at the end of the tunnel. He looked at her, but she was only a grey shadow. He crawled away, and Ziegler reached for his hands.

'Thank God,' Ziegler said. ' I thought you'd had it. Oh, the bastards. If I could lay hands on the one who planted that booby-trap.'

Frederic crawled out of the hole.

The drizzle stopped, and might never have been. The sun shone, the afternoon was warm. Johnson took off his rain-coat, gazed at yet another concrete-and-glass mausoleum.

The Orbis car came slowly towards him, splashing water from the puddles. The guide put his head out of the window. 'You did not find the man you were looking for? Perhaps it was the wrong block.'

Johnson pointed. 'There used to be a cemetery.'

'Rokonow cemetery. It was bulldozed in 1946.'

Johnson got into the car. He had never doubted that the cemetery would still be there.

'Where would you like to go now, Mr. Johnson?'

Johnson shrugged.

The guide smiled. 'Then we shall return to Warsaw, and I shall take you to visit Number Twenty-Five, Szucha Avenue. That was where the Gestapo had its head-quarters during the war. We preserve it exactly as it was then. You can still see the bloodstains on the walls, the whips and the magnetos. But it is a place that should be visited.' He gave instructions to the driver, turned to face Johnson again. He was still smiling. 'We will go from the cemetery to Szucha Avenue. During the war, the journey was always made in the opposite direction.'

5

Winter 1943-4

The Mercedes flew the swastika flag on its bonnet.
Frederic stood to attention. Beside him, Asja also stood
straight. The man in the car glanced at the soldier, ack-
nowledged the salute, frowned, and then smiled. But the
car was already past, hurrying towards Warsaw.

'Reitener!' Frederic muttered.

'You have heard of him?' Asja asked. 'He is the new
Obergruppenfuehrer of the SS in Warsaw.'

'I used to know him,' Frederic said.

'You say that so casually. Here in Warsaw the object
of our lives is *not* to know him at all.' She entered the
cemetery, her boots making gentle indentations in the
snow which smothered the huddled graves. The icy wind
rippled around her, flicked the tail of her old black coat,
plucked at the hem of her dress. She wore silk stockings
with not a ladder, in contrast to the shabbiness of her
clothes. Incredibly, she was more beautiful now than two
years ago. She had lost still more weight, and her bone
structure was exposed as if in a drawing of the perfect
female face. Black suited both the pink-brown of her
complexion and the tawny splendour of her red-gold hair,
peeping in a fringe from beneath the headscarf.

Without warning, she knelt. There was nothing to dis-
tinguish this snow-covered mound from the thousand
other snow-smothered mounds all around them. He knelt
beside her; his elbow brushed hers as he made the sign
of the cross.

She did not weep, nor did she close her eyes. She gazed
at the grave with a peculiar intensity, as if she could see
little Antoni down there, inside. Frederic felt he was in-

truding. She had wanted to bring him here, but he should not have come. This was one part of her life he could never share, now. He looked away, up at the slate-blue sky, the pale sunlight trying to penetrate. But such a sky reminded him too much of Russia. He looked at the cemetery instead. But it had grown so much, sprawling every way over what had once been green fields, a mass of graves and freshly turned earth, that he scarcely knew where he was.

Asja seemed to awake from a deep sleep, put her hand on his. He stood up, carrying her with him. 'He has been there two years,' she said. 'And I feel it was yesterday. I suppose, living in the midst of so much death, an individual can no longer mean that much to you, Frederic.'

He looked over her shoulder. There had been another group in the cemetery, perhaps a hundred yards away, kneeling beside a grave. But now they were leaving, and he and Asja were alone, in the centre of the vast park, with only the dead for company.

She left her hand in his as they walked. 'Antoni was not ill, you know, Frederic. Not so ill he could not have been cured by a doctor, or by a trip down to Zabie. You could almost say he died of exposure.'

'And you blame the Germans?'

'Who else am I to blame, Frederic? Your Germans have launched us on the end of the world. To have the Nazis ruling all of Europe was going to be terrible, but at least it promised stability. But now . . . is it true the Reds have recaptured Smolensk?'

'No war was ever won by snapping the fingers, Asja. There has to be an ebb and a flow.'

'This war is lost, Frederic. It was lost at Stalingrad. And if you cannot see that it is either because you are blind or too loyal for your own good. Nothing is going to stop the Russians now. Nothing is going to stop the English and the Americans, either. Your Fuehrer's only chance to make peace was when Italy surrendered.'

He stopped walking, held both her hands. 'We always knew Italy was the weakest link in the chain. But the Allies can never get across the Alps. They are the greatest natural barrier in all Europe. And we have new weapons coming off the drawing board every day. This time next year . . .'

'We shall all be dead. Weapons! Weapons are nothing, Frederic. They are useless lumps of steel. They have to be worked. So they are no better than the men who hold them. Did you hear about the ghetto last summer?'

'Some things.'

'After three years of being treated like insects, of watching their friends and their sisters and their sweethearts carted off whenever someone in Berlin got the mood, the Jews finally decided they would fight. If only they had fought with such determination in 1939.'

'Hush, sweetheart,' Frederic said uneasily. They were alone in the middle of a cemetery on a January afternoon. And yet you could never be sure.

'If only we had all fought to the end in 1939,' she said. 'If only we had all fought this summer. They appealed for help, you know, Frederic. They asked the Home Army to help them. Have you heard of the Home Army, Frederic?'

'A partisan movement. I hope you have never had anything to do with it, Asja?'

'It is *there*, Frederic, and everyone knows it. And everyone knows it has arms and ammunition, and is only waiting for the opportunity, so it says, to rise up against the Germans. Well, it had its opportunity last summer. And it refused. It did not even send in weapons. So the Jews fought with what they had, what they could steal. They were exterminated, Frederic. The ghetto just isn't there, any more. It just isn't there.'

'And if this Home Army, as you call it, had helped

215

them, then all of Warsaw would have been wiped out. All of Rokonow too, probably. And you'd be dead.'

'We are all going to die, Frederic. And those Jewish boys died with pistols in their hands.'

'You would prefer to be killed like that? Have you ever seen a man hit by an expanding bullet, Asja? Or by shrapnel?'

'Have you ever seen a little boy just die, Frederic?'

'Asja, I can't tell you how sorry I am about Antoni, because nothing I could say can possibly comfort you. But our duty as human beings is still to survive. It has to be that. When Dombrowski wrote: "Poland is not yet lost as long as we are alive", he meant people like you and me. I asked you to wait for me because I didn't want you to have to undergo the sorrow of being widowed twice before you were twenty-five. Now I think we have waited too long. I can get us a special licence. We can be married tomorrow. We can even have a honeymoon; I am not due to return to the front for a week. Would you like that, Asja?'

She freed her hands. 'I believed you once, two years ago, Frederic. Antoni was dying, even then. But I believed you, that survival was the only thing that mattered. So I kept him alive until the following February. Do you know how I kept him alive? I took him into the main part of the house every night, when it was cold, and he slept on the hearthrug in front of the fire. The German officers, your German officers, were very kind. They kept a fire going all night for us. And they took turns at staying down to watch over my little boy. Of course, I stayed too. That was part of the bargain.'

He reached for her, and she stepped backwards, moved behind a headstone, an old headstone, this, commemorating a death which had occurred before either of them had been born.

'So what would you like from your wife, Frederic?

216

Those officers were very decent fellows, you know. A bit pompous, but all commissioned officers are pompous. Antoni was pompous. They have left Poland now. One has gone back to Germany, the other has been sent to the eastern front. Oh, yes, they were nice chaps. Nothing to do with the Gestapo, or the SS. They gave me presents. They gave me so many pairs of silk stockings I still have some left, after two years. But they could do what they liked with my body, because I'm a Slav, and they were German. And you are a German now, Frederic.'

Anton Janski carved as a woman might knit, scarcely looking at the wood in his hands, whittling and scraping and gouging with utter confidence. He called, 'Come in,' without moving his head, watched the olive-green uniform out of the corner of his eye. 'I thought you were walking with Asja?'

Frederic sat down. 'Asja prefers to walk by herself.'

Anton raised his head. He did not smile. He kept his smiles inside his head. Recently he had smiled quite often, inside his head. 'She is a strange girl. Her life has been unhappy.'

Frederic got up, fingered the toy soldier. There were seven toy soldiers on the table, not yet painted. But these infantrymen wore neither curved helmets nor forage caps; their caps were peaked. 'She hates me.'

Anton Janski carved. 'She wishes the war would end.'

'Papa, what really happened in the ghetto?'

'I believe it was very sad.'

'Would you have liked the Poles to go to the aid of the Jews?'

'Sad,' Anton Janski said. 'Very sad.'

'It could not have worked, you know, Papa. Where a few thousand Jews were massacred, a million Poles would have died. A rabble armed with pistols cannot fight the Wehrmacht.'

'There were more than a few thousand Jews,' Anton remarked softly.

Frederic walked round the room. 'Once I was drowning, and so I clutched at the first hand stretched out to me. Can you understand that, Papa?'

'Yes.'

'So what can I do now, Papa? I am a soldier. I cannot desert to join this, this Home Army people talk about. I would be shot. I do not know that I wish to desert. If the Wehrmacht does not fight the Russians the communists are going to invade Poland. Would you wish that to happen, Papa?'

Anton Janski sighed. 'Obergruppenfuehrer Reitener is more feared than Tuchachevsky was,' he said.

'How *does* a man correct his mistakes, Papa? When you have given your life to something how do you admit it was a mistake? You cannot.'

'It is sad,' Anton Janski said.

'And yet Asja hates me for being a German. Christina hates me for being a German. Although I think Christina hates everyone, whether or not they are German. One should not hate at eighteen.' He glanced at his father. 'What do *you* feel about me, Papa?'

'I hate you too,' Anton Janski said.

II

Father Paul looked very sad. But he was as kind as ever. 'You must come and see me, Colonel,' he said. 'To-morrow morning, perhaps. And we'll discuss the details.'

'It will be my pleasure,' said Colonel von Bardoman.

'And thank you, Father.' Liese knelt in the aisle, made the sign of the cross. Paul stood beside her, the rest of the congregation watched. She wondered if the Father was sad because she was going to marry a Protestant, or because she was going to marry a German.

She stood up, instinctively moved to Paul's left, corrected herself and held his right arm instead. He smiled, half lifted the sling. 'Mustn't complain, my darling,' he said. 'If a Russkie hadn't put a bullet through my arm I wouldn't have this fortnight for you.'

They stood at the top of the steps, shivering in the crisp air of the February morning. The staff car waited beside the kerb below them, the driver stood to attention. Liese released Paul's arm to allow him to return the salute. On the other side of the street a small boy, ragged, terribly thin, cheeks blue with the cold, stuck out his tongue at her.

'Little beast.' She accepted a cigarette, leaning back on the cushions and drawing off her gloves with a nervous flick. 'Father Paul is very nice.'

'I'll allow him that. But as soon as we're married, my darling, I'm sending you to Germany.'

'To Germany? Oh, that would be marvellous. But why send me away if you're going to be stationed at Brest Litovsk?'

'Because Brest is going to be in the front line very shortly.'

'That's impossible. Isn't it?'

'I wish it were, Liese. God, how I wish it were. But the Russians seem to become stronger every day, while we grow weaker. They have air superiority, now. They have had ever since Kursk. Their T34 tanks are better than anything we have. Much better. And their morale is better.'

'There was a change in Frederic when he was here last month,' she said. 'He didn't laugh any more.'

'What did he think of the situation?'

'Oh, Paul, he's only a private soldier. After three years he's still only a private soldier. He can't be very good.'

'In the last analysis, my darling, it's the private soldier who wins or loses wars.'

'Oh, I don't think losing ever entered Frederic's mind. We are going to win, aren't we, Paul?'

Bardoman gazed at the windswept pavement, the bare trees, as the staff car drew up in front of the house. 'What bothers me is the way the new recruits have no stomach. The army of 1941, Frederic's army, was the finest the world has ever seen. But these new men, do you know, they would rather shoot themselves in the leg or the hand than fight? And the Russians, of course, are making the most of it. Their aircraft shower our lines with leaflets, telling the men exactly how to injure themselves so it will look like an honest wound.' He sighed. 'We will win. We must win, my darling. We have no alternative.'

The driver opened the door, the sentry presented arms. Bardoman saluted, ushered Liese into the hall. 'I want to tell Mama,' she whispered. 'Can we do it now?'

He snapped his fingers, and the bar orderly came out of the drawing room. 'Bring a bottle of champagne, Weiss.'

The orderly clicked his heels. Liese had already opened the baize door, was rushing into the servants' sitting room. 'Mama! Asja! We've been to see Father Paul. We're going to be married on Saturday.'

Anna Janski stood up, her face pale. 'On Saturday?'

'Oh, we shall be married in the church, Mrs. Janski,' Bardoman said. 'I will obtain a special licence.'

'But are you sure, Paul? Are you *sure*?'

He smiled gravely, and his right hand came up to touch the Iron Cross at his breast. 'The Fuehrer himself gave me this. And I told him, I am going to make you very angry, my Fuehrer. I am going to marry a Polish girl. He frowned, and I said, of course she is an Aryan, and her mother is a German, and he smiled, and punched me on

220

the shoulder, and said, be careful, Bardoman, or I shall give the bride away myself.'

'The Fuehrer said that?' Mama cried. 'Oh, you darling boy! You have made me the happiest woman in the world.' She threw both arms round his neck, kissed him on the cheek.

Asja came forward. Her face was as cold as always. But no one expected Asja to smile, nowadays. 'I am very happy for you both.' She kissed Bardoman on the cheek, embraced Liese.

'And what about you, Christina?' Bardoman smiled. 'I don't think Christina approves, Liese.'

Christina, so pretty, almost the twin of her mother now except for her ash-blonde hair and her height, stared at her sister.

'Oh, Kitgirl,' Liese begged, 'be a sport and celebrate with us. Paul has ordered champagne.'

Weiss released the cork.

'Not Kitgirl,' Christina shouted. 'Never Kitgirl to you.' She ran out of the room.

'Oh, let her go,' Mama said. 'We four will celebrate. You'll toast the bride and groom, Asja?'

Asja raised her glass. 'I drink to your happiness, Colonel von Bardoman.'

'And I thank you, Mrs. Janski. Weiss, fetch another bottle.'

Weiss clicked his heels, left the room.

'And Liese, my darling, do you think you could help me with these belts?'

'Of course, sweetheart.' Liese lifted the belt and holster over his shoulder, opened the door, placed them on the table in the hall.

Bardoman refilled the glasses. 'I will give a toast to the Janskis, wherever they may be.'

'To us all,' Mama said.

'Wherever we may be.' Asja's eyes glistened.

'To us all,' Liese said, and watched Christina standing in the doorway, her hands behind her back. 'Come here, dearest.'

'I hate him,' Christina said. Her hands came round in front, holding the pistol she had taken from Bardoman's holster. The noise hardly sounded louder than the popping of the champagne cork. But Bardoman was on his knees, trying to reach his back with both hands, even the one shattered by the sniper's bullet. And the champagne cork was popping again.

Her face reminded Frederic of a monkey's, and was surrounded by tiny, tight brown curls. Her breasts were small and round; it was chilly in the large room and her nipples pointed upwards like beacons, very red. She had a thick waist, which was surprising, because every rib was visible. Her groin was covered by a mass of thick black hair; there would be lice in there. Her thighs were plump, her calves were covered in another layer of hair. She was desperately anxious to please, wriggled her bottom on the mattress, poked out her tongue and then hid it away with pitiful earnestness. She *had* to please. The road from the brothel led only downwards.

He knelt between her legs. 'Soon,' he said in Russian. He hoped he was right, for her sake. This was worse than Ruth. With Ruth there had been at least passion, even if there had been no love.

Her fingers were anxious. To have a soldier go impotent on her would be the end. She gasped, and massaged his belly with hers. Sweat rolled out of her hair, tears from her eyes. Terror gripped her mouth. Behind Frederic the guard moved to and fro and up and down the corridor between the beds, whip tucked under her arm. She waited for complaints. Her presence kept the girls eager.

He wondered if Ruth looked like this, lying on the floor

in Josef's studio. He had thought a great deal about Ruth these last few weeks. To think about Asja was too painful. Asja was only a dream, and it was impossible to take hold of a dream. Ruth had been real, on the floor, even if he had been unable to see her. And she was still real. He felt this in his bones. Josef had shown him the photograph, taken by chance, of the Jewesses marching into the railway station. Three years ago now. Three years in a concentration camp. Because that was where she would have gone. Three years in hell. He would not have survived them. But Ruth had survived them. Ruth *had* to have survived them. Ruth, in her utterly nebulous relationship with him, epitomised the disaster of being alive in the second quarter of the twentieth century. Only Ruth, surviving, and Frederic, surviving, and meeting, and if possible exchanging a smile, could hold out any hope for the third quarter. And perhaps Asja would be around as well.

It happened so suddenly it took them both by surprise. The terror faded from the monkey face, was replaced by relief, which was in turn replaced by a fresh anxiety. Ejaculation did not necessarily mean enjoyment, or even satisfaction. Rather was ejaculation the real crisis. No man was going to complain before. Every man was a potential executioner afterwards.

His forehead touched the pillow; his lips brushed her ear. He listened to her breathing. Perhaps he had just kissed her. She was exhausted, and feeling his weight now. Her belly swelled into his as if her lungs were bursting. He thought of the lice, crawling along one hair, leaping to the next, fighting through the jungle, living out their lives in a science fiction world of jostling bodies, drowning in sweat or semen, missing their hold and plunging into vast chasms, looking enviously at those who had reached the other side, the safety and the promise of new hair and new flesh, of well-nourished blood, with the prospect

223

of making their way through a whole regiment. If he could trace the aspirations of a louse, he wondered who, or what, as large to him as he was to the louse, could trace his aspirations. Something. There had to be something. But it did not direct, and it was not interested in saving. To it, Frederic Johaasson was a louse, and when it was finished whatever it was doing it would go to the baths and drown him.

He pushed his knees downwards, took the weight from her belly. Her flesh was dead white, each pulse as visible as each rib. She stared at him, her tongue circling her lips. 'Please, sir!

'I will tell the *Kapo* that I wish you again the next time.'

Her fingers were like claws, biting into his wrist. 'Thank you, sir. Thank you.'

How easy, he thought, to make a human being happy, when the human being is reduced to wanting so little.

He sat in the bath. There were twelve men in the vast tub with him, and no doubt a hundred men had used this water before them. Yet it was still hot, and the disinfectant still cloyed the nostrils. Life would still be pretty grim for the lice. He scratched himself. Another one gone.

Kolisch splashed towards him. 'That's a cute number. I had her the last time.'

'She's terrified,' Frederic said.

'That makes her better.' Kolisch's eyes were sad. He knew Frederic too well to ask why, after two and a half years, Frederic had at last gone to the brothel. Maybe he could tell what had really happened. But Kolisch was not interested in women, and no one waited for him in Hamburg. His dream was a boat to America. And that dream also was now a nightmare.

Vice-Sergeant-Major Ziegler came into the bathhouse, blew his whistle. 'Out! Out!' he bellowed. 'Collect your uniforms. There's a war on.'

224

Anna Janski took off her coat, threw it across a chair. She draped her gloves on top of it, rubbed her fingers together. Once they had been slender fingers, with long, manicured nails. Now the nails were cut short, the fingers themselves were blue, the knuckles swollen.

She stood in front of the mirror, rubbed the tear stains from her eyes. She took off her hat; grey wisps of hair trickled around her ears. Her right hand instinctively closed on her rosary. Then she took that off as well, laid it on the table; Father Paul had not been able to offer much help. She was not sure he had wanted to.

She went into the kitchen. Asja was on her knees in front of the oven. Asja made bread every week, but with even the flour substitute now a substitute, she was never sure how it would turn out. 'What did he say?'

Anna Janski sat in the straight chair beside the kitchen table. Her hands lay on her lap, her snow-flecked boots were turned inwards 'I have been to church.'

'But did you see the colonel, Mama?'

Mama sighed. 'He says there is nothing he can do. He says we are fortunate the Gestapo did not take all of us to Szucha Avenue. He says it could still happen, although he agreed that Liese's love for Paul is so well known it is incredible that she could have had any part in it. He says . . .'

'Then he is dead? Bardoman?'

'He died this morning. They say he never regained consciousness. He was so sweet. They were going to be so happy.'

Asja opened the cupboard above the stove, took out the last bottle of wine. 'It will warm you up.'

Mama held the glass in both hands, sipped. Some colour returned to her cheeks.

'When are you going to tell Liese?' Asja asked.

'How is she?'

'She won't eat. She just lies in bed weeping. She hasn't even a blanket. I think she really did love him.'

'You're glad it happened!'

'Not glad. Never glad about something like that. But it had to happen. If only it hadn't been Christina.'

Tears rolled down Mama's cheeks, plopped gently into the half-empty wineglass. 'What is going to happen to her, Asja?'

Asja took the tray from the oven, laid it on the stone hearth. 'You must not think about Christina any more.'

'I must not think about my own daughter?' Mama's voice was unnaturally quiet.

Asja stood up. 'She is dead.'

'Asja!' Mama scrabbled for her hand. 'We will have to get her a lawyer. Yes, the best lawyer in Warsaw. If only Jan were still alive. Anton is so helpless. He just will not say a word. I tried, you know. And he wept, and then went off to the workshop. I know! Josef! Asja, you must go into town and tell Josef what has happened.'

'Josef already knows, Mama.'

'Then he must find us a lawyer, and he and the lawyer must go to the Gestapo. They must explain. About Christina being weak in the head. Diminished responsibility. That's what they must say.'

Asja rested her hands on Anna Janski's shoulders, squeezed the taut muscles. 'You still don't understand, do you, Mama? Christina has been taken away by the Gestapo. There will be no trial. When they have finished with her she will be dead or they will send her to a concentration camp. You will never see her again.'

'You expect me to believe that, Asja?'

Asja refilled their glasses, drank her own at a gulp. Asja drank like she smoked, Mama thought; anxiously,

as if unable to believe she was really doing these iniqui-
tous things.

'It is true, Mama.'

'Oh God! Oh God in Heaven! Oh Mary, what to do?
She's just a child.'

'Only to you, Mama. She's eighteen years old.'

'But she's backward. Everyone knows she's backward.
You know she's backward, Asja.'

'Everyone who is taken to Szucha Avenue pretends to
be backward, Mama.'

'Oh, God! Asja, *help* me. Help Christina. She loves
you, Asja. These last two years, she only smiled for you.
You cannot just let her die.' Mama leaned across the
table. 'I gave you a home, Asja. I gave you my eldest
son. I've always treated you as a daughter.'

'There is nothing I can *do*, Mama.'

'You can go to them, Asja. You can explain. About
Christina being weak in the head. About . . . about it being an accident. Yes, that's it. That man Weiss wasn't
actually in the room when it happened. He doesn't *know*
what happened. There were only the four of us. We're
Janskis. We'll stick together. We'll swear it was an accident. You must go and tell them.'

'No, Mama.' Asja's face was cold.

'You're afraid,' Anna Janski whispered.

'Yes, Mama. I am afraid.'

'You, Asja? You're not afraid of anything.'

Asja raised her head. Her cheeks were flushed. 'You
have been saying that, and Josef and Liese and Christina
and Frederic have been saying that, for five years. Why
do you keep saying it, Mama? Is it because you are all so
afraid that even second hand courage is important to you?
Afraid! God, how I am afraid! Of so many things. Of
you. Of Liese. I was afraid of Antoni. I'm afraid of illness, of pain, of being embarrassed. I'm afraid of men.
I'm afraid of thunder, Mama. I'm afraid of dying. And

227

most of all I'm afraid of the Gestapo. Oh God, how I am afraid of them.'

Anna Janski stared at her, the tears suddenly disappeared. Then she divided the last of the wine. She patted Asja's hand. 'We are all afraid. It is human to be afraid. But the Gestapo aren't going to trouble you, Asja. There is no suggestion that you had anything to do with Paul's death. All you have to do is to explain about Christina, so they will understand.'

'You have not the right to ask me to do this, Mama.'

'No right? No right?' Anna Janski stood above her. 'And who do you think has protected you and looked after you these four years? Who stepped in and prevented Colonel Bruckner sending you off to the Russians? Who has treated you as one of the family, no matter how bad things have become? You, not even an Aryan. You belong in a labour camp in Germany. But we have kept you here, and fed and protected you. How do you think that was done, Asja? I don't suppose you have thought about it at all. People like you, poor people, just suppose that wealthy people rub their hands together and money mysteriously appears. Or perhaps you think Anton is doing a thriving business with his little pieces of wood? He sells them now and then, to soldiers, as souvenirs. Perhaps you think the money the army pays me for occupying my house is enough to live on? With prices the way they are? We have been living off capital these last four years, Asja. Our savings, Anton's and mine. Not yours. We have been making ends meet by dipping into the money we were going to enjoy in our old age. To feed you. There is very little left. But we will go on sharing it with you, looking after you protecting you from the race laws, for as long as we have to. And now I ask you to do this little thing for me. And you are afraid! I hate you, Asja. I loathe and despise you. The Fuehrer is right. He has always been right. You Slavs are an inferior species.'

Asja left the room.

'The battalion will defend this position to the last man, the last bullet.' Kolisch grinned. 'How often have they told us that, Frederic?'

Frederic nestled in his rifle pit, on a layer of snow which even his body heat could not melt. The temperature was dropping as the morning advanced, instead of rising. Above them the sky was a vast, cloudless mauve, with the minutest drop of yellow far away to the south-east. Two years ago they had pointed at that sun with childish wonder. Two years ago they had expected each day to get warmer, at least up to noon. Two years ago they had been afraid of frostbite. Now they dug themselves into the snow, made themselves snug, peered across the white plain, not a square inch of flesh visible, even their eyes concealed by goggles.

Behind them the town reminded Frederic of pictures he had seen of Ypres during the first world war. The Luftwaffe had started the destruction in June 1941. How long ago that seemed. How long in the past had his first visit to this town been. But they were here again, and only a couple of marches away was the Lithuanian border. Next door to Lithuania was Poland.

They heard the aircraft at the same moment, and Kolisch pointed it out, flying slowly over the town, not high, wheeling and turning. 'Bastard,' Kolisch said. Frederic thought of a vulture, waiting.

The aircraft angered them more than anything else. Three years ago there had been no Russian aircraft at all, and no single German planes, either. There had only been squadron after squadron, rising in the west, disappearing to the east. But now a single Russian reconnaissance machine could spend all morning photographing the town, ascertaining whether it too had been abandoned, or whether it might be defended in force.

A dog barked eerily in the distance. 'Some bastard will have a good dinner,' Kolisch said. 'You keep dogs, Frederic?'

'My mother never allowed any animals in the house.' He resented that now. He was fighting for her side, and still he hated her.

'I'm going to breed dogs one day,' Kolisch said. 'Better than breeding humans to be shot up.' He rubbed his scarf with his gloves. Yesterday they had sat in the baths, and their clothes had been disinfected. Today the temperature was twenty below, and the lice were back. 'Special breed, Russian lice,' Kolisch had said. But he had said it last year, when it had still been possible to joke. 'You know what,' he said now. 'You and me, and old Hans, are the only members left of the original company.'

'You make it sound as if they'd all been killed.'

'Might as well. When your hands go like Wohnt's you never use them quite the same. And what about poor old Walbrodt, eh? Imagine that sod blind. I can just hear him, stomping up and down the hospital, shouting, "Out, out, up, up". Maybe the ones who stopped a bullet were the lucky ones.'

Frederic gazed along the barrel of his rifle. The snow was empty. Still.

'Supposing something turns up, Frederic, and we get out of this mess, what do you mean to do afterwards?'

'Let's get there first.'

'Get where, that's the point. You went to Warsaw for your leave. I went to Hamburg. By God!'

'We blew London flat. And other English cities.'

'Not that flat. And they're still coming, every night. I'll tell you something. I felt safer when I was back here.'

'Well it looks to me like they followed you.' Frederic pointed at the aircraft, rising out of the east.

230

IV

Asja shaved her legs. Liese always shaved her legs when she had an important date. Then she put on her best black underwear, her last pair of silk stockings, buffed her black suède courts with the silver buckles. She brushed her hair until it shone, and each wave slipped gently into the next. She put on her black dress, tied her head in her black silk headscarf. She frowned at her coat, so shabby; but so was everyone else's coat. She pulled on her black gloves, left her handbag in the drawer. She was going to need neither lipstick nor money.

She stood in front of the mirror. Asja Janski, dressed to kill. That was backwards. Her throat was dry, but she dared not take a drink of water. If she was certain of anything it was that she was enjoying her last moments of privacy, as a woman, as a human being. She took a sip of brandy instead, held it in her mouth for a long minute, allowed it to slip down her throat, caress her stomach. Her stomach needed caressing.

She opened the back door, stepped into the cold. She put her hands in her coat pockets, walked round the house, and on to the snow-covered road. She did not wait for the bus; it ran very late, in winter, and it was always full of German soldiers. So she walked, in high heels, through the snow.

Why? she wondered. Not because of what Mama had said. She had known how Mama had felt about her long before her marriage. Not because of what she had said to Frederic, either. She regretted saying it. She had thought, maybe, after she had said it, he would still take her in his arms. But she had said it too well, too convincingly. Still, it was not because of that. It was because she had known, for four years, that she must die in this war. Frederic had deflected her away from that certainty, had made her believe it might be possible to survive under the Nazis. But Frederic had been a delusion. The death of little Antoni should have taught her that. Instead, she had held on for two more years, still pretending there might be a sunrise somewhere. Now she knew how foolish she had been. Nazi night, communist night, each was black, each had no dawn.

Besides, now she could die usefully. She did not know if anything she could do would help Christina. But she wanted to be with Christina. Now and always.

She supposed she was choosing a particularly horrible way to commit suicide. There were enough drugs in the house for her to have retired to bed and stayed there. But suicide was a deadly sin. It could not be undertaken in the comfort of your own bed. This way, she would suffer, and the fact of her suicide would be known only to herself. But it *was* suicide. It was essential for her to remember that there could be no surviving this walk, that even to think she *might* survive this walk was out of the question. She had to understand that she was, as of this moment, dead. That whatever was going to happen to her over the next twenty-four hours, over the next twenty-four days, perhaps, was happening to a corpse, and therefore had no meaning. If she could remember this she would be able to sustain her dignity to the end. To die with dignity was very important.

People stared at her. Asja Janski, dressed all in black, walking along a snow-covered Ujawdowskie on a February afternoon, was always worth a second glance. A soldier spoke to her. She ignored him, continued on her way, and at last saw the barbed wire in the distance, the swastika flag fluttering in the breeze off the river.

She approached slowly. For how many dreadful nights had she dreamed of this place. She wondered if it were possible to see into the future in your subconscious. If

232

all her dreams had been leading her to this street. And now she was here, she was conscious less of fear than of excitement.

The sentry watched her approach, his gloves tight on his rifle barrel. He was looking at a handsome woman, admiring her legs and yet instinctively mistrusting her, because this was Szucha Avenue and she was a Pole and he a German, wondering if perhaps the hands in her coat pockets were each clutching a grenade, turning towards her in open-mouthed surprise as she crossed the street.

Her throat was dry again, but the taste of the brandy lingered. She felt sick. She said, 'I wish to speak with Obergruppenfuehrer Reitener.'

The sentry backed away from her, bayonet thrust at her belly, picked up the telephone inside his box, spoke in German. Asja stamped her feet. Her shoes were coated with snow, and she could no longer feel her toes. But cold toes were scarcely material when you were dead.

The door behind the sentry opened, three men came out. They wore black uniforms, and did not look un-pleasant. The Gestapo never looked unpleasant. 'Come here, Slav.'

Asja walked forward, shoes silent on the snow. The sickness spread, outwards from her stomach.

'Inside.' The man pointed to the open door.

Asja stepped inside. The corridor was bare stone. But it was warmer than the air on the street. She waited, drawing long breaths to settle her stomach. Behind her the door shut with a bang. Asja Janski had entered her tomb.

'Put your hands flat on the wall,' said the man.

Asja obeyed, leaning forward from the waist. The man stood close to her head, staring at her. She could smell the tobacco on his breath. Hands moved over her body, lifting her coat and skirt and petticoat to her waist, slid-ing over her thighs, between her legs, round her belly and up under her breasts.

233

'What do you wish with the Obergruppenfuherer?' asked the man beside her head.

The fingers pulled off her headscraf, ran deeply into her hair, disturbed the smooth waves, scratched the scalp.

'I have information,' Asja said.

The man standing beside her brought up his closed fist, slamming into her stomach with a force that lifted her from the ground; she felt herself kneeling, her face scraping against the stone. Her heart hammered on her throat, clamouring for release. She thought she would strangle before she managed her first breath. The fingers were taking off her shoes.

'Informers do not come to us,' said the man who had hit her. 'We go to them.'

Asja panted, licked her lips. The fingers had stopped prodding and stroking. 'I am not an informer,' she gaped. 'I wish to confess to the murder of Colonel von Bardoman.'

She became terribly aware of boots. They seemed all around her, and, above the boots, voices spoke in German. Then one of the boots kicked her in the thigh. 'Up!'

She drew herself up the wall. The floor was cold on her stockinged feet. She shook her head to throw the hair from her eyes.

'There.' The man pointed to the steps. She walked in front of them. The pain in her stomach was receding, her breathing was almost normal again. She thought she had scored a minor victory; they were surprised, disturbed.

She went down the steps, found herself in another corridor. But this one smelt unpleasant; unwashed bodies mingled with disinfectant. Halfway along there was a table, on which rested a radio set; the radio played softly, music which dulled other sounds. There were other sounds, but she could not be sure exactly what they were.

'Into the tram.'

She went through a doorless opening. Here was a large

cell containing a dozen benches, arranged in two rows. here were six people already here, three men, two women, and a boy. They sat on the benches, upright, their backs to the door, staring at the inner wall. When Asja came in the boy turned round to look at her. One of the guards stepped past her, slashed his whip across the boy's head. The boy screamed, fell to the floor. 'Up!' The guard hit him again, three times. The boy struggled back to the bench. He wept, and blood trickled down his neck; he whimpered as he tried not to make a noise. 'Sit still. You! Sit there.'

Asja sat down. The whip thudded across her shoulders, penetrated coat and dress to burn her flesh. 'Sit straight!'

Asja sat very straight. She stared at the back of the woman in front of her, and beyond the woman, at the wall. It was very cold down here, beneath the street, but she was sweating. She listened to movement behind her. But she did not turn her head.

Kolisch raised his head. 'They've gone.' The ground still seemed to shudder, the air was still filled with the whine and the thud of the bombs. But the planes were gone. Frederic rubbed his ears, looked over his shoulder at the town. The planes had made no visible difference. When you bomb a rubbish heap you cannot create additional rubbish. Yet the difference was there. Men would have been killed, outright, and others would have died, inside. The ones who died inside were the worst. You spoke to them, you trusted them to take your places beside you and resist the enemy, because they seemed the same as yourself. But they were only shells of men, and without warning they would go mad, or run away.

Vice-Sergeant-Major Ziegler tramped through the snow. 'You all right, Berthold? Frederic?'

'We're immortal,' Kolisch said.'

'Well, stay awake.'

'Tanks?' Frederic asked.

Ziegler shook his head. 'I doubt it. Snow's too deep. But they'll want to get us out of here, so it'll be infantry.' He squatted beside the slit trench. 'When you see them, open fire, and then fall back to the perimeter. Fast! That's an order.'

He tramped on to the next outpost. Frederic stroked his gloved fingers up and down the barrel of his rifle. Just the three of them out of two hundred and forty. No, there were four of them; Captain Winz was a general now. He wondered what had happened to Captain Koehnlein. Koehnlein had been cut off with his patrol. Koehnlein was somewhere in Siberia. If he was still alive.

Kolisch fired, once, twice. The snow was moving, entire large masses of it, along the cratered road, over the snow covered fields. It moved slowly, but steadily. The Russians had come like this two years ago. Then they had been desperate and afraid. So they had been drunk with vodka, and had staggered towards the line, shrieking their 'Ourrah!' 'Ourrah!', on more than one occasion driving elderly civilians in front of them. Such a method of waging war had been utterly repulsive. But it had been less terrifying than this advance. Now the Russians no longer needed vodka, and they no longer needed shields.

'Let's go!' Kolisch scrambled out of the slit trench, ran for the line of rifles behind him. Bullets kicked up puffs of snow from his heels, and to left and right the German machine guns began to chatter in reply.

Frederic watched him jump over the barricades, the heaped stones and piled ration boxes, disappear into safety. The Russians were much closer, their faces visible now, a long jostling line of red across the snow. And he could hear their shouts. He drew a long breath, climbed

236

out of the trench, ran for the line. He fell. He sat on the snow, listening to the rattle of the machine guns, watching the blood oozing from his trousers, already coagulating in the freezing air. He felt only surprise. To have survived two and a half years with his most serious injury the shallow scalp wound from the booby-trap, and now to be shot in the leg.

The Russians were very near. Frederic crawled, and Ziegler left the barricade and ran towards him, followed by two other men. They seized Frederic's arms, dragged him across the snow. Other men leaned over the parapet to pull him to safety. He dropped to the ground. 'My rifle!'

'I have it,' Ziegler said. 'You get to the rear.'

'Rear, hell,' Frederic gasped. 'I don't feel a thing.' He put his good leg on the ground, pushed himself upright. Ziegler placed the rifle in front of him. He closed his hand over the trigger, watched the bobbing faces coming closer.

V

'Up, Slav!' The whip cracked across Asja's shoulders, dragging them straight, bringing her head back. Of course she had not been asleep. No one could sleep in the tram. Rather had she been in a state of self-mesmerism. The pain in her buttocks, the pins and needles in her feet, had merged.

'I said up.' The guard seized her arm and jerked her to her feet. Her knees gave way, and she knelt. The whip seared across her back.

'No!' she shouted, and hated herself. She had not meant to cry out. No matter what happened. You could not be hurt when you were already dead. But if she did not get up he would hit her again. She held on to the

237

bench in front of her, reached her feet. Her shoulder
brushed the woman sitting on the bench. The woman
never moved.

She went into the corridor, placing each foot in front
of the next with a conscious effort, praying for her life to
return to her muscles. The radio hummed on the table.
'In there.'

She entered an office. There was a desk, behind it a
cupboard. An officer sat at the desk, writing; his cap and
belt hung from a stand behind him. In front of the desk
was a stool; the legs of the stool made an X, and rose
above the seat to form the arms.

'Name?' The officer did not look up.

'Asja Janski.'

'You will address me as Herr Hauptsturmfuehrer. Occupation?'

'I am the widow of a Polish air force officer, Herr
Hauptsturmfuehrer. I live with my mother-in-law in
Rokonow.'

The officer raised his head. He was not Reitener. This
man was very much the Prussian. He even had a scar on
his cheek. 'Why are you shaking, Frau Janski?'

'I have been sitting still too long, Herr Hauptsturmfuehrer.'

'But you are not afraid?'

'Yes, I am afraid, Herr Hauptsturmfuehrer.'

'Why have you come to see us?'

'I wish to see Obergruppenfuehrer Reitener, Herr
Haupsturmfuehrer.'

'He is not here. And if he were you would not see him.
You have to see me instead. So, now, tell me why you
are here?'

Reitener had been only a dream. Because he knew
Frederic. Because he had smiled at Frederic. But very
possibly this man would also smile at Frederic. 'I wish

238

to confess to the murder of Colonel von Bardoman, Herr Hauptsturmfuehrer.'

'Christina Janski murdered von Bardoman.'

'No. I did, Herr Hauptsturmfuehrer.'

'Her fingerprints were on the gun.'

'She picked it up afterwards, Herr Haupsturmfuehrer.'

The officer laid down his pen, leaned back in his chair, looked her up and down. 'And having thought it over you have decided you cannot let an innocent girl suffer for your crime. You are not afraid, Frau Janski. You are a very brave woman.'

'Christina is my sister-in-law, Herr Hauptsturmfuehrer.'

The officer lit a cigarette. 'Von Bardoman's murder was the work of the resistance. Christina Janski was their instrument. Are you confessing that you are also a member of the resistance?'

'No, Herr Hauptsturmfuehrer. It was the work of an impulse. It was the thought of Liese marrying a German.'

The officer pointed. 'You are not a Pole. Where do you come from?'

'I was born outside the village of Zabie, Herr Hauptsturmfuehrer. I am a Huzulin.'

'The Huzuls are subhuman shitbags. Say it.'

'The Huzuls are subhuman shitbags, Herr Hauptsturmfuehrer.'

'And you, a Huzulin, think you can waste the time of the Schutzstaffel? I wish the names of every member of your group.'

'I belong to no group.'

The officer got up, came round his desk, staring at Asja. He walked behind her, and she tensed her muscles. Even so she was taken by surprise when he pressed the lighted cigarette into her neck, where it joined her shoulder. She inhaled, and seemed unable to stop, so that she visualised her lungs expanding until they exploded.

'Stand to attention.'

239

Asja obeyed.

The officer returned behind the desk, opened the cupboard. With the air of a child taking out his most prized toys, he laid on the desk a short, thick stick, a longer stick with a leather thong attached, and what looked like a telephone box, with a handle attached. From the box protruded two thick wires, each of which ended in a small toothed clip. The officer sat down. 'You belong to me, Huzulin. I wish you to understand that. Every inch of your body, every cell in your brain, is mine. There can be no appeal, no relief for you unless you answer my questions. Do you understand what I am going to do to you?'

Asja gazed at the magneto, licked her lips. 'I have no group,' she said. You cannot hurt a dead woman, surely.

The radio suddenly gained in volume, blaring forth with jazz music.

The exhaustion of battle, Frederic thought, has no equal. The emotional flashpoint, compounded of courage, hatred, fear, despair, self loathing and sheer physical energy, saps a man as nothing else could possibly do. He lay on his rifle, against the half-destroyed parapet, and stared across the white plain. It looked white now, because of the darkness. But only an hour ago, just before sunset, it had been a churned surface of white and red and brown. The bodies had lain in clusters right up to the earthworks; one lay immediately under Frederic's rifle, an 'Ourrah!'-shrieking Russian whom Kolisch had shot at close range.

How long ago had that been? One hour? Two? The Russians had come four times, and four times they had been repulsed. This was Verdun, the Marne, the assault on the Malakov, or on Hougoumont Farm, all over again. This was a shameful waste of life. But these Russians had not been drunk.

240

He moved, slowly, painfully. At some time during the afternoon the medics had come along and bandaged his leg. They had cut their way through his thick winter pants to reach the wound, and then they tied a piece of felt round his leg, outside the pants. No use in patching up a man's leg if it then dropped off from frostbite. As if that were possible. He sweated. The sweat turned solid as it left his pores, hung from his face like snow. But he was still sweating.

Ziegler stood behind him. 'Are you all right, Frederic?'

'Immortal, that's us,' Kolisch said.

'I'm beginning to believe you. Anybody else?'

'Yes, Sergeant-Major,' said another voice out of the darkness. And then another.

'Get your gear and follow me.'

'You mean we've orders to pull out?' Frederic asked.

'Not this time, Frederic. But we haven't the strength to hold the perimeter any longer.'

Frederic limped. Kolisch put his arm round his waist, and they trailed into the darkness. 'Looks pretty grim, this time,' Kolisch said. 'Had to happen, I suppose.'

'We'll hold,' Frederic said. 'We always have done. Reinforcements will be up in the morning.'

'That's what they said at Stalingrad.'

In the centre of the town there was a cluster of buildings: the town hall, the post office, the police station. Here walls still stood, and stone foundations still protruded, and, more important, cellars were still intact. Here they sat and waited. It was difficult to estimate, in the darkness, but Frederic figured maybe three hundred men. Only one officer, Captain Wagner. An appropriate name, Frederic thought, for the end of the battalion. He knew Kolisch was right. The last of the civilians had fled. They waited out there, in the snow, for the Red Army to complete its job.

They listened to the rattle in the distance. 'They've got

241

tanks up, after all.' Kolisch rose to his knees. The town centre rustled, a gigantic mechanical stirring. The battalion loaded the last of its anti-tank guns, armed the last of its machine guns. Men took their places amidst the stones, waited. Frederic was suddenly content. Here he was going to die. He had run away from his first tank; his last would kill him. And he was going to die amidst rubbled buildings. For two years he had hunted men and women through such destruction. Men and women who had only been trying to defend their homes. For two years the knowledge had been growing within him that half an hour on the stool beside Rosenthal had been preferable to this. For two years he had resisted the knowledge, accepted the vague certainty that only life was important. But now the wheel had come full circle, and he would die, amidst the stones.

A tank rolled up the street, sifting through the snow, cannon staring into the square. Captain Wagner gave the order; the anti-tank gun fired. The shot ploughed into the rubble. The tank stopped, another appeared beside it, and they opened fire together, with machine guns as well as cannon. Tracers cut through the darkness, the small-calibre shells burst like firecrackers amidst the defenders. But they weren't firecrackers, and already the anti-tank gun was dead, thrown on its side amidst the ruin of its crew. Now there were half a dozen tanks, occupying the heads of all the streets which converged on the square, firing at point-blank range into the German position. Frederic lay on the ground, his rifle underneath him, pressed close to a stone buttress. The world became a place of noise, bangs and whines and screams and thuds and flashing lights. But here he was safe, until something hit his barricade. Until Frederic died.

VI

The sound of the peephole opening made Christina start. For the wall exactly opposite the peephole was pitted and torn by bullets, and beneath the gashes in the brick were brown stains, spreading down to the floor. She hoped they weren't going to shoot *her*. The radio still blared in the corridor. That meant they were questioning someone; they had turned the volume high when they had been questioning her. On the other hand, they might also turn the volume high when they intended to shoot someone.

But as she listened the sound of the radio dwindled to a murmur, and she heard the rasp of the bolt being drawn. She knelt on the cot, the blanket wrapped round her shoulders; it was very cold. The door opened, and Asja collapsed on the floor. The guard threw her clothes and shoes after her, slammed the door. The peephole closed.

Asja's eyes were clamped shut, but even so tears leaked out from under her long lashes, dribbled down the full cheeks, dripped from the strong jaw. She made no sound, but crouched on the floor like a frightened dog. Her hair was soaked in sweat, and lay plastered against her shoulders. There were black marks on her breasts and on the insides of her thighs.

'Asja!' Christina cried. 'Oh, Asja!' She put both arms round Asja's waist, and Asja shuddered. Christina helped her on to the cot, spread the blanket over her, added the shabby black coat. 'Oh, darling Asja,' she whispered. 'Don't take it so hard. It's over. At least for now.'

Asja's eyes opened. The whites were streaked with blood, and the pupils gazed at Christina as if they were staring into a powerful electric bulb.

'They questioned me too. For hours, it seemed, although I suppose it wasn't very long.'

243

Asja made a noise which might have been a sigh. Her head slumped to one side. Her back touched the wall, and she winced, then lay still, gazing at Christina.

'I called them names,' Christina said. 'Uncle Jan taught me ever so many names I've never dared use. Every time they turned on the current I called them another name. They were *furious*.'

Slowly, very slowly, Asja pushed herself into a sitting position, back against the wall.

'Of course, I was really scared,' Christina confessed. 'But I wasn't going to let *them* see that. So the angrier they got with me, the angrier I got with them. It was easy, really. I've always become angry when I'm hurting. Did you become angry, Asja?'

Asja drew the back of her arm across her eyes.

'Oh, Asja, darling, I'm so glad you're here. I was so lonely. Do you think they'll arrest Mama and Liese too? I wouldn't like to think of them questioning Mama. But Liese, she'd deserve it. Did you know Liese is a virgin, Asja? I bet you never knew that. She keeps a diary, you know. Has done for years. And when she's out I read it. And she always puts down everything, like when she wanted to, so badly. Especially with Paul. But she never did. She never had the guts. Oh, I hope they arrest Liese.' Christina put both arms round Asja's neck, kissed her on the cheek, leaned back, frowning. 'Why are you staring at me like that, Asja?'

Asja smiled, an incredulous glow coming through the utter collapse of her face. 'I was just thinking, sweetheart. I'm glad I'm here too, with you.'

'Fritz! Hey, Fritz!' The voice, issuing through the loudspeaker, wailed eerily across the night. 'You are surrounded, Fritz. The rest of your army is miles away by now, and they are not going to come back. You have been abandoned, Fritz. If you wish to save your lives you must come out now. Come out with your hands behind your heads. Walk into the light, Fritz. We have food and drink here, warm clothing, and blankets. Walk into the light, Fritz.'

A single beam played across the charred rubbish heap which had been the town centre; it was snowing again, and the flakes cut through the beam and lay softly on the dead bodies and the empty cartridge cases and the discarded helmets and equipment. Behind the light the darkness was utter.

'Bastards,' Ziegler said.

'But if we *are* surrounded, Sergeant-Major,' someone said.

'There'll be a relief, come morning.'

They occupied what had once been a kitchen, and the air was heavy with the fear sweat which always seemed so much more pungent than any other odour. Frederic crouching on the left of the line, his rifle on a shattered window-sill, counted a dozen men beside him. He wondered how many other pockets of Germans were scattered about the town. He wondered, too, at his lack of emotion. Presumably he was afraid. Certainly he was sweating like the others. But he was conscious only of exhaustion. He wanted to die, for the sake of being able to close his eyes.

'Fritz!' said the voice. 'This is your last chance, Fritz. The army is moving on, Fritz. In one hour's time this town will be in the hands of the partisans, Fritz. There will be no surrendering to them, Fritz. Surrender now, and live.'

'Look there,' someone said.

A man walked into the light, a gaunt, ragged figure, distinguishable as a member of the Wehrmacht only by his helmet. His gloved hands were clasped on the back of his neck, and even from a distance they could see that he shivered as he walked, as the snow and the glare of the searchlight swept across his face.

245

'And there,' Kolisch said.

Now there was a crowd, in small groups of tens and twenties, shambling through the snow-muck, reaching the light and disappearing into the darkness. They made Frederick think of specks of dust being sucked into the maw of a vacuum cleaner.

'Sergeant-Major?' someone asked.

Ziegler sighed. 'Any man who wants to surrender can do so.'

Three men left immediately, without a word, slinking through the doorway and across the square towards the light. Six more followed.

'But you're staying, Hans?' Kolisch asked.

'If I'm going to die,' Ziegler said, 'it'll be right here. Not in some bloody Siberian salt mine.'

'You figure there's a chance?' Frederic asked.

'There's always a chance. You heard what the Russkie said. They're just as thin on the ground as we are. And there's nothing left in this town to keep the partisans hanging around. If we can sit it out for forty-eight hours they'll have pushed on too. Then we'll move out by night and try to regain the line. It's not far. The Captain told me the division is entrenched just beyond the river. That's to be our defensive position until the thaw. Our job was to hold this town while they got dug in.'

'Then we stay with you,' Kolisch said. 'Eh, Frederic?'

'Yes,' Frederic said. He had no choice, anyway. He had seen enough of prisoner columns, Polish and Russian, to know what was involved. To survive the sort of march which lay ahead of Captain Wagner's company you couldn't afford to be wounded. 'But maybe we should take cover.'

'That's right,' Ziegler said. 'Grab as much ammo as you can, and we'll try the cellars.'

'And let's hurry,' Kolisch said. From outside there came a babble of conversation as the first Russians came

246

into the light, kicking their way through discarded equipment, checking flaccid bodies for signs of life. Frederic hugged two spare ammunition pouches to his chest and crawled back into the darkness, through another room, down stone steps, and through yet more rooms. The darkness seemed to close in on him. Ever since the explosion of the boody-trap he had hated cellars. He felt as if he had spent all his life crawling through a Russian underground. How strange, if one could crawl for ever, and come up in Warsaw.

'This is as far as it goes,' Kolisch said. In the darkness his voice seemed everywhere.

'You okay, Frederic?' Ziegler asked.

'Yes.' Frederic sat just inside the door. Here I sit and here I die, he thought. We have entered our tomb, voluntarily. You do not leave your tomb.

'Psst!' Incredibly, the hiss woke him up. His leg was stiff and aching, his body was chilled, and he was terribly thirsty, but he had been sleeping soundly. 'Is that you, Berthold?' he whispered.

'Listen.' Kolisch lay beside him. And now he could hear the scrape of feet, echoing through the cellars. He could hear voices, too. 'Think they're coming downstairs?' Kolisch whispered.

'I can't make out the words,' Frederic said.

'There,' Ziegler said. They could see the light now, shining down the steps, cautiously.

'We'll drop a few of them first,' Frederic said.

'We won't, you know,' Kolisch said. 'Once they're sure we're here they'll roll in a couple of grenades, and that will be that. You fellows ever do any reading?'

'For Christ's sake,' Ziegler said.

'I read a book once,' Kolisch said. 'It was called *The Scalp Hunters*, and it was about Indian fighting in the American south-west.'

'These aren't Indians,' Frederic said.

'Not much difference. Somewhere in the book the hero, a chap called Henry, I think, was stuck down a mine shaft with an old Indian fighter named Rube. And the Indians knew they were there and were getting set to smoke them out. So Rube said to Henry, "No use choking to death down here. We may as well rush out with guns blazing." Henry thought that was a good idea. So Rube said, "Let's go," and Henry drew his six-gun and off he went, to be knocked down and captured. And guess what, Rube sat tight, you see, and the Indians, who knew there was somebody in there, but not how many, pushed off with Henry. Rube got away.'

'I'm not with you,' Ziegler said.

'Suppose two of us were to go out, shooting, take as many of them as we can with us. The chap who stays behind has a pretty fair chance of getting away with it.'

'So what do we do?' Frederic asked. 'Draw straws?'

'Straws are for kids,' Ziegler said. 'How old are you, Berthold?'

'Thirty-two.'

'I'm thirty-six. Frederic?'

'Well, I'm twenty-two.'

'And you have that Slav bit waiting for you.'

'No,' Frederic said. 'Not any more.'

'Well, then, you go get her back. What do you say, Berthold?'

Kolisch sighed. 'Makes sense.'

'No,' Frederic said. 'We draw lots or all three of us go out together.'

'You seem to be forgetting you're a soldier, Johansson,' Ziegler said. 'And I'm your sergeant-major. I'm ordering you to remain here until you have a chance of getting away, and then to make your way back to the division and tell the general what happened here. You understand me, soldier?'

'Yes, Sergeant-Major,' Frederic said instinctively.

'Then I'll wish you good luck.' Ziegler held out his hand.

'And to you, Hans.'

'Now you listen to me, Frederic,' Kolisch said. 'When you get out of this mess, and the war is over, you go to the States, boy. Germany's not going to be any place to live. Not Poland either, when the Russkies get through with it. You go west. And take this with you.' He passed his Colt revolver into Frederic's hand.

Sturmbannfuehrer Schmidt drank brandy. 'There was an air raid, and he never came. Kleist was left holding the raincoat and the bomb.'

'Then we will have to try again.' Reitener said. 'Next time we will succeed. I have applied for a transfer to Berlin. I would have done so anyway; this war is coming too close to home.' He tapped the file on his desk. 'Did you know Paul von Bardoman, Schmidt?'

'I've met him, Herr Obergruppenfuehrer.'

'Well, he's dead. Murdered by Christina Janski.'

'That half-witted child? I don't believe it.'

'She may be half-witted but she put two bullets in his spine.'

'My God! He was going to marry her sister Liese. A lovely girl.'

'So I'm told. Werner keeps trying to make it a political affair, but of course, as you say, we are dealing with a half-wit. I'll be glad to be out of it.'

Schmidt finished his brandy, massaged the glass. 'Herr Obergruppenfuehrer, what are we doing?'

'Our duty, Schmidt. Believe me, it is harder for me than for you. I worshipped that man. I thought he was a genius. I still think he is a genius. But the margin between genius and madness is too small. Germany was created by God to defend Europe against Asia, and any man who forgets that is a traitor to his race. And if the Fuehrer intends that Germany should be nothing more than his funeral pyre then he must be stopped.'

'I meant you and me, Herr Obergruppenfuehrer. When you consider what we *have* done. God, if we are ever called to account. I have nightmares about that. And people like Moltke and Stauffenberg loathe us. They are only using us because they need us.'

'They will always need us, Schmidt. And since when have you let personal considerations come between you and your duty? Now go on back to Berlin. I have work to do.'

Reitener drummed his fingers on his desk, studied the file. Christina Janski; Asja Janski. Frederic Janski; as if it mattered. Only duty mattered. To abandon duty now would be to follow Schmidt into a private hell of doubt and self horror. Or was he already in that hell, sent there by a force greater even than Germany, a force which had made him fall in love with a boy, who had sisters, who hated. He stubbed out his cigarette, picked up the telephone. 'Werner? Anything?'

'They slept in each other's arms,' Werner said. 'And spent this morning prattling like two schoolgirls. But they have both confessed.'

Why did he sweat over a personal matter when there were such tremendous events to be planned. He stuck a fresh cigarette in his mouth, flicked the lighter. 'This is a strange case, Werner. There is more to it than you'd suspect at first glance. I think I had better see the older one.'

'You, Herr Obergruppenfuehrer?' Werner's voice was incredulous.

'Up here. Immediately.'

'Yes, sir. And the girl?'

'I will have an order for her when you come up. Immediately, now, Werner.' He replaced the receiver, took a printed form from his desk drawer, wrote rapidly. He leaned back, pressed the bell on his desk. The door to his right opened, a good looking young man came in. 'You will go off now, Carl.'

'Now, sir?'

'I will not need you again this afternoon. Be back by seven.' Reitener watched the other door open. Asja Janski's clothes had been thrown on in a great hurry, and with her untidy hair she looked like a large rag doll. The officer walked at her elbow.

'Good afternoon, Carl,' Reitener said.

The young man gazed at Asja with undisguised hostility, bowed to Werner, went outside.

'Stand in front of the desk, Janski,' Werner said.

Asja stared at Reitener.

'Here is your order, Werner. See that it is carried out immediately.'

Werner clicked his heels, took the folded piece of paper. The door closed. Reitener gazed at Asja, saw Frederic beside her on the snow-covered pavement, his hand in hers. Had he been hurt by that? he wondered. Surprised? Envious? This was a woman made to suit Frederic, tall and strong. They would couple well together. Presumably they already had. Her face was strong, too. And undeniably handsome. Yet according to Werner she had collapsed completely when interrogated.

'Do you know who I am?'

'Obergruppenfuehrer Joachim Reitener.' Her voice was low. But it fitted the rest of her. He wished he had gone down to listen to her screaming. He could not believe it was possible.

'Why did you wish to involve yourself in so terrible a crime, Frau Janski? When you know your sister-in-law is guilty?'

251

'She is not strong in the head. She has been so since birth.'

'That is not a defence.'

'I came here to beg you for mercy. But I was not allowed to see you, and I knew that to beg for mercy from that ... that man would be useless.'

'And now you have met me?'

Her gaze was steady. 'My brother-in-law said he knew you. He said he thought you liked him.'

'He thought I liked him.' Reitener got up, opened the inner door. 'Go in there.'

She hesitated, then went into the sitting room. Her shoes seemed to stick in the sudden thickness of the carpet; her eyes took in the crimson drapes, the low-slung chandelier, the polished cherrywood of the piano.

Reitener closed the door, sat on the settee. He crossed his legs, lit a cigarette. 'There is brandy on the sideboard. Pour two glasses.'

Again she hesitated. 'You are amusing yourself, Herr Obergruppenfuehrer.'

He shrugged. 'If it is any consolation to you, madam, I have only once in my life ill-treated a woman, and then the circumstances were exceptional.'

Her tongue came out, slowly, circled her lips as she looked around the room. He thought it was impossible to discover true intelligence with true beauty. The one too often made the other unnecessary. She was bewildered. Hers was a strength which needed constant direction. She filled the two glasses and came towards him.

'Your health, madam. Are you afraid of me?'

'I think I used up all my fear, Herr Obergruppenfuehrer.'

Reitener smiled. Not afraid, apprehensive. Sufficiently intelligent to mistrust her surroundings, not sufficiently sophisticated to understand Carl's look. He remembered standing like her, a long time ago, before a man. But then both of them had known what was going to happen next. Now they were both uncertain. Both uncertain what they wanted to happen next. 'Then drink,' he said. 'I am glad you are not afraid. I have brought you up here because I know you are not guilty of any crime, Frau Janski. It was a very foolish, if very brave, thing to do. I enjoy talking to very brave people.'

The brandy brought colour into her cheeks. 'What will happen to Christina?'

'We will discuss her later. What we have to say about her depends on what we have to say to each other.'

Asja's nostrils dilated, and she looked very tired. She nodded.

'Good. So we understand each other. But frankly, Frau Janski, I can smell you from here. I like my guests to smell as sweet as they look. There is a bathroom through there.'

She turned her head, slowly. The colour spread to her neck. And his neck, too? His heart-beat had quickened. Because of Frederic? Or because of what Frederic had seen, of what Frederic must have seen, in this woman.

'There is hot water, and sweet-scented soap,' he said. 'And we will talk.' He got up, took the brandy bottle with him, led her into the bathroom.

A sound, seeping through the gloom of the cellar. A fresh sound, this, because for some time there had been no sound at all. Not since the screaming stopped. But Frederic did not dare think about the screaming; he had been able to identify every note. So instead he had thought about Asja. Thought about Asja so hard he had dreamed of her, except that her face had kept changing into Ruth's, and her body too. And now he had dreamed about Ruth-Asja so hard she was here. Surely.

'Frederic?'

There was a light, at the foot of the steps, and behind

253

the light there was a woman. And she was calling his name. Therefore he was dead. And that meant Ruth was dead too, and perhaps Asja as well.

His right leg was a sheath of pain. He pushed himself upwards on his left knee, wrapped his fingers round his rifle, moving slowly, carefully, anxious not to make a sound.

'Are you alive, Frederic?' The voice was clearer, now. And it was not Asja, because it spoke in Russian. A Russian angel, perhaps. Then he remembered Kolisch, screaming. There was no such thing as a Russian angel.

'Do not shoot me, Frederic,' the woman said. He could see her now, silhouetted against the light, a short, stocky figure in her thick winter clothing. Only the voice confirmed her sex. 'My name is Galina.'

His fingers, driven by surprise, cocked the rifle.

'Don't shoot,' she snapped. 'I have come to help you.' Now the light came towards him, flickering over the empty cellar. 'Don't you remember me, Frederic?'

'I have never seen your face,' he said. 'And it is not possible.'

'But I have seen your face, Frederic. Often. We have lived in your company for two years now, watching you. Watching your friends, too, Kolisch and Ziegler. And when they came out of the cellar yesterday I knew you would not be far. They gave their lives for you, Frederic.'

'I am not proud of that.'

'It is a matter for pride to have known two such brave men.' She knelt beside him, played the torch beam over his face, then down at his wound. 'I have some bandages and antiseptics upstairs.'

'How did they die, Galina?'

'Come,' She unfixed his bayonet, left it on the floor. 'Use your rifle as a crutch.' She put her arm round his waist, helped him to his feet. She exuded a variety of odours, none of them perfumed.

254

He hobbled across the floor. 'How, Galina?'

She sighed. 'When you die, Frederic, you die. It is a moment here, an eternity there. But it is a happy ending, perhaps.'

They climbed the steps into the kitchen. The cold leapt at him, seethed around his face. It had snowed again during the night, and the wrecked town had taken on a ghostly beauty. Except for Kolisch. He hung, upside down, from a broken wall, his head a few inches from the ground. He was naked, and he was dead. It was difficult to say whether he had frozen to death or bled to death. There was a great deal of blood, frozen to his body, dusted lightly over with snow. But he had been alive then they had cut off his toes, when they had castrated him and stuffed his genitals into his mouth.

Frederic sat down, vomited on the snow.

'There is no compassion left any more in Russia,' Galina said. 'None in the world, perhaps. Our people remember Tereskaya. And she was only one.'

He wiped his mouth on the back of his sleeve. 'Ziegler?'

'The sergeant-major was shot through the head and died instantly. He is over there somewhere. The children were using him as a sled.'

'As a . . .?'

'War is all they have known, some of these children, Frederic. This was your Fuehrer's wish.'

'But you do not hate, like the others.'

'You cannot imagine how I hate, Frederic. But I am an old woman. When I was Tereskaya's age I was tortured, much as she was. Although obviously I was not hanged, so perhaps I was more fortunate than she. But the men who raped me and treated me as a plaything were Russians. White Russians, we called them. But still countrymen. When your own countrymen have so treated you, hatred becomes a part of you.'

He turned his head, slowly. She had large cheek-bones,

and a thrusting chin. Here *was* strength. But the dominant features were lost in the lines, like drainage ditches, which streaked away from her eyes, carved downwards besides her nose, continued her mouth in a deep curve like a mandarin's moustache. And he realised they *were* drainage ditches, etched out by twenty years of tears. Wisps of hair peeped out from under her fur hat; it was a gentle silver. She looked perhaps seventy, except for the power in her hands and shoulders. But she had been a girl in the Civil War, say eighteen in 1920. She was a little younger than Mama.

She unwrapped his bandages with deft fingers. Her pack lay by the kitchen door, and from it she took lint, and even iodine. 'You may scream if you wish,' she said. 'No one will hear you. And I must hurt you. This is in a very bad state.' She poured.

Frederic did not scream. He wanted to, but no sound came. He doubted if he had the strength left to scream when they started to cut him up. 'I don't understand,' he said. 'About you.'

She smiled, moved the fur cap to show the red star on her hat. 'It is necessary to do something with your life. And to do it well. Without authority I could not be here.'

'And you, a commissar, will help a German soldier?'

'I owe you my life.'

'And now I owe you mine.'

She rebandaged his leg. 'Not yet, Frederic. But I will put you in my debt if I can.'

'Why?'

Galina thrust her hand inside her fur jacket, pulled out two cigars. 'I took them from your Captain Wagner.' She bit the end off one, chewed it, spat. She lit it, passed the other cigar and a box of Swedish matches to Frederic. She leaned against the kitchen door, sucked smoke into her lungs. 'I prayed for my life, once, by instinct, because I am afraid of death. You answered my prayer. I do not

256

now why. I had just killed one of your comrades.'

'I did it for Tereskaya.'

'That is *your* reason, Frederic. But it was my prayer. It made me think.' She smiled. 'You know, a good communist should not believe in God. Tell me, you are a German, or perhaps a Hungarian, or a Rumanian?'

'I am a Pole.'

'A Pole? That makes it better. We are hereditary enemies, you and I, Frederic. But we are also children of God. I think it is a good thing to acknowledge, now and then, between enemies.'

VIII

Asja shampooed her hair. She sat in the near boiling water, up to her shoulders. The heat scorched the cigarette blisters on her body, reawoke the dreadful tingling where they had attached the electrodes. And yet she was happy. How long was it since she had soaked in a hot tub?

Reitener leaned back on his chair, smoking a Turkish cigarette, sipping brandy, watching her. 'Tell me about Frederic.'

'We were going to be married.' What would she do when he touched her? Would she scream? Would every nerve end leap outwards, through her skin, as they had felt they were doing in the office downstairs? Did he mean to touch her at all? As a lover. Was this some yet more refined method of torture? Were there other implements of which she could not even dream in the next room? She wished Christina were here. It was so easy to be brave in Christina's company. When the cell door had opened and the guard had said, 'You! The Obergruppenfuehrer will see you,' Christina had giggled, and said, 'It's you for the ceremonial screw.'

'*Were* going to be married?'

Asja rinsed her hair. She had taken nearly an hour over this bath, had done everything she could think of. 'We quarrelled.' She watched him through the cascading water. 'It was the day he saw you in the car. Outside Rokonow cemetery.'

Reitener finished his brandy, stood up. 'He is a fool. You are a very beautiful woman, Frau Janski. And a very innocent one. Dress yourself and go home. I will write you out a discharge.'

He left the bathroom. Asja scrambled out of the tub, snatched a towel from the rail, followed him into the office. He gazed at the water running down her thighs to gather in a pool between her legs. 'Have you no shame, Frau Janski?'

For a moment she did not understand what he meant. 'You took it away from me,' she said. 'You Germans. I had shame, once. I think I did. When I was first married.'

He completed what he was writing. 'Go and get dressed. We do release people, you know. Now and then.'

'And Christina?'

He sighed. 'Christina killed a German officer, Frau Janski. I accept that it was an impulse rather than a plot. So I will not have her shot. But she will have to go to prison.'

'You mean a concentration camp?'

'Yes.'

'You cannot.' She fell to her knees beside his chair. 'Not Christina. She's just a child. Please, Herr Obergruppenfuehrer, send me instead. I would have killed Bardoman if I'd thought of it.'

Reitener stood up. 'You did not think of it, madam. And unlike Christina you have a purpose in life. Now get dressed and go home, and when Frederic returns from the front, marry him and make him happy. I give you that privilege. You may tell him so.'

But he was staring at her, kneeling, the water still spilling from her hair. How strange, she thought. She had seen lust in so many men's eyes when they stared at her. Here it was absent. No lust. But something else, she had never seen before in a man's eyes.

She stood up, and he turned away from her, went into the sitting room. She dropped the towel, followed. He stood at the table, pouring himself a brandy. 'May I have one too?' she asked. She tossed her head to throw hair from her eyes, scattered water over his face. She took the glass from between his hands.

He put his finger under her chin, tilting her head backwards, looking into her eyes. 'Melodrama,' he said. 'It is the curse of all Polish history, Frau Janski. And it accomplishes nothing. Did you not know that?'

No lust. But desire. Inverted desire. Joachim Reitener, probably the most powerful man in all Poland, wanted to surrender, to a Huzulin.

She put her arms round his neck, kissed him on the mouth. She drove her tongue to the back of his throat, thrust her hands down to his thighs. She had submitted for so long. But now, on a sudden, she was the hunter. And like Reitener she was hunting herself. The jangling electricity which coursed through her body could only be relieved by sexual exhaustion.

She sat up. Now the bath water had dried, but still her body was wet, with sweat. As was his. And there was blood on his neck where she had bitten him. She could taste it on her lips. And still she seethed and wanted. He was no longer Reitener. He was Antoni, and Josef, and Frederic, and Brandt, he was Papa and he was little Antoni and Uncle Jan, he was the sentry on the door who had stared at her legs while he presented his rifle and he was Hauptsturmfuehrer Werner who had clipped the magneto to her body. He was the guards and he was Kopa. Oh, yes, he was Kopa. He was every man who had ever looked at her, every man she had ever feared, every man she had ever hated, every man she had ever wanted, lying here, under her hands, incredibly virginal, incredibly beautiful, incredibly responsive, bursting with latent desire, here, between her thighs, inside her belly.

She lay on the floor, gazed at the ceiling. The bed was above her, and he was on the bed. But now he was Reitener and she was Asja. And she was tired. Her strength had followed her fear, and drained away from her system. She sat up. 'Now execute me,' she whispered. 'And send Christina home.'

He got off the bed, stepped over her, walked into the bathroom. He returned with her clothes, dropped them on her. There was no self-desire left in his eyes. They were the coldest eyes Asja had ever seen. 'Christina left here over an hour ago,' he said. 'For Auschwitz.'

'It is a way of happiness,' Galina said. 'In war, in winter, it is the only possible way of happiness. When my group has been out in the winter night, and we return to our camp, the men each take a woman, and there is warmth, and comfort.'

Inside the sleeping bag there was warmth, and comfort. Outside the afternoon temperature had dropped to perhaps thirty degrees of frost. It was too cold to snow, and the snow itself was frosted over, hard and brittle. In the shattered kitchen the frost coated discarded rifles, crumpled haversacks, empty helmets. But inside the sleeping bag it was warm. How strange, Frederic thought, that I should find my first happiness with a woman old enough to be my mother, with death and destruction all around, with my life in ruins. Or perhaps you can only find true happiness when your life is in ruins, when there are no ambitions and no fears and even no hopes left to distract you.

'What do you think about?' Galina asked.

'I wish that time could stop, here.'

'Time never does that. Soon it will be dark, and we will make a move. How is your leg?'

'It'll hold up for a while.'

'And where do you wish to go?'

'I wish to regain my regiment. If it is possible.'

'They are beyond the river. I will take you to the river and show you a ford. You should reach them by tomorrow morning.'

'Why, Galina?'

She smiled. 'You will not accept my explanation? Perhaps you no longer believe in God. Well, neither do I. It is a difficult thing, to believe in God, in war.'

'God is there. God saved Russia.'

'There are a hundred million Russians would dispute that, Frederic.'

'God sent that rain and then that frost to bring our advance to a halt within sight of Moscow two years ago.'

'And are we, then, unaffected by rain and frost?'

'You are used to them.'

'And your Fuehrer chose to ignore them. There is nothing supernatural in that. Just human stupidity. Two days ago, Frederic, we took this town with tanks. When it snows your tanks sit by the roadside.' She kissed him on the nose. 'I have offended you.'

'No. You make me wonder where it will end.'

'With the destruction of Nazi Germany.'

'For me, Galina. Where will it end for me.'

'It will end where you wish it to end, Frederic.'

'You make it sound so easy. I am a private soldier. I am bound by rules and by laws, by superior officers. By an oath I took.'

'To Hitler? God will forgive you for breaking that oath. It ends where you wish it to end. Where do you wish it to end, Frederic?'

'In Warsaw.'

'You had a wife in Warsaw?'

'No. I had a fiancée. But we quarrelled.'

'Because you are fighting with the Germans? But you can still make it end in Warsaw, Frederic. Go to her.'

'Desert? I would be shot.'

'And are you not going to be shot here in Russia? At least you would die doing what you wish.'

'You don't know me, Galina. I have always been a coward.'

'I will tell you something, Frederic. I hate the Nazis. What your Wehrmacht has done here in Russia is the blackest page in history, and will remain so for all time. But I could call no man who has fought in this war a coward. And any man who has survived on this front for two years has to be a hero. It is sad, to see so much heroism, so much stamina, so much determination, wasted in the pursuit of so much horror, so much destruction, so much evil. You are a hero, Frederic, and you have it in you to be a good man, or you would not have given me my life two years ago. If I repay you for that now it is in the hope that you will die as what you are, not as what Hitler made of you.' She buckled her belt. 'It is nearly dusk. We will make a move now.'

Johnson sat at the bar, drank a whisky and soda. It was still light on the street, but Warsaw was relaxing for the evening. From the hotel dining room came the sound of swing music. They were dancing in there, swirling their short skirts, catching the eye with shapely nylon. Polish women were the most beautiful in Europe. Who had said that? Kolisch.

The woman behind the bar had missed the short-skirt era by several years. She wore a grey suit, lit a fresh cigarette from the stub of the last. Her hair was tinted red, her lipstick was thick. 'And what did you do today, Mr. Johnson?'

Johnson offered her a cigarette. 'I went out to Rokonow, and then I took a look at Szucha Avenue.'

She gave a mock shudder. 'A terrible place.'

'Were you in Warsaw during the war?'

She frowned, and then smiled; he was obviously much older than she. 'I spent the war in Cracow. I was only a little girl then, so I cannot remember much about it. But times were very hard.'

'Not so hard as they were in Warsaw, surely?'

'Perhaps. Things were very bad in Warsaw, at the end. There was nothing left.'

'I visited Warsaw before the war.' Johnson smiled. 'All I remember about it was a toyshop. A huge toyshop. Where they sold carved wooden ships, and soldiers. Lovely things.'

'Janski and Son. I went there once in 1938. I thought I was in heaven. Such toys. It was destroyed on the fist day of the war.'

'What a shame. The man who owned the store was very tall, as I remember, thin, mournful-looking.'

263

'They still call him the old toymaker.'

Johnson pushed his empty glass across the bar. 'Join me, won't you? Did you say still? He must be very old.'

She poured a more liberal measure this time. 'Oh, yes. He is what you call a character, eh? The old toymaker. Of course, he does not sell toys any more. But just after the war, when there was no money circulating, you would see him sitting on a street corner, with his tray of wooden soldiers. It was rather tragic, because once he was quite wealthy. He used to have a lovely house in Rokonow. Where you were today. But the Germans knocked it down.'

Johnson dried his fingers. The glass was wet. 'And this man is living in Warsaw now?'

'Oh, yes. Somewhere over in Praga. You know, on the east bank of the river.'

'He lives alone?'

'Oh, I don't know. You sometimes see him on the street with a woman. You should ask Adam. He parks his taxi right outside the hotel. He'll tell you about the old toymaker. He even knows where he lives.'

'Have another drink, on me.' Johnson left the bar, crossing the huge, high-ceilinged lounge, his heels echoing from the marble floor. He straightened his tie, drawing the knot tight so that his neck felt the collar.

6

Summer 1944

'Private Johansson!'

Frederic heard his boots hitting the floor. The vast room waited, hushed, save for the sound of his boots. The uniforms gleamed on every side; the nurses smiled, endless rows of equally brilliant teeth. But it was important to stare at the men in front of him. At *the* man in front of him. He halted, saluted. 'Heil Hitler!'

The Fuehrer raised his hand. It was hard to believe that not two weeks before he had escaped death by the thickness of a table leg. His right shoulder dropped, so that his whole body took on a lopsided appearance. And his face twitched. But the eyes still glowed. And now they were glowing at Frederic.

'Private Frederic Johansson,' the general read. 'Naturalised German citizen. Joined the Wehrmacht, April 1940. Served on the Russian front from June 1941 to February 1944, when he was severely wounded. Private Johansson was the only survivor of an entire battalion overrun by the Russians during the Battle of Vitebsk. With unsurpassed devotion to duty, Private Johansson, although wounded in the leg, concealed himself while his comrades surrendered, and after remaining hidden for forty-eight hours, with the Red Army all about him, made his way through the enemy ranks to rejoin his regiment.'

'I wish I had a few thousand more men like you.' Hitler stepped forward, hung the cross around Frederic's neck, adjusted the ribbon. It took him a long time, because his hands trembled. 'And your wounded leg, Johansson? It is well again?'

'Yes, my Fuehrer.'

'Then you shall have a week's leave before rejoining your regiment. You'll want to be in at the kill. When my new secret weapons are ready to go into action, and we begin our new thrust towards Moscow, eh?'

'Yes, my Fuehrer.'

Hitler nodded, glanced at the general. Frederic brought his heels together. 'Heil Hitler!' His boots hit the floor as he returned to the ranks. The ribbon rose above his collar, tickled his skin. Galina had said he was a hero, and now he was a hero, officially. He was alone, in the huge room, surrounded by hundreds of his comrades. During four months in hospital, in cleanliness and comfort such as he had never hoped to know again, he had at last convinced himself that Galina had never existed. He had no proof of her existence. She had been only a shadow in the cellar, and when she had returned he had been delirious. But if she had been nothing more than a figment of his imagination how was he able to remember her face, the feel of her body, so perfectly? And if he had been delirious how had he regained the German lines without help? So she was real. The feel of the ribbon made her real. But if Galina was real, then Ingrid had to be a dream. She waited for him now, as soon as the invalids were dismissed. She smiled, and her eyes laughed, and she kissed him on the mouth. 'I congratulate you, Private Johansson. I have never had a hero as a lover before.'

She was a Bavarian, like Mama. Her hair was black and short. Her features were crisp, and came together in an edge, but remained far too feminine to be dismissed as a hatchet face. Her eyes were black, and sparkled. She belonged in uniform; it was impossible to imagine her in civilian dress. She had joined the Strength Through Joy movement at twelve, had been a military nurse since seventeen, conducted her affairs with an amoral delight in physical satisfaction. But she could only be real if Galina

266

was a dream; and if Galina was real then so was Asja.

Dr. Antze shook his hand. 'This is the first engagement the Fuehrer has undertaken since his accident. And you are the reason.'

'One of the reasons, Herr Doctor.'

'Heroes should never be modest, Frederic,' Ingrid said. 'They should wear their heroism like a second skin.'

'Now tell me where you wish to spend your leave. I can give you a rail ticket to anywhere in the Reich.' Dr. Antze winked. 'How remarkable it is that Ingrid should also be due for leave. You should take her down to the Alps, Frederic.'

'I am going to Berlin,' Ingrid said. 'You come with me, Frederic, and we will honeymoon, eh?'

But the Iron Cross was growing heavier every moment, hanging like a millstone. 'I would like a ticket for Warsaw, Dr. Antze.'

The girl stood in the doorway, a pale shadow in the darkness. Josef reached beneath the pillow for his pistol, but even as he did so he knew what she was, what she wanted. The amount of blood in his arteries seemed to double.

'You are Colonel Kopa?'

Asja woke up. Josef could hear her breathing.

'Colonel Kopa is not here.' He put on his spectacles. 'I am Captain Janski.'

'Then I am to say this, that X day is tomorrow, 1st August, and X hour is five p.m. I wish you to repeat that, Captain.'

'Tomorrow, at five p.m. I had expected dawn, or sunset.'

'At five o'clock everyone will be on their way home from work. The streets will be crowded, so a few more will not be suspicious. Good luck.' The doorway was empty.

Asja's arms went round his waist. She was insatiable,

267

but she did not make love with tenderness. She was brutal. She pummelled his back. You could not exhaust Asja. You could only allay her anxiety for an hour, perhaps two.

He got out of bed, lit the candle. She lay on her face, her hair trailing forward to brush the floor. He wondered if she had understood what the girl had said, if she had heard what the girl had said. She had not left this room for four months. She had not seen daylight for four months. She had not put on her clothes for four months. And yet they had not tired of her. They had wanted her, so badly, so long, that when at last she had come to them they had not believed their eyes. Then they had quarrelled. She was Asja, and Asja had to belong. It had taken them a week to understand that this Asja was not the woman who had shared the studio two years before, that this Asja had become plural, in her senses, that no single man could ever possess her again, that for one man even to try would be to drive himself mad. Even together, share and share, they could not possess Asja.

Kopa came in. 'The girl was here?'

'Not ten minutes ago. I shall call you colonel now.'

'God! Give me a cigarette. So soon. So unexpectedly.' Kopa sat on the bed. His hands trembled.

Asja rolled on her side, reached for him. She made Josef think of a python, uncurling itself for its midday meal. Her eyes were dark pools. Her lips were tight shut. Asja parted her lips only to eat.

'Not now,' Kopa said. 'Not now, for Christ's sake, woman.' He freed himself, paced the room. 'It is too soon. Bor has allowed himself to be pushed into this. Too soon.'

'I heard the guns last night,' Josef said.

'A still evening. Rokossovsky is still a hundred miles away.'

'We have supplies for a week.'

'The AK may hold Warsaw for a week,' Kopa said.

'But we will not hold Rokonow that long. We will be isolated, and they will cut us off. You had no right to volunteer this group. I am the colonel. It should have been left to me.'

'Rokonow?' Asja asked. 'Are you going to Rokonow? The two men exchanged glances. From being a bedmate she had become a problem.

Asja got out of bed, emptied the last of the water into the basin, washed her face. 'That girl gave you a message, Josef. What did it mean?'

Josef looked at Kopa. Kopa shrugged, and nodded. 'It was from General Bor, Asja. The Home Army is going to seize Warsaw from the Germans tomorrow afternoon. The Russians will soon be here now. But we must take control of the city before the Reds come in.'

Asja dried her face. 'We are going to fight? After all these years? We are going to kill Germans openly, in battle?'

'Not you, Asja.' Kopa said. 'My command has been instructed to capture Rokonow, to control the road to the reservoir. There is a German barracks close to the reservoir. You know that, Asja. We have been given a suicide mission.'

'I am going to kill Germans,' Asja said happily. It was the first time she had smiled in four months.

11

There were fifteen people in a compartment intended to hold eight. But it was the 1st of August; the windows were opened wide and the breeze hurried stale tobacco and stale breath and stale sweat into the corridor, tugged at ties and ruffled skirts. And Frederic, being a soldier in uniform and wearing the Iron Cross, had the window seat. Ingrid sat on his knee, her elbows on the sill, eyes half

269

shut as she watched the trees racing by. 'I think you are mad.' The words came sideways from her mouth, reached his ear just before they were torn apart. 'The Russians are already at Brest.'

The breeze rippled her hair as if it were grass, close-cut and sweet-smelling. When she moved her bones hurt his thighs. 'It just doesn't make sense. You'll be sent there anyway, when you rejoin your regiment.' She leaned back against his chest, closed her eyes; there was a smut on her nose. 'Why take leave at all?'

The other thirteen people in the compartment, sitting on each other, leaning in the doorway, were civilians. They tried hard not to look at the handsome soldier and the pretty nurse. But they were so attractive to look at.

'There is someone I have to see in Warsaw.'

'You spoke of her often in the night, when you first came to the hospital.'

'What did I say?'

'You used to weep in your sleep. One should not weep when dreaming of a woman.' She nestled in his arms. 'You will never weep when dreaming of me.'

He clasped his hands on her lap. Just to touch her skirt gave him a curious pleasure. Down there, beneath the heavy drill and the two layers of thin cotton, were no lice, but only perfume and powder. He wondered if he would judge women for the rest of his life not on their looks or their intelligence or their clothes, but on their smell and whether they had lice.

Her ear nuzzled his lips. She lit two cigarettes, placed one in his mouth. He tasted her lipstick, as his hands, resting on her groin, felt her breathing. She was living the 1st of August, as she was planning to live the 2nd of August. But she had already forgotten the 31st of July, and she had no interest in the 3rd of August, nor would have, before tomorrow afternoon. This was her world.

What would happen to the Janskis when the Russians

270

came? Would the commissars remember that Anton Janski had fought against Tuchachevsky twenty-four years ago? Would they need to remember? Anton Janski was the most bourgeois of men. And he had a German wife, who had flown the swastika flag from her window. There would be many people to tell them that, as there would be thousands of people to tell them that Josef was the Nazis' official photographer, and hundreds of people who would remember Liese as the darling of the German officers, and even a few who would denounce Asja as their whore.

Ingrid sat up, threw the cigarette out of the window. 'We are coming into Berlin.' She turned on his knee, put her hands on his shoulders, kissed him on the mouth. She glared at the man sitting next to him. 'Look the other way, filthy swine.' She kissed Frederic again. 'Come with me.'

'I have to go to Warsaw. Just once more. I have to say goodbye to some people there. Not only the woman. All of them. I'm never going to see them again after this time.'

She pouted. 'They must be very important to you.'

'They are. Were. I couldn't just turn my back on them without saying goodbye. But I'll be there by tomorrow morning, and I'll be ready to leave by tomorrow evening. I'll get a train back. If I have to stand the whole way I'll be back again on Thursday morning. We'll still have five days. Will you wait for me, Ingrid?'

Her thighs brushed his face as she reached above his head for her bag. 'I'd intended to sleep the first twenty-four hours, anyway.' She rested the bag on his lap, sat on the knee of the man beside him, scribbled on a piece of paper. 'There's the address. I'll have a room on the top floor. I'm going to stay in bed until lunchtime on Thursday.' She adjusted her cap, chucked the man under the

271

chin. 'You want to get a girl of your own.' She squeezed Frederic's hand, wriggled through the other people, joined the throng in the corridor.

'You are very lucky,' said the man.

Frederic watched the platform; there was bomb damage to the roof, and the street beyond was cratered and rubbled. The crowd filed towards the barricades, trying not to look at the destruction on every side of them, trying not to think what it meant for them. Only Ingrid did not seem aware of her surroundings. She marched for the street, head held high. She did not look back, and the train was moving again. The time was four-thirty on the afternoon of Tuesday, 1st August 1944.

Liese knelt on the edge of the croquet lawn, plucked grass from around the rose bushes. Colonel Krause liked the flower beds to look nice, and there was a lot of rain about; the weeds were sprouting like beanstalks.

It was a magnificent afternoon, despite the cloudbank to the south-east. The Russian planes droned overhead but Liese ignored them. The Russian planes were a part of life nowadays, and they never bombed Rokonow. She wore her oldest slacks and a white cotton shirt and sandals. Her hair was tied in a knot on the back of her head. She felt sweat trickling down her neck, was pleasantly thirsty. Her face was hot. She seldom tanned, developed freckles instead. They were tiny freckles, and when she went out in the evening they were easily disguised by powder. But freckles were important during the day. All German women should have freckles, to show how healthy they were, how they enjoyed living in the open air.

Liese preferred weeding to housework, and now that only Mama and herself were left at home there was a great deal of housework to be done. But she could spend an entire afternoon kneeling on the croquet lawn, sheltered from the worst of the sun by the huge poplar over the front gate, knowing she was being admired by the sentry on the steps, thinking, planning.

What did you think about? You thought about the future. Mama had said, 'There is nothing for us here any more, and the Russians are coming. We will go to Germany, Liese. We will go and live with Kurt.'

Uncle Kurt was the only part of the past to be remembered. At Uncle Kurt's house in Munich she had first met German officers. She was still only twenty-four. Mama kept reminding her of this, kept reminding her that she had all her life in front of her. Mama thought it best for her to forget everything that had happened between that visit to Munich in 1938 and this summer. Mama was very brave. When she had told Liese that both Christina and Asja had been taken by the Gestapo and wouldn't be coming home again, Mama had never even cried. She had rested her hand on Liese's shoulder and said, 'Now there are only you and me, Liese. And Frederic. Us three out of all the Janskis.'

And when she had said, 'There are Papa and Josef too, Mama,' Mama had curled her lip contemptuously. 'Papa? I wonder if he has not entered his second childhood. And when last has Josef been out to Rokonow? Not since the girls were arrested. Oh, not him. Josef is afraid of his own shadow.'

So they three would begin a new life in Germany. It made the future exciting. Liese envisaged Germany as a beseiged city, defying the world. And she would be a part of it.

Her knees ached, and she got to her feet, stood at the gate. There were a great number of people on the street, and this was strange. Rokonow had always been a sleepy little place, and since the occupation had been sleepier yet, except for the German soldiers from the barracks near the reservoir. But these were civilians, walking in a

273

group, looking extraordinarily self-conscious. They knew they should not be here. She hoped they weren't going to demonstrate. Because then the soldiers would come along with machine guns and drive them away, and it would be terrible. Those things had happened once or twice in Warsaw, in the early days, but never in Rokonow.

She crossed the croquet lawn, looked over the hedge. There were people in the orchard, too, almost as many people as on the road, and as strangely dressed, for a warm August afternoon. The tall woman walking in front wore a black woollen dress and carried a winter coat over her arm. It occurred to Liese that if she had walked all the way from Warsaw dressed like that she must be sweating like a pig. The woman had red-gold hair, loose and untidy, blowing in the breeze. And the tall, fair man beside her wore spectacles. Asja and Josef were coming to Rokonow, accompanied by dozens of grim-looking people. But Asja? Asja was in a concentration camp.

She ran across the lawn, up the front steps. The sentry checked her. 'No, please,' she gasped. 'There is going to be trouble.'

She had given the signal. The afternoon exploded. Liese gazed at the fence. The people from Warsaw were lined up there, and they had dropped their coats and bags, and were pushing machine pistols and tommy guns and even revolvers through the uprights and firing. She was reminded of a vast fairground, with hundreds of holiday-makers standing at the shooting booths. But she was the target. The sentry struck her on the shoulder to throw her flat on the steps, and raised his rifle. He fired, once. Liese looked up. The sentry's body shuddered, his tunic turned pink, his knees gave way and he went rolling down the steps, thump, thump, thump. His helmet came off.

Liese stayed on her belly, wormed in the front door. Weiss the barman came running out of the drawing room, saw her there, hesitated. Feet thudded on the steps, subdued amidst the chatter of the tommy guns. The front door crashed back on its hinges, and Weiss turned to run. His white jacket became crimson, and he hit the floor as if someone had jerked his legs out from beneath him. Liese put both hands over her head, pressed her body against the skirting board, closed her eyes. Her bowels exploded with fear, and she hated herself. The floor trembled as people ran past her. Someone trod on her, and she moaned, but did not move. She inhaled gunpowder and dust. She heard Mama screaming. Were they killing Mama? She heard Colonel Krause shouting orders, and then his voice seemed to choke as it died away.

The noise became more distant, and she crawled for the drawing room, keeping her face pressed to the floor, using her knees and toes to propel herself along. Her head bumped into Weiss, sprawled across the doorway. She rose to her knees, and something hit her on the back with tremendous force.

III

'Out! Out!' Frederic awoke with a start. The train had stopped, and for a moment he was back in 1941, with Ziegler and Kolisch sleeping beside him, and Walbrodt looking in the door and shouting. But this man was not Walbrodt, and Ziegler and Kolisch were dead.

He climbed down. The night was very dark, but at some distance up the track he could see lights flashing, and even above the hissing of the engine there arose a hubbub of voices. But there had been no explosion, no gun-fire. 'What has happened?' he asked a shadow.

'They say the train is to go no farther.'

'Then where are we?'

'God knows, soldier. Somewhere in Poland. There is a town over there.'

275

He could see the shadow of a church steeple, of houses down the embankment, blacked out to conceal them from the Russian bombers. He shouldered his haversack, walked towards the lanterns. There was a station, and another train. The platform was crowded with men. 'Why are we stopped?'

'Find your section, soldier. They will tell you what to do.'

'I have no section, here. I'm just out of hospital.'

The sergeant-major raised his lantern, saw the Iron Cross at Frederic's breast. 'And you intend to take your leave at the front, soldier?'

'I have a pass for Warsaw.'

'Warsaw is off limits, as of now. There is some kind of a civil disturbance going on. Give me your name and number and I will find you a place on a train for Frankfurt.'

'Thank you, Sergeant-Major.' Frederic stepped into the darkness, walked along the line.

A man sat on the step of the last carriage. 'There is nothing beyond this train,' he said.

'But you have come here from Warsaw?'

'Just over there. We left at five o'clock yesterday afternoon.' He scratched his head. 'Got a cigarette, soldier?'

Frederic gave him a packet. 'What is happening there?'

'The partisans are attempting to take control of the city. So we were told to get the rolling stock out of Gdanska, and quick.'

'But *can* they? A few partisans?'

'More than a few, soldier. More than a few thousand. As to whether they can hold the city, now that is another matter.' The engineer's teeth gleamed in the darkness. 'This will be the end of the Home Army. They are like those things, what do they call them?'

'Lemmings?'

'That's right, lemmings. They are rushing towards a

national suicide. I have seen it coming for a long time. And the Fuehrer will show them no mercy this time.'

'Them?' Frederic asked. 'You are a Pole.'

'I was a Pole. I am a German now.' The man's voice was proud.

Frederic walked into the darkness. Now the hubbub behind him was dulled, and he could hear the growl of thunder in the distance. There was a storm over Warsaw. Wagner would have written the script, Chopin the music. I was a Pole; I am a German, now. You have always been a German, Frederic. No, I have always been a Pole. My blood tingles more to the names of Poniatowski and Kosciusko than to Bluecher and Gneisenau. I would rather follow a Pilsudkski than a Hindenburg.

What happens to historians when the past becomes the present, when it is no longer a matter of analysing a sentence in a book, when it becomes a business of living the sentence. He could see the sentence now. 'In a brief month's campaign, commencing 1st September 1939, the German armies conquered Poland. From then until occupied by the Russians, Poland was a German colony. There were abortive risings, by the Jews in the Warsaw ghetto in the summer of 1943, by the so-called Polish Home Army in the summer of 1944. Both were put down with ruthless severity by the German forces.' But what about the Poles?

He stared into the night. Over there, under a thunderstorm, a nation was dying. His nation. Because that would be the Poland he knew, and loved. Whatever survived, to be resurrected by the Russians, would be something else again. Perhaps it would become great, perhaps it would stay free, which Frederic Janski's Poland had not accomplished. But it would be a different country.

He walked towards the thunder.

Anton Janski sat on the floor, beneath the window of his

workroom. It was not altogether dark. The lightning flashed, and the guns flashed as well. The heaviest fighting was over at the reservoir. The Germans were trying to recapture the pumping station.

The rain teemed, sullenly; there was no breeze to hurry it along. It had started raining about an hour ago, and the accompanying thunder was so continuous it was difficult to isolate the gunshots. Earlier it had been a sultry August evening. It had promised the storm, well before dusk. And a storm had broken, well before dusk. He had watched them from his window, chopping down trees to use as barricades, pushing cars to the street corners, and there turning them over, boarding windows. He had watched the women hurrying to and fro, every one with a pistol on her belt, carting ammunition and food and medical supplies. He had watched the children pedalling up and down the street with messages.

The Germans had been taken by surprise. The only soldiers left on the street the last time he had looked had been dead; he had counted six crumpled olive-green heaps on the pavement on this one street. The partisans had been firing at anything which moved. One of them had seen him looking out of his window, and put a bullet six inches from his head. Since then Anton had sat on the floor. That had been several hours ago. And still he sat there, not hungry, not thirsty, not even afraid, really. He was waiting.

Now at last they had come into the Landski house. The firing from the reservoir had died down. The Home Army had taken Rokonow, was holding Rokonow. Now they had the time to search the houses. He could hear them banging about, downstairs, kicking open doors, shattering windows. He supposed there was a considerable hooligan element in the Home Army, attracted by the prospect of creating mayhem. But every army relied on its hooligan element. Pilsudski's army had contained a very large hooligan element. War was the natural condition of the hooligan. And when they were on the winning side they were decorated as heroes.

He stood up, took his place by the table on which waited his toy soldiers. Anton Janski, commanding his men into battle. He wondered why he had not remained in the army, adopted it as his career. He might have been a general. The door crashed open, four young men came in. They were wet. Two carried tommy guns, the other two carried machine pistols. Anton raised his hands as the beam of the torch played over him.

'Anton Janski. A known collaborator.'

'Oh, no, no,' Anton said. 'I hate the Germans.'

'You married one.'

'That was a long time ago,' Anton explained.

'He is a relative of Captain Janski's,' said another man. 'He cannot be shot out of hand. You, take him to headquarters.'

The man pointed his tommy gun at the door. Anton clasped his hands on the nape of his neck, went down the stairs. He walked along the street, raindrops soaking into his hair. People called out to him, shouted names at him. He smiled at them as he walked. He was not afraid. He was not even ashamed. He was Josef's father.

The sentry still lay at the foot of the steps; his helmet was half full of water. The rose bushes were trampled into shapeless weeds and the croquet lawn was scarred with the imprint of heavy boots. The front hall smelt like the interior of a sewer. A lantern hung from the electric light cord. Anton gazed at Weiss, lying in the drawing-room doorway. 'In there.'

Anton Janski stepped over Weiss. The girl lay in the shaft of light coming through the door, her head turned to one side, her eyes staring. The back of her white shirt had turned red, and the blood had spread to either side of her. He had never suspected that Liese's pale flesh con-

279

tained so much blood. Liese? He sat down.

'Up!' snapped his captor.

Anton remained seated, gazing at the girl. All gone, he thought. All gone.

'This is Anton Janski,' the guard said.

A man stood in the doorway. He was of medium height, had lank dark hair and narrow features. He wore an automatic pistol on his belt, a band round his left sleeve. He came into the room, saluted. 'I am Colonel Ladislas Kopa. This company is under my command. I am sorry to say that Josef was killed by the sentry on the door. The very first shot fired in this action. Would you like to see him?'

'I have already seen my daughter.'

Kopa knelt beside the girl's body. 'I did not know. How did this happen?'

'She gave the alarm,' said another man. 'Then she ran in here to get a weapon.'

'Liese did not know one end of a pistol from the other,' Anton said.

'But she was engaged to a German officer.' Asja's dress was torn, and was stained with blood. Her face was stained, too, and she carried a machine pistol. She made Anton think of one of the furies, with her red-gold hair and her hate-filled eyes.

'We thought you were dead,' he said. 'Why aren't you dead?'

'Because the Germans decided not to kill me, Papa. They tortured me and then they let me go. They wanted me to live. So I lived. To kill Germans. And those who love Germans.'

Anton stood up. 'Anna! Where is Anna? Have you shot her too?'

'Where is Frau Janski?' Kopa demanded.

'In the back. She has not been executed. Yet.'

'There will be more than enough killing to satisfy even

you before the Russians get here. Take Mr. Janski to be with his wife. And Asja, there are to be no more executions without my order.'

A man ran up the stairs, saluted. 'The Germans are counter-attacking the reservoir again, Colonel. They have an armoured car.'

'Reopen contact with Warsaw, Asja. Tell them that we are holding the pumping station and most of Rokonow, but that the Germans have brought up armour. And remember what I said. No more executions. Not a hair more to be harmed.'

Asja laughed. 'Yes, Colonel.' She waited while the men hurried out, raised her pistol. 'Come along, Papa.'

'I would like to bury Liese.'

'My girls will look after her when they get a moment. You may say a prayer over her.'

Anton knelt beside his eldest daughter, closed her eyes. He walked in front of Asja, through the baize door. But the baize door was no longer there. It had been knocked flat, its material shredded. The corridor beyond was dark, but a lantern gleamed in the servants' sitting room. A young girl waited here, armed with the inevitable machine pistol. Anton thought she could not be a day older than sixteen. There were female hooligans as well as male. 'A prisoner, Marie,' Asja said. 'Put him with the other.'

Marie opened the door. 'Hey,' she said. 'You awake?'

'Go away,' Anna Janski whispered. 'Leave me alone.'

'I've brought you company. You, go in there.'

Anton Janski stepped into darkness.

IV

The darkness was beginning to fade when Frederic heard the train. He had walked along the track for several hours. The thunderstorm had drifted towards him, the

281

clouds had opened and soaked him, the storm had passed on. And still the skyline glowed. Amazing that there should be enough left of Warsaw to burn.

The train roared at him. He slid down the embankment, crouched there while the trucks rattled past above him. It was a warm night, now that the thunderstorm had gone and the doors of the truck were open. Men sat, lay, hung their feet over the still, laughed, joked. His comrades, happy, because they were not being called upon to face the Russians this time.

The train hurtled towards the glow. Frederic crossed the track, walked south-east, now, keeping the light on his left hand. Dawn found him standing on the banks of the Utrata. Now he could see the smoke, and he could hear the pop-pop-pop of the rifles, the chatter of the machine guns, and the deep thuds of the mortars. The sound, like the smoke, made a continuous pall across the eastern horizon, and as he watched it, spreading far enough south to cover Rokonow and even neighbouring Wilanow, he heard the most familiar of military sounds. He knelt in the shelter of the trees, and watched the tanks rolling across the meadows to his right, making for the bridge. Five years had been taken away in the wave of a morning breeze. But there were differences. This morning he wore an olive-green uniform and he could get to his feet and walk towards those tanks, and even hail them, and the men in them would greet him. He could ask for a rifle and take part in the crushing of the dreadful Poles. He wore the Iron Cross, and any detachment would be glad to have him.

Or he could turn round, having come this far and seen the last of his city, his people, his family, and walk back to the Mazowiecki Junction, and take up the sergeant-major's offer of a place in a train to Frankfurt. Frankfurt was only a couple of hours from Berlin, and Ingrid of the burning white thighs.

Or he could sit here until nightfall, and then make his way into Rokonow. Why should he do that? For a father who hated him? For a mother who despised him? For a sister who was scarcely aware of his existence? For another sister who was scarcely aware of anyone's existence? For a brother who would be opposed to the revolt anyway, was probably at this moment taking photographs of the dying patriots? For a head of red-gold hair and a strong face and two long, powerful legs and . . . but there was the real difference between going forward and returnnig to Berlin. Ingrid's thighs were gleaming white, and they burned. He did not know the temperature of Asja's thighs.

He sat down, snug in the long grass, his back against a tree, and watched the river. To his right the tanks moved in an endless procession over the bridge, and behind the tanks there came truckloads of infantry, and behind the infantry the guns rumbled along the road. A full division was being moved into position for an assault on Warsaw, to exterminate a few civilians armed with hand guns. All that was needed to complete the job was a squadron of Heinkel bombers. But there were no Heinkel bombers left to risk in the air over Poland. And now he understood what was strange about this morning, what had troubled him since dawn. For the first time in six months the sky was empty. The storm had passed on, and the blue above was punctuated only by little clusters of white fleece. But there were no aircraft. As if a giant hand had swept all the troublesome insects out of the sky, the Russian Air Force had disappeared. On the morning their very presence would have been invaluable to the partisans. Did that mean the Red Army was poised on the other side of the Vistula, waiting for the command to launch the assault that would free the city? But if that were the case the Germans would be rushing far more than one division towards the river. So perhaps it meant something far more sinister, that the Soviets were aware that the men who would rebel against their Nazi conquerors were the same men who, in time, would rebel against their Russian saviours.

He chewed a bar of chocolate. He was so terribly tired. He had been up all night, except for that uneasy doze just before the train had stopped, and he had been walking for hours. The morning was warm, and he was hidden by the long grass while only ten miles away people were dying. His people. His people now or his people never again. He had joined the German Army to fight the Russians. Poland had no longer been involved then. But Poland was involved now, and he must either be a German or a Pole, and what he was now he would be for the rest of his life. Except that to become a Pole at this moment meant there would be no rest to his life. But could a Pole-cum-German have any rest either?

He slept. And as usual he did not dream of Galina, or even of Asja or Ingrid. He dreamt of Ruth.

'Fall in! Fall in!' Wanda looked over the barracks with an air, if not of kindliness, at least of good humour. But Wanda's good humour was often more dangerous than her rages. She pursued her pleasures with a sensual delight, whereas when angry she bubbled with vicious violence, her yellow hair bristling, her plump thighs and shoulders quivering with unrestrained power. When she had whipped Christina, the other day, she had paused between each blow to massage the bleeding flesh. It was the only time Ruth had seen Christina cry.

Now the whip was out, not flailing as yet, but cracking through the air, Wanda, with her polished boots and her tight belts and her whip, imagined herself as a lion tamer when she came in here, wearing her courage in her hands, ready at any moment to defend herself against a concerted assault. As if any of those toothless, white-maned, emaciated lionesses could cross the room quickly enough even to reach her.

'Up! Up!' The whip stung. Ruth was on her feet, standing to attention. Wanda was far earlier than usual. Something was going to happen. Something terrible. Only terrible things were happened at Oswiecim.

Wanda smiled at them. 'I have good news for you, Fräuleins. You are to be evacuated. The Russians are advancing in this direction, and we cannot let you precious ladies fall into their hands. Because they will ill-treat you. Oh, yes. There will be Cossacks, and Cossacks like nothing better than to rape ladies of quality. So we are going to save you from that fate. We are good to you, eh? Come along now. Fall in.'

Esther began to weep. She supposed that Wanda was indulging her fiendish sense of humour. But Esther was always weeping. She had spilled so many tears over the past three years it was incredible there could be any moisture left in her shivering body. She was down to the dregs now. Three years ago, when they had first arrived here and Esther had wept, her breasts had jiggled and her thick black hair had shaken. Now that she had no breasts left her ribs jiggled instead, and her thin white hair shivered. Esther, like Abbi, like Ruth, was a veteran of this barracks. They were the only remaining veterans. Three years in this barracks. Esther was the youngest. Esther, Ruth calculated, would be twenty-two next month. This was a disturbing thought, that such an ugly old crone should be approaching her twenty-second birthday. Because, of course, Ruth did not look like that. If her breasts had also shrunk into nothing at least her hair must still be black. So long as she had no mirror, her hair could still be black.

Abbi was still over at the brothel, with Christina. Ruth had always envied Abbi, as she had envied Christina since her arrival. How strange that Christina Janski should

285

have finished her life in Oswiecim—because this was the end of life; not even Ruth still believed in an afterward—with Abbi Landski and Ruth Blass. But so long as she was alive, Christina, like Abbi, was a woman to be envied. They both still had breasts, and buttocks, and calves, and even little pots on their bellies, because the guards liked women that way and saw that they got enough food, and if Abbi's hair was streaked with grey it was still long and clean, and Christina's fine yellow tresses were as pure as the day she had walked through the gate, her head high, smiling even at Wanda with that childlike innocence she preserved under almost every circumstance, had regained the moment Wanda had stopped whipping her.

But Abbi wasn't here this morning. After so much joint suffering they were to be separated. She licked her lips, preparing herself for the blow; Wanda always struck those inmates who addressed her first. Ruth's voice was as thin as her body. 'My friends, Abbi and Christina . . .'

Wanda did not hit her. Wanda laughed, a hearty explosion of mirth. 'They're still on their backs. Oh, the Russkies would make a meal off of them, Ruthie. Oh, yes. But they'll be along with the next load. You take my word for it, Ruthie. You'll meet them again. Oh, yes. Have I ever lied to you, Ruthie?'

Wanda loved her little joke. Ruth walked behind Esther, shuffled across the compound and through the gate. She had watched many other columns shuffling through this gate, off to somewhere else. Somewhere better. The most ghastly place on earth would be better than Oswiecim. Hell would be restful after Oswiecim.

There were male guards out here, a great number of them, fingering their weapons and looking anxious. Perhaps they expected the women to attempt to resist deportation. And there were the trucks, waiting. Ruth's heart actually found the strength to pound. She had not really believed they were going anywhere. Like Esther, she had presumed it was all some trick on the part of Wanda. But there were the trucks, waiting. And above the trucks floated the clouds. Beautiful clouds, this morning, all white and fleecy, mincing past. She thought, if she could just summon the strength, she could rise above Esther and join the clouds, and disappear across the river and into the mountains. She hated the thought of leaving Abbi. But she wouldn't really have left. She'd hover up there, over Abbi and Christina, for ever. Clouds never died. They broke up, sometimes, but they came back together again. There were always clouds in the sky, somewhere. They filed past the trucks. Now why were they doing that? They walked along a flower-lined path towards rectangular buildings made of concrete, like large public conveniences. 'Come on, come on,' shouted the guards. Into the baths with you. We're not having any filthy shitbags in our trucks.'

These people were so clean. She wondered if there was something about working in a concentration camp which made the guards want to be cleaner than ordinary human beings. If only they would do something about the smell. Because not far beyond the bath was the crematorium. Wanda often talked about the crematorium. 'You'll wind up there,' she jeered. 'We've no room to bury the likes of you. You'll burn, when you go. Oh, it's a good way to go, Ruthie.' The crematorium was always working, belching black smoke, evil-smelling, thick, nauseous, into the sky. But when the smoke reached the sky it mingled with the clouds, became part of the clouds. To die was one way of becoming a cloud.

'Strip! Get them off! Quickly, now.' They dropped their clothes on the ground, filed through the great steel doors. It was less like a shower bath than a fortified bunker. And there were no drains. A gigantic shower bath, with no drains. Esther had noticed it too. Esther was turning round to point this out. Esther was preparing to weep

287

again. Anything out of the ordinary had Esther weeping. But more and more women were crowding into the bath, until there was not room to move an arm, and the doors were clanging shut, and a hubbub rose towards the concrete roof, a noise accompanied by smells and rustling, and suddenly by a scream, which began under one of the ventilators and rippled through the packed women towards the door, impelling them backwards, as if they could move at all, as if there was anything they could do, and yet they moved, receding from the ventilators, thrusting against the iron door, while the screams and the smells thudded against the roof, over-laden now by another smell, a difficult smell, an incredible smell, which tormented the nostrils, scorched the lungs. Ruth found Esther in her arms, choking and weeping, pressed tight against her by the weight of bodies on every side. But Ruth was no longer interested in the weight of bodies. Ruth knew what was happening now. And for the first time in five years she was happy. She was on her way to the clouds.

V

'Halt!'

Frederic halted. He was surprised to have reached this far without challenge.

'Advance!'

He could see the bayonet, glinting in the darkness. And he could hear a man breathing. In Rokonow there was a lull in the fighting. The night was almost quiet, save for an occasional rifle-shot.

'Name and rank.'

'Private Frederic Johansson. I am on hospital leave.'

A light flashed, the beam played over him, rested for a moment on the cross at his breast. 'On leave, here?'

288

Frederic held up his pass. 'I have a brother in the Rokonow garrison.'

'It has been withdrawn. What was left of it. They were taken by surprise, you see, and the insurgents are in strength. They even beat off our first counter-attack. But there will be another in the morning. The Rokonow business will be the first finished; we have cut their link with Warsaw.' He pointed. 'If you follow the road you will find company headquarters. They will be able to tell you about your brother.'

'Thank you, comrade. But there is something about this situation I do not understand. You say that we have cut Rokonow off from Sielce, and will attack again in the morning. What is to stop the Poles withdrawing through this gap? I have been walking for over an hour and you are the first patrol I have encountered.'

The sentry grinned. 'We want it to appear like that to the Poles. There are two tank squadrons in the hollow over there. That is the point, you see, to put sufficient pressure on the river side of Rokonow so that the insurgents will seek to withdraw. Once they leave the shelter of the houses the tanks will have them.'

'Ingenious,' Frederic said. 'I'll wish you every luck. Company headquarters is over there, you say?'

'About a quarter of a mile,' the sentry said.

Frederic walked along the road until he estimated he had covered about a hundred yards. Now he could see a light in the distance. To his left the wood which clustered to the west of Rokonow loomed in the darkness. But according to the sentry there would be no soldiers in there. He looked over his shoulder, saw nothing. Beyond the trees a fire burned, sending flames high into the sky. He would use that as a beacon.

He left the road, climbed through the wire fence that bordered the wood. He walked through the trees. No more thinking, now. He had taken his decision. Or perhaps it had been taken for him. It should have been taken five years ago, but even at this late date it was remarkable what peace of mind it gave him.

The trees ended, and there was a road. It was a splendid night, cool, and quiet save for the persistent pop-pop in the distance, and for the flames which now were much closer. He passed a white gate, guarding a curved drive through a shrubbery to his right. He remembered this house; he had passed it on a dozen occasions as a boy, on his way to hunt birds' nests in the wood, with Josef. An eternity ago. A different existence. But he could not remember the name of the family who lived there. On his left was another gate, wrought iron this time, and more extensive gardens. He could see no lights. He wondered what had happened to these people. They had accepted the Germans for five years, happy to be able to go on living in beautiful Rokonow. What had happened to them, now?

He passed a shattered street lamp, and the gardens began to dwindle as the houses became closer together. Frederic Johansson, keeping a belated appointment with death, in a dead town. He could smell it now, the scent of death, of bodies waiting to be buried.

He came to a car, burned out, a crumpled heap of twisted metal. There was a shoe protruding from the passenger door. Inside the shoe was a blackened leg. He turned the corner, saw the barricades, the felled trees, three upturned cars, and a variety of other rubbish. Oh, yes, these were insurgents. Amateur soldiers. The poor bastards had never seen tanks in action.

'I have contact.' Asja kicked the table on which the set rested, made the static worse.

Kopa sat down. 'This is Rokonow calling headquarters. Over.'

He drummed his fingers on the table, watched Asja as

290

she flopped on the bed, legs spread wide. It was a warm night, and she wore only her slip. Her legs were bare, and she had gathered her hair in a bow on the nape of her neck. She was all his now. Kopa's woman. After five years of wanting she belonged only to him. As if it mattered now. 'Rokonow calling. Rokonow calling headquarters. Over.'

A reply at last, very faint. 'Go ahead, Rokonow. Over.'

'We have suffered forty-six casualties, nineteen dead. There is a large German force concentrating to the south. We have heard tanks out there. Over.'

'Do you still hold the reservoir? Over.'

'We hold the pumping station, for the time being. Over.'

'Do you still have adequate stocks of ammunition? Over.'

'We captured some at the reservoir. But morale is low, General. There is evidence that the Germans have cut the road to Sielce. Over.'

'Your information is correct, Colonel Kopa. Rokonow is isolated. Over.'

'Then I would like permission to withdraw to the west, should the position require it. My patrols inform me that there are no enemy detachments in the wood, or even beyond, as far as Okecie. It should be possible for my command to split up into small groups and infiltrate into the open country. Over.'

'There will be no withdrawal, Colonel. You are pinning down a large German force which otherwise would move on the city from the south. You will regroup on the pumping station. This must be your citadel, and it must be held to the last man. The Germans will hesitate to shell the pumping station itself. Repeat those orders, Colonel Kopa. Over.'

Kopa sighed. 'I will concentrate my company on the

pumping station. I will defend the pumping station for as long as possible. Over.'

'Thank you, Colonel Kopa. We have information that the Red Army is much closer than we had hoped, and is at this moment preparing to launch an assault on Praga. They may well be across the river by tomorrow night. Good luck, to you and your command. Over and out.'

Kopa lit a cigarette. His hands trembled.

'Voices, giving orders over the radio, always make me think of God,' Asja said. 'Or perhaps the devil. Because there is no God, eh, Ladi?'

'Promises, orders,' Kopa said. 'He has been dangling the Red carrot in front of our noses for days. It might make some sense if we controlled even one of the bridges, if we had seized even one of the railway lines. This operation was lost on the first day, Asja.'

'My God, that I would lie here and pray for a lousy Cossack to walk through that door. I should find that funny.'

'Where have all the planes gone, Asja? Tell me that.'

'If one could see his face, to know how much of what he says is the truth, whether or not he is afraid.' She took the cigarette from Kopa's mouth, dragged smoke into her lungs.

'He isn't afraid,' Kopa said. 'He doesn't know about fear.'

'But you are afraid, Ladi.'

Kopa tried to light another cigarette. If only his hands would keep still. 'This isn't what I expected.'

'Nothing is ever as you expect. Are you going to tell our people what he said?'

'No. I shall give orders to concentrate on a line from this house to Grybowski's Store, and then another line from the store to the pumping station. That will give us a triangle, with the river as our base and the store as the apex. It is not good, but it is the best we can do. You'll

292

stay here with the radio. When I sent you orders to withdraw, use grenades on all this equipment. Nothing must be left. But you'll bring the portable set and as many batteries as you can carry.'

Asja scratched her thighs with the flats of her hands. 'Leave me Marie and Jutka. And three tommies.'

'Then give me your pistol.'

Asja shook her head. 'I will keep that too. Something may go wrong, and you cannot shoot yourself with a tommy gun. It is not conceivable.'

'You will come when I send for you?'

'The first time.'

Kopa bent over her, kissed her mouth, straightened as figures crowded the doorway. 'Why have you left the barricades?'

'We have a prisoner.' They threw the German soldier forward. His boots caught on the carpet and he sprawled on his belly. He had lost his cap and there were bruises on his face. He gazed at Asja's bare feet, hanging over the side of the bed.

Kopa stood above him. Here was a typical German, he thought. Yellow-haired and arrogant. A blond beast.

'He walked towards us,' they explained. 'With his hands above his head.'

'He deserted, to us?' Asja sat up.

The German licked his lips. 'I have information.' He did not raise his head.

'You?' Kopa stooped, frowned. The lantern made a poor light, but there was something familiar about this German' face. Or were all German faces familiar.

'The wood is not defended. But there are tanks concealed in the hollow beyond, for if you should attempt to break out.'

'Break out? We are not going to break out, Fritz. We are going to hold Rokonow until the Reds get here. The day after tomorrow. Shoot him.' He went to the door.

'Leave him here,' Asja said. 'Marie and Jutka and I will take care of him.'

Kopa hesitated. But the prisoner was a German, and no German deserved an easy death.

v

Asja's bare feet. And Asja's body above, wearing only a thin cotton slip, tantalising in the semi-darkness. But not Asja's voice, surely.

'He was born in this house,' she said. 'You remember Frederic Janski, Jutka.'

'I remember Frederic very well,' Jutka said. He did not remember her. Jutka was one of those indeterminate women you meet and know and perhaps even flirt with and then forget. But he was lying on the floor, and she was standing above him, today; she carried a tommy gun, under her arm, as once she must have carried a handbag.

'He ran away.' Asja sat on the edge of the bed, looking down at him. 'He changed his name to Johansson and joined the German army.'

'Let *me* shoot him, Asja,' said the young girl, Marie. 'I haven't shot anybody yet. I aimed at one man, but he ducked.'

I am in a madhouse, Frederic thought. Where they can talk about stamping on a man as if he were a cockroach. But I have been in this madhouse for five years.

'You're not shooting him in here,' Jutka said. 'I'm not sharing this room with any dead Fritz. How long are we here for, Asja?'

'Until Kopa sends for us.' She was gazing at him. If only he could see her eyes. He rose to his knees, could see her hair, the outline of her face. But her eyes, like her thighs, were lost in darkness.

'We could do it in the yard,' Marie said. 'We'll have to

294

do the others, too. We could do them all in the yard.' She stroked her tommy gun, as if she was drawing strength from the cold steel barrel. Strange, Frederic thought; I used to stroke my rifle just like that.

'Oh, yes, the others,' Jutka said. 'Frederic would like to see the others. Up, Fritz.'

Frederic stood up.

'And keep your hands up.'

Frederic clasped his hands on the nape of his neck.

'I'll take him.' Asja picked up the third tommy gun, pointed at the door.

'Let me come with you,' Marie begged.

'You'll both stay here. Frederic, take the torch.'

Frederic lowered his hands, switched on the torch, stepped into the corridor. The muzzle of the tommy gun jammed into his spine. 'Josef is dead,' Asja said. 'He was one of us, you know, Frederic. No, you never guessed that. His working for the Nazis was all a front. He worked for us, and he led the assault on this house, his own house, Frederic. He was shot through the head when he was climbing over the fence. I couldn't stop to help him, then. When I went back he was dead. Go down those steps.'

Frederic went down the steps.

'And Liese is dead. She tried to give the Germans the alarm. One of our men shot her in the back. She was always the lucky one, eh, Frederic? She lived her entire life in a daydream, and she never knew she was being killed. Go into the servants' quarters, Frederic.'

Frederic followed the beam of the torch through the remnants of the baize door. No use thinking now. No use doing anything except wait for Asja to finish. She was going to tell him about all of them. And when she was finished she would tell him about himself.

'And Christina is dead. I don't know *how* Christina died, Frederic. But you do. She was sent to the concentration camp down at Oswiecim. The one the Germans call Auschwitz. She was sent there for shooting a German officer. You never met Paul, did you, Frederic? Paul von Bardoman? You would have liked Paul. He was charming. He was going to marry Liese. So Christina shot him. Tell me how Christina died, Frederic?'

They had reached a locked door.

'Open the door, Frederic. Shine your torch inside.'

Frederic turned the key, hesitated, threw the door inwards. But the smell in here was of living bodies, not decaying flesh. He shone the torch into the room. Anton Janski sat up, shading his eyes from the light. The woman beside him cowered on the mattress, trying to conceal herself with her hands, for there were no sheets and no blankets and no pillows.

'Mama?' Frederic whispered. How much store do we put by hair in women, he thought. He would always recognise Asja, even in the dark, because of her hair, red-gold, wavy thick. He would always know Christina, even when he met her in hell, because of her hair, white-gold, fine, straight. He would always know Mama, because of her hair, jet black, clinging to her neck like a shawl. So this woman could not be Mama, this gleaming egg, this bare neck. 'Mama?' he said again.

'My girls shaved her,' Asja said. 'Had I touched her I would have strangled her. But shaving is the only treatment for collaborators, eh, Frederic? Had Liese lived, we would have shaved her too.'

'Liese is dead,' Anton Janski said. 'Did you know that, Frederic? They showed me her body. And Asja is dead too. She was executed by the Gestapo. I don't know what she is doing here at all.'

Frederic knelt on the bed, held his mother's shoulders. 'Don't be afraid, sweetheart. Your hair will grow again.'

'He is a hero now,' Asja said. 'Do you see the cross, Mama? Who gave you that, Frederic? Was it the Fuehrer himself?' He shone the torch into her face, and at last could see her eyes. The tears streamed downwards, clouded the smooth cheeks, hung from her jaw like raindrops.

'Bastard.' Her fingers were tight on the trigger, and the muzzle pointed at his belly.

'I'll come back for you, Mama. And you, Papa. I swear it.' Frederic stepped outside, closed the door, kept the torch shining on Asja's face. 'What did the Gestapo do to you, Asja? What happened at Szucha Avenue?'

He watched her fingers relaxing on the tommy gun, watched it slide from her hands, catch for a moment on her thigh, fall to the ground. Her knees trembled, and she slumped against the wall. 'Oh, you fool, Frederic. Oh, you fool.'

She sat on the floor, in the servants' living room, her back against the old settee. The night still trembled, now and then, with isolated shots, rumbling explosions. Out there men and women, her men and women, were being killed. Their stench hung on the air, corroded her nostrils. Josef and Liese were out there, lying on the same heap, their hands touching. She wondered if they would ever be buried. But Asja was here, the tears still wet on her cheeks. The fire which had burned inside Asja for six months had suddenly run out of fuel. She should hate him for doing that to her. Hate him more than ever.

He was kneeling beside her, holding a cup of water to her lips. She wondered where he had found the cup, where he had found the water. But, of course, he had been born in this house, as she had conceived in this house, as her son had died in this house.

'Tell me, Asja,' he whispered. 'You have to tell me. You have to speak about it.'

The torch lay on the floor, shining on them. 'They raped me, Frederic. They raped me with magnetos and whips and cigarette butts. And with words. The words were the worst, I can*not* explain it to you. The pain was nothing. I screamed, and I banged my head on the floor, and I wept, but the pain was nothing. I suffered more continuous pain with little Antoni. It was the *thought*. Can you understand anything about that, Frederic?'

'Nothing like that has ever happened to me. I have watched my best friend flogged to death. I have raped women. I have listened to my second-best friend being castrated. I have lain on a girl's belly while she hated me. I have seen men, and women, blown into several pieces and I have watched children die of starvation. But nothing has happened to *me*, save a bullet in the leg. I do not even hate any more. Why did I *watch* all those things happening, Asja? While you had to *feel* them?'

'Why does one person survive a plane accident, Frederic?' She smiled through her tears. 'Maybe there is a God, after all. Maybe God selects the one person, out of all the rest. He stood above Europe, in September 1939, with a long stick with a pin in the end, and He jabbed it down with His eyes shut, and He said, "Now, you, and you, and you, will survive the coming war, physically and mentally. No matter what happens, you will come through." ' She ran her fingers into his fair hair. 'Untarnished.'

'Why, Asja?'

'To tell the unborn ones, Frederic. To put an end to hatred, when it is possible to do so. I would be no use for that. I am as vicious as any Gestapo officer, as immoral as any whore. Maybe we all are, inside, but my viciousness has been exposed, and I cannot hide it again. The war has done that to me. So I will always hate the Germans, and I will always look over my shoulder when I see a policeman, of any nationality, and I will always know guilt when I eat a square meal, and I will never dare fly. The war killed me, Frederic. Like your father said, I am dead, so why am I here? Even if I should sur-

vive I will still be dead. For ever and ever. And there
will be millions and millions and millions of people like
me, walking the street, ten, twenty years after the defeat
of Germany, still dead. And do you know the most terrible thing about it all? They will be the people running
the world, then, because they are our ages now, and they
will be dead, capable only of hatred and mistrust. That is
what happened after the last war, that is what is going to
happen after this war. So without men like you, who can
come through it without dying, inside, there would be no
hope for the future, would there? And you, you poor be-
sotted fool, had to come back here. You must have walked
right through the German lines, Frederic. Why did you do
that?'

'Maybe because I've at last realised that if I can survive all I have seen over the past five years, without dying,
there must be something wrong with me, not right about
me.'

'And what made you choose here, Frederic? Here in
this stench and this filth and this despair. Here, where
there is no hope save from the Reds. There is our star,
Frederic. Stalin and the Cossacks.'

'I wanted to see you, before I died, Asja. Before we
both died.'

She sighed. 'A man once said to me that melodrama
was the curse of Polish history. I think he was right. He
was right about a lot of things. Melodrama and romance
are the curse of all history. They lead to hope. What is
romantic about love, Frederic? It is so close to hate. I
love you, Frederic. I have always loved you. Even when
I hate you I love you. But when I hate you I want to
hurt you. Just now, in the wireless room, I wanted you
to kiss me while Jutka and Marie shot you. There is
nothing romantic about that. It is hideous.'

'We are all hideous, that far down. We don't look that
far, as a rule, Asja. And when we do, like you, just now,

we look up again. Quickly. It's only when you can't look up that you're in trouble.'

'And I'm in trouble, Frederic. I know I'm in trouble. I went to Szucha Avenue to die. I wanted to die, doing something effective. You see, I'm just as romantic as you. Do you know who was in charge at Szucha Avenue?'

'Reitener,' he whispered. 'I'd forgotten.'

'He sucked me dry, Frederic. Not during the interrogation. He had nothing to do with the interrogation. But afterwards. I could have survived the interrogation. Christina showed me how to survive that. But not the afterwards, with Reitener.'

'Reitener? It doesn't seem possible.'

'Oh, he was experimenting, with himself. I know that now. I think I understood it then. I was just a thing to him. And when he was finished he tossed me my life, contemptuously. He took Christina's, and he gave me mine. But I had already given myself to him, because he was like no man I have ever known. No man, Frederic. And I know that if he walked through that door I would give myself to him again. Did he do that to you, Frederic?'

'Yes,' Frederic said.

'So you understand, Frederic. So if you have come back, to claim me, Frederic, you must make me forget Reitener. You must make me do that, Frederic. Or we are both dead. For ever.'

VII

Dawn came slowly to Rokonow. The light streaked out of the east, warmed the hurrying waters of the Vistula, penetrated the rumbling dust cloud that was Warsaw. It seemed reluctant, aware that it was unlikely to illuminate anything very pretty. Yet this morning there was a hush in Rokonow. From the north, from Sielce and

300

Mokotow, there came the rattle of machine-gun fire and the thud-thud of mortars. Perhaps the Germans had forgotten about Rokonow.

The servants' living room looked west, and so the light had to reach right round the Janski villa and come in again. The room paled gradually; the woman's face led the way. Her cheeks were still stained with tears. Her lips were puffy, her hair and forehead wet with sweat. Her nipples were inflamed, her belly mottled red and white. Her thighs were cool. Now. But they had been hot. They had caught fire with a molten vehemence which made Ingrid only a picture in a book, lovely to look at, impossible to know. He was glad he had come back, to these thighs, to learn how much they wanted, how much they could take, how much they could give.

She sat up. 'Do you have a cigarette? Or would you prefer a more solid breakfast?'

His jacket lay on the floor beside them. He took the packet from his breast pocket, lit two.

She dragged smoke into her lungs, rose to her knees, then her feet. 'There is food, you know. Some food.'

He lay on his back and looked up her legs to the dark splendour of her love forest. Her legs, clinging to the flanks of her pony, had been the first thing he had known about Asja. Even then he had suspected what lay above. And for all his innocence, then, he had known that to be held by those legs, to find his way through that forest, would be an unforgettable experience. From that moment he had been jealous of Antoni. And he was still jealous of Antoni. The legs were as lovely as ever he remembered them, and their grip was as consuming as ever he had hoped. But the forest did not belong to Asja any more. He wondered if any part of her still belonged to Asja.

She stood at the window. The cigarette smoke drifted back into the room. 'It is not your fault.' She sighed. 'Kopa asked me once if I had ever caught fire. I did not know what he meant, then. But the Gestapo, and then Reitener, lit a fire in me. So what am I to do, Frederic? Nothing can change me now. I am a woman who grieves continually, and who hates continually, and who lusts continually. That is my legacy from this war.'

Jutka opened the door, looked from one naked body to the other. 'Oh, you whore,' she said. 'Oh, you lousy bitch. I should shoot you both.'

Asja flicked her cigarette out of the window. 'What do you want?'

'Headquarters is on the air. They say there are severe counter-attacks being launched on Mokotow. They wish to know if it would be possible for Kopa's company to strike north, as a diversion.'

'Don't they want to know when our wings are going to sprout and our heavenly host appear? You will have to deliver the message to Kopa. Send Marie.'

Jutka sneered. 'Only that message?'

'Only that message is important now.'

Jutka closed the door. Asja dropped her slip over her head. 'You make me forget my duty. I wish to forget my duty sometimes.'

'Is that not sufficient?'

'No. Because I crave so many things. Frederic. Things you could never give me, so long as you loved me. Because I want man's contempt, man's distaste, man's horror. I want his body as well, but only hidden beneath those emotions. Because tenderness fills *me* with contempt. Because I want my man to treat everyone in the world with contempt, to march across them in his jackboots as he marches across me. Because, last February, I fell in love with Reitener.'

'So did I, Asja. Once. It is not the man. It is the *idea*.'

'And because you are Frederic you have survived. But because I am Asja I have succumbed. The world is full of Reiteners, Frederic. And because of their glamour, and

302

their personality, and their ruthlessness, we always know they are there. Without them the world might be a better place, but it would not go round quite so fast. They are in every country, every society. Hitler's secret, perhaps his only secret, is that he clapped his hands like some wizard, and brought all the Reiteners in Germany together, and said to them, "Now do my will." So put on your clothes and go back to them, Frederic. Quickly. That girl is going to tell Kopa what has happened here.'

'But you will come with me when I go, Asja. You must; those barricades of yours will not stop a tank for five minutes. We will escape, you and I. We'll swim the Vistula, and surrender to the Russians. Don't shake your head. Nothing can be worse than the past five years. And when the war is over we'll leave Europe and go to America. We'll make a home over there, Asja. We'll work together and play together and love together. It is a huge, wonderful country, and it is a free country, and we will find the part of it we lost best, and we'll live there, and we'll be happy. This I promise.'

'And will they wish to have us?'

'Yes. This, too, I promise.'

She smiled. 'Yes. There was one thing which Reitener lacked, and you have found it out. Reitener knew nothing of hope. He had no interest in hope. Like all his kind, he was a nihilist. And can you promise me hope, Frederic? Despite everything?'

'Despite everything.'

And the five years need never have been, and Antoni need never have been, and they were back in Zabie, as children, together. And it was very warm, and very quiet, save for the tractor in the distance, coming ever closer as it cut the earth to ribbons.

Many tractors.

The telephone jangled. Hanna flicked the receiver from

303

its hook with one finger, cradled it between cheek and shoulder while she continued typing. She did most things well, gracefully. Presumably she had been as graceful, in Paris. 'Yes,' Hanna said. 'I will tell him.' She cupped her hand over the mouthpiece, smiled at him. 'There is a Standartenfuehrer Schwartzman here to see you, Herr Obergruppenfuehrer.'

Reitener raised his head, more sharply than he would have wished. 'Schwartzman? Give it to me.' He took the receiver. 'Carl? Is the gentleman alone?'

'He has three men with him, Herr Obergruppen-fuehrer.'

'Ask him to give me ten minutes, will you, Carl?' He handed the receiver back to Hanna, gazed out of the window. It was a delightful August morning, warm and sunny. A good day to be alive.

He lit a cigarette, opened his middle drawer. Here was a Mauser automatic pistol, easier to reach at short notice than the one in his holster. And here, too, was the capsule. He touched it, curiously, with one finger, took it from the drawer, let it roll across the palm of his hand. Hanna watched him with her mouth open. She was a remarkably attractive girl. And now she was more confused than she had ever been in Paris. But she had never let her confusion interfere with her devotion to him.

'How long have you been in the service, Hanna?'

'Seven years now, Herr Obergruppenfuehrer.'

'Always on the clerical side?'

'Oh, yes. I joined as a stenographer.'

'Then you have never seen a man, or a woman, in-terrogated?'

'Once or twice, in Paris. They used to make all us girls go down sometimes. It was psychological, you know. We were supposed to laugh at the prisoner, and make re-marks.' She shrugged, prettily. 'I don't think it was very effective.'

He tried to envisage her, at the mercy of Werner. And succeeded. 'Have you ever thought what it must be like, to be interrogated?'

She gave a mock shudder. 'Ugh! But I mean, it couldn't happen. I'm not an enemy agent, am I? Or a traitor. So I have never considered it.'

'You are my private secretary, Hanna. The security of your future depends on the security of mine.'

She smiled. 'I know, Herr Obergruppenfuehrer. When you asked for me to be sent to you again, I remember Elsa, our senior typist, was quite green. She said, "Hanna, you're on your way. Because Obergruppenfuehrer Reitener is going to be one of the leaders of the Reich, one day. One day soon."'

Could she really be as innocent as she seemed? But he had known her for three years, had never known her different. He wondered if this was not Hitler's greatest achievement, and his greatest crime, that he could create a nation of Hannas, so innocent, so deadly. But he had also created a nation of Reiteners, and for Reitener there could only be women like Hanna. So for three years, at the very least, he had been a fool. He thought that every-thing might have been different, had he thought more about Hanna and less about Germany, three years ago. 'Would you care to dine with me tonight?'

'Me, Herr Obergruppenfuehrer?' Her cheeks were pink.

'We could go to the opera. I think they are doing *Tristan und Isolde*. It is not one of my favourites, but it makes an occasion. Yes. We will do that, Hanna, you and I. Perhaps I will call for you, perhaps I will send for you. We shall know later. But there is something I'd like you to do for me, now.'

'Oh, yes, Herr Obergruppenfuehrer. Anything you wish.'

He held out his hand. 'Take this pill.'

305

She frowned, picked it up.

'It is a special kind of aphrodisiac. It will take away all your inhibitions, make tonight the most memorable of your life.'

'Oh, yes, Herr Obergruppenfuehrer.' Her tunic heaved. She closed her hand tightly, went to the water cooler.

'No, no,' he said. 'No water. Just put the pill between your teeth, and bite.'

'Yes, Herr Obergruppenfuehrer.' Her mouth closed. She grimaced. 'It's bitter.'

'I would sit down, if I were you. It may make you a little giddy.'

She nodded, sat at her desk. She smiled, and then frowned. Her hands grasped for her tie knot, pulling it loose. She sighed, and her head rested on her typewriter. Her hands dropped from her tie, hung beside her chair.

Reitener got up, opened the door. 'Max! How good to see you, after all these years. Tell me, how is Gerda?'

Schwartzman cautiously entered the room, sniffing the air. He signalled his men to wait, and closed the door. 'We are divorced, Herr Obergruppenfuehrer. That time we spent at the camp affected her, and she became a regular wanton. She drank, too.'

'Oh, dear me.' Reitener sat down. 'How tragic. And now you are a Standartenfuehrer, and you have come for me. I find that a very odd coincidence.'

Schwartzman's frown deepened. 'No coincidence, Joachim. I volunteered for this assignment. For old times' sake. You are dying?'

'Unfortunately, no. I gave the capsule to my secretary.'

Schwartzman glanced at the dead girl, then leaned over the desk. 'Then you must use your pistol. I will step outside for a moment.'

'Call your men, Max.'

'You must use your pistol, Joachim. This is no ordinary business. I received my instructions from the

306

Fuehrer personally. There is no hope. You are going to be taken apart, and then you are going to be publicly shamed, and then you are going to be hanged. Hanged, Joachim, not shot. Strangled with piano wire. I will leave you alone now.'

Reitener sighed, stood up. 'Life is a compound of experiences, Max. I have managed to sample most things. Save only what I have inflicted so often. So I do not think I could cheat myself of that.' He smiled, clapped Schwartzman on the shoulder. 'Besides, when you have finished with me, hell may not seem so terrible, eh?'

VIII

Four men climbed through the fence from the orchard, ran across the yard. They panted, and their faces were grey. But they still carried their rifles, still wore their bandoliers. 'They're coming,' they gasped, as they ran up the back steps. 'Tanks. Through the wood.' They paused in the doorway, gazed at the uniform which was the symbol of their defeat. 'A Fritz.'

'Fighting for us.' Asja deliberately handed her tommy gun to Frederic.

'But we cannot hold a house like this against tanks.'

'We cannot retreat without orders. Open fire the moment you see them. I will send for help.'

'We need an anti-tank gun,' Frederic said.

'Kopa captured one. I'll ask for it. You stay here and wait for me.' She ran along the corridor, through the baize door, up the stairs. Jutka lay on the bed, smoking a cigarette. 'Tanks!'

'Where?' Jutka started to her feet, gazed at the doorway as if she expected to hear caterpillar tracks on the steps.

'They're coming through the wood. Find Kopa, tell

him we need men and we need machine guns. And we need that anti-tank gun he captured at the pumping station.'

'And how is your friend?'

Asja hit her, a swinging blow across the face which knocked her against the wall. 'He is on our side. Frederic has always been on our side, in his heart. Now go and fetch Kopa.'

Jutka licked her lips, reached for her tommy gun.

'I'll keep that. Here.' Asja reached into the pocket of her coat, draped over the chair, handed her the automatic pistol. 'Now hurry.' She sat at the radio set, listened to Jutka's feet on the stairs. She wanted to call for help. Help for Rokonow. But Rokonow was beyond help. As Kopa had said, three days ago, theirs was a suicide mission, to distract the Germans into regaining control of the pumping station while Warsaw prepared to stand siege. There would be no help for Rokonow. Rokonow had served its purpose.

She tucked the tommy gun under her arm, went to the window at the rear of the corridor, next to the bathroom, and looked out, over the backyard, and the orchard, and then another backyard, and then a street. Beyond the street a garden shed and a garage were trembling, as if there was a private earthquake going on over there. She watched the walls cave outwards, the roof slide inwards. She watched the long barrel of the gun, like some monstrous penis, come snaking through the dust and the debris. Then the tank followed, slowly, seeming to delight in crushing the earth and the stones and the wood. The turret was turning, from side to side, seeking its next victim, until it stopped, and she was able to look directly into the black barrel.

She ran, desperately, sweat-wet bare feet slipping on the polished floor, tumbling down the stairs, the tommy gun clattering beside her. She lay on the hall floor, her hands over her head. From above her there came a dull rumbling sound, and pieces of plaster fell around her. Dust billowed down the stairs, made her cough, and through the dust she smelt scorching wood. The tank would sit out there and pound the Janski villa into rubble. There was no hope of the anti-tank gun getting here in time.

She crawled along the hall, into the living room, found the box of grenades. She tore open drawers in the sideboard, took out a table cloth, used it as a bag for a dozen of the deadly little balls. But the wireless equipment came first. She went back up the stairs, paused to stare at the back of the house, now a vast hole with flaming edges. She fell to her knees as the house trembled again, but where this shell had exploded she did not know. Not the kitchen yet; she could hear the chatter of Frederic's tommy gun. They were consummating their love, killing, and being killed. She hoped Frederic managed to get away. She prayed that. But if he was going to die she hoped they died together. At the very same moment.

She stood in the doorway to the wireless room, trembling. She had never done this before. Kopa had shown her how, but only in mock-up. She rolled the grenade inside and slammed the door. She ran for the steps, crouched there. The noise was surprisingly soft after the explosion of the shells. But the door had been blown out.

She went down the steps, instinctively turned to her right, and checked. Frederic did not understand. He looked on her only as his lover, his woman. To go back into the kitchen would be to imprison herself, to make dying doubly difficult. She turned left instead, picked up the tommy gun and the grenades, went down the front steps. The sunlight danced on the croquet lawn.

Even the pool of dried blood where the sentry had lain looked right. Why shouldn't people have red lawns as well as green lawns? Nature was too conservative.

She went round the side of the house, between the library and the hedge, her back against the wall, her tommy gun under her arm, the bag of grenades carried in both hands. She paused, listening. The rifles and the tommy gun barked with frantic ineffectiveness from the kitchen, and there were explosions and crashes from farther down the street. And now she could hear the clank of the tracks. She crouched in the shelter of the house and watched the trees in the orchard trembling as they were swept from left to right.

She ran across the yard, and the firing from the kitchen stopped. She heard Frederic shouting. She paused by the well, held the grenade in her right hand, looked at the tank. It had to come closer. But it had stopped again, and the gun barrel was swinging to and fro, no, only to, to her. Oh God, she thought. Oh God! Not me. Not me, alone.

She threw the bag of grenades away from her, stepped clear of the well, hurled the one she was holding. She threw it like a veteran, terror giving her arm a strength and an accuracy she had never suspected she might possess. The grenade landed squarely on top of the hatch cover, and exploded. She wondered if it had dented the armour, and dived for the shelter of the well. But the short flame of the grenade explosion was already obliterated by a larger flame, a brighter flame than she had ever seen. She seemed to be in the centre of a whirling world of stone and water, and it occurred to her that but for the stone buttress of the well she would have been blown into very small pieces. Oh, damn the well.

Liese had not known she was going to die, had not known she was dead. Liese had always been the lucky one. Asja lay on stones, under stones, had stones inside her. She dared not look down. To see would be to feel, and to feel would be impossible. Agony hovered on the edge of consciousness, broken bones, shattered veins, mangled flesh. To look down would be her last act. She looked up at the enormous caterpillar tracks rising above her.

Asja screamed.

They held Frederic's arms, pinned him to the floor. 'She is dead,' they said. 'And every life is important, so long as it remains alive.'

And still they listened to the scream. They watched the tank, rolling over the remnants of the well, crushing the stones and what lay amidst the stones, moving on, towards them now, leaving the scream behind to drift towards the wood. They watched the tank roll over the tablecloth full of grenades, and they watched the flash of light as they listened to the explosion. The tank slewed sideways, came to a stop. One of its tracks had been blown off. They wanted to cheer Asja the heroine. But they didn't. They still listened to the scream. And if the tank couldn't move its gun could. The gun was turning again.

Marie panted into the room. 'The colonel says we are to withdraw. He says the Germans are attacking on the reservoir side, too, and he can send no help. He says we must concentrate on the pumping station. Quickly now.'

The kitchen was empty. Frederic gazed at the tank and the shattered well. Marie had come just five minutes too late.

There was a flash and a whine, and plaster fell on his head. He smelt smoke, and thought he could hear flames. He could just sit here, and die. He wanted to do no more. There were so many people waiting for him. There was the Russian officer who had surrendered on the first day of the war. And there were Rosenthal and Mittwitz. And Groetz. And there was Tereskaya, and Kolisch and Ziegler, and the woman who had defended the church door. And there was Smorodin and there was Asja. But **Mama** and Papa were still alive.

He rose to his knees, reached for his tunic. The cross

glinted, and he dropped it again. He ran down the corridor, to the bedroom. But the door was open, and the bed was empty. Good old Papa. Asja had forgotten to relock the door, and while she and Frederic had searched for each other on the kitchen floor Mama and Papa had got out. He hoped they had got far. He did not know how they could possibly have got far enough.

He ran through the house and down the front steps. At the gate he looked back, saw the upper floor dissolve into crumbling ruin as the roof fell in. How hot it was. The flames leapt from the burning house, seemed to be trying to add their orange to the yellow of the sun, hovering overhead. He ran. People moved about him, also running, shouting, shooting. He thought he saw Jutka, but she did not see him. She was sitting on the pavement, weeping, pawing at the blood on her legs like a wounded animal. He came to a street corner, and saw two tanks firing into the houses on either side of them. If tanks were here, in the very centre of Rokonow, then Kopa's company was destroyed. He wondered who this Kopa was, what this Kopa was like. He had not looked at him in the darkness of the wireless room. He had looked only at Asja. But now he remembered, Kopa's voice had suggested that he, too, loved Asja. That he trusted her.

A man stopped him. 'We must abandon Rokonow. The pumping station is lost, and the colonel says we have done all we can here. We must go down into the sewers, and try to make our way north, to Sielce. Do you know the way through the sewers, comrade?'

'No.' Frederic ran on. Lemmings, going to a national suicide in the stench and the darkness. But he would be more true to the species. He ran on, through the smoke and the noise and the stench and the gun-fire and the morning heat, until he saw the waters of the Vistula, hurrying, always hurrying, for the Baltic.